LOVE FOREVER LINDISFARNE

Kimberley Adams

Shy Bairns Publishing

This book is dedicated to you, my Lovely Lindisfarners, who support me on social media. Without you there would be no books, so this is one small way of saying a very big thank you. Your cheerleading, unwavering support and kindness about the books packs my heart with enough love to fill
St James' Park...

Dear Reader...

Kim here again! Love Forever Lindisfarne is the third book in the Lindisfarne series. Who would have thought I'd be saying that? Each book can be enjoyed on its own, but you'll get a richer experience if you've read the first two. They're available if you'd like to read them in order—no pressure though. Hopefully, this introduction will help you tune in quickly.

Ellie Montague was living in London when she was unexpectedly dumped by her boyfriend. Seeking a fresh start, she seized the opportunity to spend a month on Lindisfarne caring for rescue animals. She arrived on the island with little more than hope and a suitcase. It was there she met Zen, with his captivating coffee-bean eyes, as she crossed the causeway for the first time. They were instantly smitten. Now, fifteen months later, Ellie and Zen are deeply in love and living together in the attic of Zen's sister Aurora's café. Many beloved characters from the first two books make an appearance. Meg, Bert, Ethel, and Maurice—stalwarts of the island—continue to play pivotal roles. The Crafty Lindisfarners, the dedicated group working tirelessly for the island, are as active as ever. And, of course, we meet The Right Honourable Aidan Bamburgh again, all six aristocratic feet of Viking heritage! In the first book, we were introduced to Ellie's closest friends— her inner circle. Sophie, her bestie; Jake, Sophie's fiancé; and Tara and Toby, who have since moved to the island and now have a toddler son called Farne. They all play integral roles in Love Forever Lindisfarne.

As always, the island is bustling with activity, and you'll meet some brand-new charming and colourful characters (and animals!) in this book, but I'll leave those surprises for you to discover on your own! I hope you enjoy your visit to Lindisfarne. May it stay in your heart forever.

Love and stotties, Kim x

Chapter 1

I gazed around the tiny bedroom affectionately known as the broom cupboard. It was where I had spent my first night on the island, and so much had happened since then. Life moved along like the tide, ebbing and flowing with regular certainty and stopping for no-one. Pushing open the door, I stepped into the kitchen where Meg, Tara and Aurora were sitting around the farmhouse table, the usual big brown teapot, notable by its absence, replaced with a bottle of Champagne in honour of today's special occasion.

'Well,' I asked sheepishly, 'will I do?'

Three pairs of eyes filled with liquid quicker than they would had they endured a battering from the brutal North Sea winds. Meg grabbed the box of tissues and handed them around.

'You look beautiful, Ellie,' sniffed Tara.

'Is it not too much?' I asked. 'Not too fussy? It's not all about me, is it?'

'Pet, you look stunning,' said Meg.

'None of us can cry,' Tara yelled. 'We'll ruin our makeup. The beautician who did us will be halfway back to Alnwick now, and the tide's in.'

'And you'll soak baby Hettie,' Aurora laughed. 'Mind you, she may as well get used to water – Jack's itching to take her out on the boat.'

Meg held the precious bundle like she was made of porcelain and dabbed the baby's face gently with a tissue.

'The name Hettie does suit her, Aurora. I know you weren't that keen when Jack said he wanted to name her after his family's first boat,' I smiled.

'Well, would you want to call your firstborn after a smelly old fishing trawler called the *Happy Hettie*?'

'Erm, that's kind of pot calling kettle. Remind me, didn't you insist on calling her after an old boat too – the *Henrietta* of Amsterdam from that model ship hanging in the castle?' Tara laughed.

'Okay,' Aurora grinned, 'you got me! That was a compromise, and at least little Henrietta here, or Hettie as she is now known, is named after a proper posh boat too. Your great-granddaughter is three weeks old today, Meg. Can you believe it?'

I could see Meg's face twitching, trying to stop the tears from flowing. At that, Farne wriggled out of Tara's arms to the floor and crawled towards me, his pudgy sticky fingers heading perilously close to the dress.

'Hey, little man, I'll take you to see the alpacas as soon as I get back in my work gear,' I said, grinning at him as Tara scooped him up, saving the dress from a coating of chocolate digestive fingerprints.

Meg stood up, handed Hettie back to Aurora and gave me a hug before turning to us all.

'You lot,' she sniffed, 'have made mine and Bert's lives even more special. There's not a drop of blood between any of us, but I tell you now, you are my family, and I adore the bally lot of you. To have these gorgeous bairns in our family, well they're the icing on the cake, make no mistake. I'm a very lucky woman. A very lucky woman indeed.'

The door creaked open and in strode Maurice, the island oyster farmer and lifelong friend of Bert and Meg.

'Your carriage awaits. Well, cart, if truth be told, but me and Nora used two cans of Mr Sheen on it, and the Crafty Lindisfarners have made it look like one of those hen do things you see trotting along the front at Blackpool. It's way over the top, if you ask me, but I'm sure you'll love it.'

'Thanks, Maurice,' said Aurora. 'Is Toby here with the car?'

'Aye, he's waiting for Tara and the bairns.'

'Are you sure you're going to be able to manage the two little ones?' asked Aurora, handing baby Hettie to Tara.

'Absolutely, and don't forget I've got Toby there too, so please don't worry. Hettie is in safe hands, and you're going to see her when you get to the church – in all of about ten minutes!'

'I know, I'm such a mother hen. Never thought I'd be like this in a million years, but the minute I held her, that was it.'

'I was exactly the same,' said Tara. 'It's perfectly natural. Now you all go, and I'll see you over at the church.'

'You look a million dollars, Meg,' said Maurice, looking at Meg in her gorgeous outfit chosen especially for the occasion.

'You mean all green and crinkly, Maurice? Bert says that all the time!'

'No, hen, I mean it. Right, let's get this show on the road. Everyone else is waiting for us over at the church. I saw the groom and best man walking along the road when I was on my way here – no donkey for them, just good old Shanks's pony!'

Meg tucked her arm into Maurice's as I held up the hem of my dress and picked up the posies, then followed them over the castle courtyard, carefully making my way across the cobbles in my heels. We went through the door in the big arched gate to the pony cart, except it was Wonky and Wilma, the donkeys, who were doing the honours.

'I see what you meant about the "carriage", Maurice,' I laughed, looking at the ancient old oyster cart which had been covered in paper flowers, ribbons and what looked like every adornment the Crafty Lindisfarners could find in the store cupboard.

'Oh, and look at Wonky and Wilma in their pretty flower-covered harnesses,' said Meg.

'Aye, pet, they look great, but you know Wonky. I just hope the training we put in was enough and that they don't decide to pull us onto the sand flats,' murmured Maurice.

'Remember when Wilma got stuck in a sand drift after the storm?' I said, recalling how Zen had worked tirelessly to free the little animal.

'Well, it better not happen again, or by God I'll send them to work on the beach at Whitley Bay,' laughed Maurice.

Once we were settled in the cart Aurora tapped Maurice on the shoulder.

'Okay, driver, put your foot down, and don't spare the donkeys!'

Chapter 2

The three of us sat in the back, with Maurice up front cajoling the donkeys to keep in a straight line and not stop every time they felt like nuzzling each other.

As we descended the steep track, I thought how amazing it was that the castle had stood perched on top of its commanding position for almost 500 years. The building was much changed from the original, after going through various upgrades during its lifetime, but the 360-degree view across the island, the fortress and lands around it never failed to raise the spirits, and today was no exception.

As we reached the bottom of the track and trotted on to the level road to the village, a gentle breeze blew Meg's feathered fascinator, so it looked like a guillemot in full flight. The island was sprinkled in spring sunshine, and the usual North Sea chill had taken a day off for a change. As we ambled along, the ruins of the priory to our left, it was hard not to get emotional as to the beauty of it all.

'The sun shines on the righteous,' Meg smiled.

'I had serious doubts we would be able to make it over to the church in the cart, yet it's almost balmy today. The landscape is looking ready to explode into new life,' said Aurora. 'I love spring with the promise of summer not far behind.'

'Aye, pet, but never fear – it'll probably be snowing tomorrow, as you know. Ellie, you've been on the island long enough to know how quickly the weather changes.'

'I've been here sixteen months now, Meg. I can't believe how fast the time has flown, and I still pinch myself every day to make sure it's really true that I ended up on the island amongst all of you. Were you nervous on your wedding day, Meg?' I asked.

'Not a bit, pet. It's fifty-five years, but I remember it like it was yesterday. We were just kids – had to scrimp and save enough to get married. And then I went and spent most of our savings on a whim.' Meg smiled, a faraway look in her eyes. 'Bert wasn't even cross with me, and I knew then I had made the right choice.'

'What did you spend it on?' I asked intrigued.

'Oh, you must show her, Meg,' said Aurora.

'I will, pet. Bert and I didn't have much of a clue about life, or money, to be honest, both being island kids who'd had a sheltered upbringing other than the occasional trip to the big city full of all kinds of exciting things.'

'I take it you mean Newcastle and not Alnwick?' I smiled.

'Yes, I do. It was overwhelming, really – the sheer volume of people, the city traffic and noise. And that was back in the late sixties, when it took hours to get there. It was like entering another world, and to this very day, whilst I enjoy a visit, I'm always pleased to be on my way back home to Lindisfarne. Anyway, we married in Alnwick, at the registry office. Just me and Bert, with Maurice and Ivy, his dear old mam as witnesses. Then we came back to the island for our do in the village hall, and they did us proud.'

'Did you not want a church wedding?'

'Yes, of course. It was all sorted, but the island was rocked with a major scandal – at least it was to us back then. A month before the wedding, the Reverend Randy Richardson as we all called him, run off with one of the flock. A proper Jezebel she was, not much older than me. Her name was Gloria. Blooming cheek being given a name so associated with the Virgin Mary, as believe you me, she was no innocent. She appeared on the island from somewhere in the west country to work at the hotel and soon had her claws into the randy rev, who was about ten years her senior – the stories about what they got up to in the vestry would make your hair curl. Anyway, they stole the church silver and disappeared together. Poor Mrs Richardson was left bereft.'

'He was married?'

'Ellie, you may have noticed already, this island has had its fair share of what Bert might call ne'er do wells over the course of history, most recently you-know-who from just over there,' she pointed towards the St Cuthbert's Way Hotel. I won't even say that woman's name on this special day,' Aurora laughed, but we all knew she meant Isla, the cause of nearly all the island scandals in more recent times.

'Yes, he was married. Thankfully they didn't have any children. He must have been good at something, I suppose, because he looked like Lurch off *The Addams Family*, and personally, I was glad to see the back of him. He had the personality of a cricket bat, as my Bert might say!'

'Did All Saints get the silver back?'

'Yes, stupid pair tried to sell it in a pawnbrokers in Newcastle and were caught red-handed. Aurora's right, you young people probably think things like that never used to happen back in our day, but believe you me they did, and this island was no exception,' Meg chuckled, 'only difference was, scandal wasn't splashed all over the blinking internet the minute it happened – just the local newspapers, probably a week later.'

The cart suddenly swerved to the right and came to an abrupt halt in front of a bench where a young woman was sitting eating a sandwich.

'Oh, no, you don't, you little bug... erm, villain,' shouted Maurice, as Wonky attempted to snatch the sandwich from out of the young woman's hand. She pulled away, and the sandwich flew up into the air then landed on the ground, its contents splattering across the road.

'I'm very sorry, lass,' said Maurice, doffing a chauffeur's cap, which kind of looked out of place on the driver of a donkey cart. He had acquired the cap specially for the occasion from the Lindisfarne Amateur Dramatics Society, otherwise known as The Lads. Their last play was *Murder on the Orient Express*, so it's a wonder he hadn't turned up in a fez.

'He's a law unto himself, is this one,' Maurice grinned.

The woman looked up, and I saw that the face peeping from under her hood belonged to a girl of no more than sixteen or seventeen. She looked at the sandwich lying on the ground and promptly burst into tears. She was as pale and pearlescent as one of Maurice's oysters. The only colour in her face came from two bright blue eyes, glistening with tears, both of which had heavy navy shadows underneath them. She looked exhausted, and she was shivering, despite the warmth of the day and the hooded tracksuit she was bundled up in.

'Eeh, pet, did you get a fright?' Meg asked, standing up and gesturing to Maurice to help her down from the cart.

Meg, Aurora and I clambered down in our finery, still holding our posies and Meg and I sat down on the bench each side of the girl.

'Now then, love, whatever's the matter?' Meg asked gently. 'Wonky's just a Hungry Horace – he won't hurt you.'

'It's not the donkey,' the girl whispered. 'I like them. Mam used to take me to the beach and I'd ride along the...'

But before she could finish the sentence she broke into deep sobs, crumpling up between us like a ragdoll.

Meg handed her posy to Aurora, fished in her suit pocket for a tissue and gave it to the girl.

'There, there, lass. I don't know what this is all about, but you're with us now and we're going to make sure you're okay.'

A sniff came from within the hood.

'It was my last money.'

'What was?' I asked gently.

'The sandwich. I've got no more money, and I don't know what to do.'

She broke into sobs again.

'Are you here on the island alone?' I asked.

She nodded.

'You're freezing, pet,' said Meg. 'We need to get you warm, then you can tell us what you feel like telling us. And don't worry, I know where there are going to be lots of sandwiches… and cakes.'

'They'll be curled up at the edges, Meg, if you don't get a wriggle on,' grumbled Maurice. 'Nee disrespect to the lassie, like,' he added quickly. 'I don't like seeing people upset.'

I could see Aurora discretely trying to point to her watch then to Meg, who caught her in the act.

'Aurora, we don't leave anyone in distress – not on this island, as you well know. The vicar will just have to wait. Is that okay with you, Ellie?'

'Erm, yes, I suppose so,' I answered, thinking of everyone waiting in the church, probably growing more impatient by the minute.

'Now then, pet, what's your name?' asked Meg.

Silence.

'Oh, okay – not to worry. All in your own good time. My name's Meg, that's Ellie and Aurora, and just ignore him in the front.'

'Maybe we can drop her at the village hall,' suggested Maurice. 'She can have something to eat and get warm while we're in the church.'

'She'll take off the minute we leave her,' whispered Meg in my ear, 'and call it gut intuition, but this young lassie needs our help.'

I agreed.

'Right, lass, how do you fancy coming to church? I need to get off this bench before the seagulls come and swoop on that sandwich and plop on my suit. It may be good luck, but this cost an arm and a leg, and I want to get a few more wears out of it before it needs to go to the cleaners. We'd really like you to come, wouldn't we girls?'

'Absolutely,' agreed Aurora and I in unison.

Meg stood up, smoothed down her beautiful aquamarine suit and held out a hand to the girl, who grasped it tightly. Then Maurice helped the three of us into the back of the cart, while Aurora sat up front. We headed for the church at a sedate pace, fashionably late, with a distressed stranger on board. Aurora burst out into a tuneless rendition of 'Get me to the Church on Time' and we all joined in, except for our mystery guest, who was probably wondering what the heck was going on.

Chapter 3

We got to All Saints and piled out of the cart. Maurice saw to the donkeys and a stressed Reverend Rosie rushed out of the church.

'Where've you all been? Do none of you answer your mobiles?'

'We all switched them off before we left, in case we forgot,' I explained.

'We're here now, pet, and we might need your advice later,' I heard Meg whisper into the vicar's ear, nodding towards our guest.

'Erm, right,' nodded Reverend Rosie. 'I'll go back in, and when you're ready, let's do this!'

Our stranger clung on to Meg's hand like a limpet clinging on to a rock and held Aurora's posy so tightly in her other hand that I wondered if it would end up as a bunch of stalks without any petals. I looked at her eyes peeping out from the hood. The girl was almost as tall as me, very slender and cloaked in an air of vulnerability.

'Maybe you could let go of Meg's hand now and we can find you a seat inside where you can watch,' I said gently, detaching her grip from Meg's hand to my own. The grip tightened the minute our hands touched.

'Aurora, go get Ethel and bring her out to me, please,' said Meg.

Aurora came back with Ethel, who was in her wheel-chair. The last few months had seen a decline in Ethel's health. It was the first time in many years that she hadn't been to Benidorm for her winter warmer, due to her mobility being affected by increasingly painful arthritis. But that didn't stop her being the Ethel we all knew and loved – and that tongue was just as acid sharp as ever!

I saw Meg nod at Ethel, then she pointed her eyes directly towards the girl. No words were spoken and Ethel nodded back knowingly. The two older women were so in tune with each other that after years of friendship, where Ethel had been a constant in Meg's life, it seemed they could communicate purely by the expression on each other's faces. Meg turned to the girl.

'This is my very dear friend, Ethel. Her bark's worse than her bite, but she's actually very kind, and she'll look after you while us three get on with why we're here today.'

I gently detached the girl's hand from mine and held my breath as I wondered if at this point she would bolt, but she handed the posy back to Aurora and undid her hood. The face that was revealed as she shook out a mass of golden blonde tresses was pretty, if a little drawn, with two amazingly bright blue eyes.

'Thank you,' she whispered to Meg, then smiled shyly at Aurora and me. 'You are all very kind.'

Ethel took the girl's hand in her own and grinned at her.

'Pet, you're freezing. Here, wrap that over your knees when we get inside.' She handed the girl a tartan rug. 'They insist I bring it with me, but the day I have to wrap up like a pensioner is the day I give up,' she cackled. 'Oh, and by the way, I can still walk, but it's canny getting a lift back in this contraption if I have a few glasses of the hooch.' She winked. 'Anyway, whoever you are pet, you're very welcome. There's a big woman in there, the one in the dress that looks like a pair of flowery curtains from an old folk's home—'

'Ethel!' hissed Meg.

'Well, that's Dora. She's the butcher's wife, and she makes the most amazing sausage rolls. What say you push me over to the village hall after the service and we can stuff our faces. You're like me – you could do with a bit of lard on your bones. Then you can tell me anything you like, or nothing at all, if you don't want to. I've been on this planet enough years that I'm sure you can't tell me anything I haven't heard before, and I'm a good listener – as long as you speak up.'

The girl gave a tiny smile, and I noticed a flush of colour had begun to return to her alabaster cheeks.

'Come on then, lass,' said Ethel, 'time for us to go in.' The girl took the wheelchair and carefully pushed it towards the door.

'Okay, girls, drama over – for now, at least,' said Meg, once Ethel and the girl were safely inside the church. 'Time to get this show on the road!' And she set off towards the door with a spring in her step.

We walked down the aisle towards the front altar, Miss Brown, the schoolteacher, belting out 'Here Comes the

Bride' on the organ, and I saw the back of my gorgeous Zen. Wearing a dark fitted suit, his hair tamed for the occasion but already making a bid for freedom, he stood head and shoulders above a sharply dressed Bert next to him. It struck me that it was probably the first time I'd ever seen Bert without his tweed cap balanced on his head. Even when he had been in hospital for his hip operation, it was back on his head the minute he recovered from the anaesthetic. Zen turned around and gave me a smile that was so full of love I thought I might just burst into confetti and rain down on the congregation. His coffee bean eyes were twinkling, his pale face bathed in colour from the light streaming in through the stained glass windows, with jewel like dust motes dancing in the air around him. I don't think I'd ever seen him look more mesmerising, and I almost stumbled as I was so focused on him.

'It's meant to be me with the shaky legs,' smiled Meg, giving my hand a squeeze and handing Aurora her posy. She took her place next to Bert, and Zen sat down in the front row with his mam and dad.

'Welcome all. It's only taken fifty-five years to get our beloved islanders, Meg and Bert, to say "I do" in All Saints,' smiled Reverend Rosie, 'so I was more than happy to deviate from protocol. Today, we'll almost be having a traditional service for the renewal of their vows – a little compensation for them being robbed of their church wedding all those years ago. If you know, you know,' she winked.

Bert took Meg's hand, whispered something in her ear, and her eyes immediately filled with tears, as did mine, seeing the love radiate from the pair of very special people I had come to love. As I glanced at my handsome boyfriend then took a moment to look around the church at the islanders, friends and family, out in force to celebrate the joyful occasion of two of their own, I was momentarily overcome by a tsunami of pure joy. Despite my best efforts to stop the tears, before I knew it the waterfall was in full flow, rolling down my cheeks, splashing onto the flowers and taking my mascara with it.

'Meg, Bert,' began Reverend Rosie, as the music faded, 'I think that's everyone here now, so I'll begin.'

Suddenly there was a kerfuffle at the back of the church at the door.

'Not quite everyone, Vicar,' shouted Maurice, who was being pulled down the aisle by the castle's canine contingent: Tri the three-legged Greyhound, Robson the lamb-like Bedlington Terrier, Flower the Collie, Duchess the ancient Patterdale, and tiny terrier Nacho, all wearing Northumbrian tartan bandanas around their necks.

'Meg, Bert, we knew that having the dogs here with you today would complete your family. Believe you me, we tried to work out how to get the rest of the menagerie here too, but those stupid turkeys and your girls,' said Maurice, meaning Meg's hens, 'wouldn't have appreciated it.'

'I heard all about the debacle at the nativity the other year,' smiled Reverend Rosie. 'Those donkeys and alpacas sounded like they were very naughty, so I agreed we would stick to dogs. Don't they all look splendid? I'm sure they're going to be well behaved, aren't they, Maurice?' she said sternly, with a twinkle in her eye.

'Aye, vicar. Exemplary,' replied Maurice, as Duchess let out a massive trump which reverberated around the church.

'That's ma bairn!' Ethel shouted from the back. The congregation were all soon laughing, which set the tone for the rest of the ceremony – perhaps the most joyous occasion I had ever attended in my life.

Chapter 4

The village hall was soon filled with the sound of chatter as the guests relaxed and tucked into a delicious buffet provided by the Crafty Lindisfarners.

'Hoy, Maurice, how many of these here oysters of yours do you recommend for a honeymoon night?' Bert shouted to his friend of many years, as he surveyed the platter of freshly collected island seafood on ice that wouldn't have looked out of place in a Michelin starred restaurant.

'Bert, pet,' retorted Meg, laughing. 'It'll take more than those slimy molluscs. No disrespect Maurice, but that's a load of codswallop which helps you sell the blooming things to people with more money than sense.'

'Meggie, how very dare you! I'll have you know Casanova himself was very partial to the little shells of pleasure, and we all know what a lad he was. If you're after why they, erm, help down the business end, me old da, God rest his soul, used to say, "Zinc to make the girls wink," and me da knew his oysters!'

Zen was on the stage singing a medley of songs from 1970, the year Meg and Bert were married the first-time round. 'Bridge over Troubled Water' happened to be number one in something they referred to as the 'hit parade' on the day of their first wedding. Zen and I had listened to the lyrics many times as he learned the song, and despite its rather ominous title, it was perfect for celebrating the lives of two people who were always there for each other – through thick and thin. As usual, just watching Zen put his heart and soul into singing such a beautiful song gave me goosebumps on top of goose-bumps. His dark hair now dishevelled, the suit jacket and waistcoat a thing of the past hanging redundant on the back of his chair, the top buttons of his shirt undone and the Northumbrian cravat loosely draped around his neck – he was every inch the rock god. He and I wouldn't be needing Maurice's oysters any time soon, that was for sure.

'Ellie, Aurora, come over here, please,' shouted Meg from the top table. 'Bert and I got you both a little some-thing to say thank you for today and for everything that you both do for us.' She handed us each a little box with a bow on the top. 'You look stunning in those minty sea foam dresses, by the way – good choice.'

Inside the boxes were two beautiful necklaces, in the same design except for the centre stone.

'We got them made especially for you both at the jewellers in Morpeth,' said Meg.

'Meg, it's in the shape of the island,' Aurora gasped, immediately recognising it.

'They are,' smiled Meg. 'They're exactly the same, ex-cept for the stone in the middle. Yours is lapis lazuli, Aurora. Such a beautiful shade of blue that reminded me

of you in the sea on a summer's day,' said Meg, helping Aurora with the clasp. 'And yours is citrine, Ellie,
because you have been like a ray of sunshine shining
into our lives.'

'Or it reminds you of her wearing the yellow hi-vis
jacket, perhaps!' Aurora guffawed.

As Meg leant in to fasten the necklace around my
neck, she whispered in my ear.

'It'll be your turn next, Ellie; you and my grandson
are meant to be together just like me and Bert. I don't
give a fig how you choose to commit to each other, pet,
because I know Zen might not appreciate anything as
traditional as this, but you're the only girl for our Zen.
Me and Bert couldn't be happier that you've joined our
family.'

'Oh, Meg, don't,' I smiled. 'I've already cried off all
the mascara.'

'You look beautiful, pet. You always do, even in that
yellow coat! Right, I'd best catch up with Bert and watch
what the old reprobate is up to – don't want him too
drunk on our honeymoon night, do I?' she winked,
as she went off in search of her soulmate, who was
propping up the bar with the men of the island.

'Ellie! Come and sit with us a minute,' shouted Imogen. 'Harriet and I want to run something past you.'

Imogen was the owner of Love Lindisfarne, the gift
shop which she had lovingly turned into a Northumbrian craft hub. It was where the Crafty Lindisfarners
met, and many a happy hour was spent in the back
shop, allegedly crafting, but mainly discussing island
gossip.

'You're both looking well, considering the time of year,' I said, as we all had a hug then sat down at their table. 'Loving the suit, Harriet.'

'It's the same one I wore for Aurora's wedding – oh, and Ethel's non-funeral and Farne's baptism. My mam calls it my hatches, matches and dispatches outfit – can't see the point of having more than one,' she laughed.

'How's lambing going?'

'Same as always. Mainly good, then occasionally we get a crisis that requires hours out in the freezing cold, usually overnight, then more hours next to the Aga trying to save those tiny wee lambs who, for whatever reason, are without their mam.'

'That bit's my job,' said Imogen, smiling. 'Harriet's hardened to the cold after living on the tops of the national park all her life, but I'm a soft southerner, so I'll happily sit up all night nursing the newborns in the warm.'

'I just wish I had more time to get up and see you. Honestly, life here on the island, as you both know, is equally as busy and there's always something to do. What with my job at the castle, the tea van, helping in the café now Aurora is on maternity leave, I'm not sure if I'm coming or going. And Zen and I are moving over to the cottage this next week to look after the animals when Bert and Meg go to Melrose on their very first honeymoon. They didn't get one the first time around as some sort of crisis happened at the castle, so I'm not letting anything get in the way of them getting one this time.'

'Well, that's kind of what I wanted to talk to you about, Ellie,' said Imogen. 'I've been spending more and more time up at the farm with Harriet as she's virtually running the place now.'

'Mam and Dad need to relax a little, Ellie. You know that farming is in their blood, and they will never step back completely, but I'm trying to take on as much as I can so that they can at least get more rest,' explained Harriet. 'I'm begging them to take a holiday, maybe to Hexham where my Auntie Sylvie lives – that's about as far as I'll get them to go.'

'So,' continued Imogen, 'we've decided that it would be much more practical if I moved up there permanently and learned more about farming – other than sitting in front of an Aga snuggling baby lambs, that is!'

'I'm really pleased for you both,' I said, 'but I'm guessing the issue is the shop?'

'Absolutely. I'm so torn, Ellie. As you know, it's very special to me and I don't really want to let go, but it's just too impractical flitting from the farm to the island. The tides don't help much either. In fact, we're about to head off soon to get back across the causeway as soon as it opens.'

'Listen, it's probably not the best time to try and think of solutions today,' I said, noticing Tara waving me across to her table, 'but let's arrange to meet at Love Lindisfarne this week and throw some ideas about before the season kicks off.'

We made arrangements and said our goodbyes, then I went across to see Tara, Toby and little Farne, who was happily mushing up food on his highchair table.

'Oh, wasn't that just wonderful,' Tara smiled, as I sat down and eventually managed a sip of Champagne. 'I hope Toby and I get to do the same one day. Maybe not wait as long – what do you say, darling?'

'I'll consult my diary,' smiled Toby. 'The way things are going at the moment I wouldn't have time to even say "I do."'

Toby had been given the temporary role of Custodian of the Lindisfarne Estate, when Sir James and Lady Grace relocated to California so that Grace could rehabilitate after a stroke. Grace was much improved when they'd eventually returned to the island but nowhere near fully recovered, so they'd decided to take more time out to do all of the things that they had wanted to do, but never had the time, because the running of a busy estate was a full-time way of life. I think the fact that Toby had been doing such a good job gave Sir James the confidence to let go of something so close to his heart, knowing it was in competent hands. They were currently in Ibiza, where James was enjoying himself sailing and Grace was dabbling in all kinds of alternative therapies. As a result, Toby had been offered a more permanent contract and was now knee deep in the full management of the island and all estate business. As Toby took his specs off and ran his hand through his hair, I noticed how tired he looked.

'Ellie,' he began, 'we need to meet up next week to begin to plan the season. The castle opens soon, and while I'm sure we're on top of it, we need to make sure everything is in place and the staff and volunteer rotas are all sorted.'

'Toby!' interjected Tara. 'What did I say earlier? No work chat today. None. You can speak to Ellie tomorrow, but today is our family day at our friends' event. The Lindisfarne Estate won't crumble without you for one day.'

'Tara's right, Tobes. You look knackered. Have a few beers and spend some time with Tara and Farne. We'll catch up in the next few days, for sure.'

Aurora came over, put a sleeping baby Hettie in my arms, and sat down with us.

'Jack's gone to catch the tide. I'm surprised he managed to come at all, but he's very fond of Meg and Bert. We're like ships passing in the night at the moment, pardon the dreadful pun,' she laughed. 'I could do with a catch up with you both this week.' She looked at Tara and me. 'Got a few things buzzing around my head that maybe you can help me with. Oh, and we need to sort out TEA at the Castle. I can't believe that's due to open soon.'

'Er, I'll add you to my growing list,' I half laughed, thinking life on Lindisfarne was sounding like it was going to get busier than ever.

Chapter 5

As the guests began to drift off, the Crafty Lindisfarners started the task of tidying up. Ethel, now holding court at the top table, rattled a spoon on her glass.

'Meg, Ellie, Tara and Aurora, get your backsides across here. We need a pow-wow.'

'Where's the girl gone, Ethel?' I asked. 'Has she disappeared?'

'No. Don was taking Amelia and William to see the alpacas, so she tagged along. She seemed quite comfortable around the kids – she's not much more of one herself.'

'So cut to the chase, Ethel – what's the story?' demanded Meg. 'I haven't got long. Zen's driving Bert and me to Berwick to catch the train to Edinburgh. Bert got me a surprise – he booked us a room in that swanky hotel next to Waverley Station, and we're catching our connection to Melrose in the morning.'

'Ooh, how romantic,' said Aurora. 'I hope you've got your sexy underwear on?'

'Can't beat M&S,' replied Meg. 'I like a roomy gusset these days.'

'Well,' said Ethel, 'our mystery visitor is from Newcastle and is called Kitti. Actually, her full name is Kittiwake, after the birds you know. Unusual name, but she gets called Kitti.'

'That's odd considering how many kittiwakes we have on the island,' said Aurora. 'And by the way, when you're called Zen and Aurora you know all about being called unusual names.'

'I like the name Kittiwake,' said Tara. 'Might call the next one after an island bird.'

'What, like Shag, perhaps?' said Ethel with a straight face.

'Ethel! Right, enough you lot,' said Meg looking at the village hall clock. 'I'm under time pressure here, and we need to get this sorted before I have to go.'

'Well, she didn't tell me much, other than the poor bairn has recently lost her mam. Her only relative from what I can gather.'

'No! That poor lassie,' said Meg. 'Do you know how old she is?'

'Sixteen,' said Ethel. 'Was her birthday recently.'

'But why is she here on the island?' Did she tell you that?' I asked.

'No, Ellie, but I tell you this – I might be old, but I'm still as sharp as Dora's butcher's knife, and that young lass has a connection to this island, I'm sure of that. It was no random trip. You see if I'm not wrong.'

'She might have come for some spiritual guidance, or just to retreat. Many do,' said Tara.

'At sixteen? All the way from Newcastle? I think not,' said Meg.

'Fair point,' Tara nodded.

'How did she get here?' I asked. 'And how is she getting back?'

'She arrived on the island last night. Don't know how she got here. She slept rough in one of your empty shelters in the paddocks as it happens, Meg.'

We all gasped.

'No wonder she was so cold this morning.' I shuddered.

'And she said she had no money left,' Meg pondered.

'Well, I think we should find her somewhere to stay tonight, then perhaps you younger ones can see if you can get her to talk, and we can go from there. See if we can get her home,' said Ethel.

'If she even has a home,' said Tara dejectedly. 'She might be in care. What if they're looking for her?'

'She can stay with Zen and me at the cottage, on the sofa tonight. Is that okay with you, Meg?' I said, my mind made up. 'I'll talk to her, though, and see if there is anyone we need to contact immediately. Don't want to get us into any sort of trouble.'

'Of course it is, pet. She'll be nice and warm, and I'm sure having the dogs around will reassure her. She seems to like animals. And speak to Reverend Rosie – she'll help too, if need be.'

'Sorted,' said Ethel. 'Bring her over to mine in the morning, She's a nice kid and I'm really fond of the lassie already. I'm missing me granddaughter.' she grinned, meaning my bestie, Sophie, from London who Ethel had 'adopted' on their first meeting, 'so young Kitti will be like a breath of fresh air. Right, meeting over. Who's going to push me and this chariot down to the Crab? The party's not over yet!'

***

After we had waved Meg and Bert off, this time in the car with Zen and not the donkey cart, I walked over to the cottage with Kitti. The earlier sun had gone in for the day, and there was a chill in the air as the wind was blowing directly from the North Sea.

'Ethel told me you slept in one of the shelters last night,' I said gently, gesturing to the wooden structures in the paddocks as we passed.

'I'm sorry,' murmured Kitti. 'I didn't do anything stupid or leave any rubbish. Just lay on some straw.'

'That's okay, Kitti, don't worry. It must have been cold, though?'

'It didn't seem it at first, but then I couldn't get warm and didn't sleep much. The wind was blowing straight in.'

We stopped and took in the view across the island as dusk descended, a slash of a tangerine sunset to the west. Kitti's eyes darted around, drinking everything in.

'I can't believe you live in an actual castle,' she said, looking up at the towering structure on top of the curved hill ahead of us. 'It looks like the top of an ice cream cone.'

I looked at the castle, the positioning of which actually did resemble a giant Mr Whippy!

'You're right – it does,' I laughed. 'The mound is called Beblow Crag. It's volcanic and really ancient.'

'Ooh, will it explode with lava?'

'No,' I laughed. 'And we don't live in the castle, but when I first came to the island I did stay in it for a while.'

'Was it like, really spooky?' she asked, eyes wide. 'I bet it's full of ghosts.'

'I thought that too, and to be honest on my first night I was scared, but I had little Nacho with me – you'll meet him and the other dogs in a minute – and I was in the guest apartment, which actually just felt like being in a very posh hotel. There were no ghosts. At least I didn't see any. I'll show you around before you go; I work there now for some of the time. Oh, and me, Tara and Aurora also run that,' I said, pointing to TEA at the Castle, our vintage campervan, which was shut up for the winter.

'Cool,' she said. 'I'd love to see inside the castle. I like history.'

I had so many questions I wanted to ask her, but best save them for tomorrow, perhaps, except for the pressing matter of whether we needed to inform anyone.

'Kitti, I'm going to show you around the yard because I need to check on all the animals,' I said, as we went through the gate into the courtyard. 'Maybe then you can tell me if we need to contact anyone?'

'Oh, I can tell you that now,' she smiled.

I raised an eyebrow.

'Everything's okay. You don't need to worry. I told the foster carer that I was going to stay with a family friend for the weekend, so no one will be looking for me.'

'You're in care?'

'Yes, for now. I know I lied about coming here, but they wouldn't have let me otherwise, and I really needed to.' I could see her eyes welling up. 'Please, Ellie, I'm telling you the truth, I promise. The foster carer's a bit, er, well she was busy so just agreed without checking. I told her I was visiting a Mrs Cuthbert on Lindisfarne, so they already know I'm on the island. They're expecting me back on Monday... if I go back,' she added defiantly.

'Mrs Cuthbert,' I laughed, choosing to ignore the bit about not going back. 'Did she not see through that one?'

'No, she didn't. She's kind but not really that clever.'

But you are, I thought, looking at Kitti. As Bert might say, Kitti was as sharp as a razorbill's beak.

'Okay, let's talk more about that later because I need to go and check on all the animals, and I thought you might like to help me. The dogs have been locked up in the kennel since Maurice dropped them off earlier. Listen; they're already barking, asking us to get them out.'

'Ooh, please. I met Pacino and Murray, the alpacas, and of course Wilma and Wonky, the donkeys. This place is just magic. I love animals. I thought that one day I might train to be a vet, but that might not happen now because...' she tailed off sadly.

'Right, let me go and get changed, and then we'll do the rounds,' I said brightly, trying to raise her spirits. I opened the porch door and grabbed the big yellow communal coat. 'Here – put this on. It's a requirement for all new starters to wear this with pride.'

It was the first time I'd seen her really smile. It lit up her face like there was a giant buttercup shining up from underneath her chin, and, as she put on the manky old coat, it struck me how naturally beautiful she was.

'I look like...'

'Yep, Laa-Laa the Teletubby,' I howled. 'Have a seat for a couple of minutes – I'll be with you in two shakes of Wonky's tail.'

We started the rounds by letting out the dogs.

'Where's the smelly one?' Kitti smiled.

'That's Duchess, and she spends most of her time with Ethel, although we all walk her and make sure Ethel has everything she needs for her. She's great company but yes, a little bit whiffy, and Tri the greyhound now lives permanently with Maurice and Nora.'

As we went from stable to stable, the dogs careering joyfully around the yard, Kitti couldn't contain herself. She was even excited to meet Sage and Onion the turkeys.

'Thanks for showing me around, Ellie,' she said, as we walked back to the cottage with the dogs. It's so nice here, and I love them all. 'Do you have a favourite?' she asked, 'or is that not really allowed?'

'I think it's allowed,' I smiled, 'as long as you treat them all the same. Don't tell any of the others, but my favourite is Hannibal, the Shetland pony. You might have seen him in a paddock earlier – you can meet him properly tomorrow, but I warn you in advance, he can be a proper little mischief-maker.'

'My favourite is Holly. She's super cute and so tiny,' she said, referring to our little pygmy goat.

When we got back to the cottage, I left Kitti sitting on the sofa, surrounded by dogs, as I went to put the kettle on the Aga. Zen was due back any minute, and it would be good to have a drink and talk a bit more to Kitti – see if we could get her to tell us what was going on. At that, the inner porch door into the living room-cum-kitchen opened, and in came Zen wearing a very odd expression that I couldn't quite read. My heart immediately began to do back flips, thinking something had happened to Bert or Meg.

'What's the matter? Are Bert and Meg okay? Don't tell me they missed the train or something?' I tailed off.

'Erm, no, all good, but I have got a surprise for you. A big one.'

'A surprise? What kind of surprise?' I asked, an ominous feeling growing in my stomach after seeing the look on his face.

And just at that, the door opened again, and a head peeped around the frame.

'Oh, my God, Sophie! What are you doing here?' I stared incredulously at my bestie as she staggered into the room, propelled by a haze of red wine fumes, the dogs nearly knocking her over in a rush for cuddles.

'Ta dah, Ellie Nellie!' she hiccupped, then promptly burst into tears as she fell into my arms.

Chapter 6

'What on earth? Where did you find her?' I turned to Zen for some answers.

'She got off the train that Bert and Meg were going on.'

'Erm, I am here and can speak for myshelf... I think,' Sophie giggled, the tears stopping mid flow for a nanosecond before they began to drip again.

I guided her to the sofa, where a wide eyed Kitti was sitting, watching events unfold like she was tuned in to an episode of *Hollyoaks*. Sophie then saw Kitti, stopped in her tracks and looked the young girl up and down.

'And who are you?' Sophie asked accusingly. 'Ellie Nellie is MY friend.'

'Erm, hi, I'm Kitti. Your friend Ellie has helped me today because...' there was a pause... 'I've kind of run away.'

'You have? Snap. High five,' replied Sophie, flopping down next to Kitti and giving the girl a hug. 'Great, we can be friends because I've run away too.'

I looked at Zen who shook his head and whispered, 'She wouldn't tell me anything on the way here other than it's to do with Jake, but what it is I don't know.'

'Make some coffee, Zen – the strongest bean you've got handy. I need to try and sober her up.'

'Would you like some hot chocolate, Kitti, or maybe you'd like to try Zen's coffee? That's what he does, by the way – he has a coffee company called Island of Beans.'

'Hot chocolate, please,' said Kitti, smiling shyly at Zen.

'I can do you one of my specials. We're currently working on a range of the best hot chocolate you will ever taste,' he grinned.

'I'm starving,' said Sophie, interrupting.

'Have you eaten anything today?' I asked.

'Erm, I can't even remember,' she replied. 'I had some nice wine, though, and think I had some of those things that taste like cheesy feet, which reminded me of work, so I threw them away.'

'I'll make you a sandwich. You stay there and talk to Kitti, but first, let's get your coat and boots off.'

I left Sophie sprawled on the sofa, Nacho on her lap, Flo on her feet and Robson tucked up next to Kitti.

'Did she have a bag with her?' I asked Zen, as he ground some coffee beans.

'Yes, it's in the car. A big holdall as it happens.'

'So, maybe not a flying visit? I'll wait until she sobers up. Probably better just leaving her to sleep tonight and talking to her in the morning.'

'And on the subject of sleeping, where are we all going to go?'

'That's a good point. We might have to use Meg and Bert's room tonight.'

'No, not happening,' said Zen firmly. 'Bert and Megs room is and always will be sacrosanct. I'd rather go home to the attic and come back early in the morning. I had just wanted to relax tonight with you and a glass of wine. You looked incredibly sexy today in that gorgeous dress,' he said kissing my neck, 'and I was looking forward to seeing it slide onto the floor.'

'Well, the dress is back on the hanger, and I'm now modelling the epitome of workwear chic in this pair of Bert's old overalls, which are not what you would call sexy. Plus, you did your back in the last time we attempted to get in the same bunk together. Mind you, seeing you in that suit today did rather give me the same idea, so perhaps we can recreate the moment sometime?' I winked. 'Don't go home, though. Have a few glasses of wine and chill out, if that's possible, considering what's going on. I need you here.' Then I suddenly had a lightbulb moment. 'Hey, we've got the castle keys. What about you crashing in the guest apartment overnight? There's no one in the building, and that way if I need you, you're just next door. Kitti seems lovely, but she is a stranger after all, and Sophie might need some muscle to get her to bed. I'll sleep in the broom cupboard with Soph, and Kitti can go on the sofa as arranged. Does that sound like a plan?'

'Pass me a bottle of red, and make it an expensive one. I'm going to be the king of the castle tonight,' he grinned.

We all sat around the roaring fire. Both Kitti and Sophie were exhausted, and neither showed any inclination of explaining why they came to be on the island. Kitti, however, was slowly coming out of her shell and looking so much more relaxed and happier than she had all day.

'So, you're really going to stay in the castle overnight all on your own?' she asked Zen, her face contorted into mock fear. 'Ellie was telling me all about the ghosts that roam around in there when strangers dare to enter,' she smirked.

'You never told me that,' said Zen, winking at me.

'It's true,' I smiled. 'They were all over the guest apartment when I first arrived, but we got to be friends. Just don't take any nonsense from the one that carries his head underneath his arm.'

'Listen, if any of them manages to wake me up then they deserve to haunt me because I am officially shattered. I will sleep like the dead after nearly a full bottle of this.' He drained his glass. 'Right, I'm off to the tower. If they chop my head off, please make sure my hair is looking it's best, will you?'

'Night, Zen,' said a sleepy Sophie.

'Night, ghostbuster,' smiled Kitti.

I went into the porch with him, shutting the inner door behind us. Wrapping our arms around each other, we said a very passionate goodnight. Had it not been for the two runaways on the other side of that door, I think I know exactly what would have happened next!

'I wish I was helping you to remove that dress, Ellie,' Zen murmured, as his hand began to work its way down my boilersuit. I pushed in to him and began to mould into his familiar body. 'Let me just find out what's under your very seductive overalls,' he said, trying to pull down the zipper, which got snagged on the material and stuck firm.

'Saved by the zip,' I grinned. 'Shame, because there's nothing under them except for some really wispy lingerie, which is far more for show than practicality. I'll leave you with that thought. Night night, gorgeous. Sleep well, and

I'll see you early in the morning.' Then, much as I didn't want to, I gently pushed him out of the door.

Chapter 7

'Who's for bed?' I asked, as I went back into the room. 'Sophie, Kitti is on the sofa, so we'd better go and let her get some sleep. Kitti, you go to the bathroom first. I've left a new toothbrush for you, and there's plenty of towels. I'll bring in the bedding. Just shove the dogs off if they try to climb on you in the night. Sophie, you're on the bottom bunk – I'm not risking you falling out of the top one.'

Kitti and I took an arm each, heaved Sophie off the sofa and guided her to the broom cupboard, where she somehow managed to pull off her jeans and jumper then flopped into bed.

'Kitti,' I said, as I got her sorted, 'you're not going to do a runner in the middle of the night, are you? You know nothing about the tides on the island, and it would be so dangerous.' I thought back to my own arrival when I was as naïve as she was now.

'I promise I won't, Ellie. I feel safe here, and I'm very sleepy. I've told Nacho he can be up on the sofa with me... is that okay?' she added quickly.

'Of course it is. I'm pleased to hear that you're feeling okay. We do need to talk more in the morning, but I'm sure we can sort everything out for you. Night night, chick. Sleep well.'

By the time I'd got Kitti settled, Sophie was fast asleep, so I climbed into the top bunk and lay wide awake, going over the events of the day. Due to Sophie's unexpected arrival, we still hadn't managed to have that talk to Kitti, and my brain was whirring as to why she was on Lindisfarne. And what on earth was going on with Sophie? Plus, it felt like everyone was wanting to meet to discuss matters pertaining to the island. Things seemed all at sea, and I felt as adrift as if I was on the tiny *Lady Eleanor* on a choppy tide. On that last thought I dozed off, thinking of Zen lying in splendid luxury in that huge bed in the castle guest apartment. I wished I was there with him, because then I wouldn't have time to think about anything else other than us.

I felt Sophie stirring underneath me. A glance at my watch told me it was just gone 3 a.m.

'Sophie, are you awake?' I whispered.

'Ellie, is that you? Where am I? It's pitch black in here! I'm scared. Have I died and been put in a coffin?'

I couldn't help but laugh.

'You're at Meg and Bert's, in the broom cupboard, in the bottom bunk bed which is why you feel a bit enclosed. Don't bang your head when you get up.'

'Need the loo,' she said. 'Where's the light? Or can you put your phone torch on. Don't even know where mine is.'

I switched the light on so she could navigate her way around the little room and find her way to the bathroom.

'Ellie, who's that on the sofa?' asked Sophie as she came back into the room. 'She's got long blonde hair sticking out. Don't tell me it's the Poison Pylon?'

'Like it would be! It's Kitti – you met her last night. Long story, which I'll tell you about in the morning.'

Sophie climbed back into the bunk, and I heard her sniff.

'Oh, Ellie Nellie, I've made a bit of an arse of myself, haven't I?'

'No more than usual. You want to talk about it or leave it until the morning?'

'It's Jake,' she whispered. 'I lost it altogether yesterday, so threw some things in a bag and went straight to Kings Cross to find a train up here. I just wanted my bestie.'

'And you've got me, Soph. What's going on?'

'We've been engaged a year and a half now and no closer to getting married. Every time I raise the question Jake just prevaricates. I'm not sure he even wants to marry me anymore.' She began to cry.

'Oh, Soph, I'm sure that's not the case. He adores you. Is there anything going on that might be contributing to his reluctance to move on the wedding? Work, for example – he's in such a high stress environment. You hear of traders in the city burning out all the time, and whilst I wouldn't expect that of Jake, who knows.'

'He's always working. I hardly ever get to see him, and since we moved to Chelsea it's got even worse. I spend most nights on my own until he comes in about ten, and then he's so tired he just goes to bed.'

'Sounds to me like he's working too hard.'

'Or maybe he's got another woman,' she wailed, 'and comes home exhausted after a shagathon.'

I really couldn't see Jake doing that to Sophie. He had never struck me as a philanderer. Far from it; Jake was a family man with strong values, who kept those he loved close.

'So, what happened yesterday to make you leave him?'

There was a long pause.

'Erm, well, I've been feeling so stressed lately that on Friday at work I couldn't concentrate, and I ended up nicking Mr Chakravarti's foot with a scalpel. It started to bleed quite badly, and he yelled at me. I don't blame him. Phil was livid, which I understand, because it's his business, and he can't have staff who aren't on the ball, but at the time I just couldn't take any more. I chucked my badge at him, told him to shove his smelly job and to go stuff his bunions where the sun don't shine. To which he said not to bother coming back.'

'You've lost your job? Surely not? He'll calm down – you've been there ages.'

'He won't. It wasn't the first time, Ellie, and I was already on a warning,' she whispered. 'I just haven't been concentrating at all lately, and I've had a few days off too.'

'That's so not you, Sophie,' I murmured.

'My official letter of dismissal arrived by email on Saturday morning, and when Jake found out he was apoplectic, and we had a huge row. I thought he might have understood, but he didn't, so now I'm here.'

I clambered down from the top bunk, drew my sobbing friend into my arms and stroked her hair.

'Listen, I'm sure we can put at least some of that right. Might not get your job back–'

'I don't want it back,' she said vehemently. 'I'm sick of smelly feet.'

'Oh, okay. Well then, that's one less thing to think about. Let's concentrate on Jake, but not now,' I said, glancing at the time on my phone. 'It's 3:45 a.m. and I need to be up at about 6:30 a.m. to sort the animals out before having a million other things to do tomorrow. I mean today!'

'Oh, of course. Meg and Bert had their second wedding yesterday. And I can't even get my first,' she said, only half joking. 'Was it lovely?'

'I'll tell you all about that in the morning. And you can go and see Granny Ethel. She'll have her very own take on your situation and will be full of useful advice... not! Try and have a few more hours' sleep, because I'm going to drag you out of that coffin to come and help me in the morning. Don't say you haven't been warned. If you're staying here then you will have to pull your weight – no slackers on Lindisfarne,' I laughed. 'Seriously, Sophie, you're going to be okay, you know. Love you loads, bestie. Now go back to sleep, stop it with the too-much-wine snoring, and let me get some much-needed shuteye!'

Chapter 8

The alarm went off at 6:30 a.m. and I heard Sophie groan from the bottom bunk.

'Did I dream it, or did you say I had to help this morning?'

'Yes, I did say it, and I meant it. Now get your carcass out of there and get ready. Did you bring any casuals with you, or can I lend you something? We might have to roll the legs up, though.'

'Listen, Ellie Nellie, I'm almost a local here. I know the score, and I brought jeans and jumpers with me. Are you sure you need me to help?'

I pulled the duvet off her and she squealed. It was just like being back in our flat in Peckham. We went through to the living room where Kitti was buried under a mound of dogs on the sofa.

'Sorry to wake you, Kitti. We're just going to have a hot drink, and then we need to go and see to the animals. You just stay there; it'll be nice and quiet when we go out.'

Kitti bounced out of bed with the exuberance of youth, scattering the dogs who had their early morning shake then lined up at the door to go out.

'I'm coming to help too,' she smiled. 'Is that okay?'

'Of course it is – the more the merrier.'

'Er, well, if Kitti is helping then maybe I...' began Sophie, until I gave her *the* look.

'Right then,' she continued, 'cup of tea and I'm ready.'

The door opened and the dogs all shot out.

'Any coffee on the go?' asked Zen, coming in and looking far too good for this early in the day.

'Hey, morning,' I said. 'How did you sleep?'

'Did the ghosts not get you?' laughed Kitti.

'Well, funny you should mention that. I don't believe in them, but something strange happened last night.'

'No way! I was only joking, you know. Ellie didn't really say there were ghosts.'

'Well,' said Zen, 'I got into bed, and then all of a sudden I heard a clanking noise. It sounded like pipes, but I know for sure Bert switched the heating off in both apartments recently because I was with him when he did it, and no one else has been in there since.'

'Maybe Toby's been up there for something?' I pondered.

'Tobes never goes in the apartments when they're empty, Ellie.'

'Maybe it was chains rattling. Perhaps an old knight in armour was captured and had his legs shackled together, then died in agony being tortured,' said a wide eyed Kitti, who was really getting into the paranormal possibilities.

'Or a decapitated monk, who was pulling his head along on chains,' I suggested.

'No, I think it would have been a hunky Viking clanking along the corridor, dragging his latest conquest to the boudoir.'

'Sophie, the Vikings were never in this castle,' I laughed, 'but I like the thought of that!'

'Hey, you lot, I've already told you that I don't believe in ghosts, but I'm telling you, I heard something. I'll go and check over the castle when we've done this morning.'

'You probably just imagined it,' I said, wrapping my arms around him and giving him a hug. 'All that talk of ghosts before you went over was probably just playing on your mind. Anyway, come on – we've got work to do. Sophie, you take Kitti and make a start on the chicken and turkey coops. Zen and I will go down to the paddocks and start down there. See you both back here for coffee later.'

As Zen and I walked hand in hand down the cinder path towards the paddocks, it gave us a chance to talk. The sun had been risen for a while, but we were now in what was described as the golden hour. As we looked over to the east, the landscape was cloaked in citrus shades which were diluting with every step we took down the bank.

'Did you manage to speak to Sophie last night?'

'Erm, kind of, at about 4:00 a.m. this morning. It sounds like her and Jake have been having some serious issues lately.' I told Zen what Sophie had said.

'Does Jake even know where she is? He might be worried sick.'

'Blimey, I never even thought about that. Would it be interfering to ring him later? Maybe you can do that. Probably better him speaking to you.'

'Why? Because I'm a man?' he grinned.

'No, because you're not Soph's bestie, and he might be more inclined to speak freely to you.'

'Okay, I will, if nothing more than to tell him she's safe. Now what about runaway number two?'

'It's mad, isn't it?' I laughed. 'Two for the price of one. You leave Kitti to me, and I'll see if I can find out what's going on there. She seems really relaxed now; I think she might trust me enough to talk a little. Right, best crack on. Would you prefer horse dung or alpaca poo? Take your pick – I'm all heart, me!'

***

Later that morning, Zen had given Sophie a lift across to the village to see Granny Ethel, and I knew just the thing to get Kitti even more relaxed and hopefully inclined to talk to me: an alpaca walk.

'Which one do you want to lead?' I asked, holding Pacino in one hand and Murray in the other. 'We can swap on the way back.'

'They're both so beautiful,' she said. I think Amelia said she likes Pacino best, so maybe I'll take him.'

I handed her the gorgeous dark coated alpaca with the giant chocolate button eyes as I held on to Murray with his grey cotton wool coat. I made sure she had her pockets topped up with carrot slices, and then we set off from the paddocks across to the village. We walked slowly, and I could see Kitti's eyes darting across the island. Every now and again she would stop to stroke Pacino and whisper into his furry ear.

'What's those funny hut things?' She pointed to the upside-down fishing boats. 'We saw them yesterday from the cart, and I wondered what they were. Look at all those birds over there.' She nodded towards the coast. 'What's that ruined thing?' She gestured towards the priory. 'Where did St Cuthbert live on a little island? I read about that. How many people get stuck in that hut on legs in the sea?'

Kitti was firing out questions like a Gatling gun!

'Whoa, slow down. Let's just enjoy the walk today, and I'll tell you all about the island later.'

'There may not be a later, Ellie. Have I got to go back tomorrow?'

'Look, there's the bench where we met yesterday. Why don't we sit for a little while and have a chat, then I'll treat you to a hot chocolate and cake in Aurora's café. How does that sound?'

Kitti nodded. We sat down on the bench, fussed over the alpacas and tied them up, then Kitti turned towards me and took a big intake of breath.

Chapter 9

'I lost my mam,' Kitti whispered, and I saw big, fat tears silently roll down her cheeks. 'She was killed in a car accident. She was only thirty-two.'

I gulped. That wasn't much older than me. She had been so young.

'Oh, Kitti, I'm so sorry,' I said. 'Can I give you a hug?' She nodded and I wrapped her into my arms and felt her thin body shake with sobs.

'How long ago was it?' I asked gently.

'Six weeks and four days,' she said precisely.

'That's no time at all. You must be numb'.

'I am. I keep thinking I feel a bit better, but I don't really. Me and mam were so close, Ellie. There was only us, and now there's only me, and I'm so scared.'

'You poor darling, Kitti. If I ask you questions you don't want to answer, then please just tell me – I won't be offended. What about your dad? Is he in your life at all?'

'No, he's not. I never met him. Mam and he were very young when I came along, and I don't think he even knows I exist.'

'Oh, okay. What about grandparents on your mum's side? Aunties or uncles?'

'Mam didn't have brothers or sisters. She was an unexpected baby; they were quite old when they had her, and she was only sixteen when she got pregnant with me. Same age as I am now. I know I would never be able to cope with a baby, yet mam did all on her own. When her parents found out, can you believe they kicked her out? They said she had brought shame on the family, and they wanted no more to do with her. Then they moved miles away somewhere without even telling mam. I never met them, and don't ever want to,' she said bitterly.

'That's understandable,' I agreed, angry on her behalf.

'The social worker was so pushy, saying that it would be in my best interests if they tracked them down and I went to live with them. And do you know what? That was because it was the easiest thing for her to do. She's awful. Why do people go into jobs like that when they aren't even kind?' She broke down into more sobs.

'I don't know, chick. Suppose the things they deal with day in day out might make them a bit brittle around the edges. That's no excuse though. You've been through a lifechanging event, and you need a lot of support and kindness.'

'I told her I hadn't even met them, but that didn't seem to count for anything, and she wasn't listening to me. She couldn't find them, though; although I think she's still looking. I said I didn't know anything about them, which is mainly true. Mam always said I had to protect myself and go with my gut about people and situations. I knew it would be the worst thing I could do to go anywhere near the people who had been so evil to my mam.'

'I get that,' I said. 'So, is that how you ended up in care?'

'Yes. Me and mam lived in a rented house, so I had nowhere to go after she died.'

'Where was that, Kitti?'

'Heaton. Do you know where that is? You and Sophie don't talk like us.' She gave a tiny smile, which was good to see.

'Hey, I'll have you know I'm a posh southerner, according to Maurice who was driving the cart yesterday. I'm from Cambridge, though I lived in London for years before I came to the island, but now I'm an adopted Geordie. I love it here. Heaton is near Jesmond, isn't it? We deliver coffee around there, and see, I am getting to know my way around!'

'I wanted to stay in our house, but they said I was too young because I was fifteen then. I only had my birthday two weeks ago. I had no money to pay for it, so they found me a temporary foster placement until they can look for a flat or hostel or whatever dump they can shove me in.'

'So, your foster carer, is she okay?'

'Yes, she's called Sue and her husband is Billy. They've fostered loads of kids, and they are kind and friendly, but there's another girl placed there too. That's why Sue didn't really take that much notice when I said I was coming to Lindisfarne for the weekend, because Paige was kicking off. I don't like her; she's mean and scary. She's only fourteen but has been in loads of trouble, so I just stay in my room as much as possible out of the way. I do see a bereavement counsellor, though. He's really nice and listens, but he can't do what I want like get mam back or at least get rid of Paige, and I don't really want to move foster carers because it could be even worse.'

My heart was beginning to break. I couldn't bear the idea of this bright young woman, who had been through hell, being passed around like a parcel and not having the stability and proper care she needed to help her through such a traumatic time.

'Pacino and Murray are getting a little impatient, Kitti,' I said, standing up and turning away. I pretended to fuss with their halters so that she didn't see the tears that were threatening to spill down my cheeks. 'Let's carry on to the café. I think we could both do with a treat after that, then we can talk some more.'

I was desperate to tell her I would help, as no doubt half the islanders would, but she had been through so much I didn't want to offer false hope until I could find out what could be done, if anything.

'You've already got friends on Lindisfarne, Kitti. There's Zen and me, Meg, your Granny Ethel,' I laughed. 'Oh, and your runaway sister Sophie. We'll all be there for you as much as we can.'

'I knew Mam would be right about Holy Island,' Kitti said cryptically, wiping her face and unhooking Pacino. As we set off towards the Priory and the village, I wondered just what on earth she could mean by that.

Chapter 10

When we got to the café garden, there wasn't much privacy to discuss Kitti's situation any further, as the tourists were out in force with their cameras, wanting to take photos of the alpacas.

'Hey, Pip, how are you coping without the boss?' I asked, as Aurora's assistant came to take our order.

'Hi, Ellie. It's pretty full on, and the season is starting officially next week. I just don't know how I'm going to cope. Are you still coming to do some shifts?'

'I'll try my best, Pip. Aurora said she wanted to see us to talk about what was going to happen. Oh, sorry – this is Kitti from Newcastle. She's staying with us until tomorrow.'

'Hi,' smiled Pip warmly. She was probably only a couple of years older than Kitti.

'Two of your special Zen hot chocolates, the ones with the salted caramel. Promise you'll love it, Kitti. You choose the cake.'

As Pip went off to prepare the order, I explained about Aurora being on maternity leave and a little about how many of us on the island had more than one job.

'That's Zen's roasting shed. It's officially called the roastery, but we just call it the posh shed,' I said, pointing to the wooden building at the rear of the garden. 'Zen and Aurora are brother and sister. Aurora and her husband, Jack, and their tiny baby, Hettie, live on the first floor above the café. And see those windows sticking out of the roof up there? Well, that's the attic where Zen and I live.'

'Where does Ethel live?' asked Kitti.

'Just on the edge of the village. Ethel's family have been islanders for generations, and she lives in the same cottage her ancestors lived in when they first came to the island. Between you and me, we're all worried about Ethel, because she's an old lady now and is finding getting around increasingly difficult, although she'd never admit to that. Her cottage is like a time capsule and hasn't got an upstairs bathroom, which is becoming a problem. She could really do with a stair lift too, if she's to stay there, but Ethel knows her own mind, so we won't interfere until she asks for help. If she ever does.'

'It must be cool to live somewhere where people look out for you,' Kitti mused.

'It is, of course,' I replied. 'But the other side of the coin is that everyone knows everyone else's business. When I first arrived on the island, everyone knew my name before I even got here.'

Kitti looked horrified.

'Will they know about me?'

'Of course not. Those of us who know won't say anything. We've just said that you're a guest from Newcastle who came to the blessing, and everyone accepted that without question. Right – are you ready to get these two back to their paddock?'

'They've been so good,' smiled Kitti. 'They seem to like having their photos taken.'

'I think it's got more to do with the carrots they're given as a reward.'

'We'll pop in to see Ethel on the way back, if that's okay with you. I want to check in with Sophie. She's got some things going on too.'

'Er, yes – she was very upset last night. Unhappy people seem to come to this island, don't they?' she pondered.

'You're not far wrong, Kitti. That's how I came to Lindisfarne. I suppose you could say I ran away too, and it was the best thing I could have done. Many of the people who come do so to look for guidance, to reflect or just try and find themselves again. It's well known for being a very spiritual place, and I hope some of its magic rubs off on you.'

As we walked past Love Lindisfarne, the gift shop, Kitti stopped to peer into the window. The shop was shut, but the door suddenly flew open.

'Ellie! Pleased I caught you – was just about to send a text message,' said Imogen. 'Crafty Lindisfarners board meeting here tomorrow at 10.00 a.m. Hope you can make it. And Kitti, you'd be more than welcome to join us if you're still around. I hear Sophie is here on the island too.'

I winked at Kitti. 'See, the island bush telegraph strikes again!' I turned to Imogen. 'Yes, she is. Hopefully, she'll call in to see you before she heads back to London.'

We continued along the main street towards the edge of the village. Whilst we had year-round tourists on the island, the bulk of visitors came in the spring and summer months, and the shops were gearing up for the influx with pretty plant displays and newly designed window dressings.

'It's very different to Chillingham Road. That's my main street in Heaton,' smiled Kitti.

'I imagine that's more like mine was when Sophie and I lived in Peckham.'

'I like this, though,' said Kitti, 'even though there aren't any takeaways that I can see.'

'There aren't, but you get used to that, and the café and pub both do lovely food to take home,' I said smiling, remembering Meg telling me when I first arrived that I'd just have to get used to the lack of eateries that I used to find right outside our flat door in London.

We arrived at Ethel's and tied up the alpacas in her back garden then went into the cottage. Sophie was sitting on the sofa, a big box of tissues by her side, her eyes red like two blood moons, and Ethel was holding court from her chair.

'You okay, Sophie?' I asked. 'Kitti and me have just walked the alpacas and are on our way back. Thought you might want to walk to the castle with us?'

'I'm going to go and see Tara and Farne. I texted her and I'm going for lunch – and more sage advice,' she smiled. We both knew Tara was only one step behind Ethel in speaking her mind out loud with no filter.

'You just bear in mind what I've said, young lady,' cackled Ethel, as Sophie stood up to go. 'He's a good man is your Jake. You find out what's going on before you burn any more bridges. You hear me?'

'I do, Granny Ethel, and I promise,' replied Sophie, sounding anything but convincing.

'Good, pet. Now then, Kittiwake – how are you today?'

'My mam was the only person to ever call me by my full name,' Kitti said sadly, 'but it's nice to hear you say it.'

'Well, if it's okay with you, I'd like to always call you by the lovely name your mam chose for you. Oh, and what's your surname, if you don't mind me asking?' quizzed Ethel.

'It's Penaluna.'

'That's an unusual name – never heard it before,' I smiled.

'It's Cornish,' said Kitti bluntly, without going into any more detail.

'I've heard that name before somewhere, I'm sure of it, but I'm buggered if I can think where,' said Ethel, her eyebrows knitted together deep in thought. 'It'll come to me. Meg, Bert and me once went to Cornwall on holiday, so it might be from there, but I don't think so. Lovely place. Pasties are okay, but I prefer me a nice Greggsies.'

'I've never been to Cornwall. Don't ever want to,' said Kitti angrily.

'Anyway, Kittiwake,' said Ethel, quickly changing the topic as we could all see that Kitti was upset by something to do with Cornwall, 'you're looking so much better, and you've got a bit of colour in your cheeks. As pearly pink as my apple blossom, they are. Are this lot looking after you? They'd better, or they'll have me to deal with!'

'Everyone has been so kind, thank you, Ethel. They've let me help, and I love all the animals – especially Holly Goatlightly, and I wish I could...'

She trailed off but I could almost guess that she would have said something to the effect that she wished she could have stayed on the island.

'Chin up, babe. Us runaways stick together,' said Sophie, as she gave Kitti a sisterly hug then went to the door.

'Hang on, Sophie, I'll come down to Tara's with you. Ethel, is it okay if Kitti stays with you a while? I've got a few things I need to do. Can you keep an eye on Pacino and Murray and take them out a drink, please, Kitti?'

Kitti and Ethel both nodded, smiling at each other.

'She can stay all day for me. Linda will be coming with my Sunday lunch soon; I'll ring and get her to bring Kitti one too. You go and give those animals a drink,' she said, turning to Kitti, 'and I'll find an episode of *Homes under the Hammer* and we can guess the prices – mind, I'll show me wrinkly old arse from the top of the lighthouse if any of them ever tell the truth about the cost of doing up those properties.'

'Ethel!' said Sophie and I in unison.'

'You're funny,' said a laughing Kitti, 'but in a good way.'

'Aye, that's been said before,' replied Ethel grinning.

Kitti went to fill a bucket with water, and I steered Sophie towards Tara's, hoping that between us we could help get Sophie and Jake back on track. If that happened without Sophie digging the heels in, then I might be showing my derriere from the top of the lighthouse too!

Chapter 11

'Sophie, Ellie,' squealed Tara. 'I can't believe all three of us are back together again in the Holiday House and that we own it now – not that we've done anything to it yet, other than Farne's room. Too busy. Talking of the little cherub, he's having his nap. Toby is in the study and on hand for daddy day care, so we can have a proper catch up. The Pinot is on ice.'

We followed Tara into the lounge, with the huge squashy sofas arranged around a roaring log fire.

'You were so lucky being able to buy the house furnished,' I said. 'I love the shabby chic effect, which I appreciate might not have been deliberate on Muriel's part, but it really suits the house.'

'Me too,' said Sophie. 'I'll be honest, I hate our flat in Chelsea. I hate all the clean lines, the clinical furniture, the neutral walls that close in on you. The place is so small, yet it probably cost twice as much as this fabulous house.'

'But it's got that beautiful view of the marina, and a balcony,' I said, trying to uplift the mood.

'Ellie, if you've seen one boat you've seen them all, and that balcony is so small you have to go out on to it sideways. Plus, you've got half of *Made in Chelsea* staring up at you when they're running past looking all tanned and lovely in designer Lycra, with their caramel ponytails swishing along behind them. It's all so bleedin' fake. I HATE IT ALL!' she shouted vehemently.

I looked at Tara who immediately sprang into action.

'Here, have this,' she said, shoving a big glass of Pinot into Sophie's hands.

'Ellie, what can I get you?'

'Can I have a coffee, please? I've got loads on today, so I'll leave it to you two to put a dent in your wine rack. Okay, Soph,' I said, coffee in hand, as she took a top up of wine from Tara. 'Better get this grilling underway before you get trollied. What on earth's going on, and more to the point, what can we do to help?'

Sophie put her glass down on the coffee table and gazed around the room. 'It is lovely in here, Tara. It's got such a peaceful vibe – a proper family home. Sorry about the outburst, but when I think about our soulless box in London, it just adds to my misery. If you both remember, I never really wanted to move there. When Jake said he didn't want me to take any of our old stuff, including our favourite sofa, Ellie, I kind of left all of my identity behind, if that makes sense.'

'It does. But Jake isn't the type of person to dictate to you, is he?' I asked, wondering if I knew him as well as I thought I did.

'No, he's not. And I got what he was saying initially. A brand-new swanky apartment and tatty old second-hand furniture don't really mix, do they? I'll admit I was sort of excited by the prospect of new beginnings after Peckham, but I'm really not happy there, and Jake is saying that we can't move at the moment.'

'For what reason?' asked Tara.

'The usual. Money. Jake seems to be working harder than ever, and I hardly see him. I think of you two, living and working alongside your partners, and then there's Jake and me, who are hardly ever together. He doesn't even seem to care, and I don't even know if he's really working or…' she tailed off.

That really didn't sound like Jake.

Sophie blew her nose and took a gulp of her wine before continuing.

'We've been engaged for what feels like ages now. I thought we would be married quite quickly, but when we got to London after our holiday up here with you all, we both just reverted to city life at a hundred miles an hour. We never seemed to find the time to even discuss planning anything. Then, when I did bring it up and began to tell Jake what kind of wedding I'd like, he just kept asking me how much it would all cost and that maybe we could wait a while. Jake earns a lot of money, so I don't understand what the issue is, and I'm now thinking that it's because he doesn't want to marry me at all.'

'What kind of wedding *do* you want?' I asked gently.

'Ellie, you know that I'm part of a massive family, and my mum and sisters got totally invested and kind of took over, me being the first girl to get married. I'd already picked out that gorgeous wedding venue in the countryside near Cambridge. You know the one I mean – it has a moat and everything.'

My eyebrows shot up until they were resting on Tara's coving.

'Soph, that place costs a fortune.'

'Well, the photos will be stunning, won't they? replied Sophie, sounding irritated. 'The thing is, Jake and me both have such big families, so it would be expensive for the guest list. I get that, so I pared it down to one hundred and twenty. But then my mum started saying we couldn't invite some cousins and not others, so it all got a bit out of hand, and the numbers crept up towards two hundred and fifty.'

'Two hundred and fifty,' I gasped. 'That's more than the population of this entire island.'

Tara stared at Sophie open mouthed before taking a big gulp of wine.

'I don't think I know that many people,' said Tara. 'Horses for courses, Sophie, but how does Jake feel about such a grand occasion? Is it the type of wedding he wants? Is it the wedding you both want? Toby and I are Irish – we've got more family between us than the Von Trapps – but we managed to have a lovely day in that fabulously run-down castle in Tipperary with our nearest and dearest, including you lot, and it didn't cost the earth. It's what you and Jake want, and not what your mammy and your sisters want, you know. You could still have the same venue but keep the costs down with much lower numbers. I bet you don't really know half of them.'

'Well, that's an option,' sniffed Sophie, 'if there's still going to be a wedding. We've really grown apart lately, and the final straw was when I told Jake I'd been sacked. I thought he would comfort me, tell me he was sorry for making me so uptight that I couldn't concentrate and that everything would be okay, but instead he just yelled at me even more, said I was living in a dream world and that my stupidity was going to put him under even more pressure.'

Sophie began to cry.

'You've been sacked?' gasped Tara.

I shook my head towards her and pulled an imaginary zip along my mouth.

'Oh, er… well, what happens next?' asked Tara, changing course and handing Sophie a tissue. 'Are you going to go back and sort things out with him?'

The look that crossed Sophie's face was one I knew well. She had dug her heels in. The stubborn Sophie of old, which I hadn't seen in a very long time, had re-emerged.

'No, I am not. Jake should be here now. I've been on the island a day and he hasn't even texted me. I was expecting him to follow me up and apologise for what he said to me. I've got nothing to go back for. If it's okay with you, Tara, can I stay in one of the spare rooms for a few days, then I'll decide what to do. But in the meantime, I'm on holiday, so top this glass up. I'm going to forget about Jake for now and have some fun.'

I glanced at Tara, who was shaking her head in bewilderment.

'Erm, of course you can stay Sophie, but maybe just phone Jake, eh?'

'Hmm, I'll see,' said Sophie. 'I might later.'

Later would be no good the way she was throwing the wine down her throat; it was a car crash waiting to happen.

'Sorry, but I've got to go and see Reverend Rosie about something,' I said, getting up to go.

'You're not planning your wedding, are you?' said Sophie, eyeing me suspiciously.

'What wedding? We're not even engaged yet. It's about Kitti. Look, come over to the cottage for your bag later, Sophie, and let's talk to Zen – he might be able to help. I'm sure we can sort this.'

'Of course we can,' said Tara encouragingly.

'Well, I'm pleased you two think it can be sorted,' replied Sophie sarcastically. 'Anyway, enough of that for now. Any chance of something to eat, Tara? I'm starving after being dragged out of bed at stupid o' clock.' Sophie adopted the face – the one I knew well enough to know it was subject closed for now. Tara was in for an afternoon of treading on eggshells.

'Don't worry about her,' said Tara as she showed me out. 'I'll limit the wine. I'll tell her we've gone almost tee-total since Farne arrived and only ever have one bottle in the house at a time.'

'She'll never believe you,' I said, giving Tara a hug. 'Worth a go, but whatever happens, don't let her go back to Ethel's. The pair of them will be on the hooch that Ethel keeps stashed under the sink, and I don't want Kitti seeing the result of that,' I grinned. 'You know, Soph – once the hurt has subsided, she'll be mortified and be on the next train back to Jake.'

One could live in hope.

Chapter 12

I walked back over to the castle. The tide was now in, meaning the island was once again cut off from the rest of the world. Zen was at the far end of the yard, pulling out chairs next to the five-bar gate which looked through to the paddocks below. It was late afternoon, and the birds were circling, calling to each other before heading to rest.

As I walked towards Zen, the noise got progressively louder, and I wondered if they were kittiwakes, who were known to be very vocal. Bert had told me the young have a black W across their wings, and I looked to see if I could spot any. He had also told me that if I listened carefully, I would hear them say kitt-eee-waaake and possibly a laugh at the end, like a ha-ha-ha. I smiled, wondering just why Kitti had been named after the birds that called this very island home.

'Hey, gorgeous,' Zen smiled. 'Busy day? I was just getting set up so we could sit and have a glass of wine and a catch up. Sound good to you?'

'Absolutely,' I said, drawing him towards me and running my fingers through his dark curls, which were catching the last of the golden rays from the sun and taking on a hue of burnished copper. As my eyes locked with his, we stood silently and hugged, and everything was all right in our world for about two seconds – before the dogs came charging up the cinder path then burst through the gate, and our bubble.

'You sit,' said Zen, kissing me full on the mouth, 'I'll go and get the wine'.

He came back with a bottle of Merlot, a plate of cheese and crackers, and two glasses.

'Honestly, Ellie, I don't know what it is, but we always seem to end up in some drama when we come to stay at the cottage, I'm still not quite over when the television production company came.'

'Me neither,' I smiled. 'I do know what you mean, though. I thought we would have a nice week together, just us and the dogs and the rest of the menagerie, and instead, here we are with two runaways.'

'Talking of, how has that been today, and actually, where are they?'

I explained about Sophie being with Tara and Kitti with Ethel. 'Did you manage to speak to Jake?'

'Yes, I did. Jake knew she had come here to the island because she left her laptop open, showing the train times and ticket purchase.

'So why isn't he here?'

Zen looked at me curiously.

'Why isn't Sophie there?'

'Touche. I just thought he would have followed her.'

'Well, it seems that they've been having a few problems of late, mainly of the financial kind. Ellie, Jake told me all of this in confidence, but I said I would tell you and he was okay with that. This is between me and you, right?'

'Yes, of course.'

'I'm really worried about him. Honestly, he sounds like a man on the edge. He's burned out. The stress of working in the city environment has taken its toll. He's been working longer and longer hours, trying to keep up, and says he feels like he is on a hamster wheel and getting nowhere fast. The financial markets have been so volatile of late that the strain on him has been huge.'

'I know it's a high stress environment, but Jake just seemed to cope with it,' I replied, shocked at hearing that he was under so much pressure.

'They bought that apartment in Chelsea Harbour, and it stretched them, but Jake was expecting a big bonus which he was going to use to reduce the mortgage. Only it never materialised, and basically they are living beyond their means. He's tried to protect Sophie from most of this, which apparently has been quite easy as she seems totally wrapped up in the wedding.'

'Well, that's kind of understandable,' I said, defending my bestie. 'If she's not fully aware of what's going on, then it's reasonable she's focusing on what should be the happiest day of her life.'

'Jake loves her; that's obvious,' continued Zen, 'and I personally don't think he made the right choice to keep things from her, but as the potential wedding costs began to spiral, I think he felt trapped in a corner. Then, of course, when Sophie got sacked, meaning her income was gone, he just saw red and lost control. He went out for a walk to calm down, intending to talk to her when he got back, but she'd already gone.'

'I understand,' I said. 'Poor Jake – he's like a proper bloke's bloke, and it must have been hard for him even talking to you about this.' I grabbed Zen's hand and squeezed it. 'I know Sophie can be quite reactive, but from what she said, she's had enough of her job too. She hates the flat, and her mum and sisters had taken over the wedding plans. She's just gone along with them for a peaceful life.'

'So, what happens next? Zen asked, leaning towards me, tucking a stray strand of hair behind my ear and kissing my neck.

'I know what will happen next if you do that again,' I smiled.

'I didn't mean that!' He burst out into peals of laughter, 'but now you mention it...'

'We need to think about Jake and Soph, then I need to tell you about Kitti, so later, tiger,' I grinned.

'Killjoy! I love you, Ellie Montague. Have I told you that today?'

'I love you too, Zen Chambers, but the answer is still no. Seriously, I do love you, and please – never ever keep stuff buried away like Jake has. I want us to share everything – the good and the bad – and work through things together.'

'Promise, and same goes for you. Right, back to Sophie...'

'She's coming over later to collect her bag. She's staying with Tara and Tobes in the Holiday House for a few days. Or until we can persuade her to go home, that is.'

'And Kitti?'

'I went to see Reverend Rosie. She's agreed to come with me tomorrow to take Kitti back to Newcastle, but first I wanted to talk to you about an idea I've had.'

'Ellie, I can read you like a book, and I've got a feeling I know what's coming.'

'Zen, Kitti came to the island for a reason. I don't know what that is yet, but both Meg and I feel it's something really important. Meg's already rung me twice today to make sure everything is okay.'

'They're supposed to be on honeymoon, having a break,' Zen exclaimed.

'Oh, you know them both well enough. They can't let go of island business that easily.'

'Meg suggested, and I agreed, that I should ask Kitti whether she would be interested in a job and accommodation here on the island. That's if it's possible, because there might be far too much red tape, although Rosie seemed to think it wasn't *im*possible.

'Yep, thought so,' nodded my very understanding, but wary, boyfriend. 'And what job might it be? And more importantly, where would she stay? She can't be on her own.'

'Exactly. She needs a proper, loving environment, with people who have her back and care about her. Listen, I know we've only just met her and still don't know what brought her here, but I have seen enough to know she's a lovely, if very sad, young woman whose gone through an extremely hard time and, erm... well, er, I thought she could maybe have our spare room in the attic.'

'Live with us? Ellie, have you gone mad? Us with a teenager? What do we know about kids of that age?'

'You might find this hard to believe, but you are the same age as her mum was, and I'm only a couple of years younger, so to Kitti we're probably parent age, even though that makes me feel older than Ethel!'

'And how would we all fit in the tiny attic? Our spare room is even smaller than the broom cupboard here, and I'm not sure I want to share my space, or you, for that matter. I mean, I couldn't just wander about in my undercrackers, and I bet she'd want to watch *Love Island* or something when the footie is on. And you two will gang up on me. Oh, Ellie, it's a massive ask. I need to think about it. It's a beautiful thing you're willing to do, and I do understand, and it makes me love you even more, but I really need to think about the implications.'

'I understand,' I nodded.

'It's not like taking another abandoned animal into the fold,' said Zen, sweeping his arms around the yard. 'This is much, much bigger. It's about a bereaved teenager, who sounds like she hasn't had much family support outside of what her mam did. I need to sleep on this, Ellie, and we can talk more, but be prepared for me saying I can't do it. I'm just being honest.'

'I know you are, and I totally get it. I'm kind of scared too, but I've just got this feeling that she needs to be here. Don't ask me how or why. Remember when I said I saw the two stars and they kind of guided me when we got together? This island is known for its spirituality, and there's often things we can't explain logically. This is one of those occasions – maybe I'll see it in the stars again,' I smiled.

'Look, if it's a no from me, it will only be the bit about her living with us, and there will be alternatives, okay?'

'Okay – I want you to be sure. I want *us* to be sure. Kitti may not be interested – I'll talk to her later. Right, I'll pop over and get some more nibbles – you refresh the wine,' and I turned to get up. 'By the way, did you check out your ghosts in the castle today?' I stuttered, looking across to the castle.

'Never had a chance. I'll go over later, but the castle is still there,' he laughed, then noticed the expression on my face. 'What's up? You look like you've seen a ghost. Pardon the pun.'

And at that the dogs started barking and shot off towards the other end of the yard.

'I have,' I replied. 'Somehow, I don't think you're going to need to check, because your ghost is walking down the back steps of the castle right this minute, and he looks very real and human to me!'

Chapter 13

Zen swung around, shaded his eyes with his hands, and stared at the stranger now walking towards us.

'I don't believe it,' he smiled, as the man arrived at the table and I got to see the 'ghost' up close for the first time. Oh, my days, I'd never seen a more handsome spectre in all my life! I'd guess he was about forty, a smidge taller than Zen with steel blue hair that was greying around the front and temples, in a way that looked like it had been styled professionally. Maybe it had, as it was Insta perfect. The man glowed. A golden tan lit up an angular face that might have been sculpted by Michelangelo. His eyes were the colour of autumn leaves in varying shades of gold and amber, his irises ringed with sooty black lines, as if drawn on with a Sharpie. As the man's face broke into a dazzling grin, it was difficult to drag my eyes from where they were dangling halfway down my face and replace them in their sockets. I don't think I'd ever seen a more striking man outside the pages of a Jilly Cooper novel. Of course, he wasn't as handsome as my Zen, but whoever he was, he was mesmerising.

'Inigo,' smiled Zen, reaching over and shaking the man's hand.

'Zen, how you doing? It must be what, about seven years since you stayed with us in Ibiza?'

'Yep, about that.'

'Sorry it didn't work out for you and Bethania,' began the man, then promptly stopped, looking directly at me.

'Inigo, let me introduce you to my girlfriend, Ellie. And it's fine talking about Beth – let's face it, she might be your family before too long, if Aidan and her decide to tie the knot. Ellie and I are both cool with the way things turned out… eventually,' he smiled and squeezed my hand. 'Ellie, this is Inigo Lindisfarne. He's Aidan's cousin, the son of Sir James's brother, Rafe.'

I grasped his hand and looked into the mesmerising eyes, and I swear I saw those autumn leaves swirling around as if caught up in a twister. I'd only had two glasses of wine – what was wrong with me!

'Er, hi,' I squeaked, wishing I was wearing something more decent than a sweatshirt and jeans, although, in fairness, it was actually a step up from most of my outfits these days. 'We thought you were a ghost, but I can see you're not,' I could still feel the warmth from his hand, and it was most definitely human.

'Thank God for that, eh? Although I can think of a few people I'd like to haunt,' he said wryly.

'I'll get you a chair. Ellie was just about to go and grab some more nibbles, so we'll get another glass, and you can tell us just what you're doing in the castle spooking me out.'

I went to the cottage, and the first thing I did was ring Meg.

'Who's Inigo Lindisfarne?' I garbled.

'Nice to speak to you too, Ellie.'

'Oh sorry, are you having a nice time?'

I could hear some sort of Scottish music in the background.

'Just having a drink before an early dinner, or in our case, a late tea,' she laughed. 'Now what's this about Inigo?'

'He's here.'

'Where?'

'Here, at the castle.'

'What the... no one told us he was coming.'

'Nor us,' I replied.

'He's a dish, isn't he?' said Meg.

I had to smile at the word dish, but Meg had hit the nail on the head. He was fit!

'Maybe they've done a house swap for a while. That's where James and Grace are staying in Ibiza – at his place.'

'Oh, I see,' I replied, the penny beginning to drop.

'And from what I gather, he's split up from his wife, so the ladies of the island can form an orderly queue.'

'Not me,' I said firmly.

'Nor me, pet. Not that he would have any interest in a woman of my age. Mind you, Ethel was telling me about this woman they call the Busty Granny.'

'Busty who?'

'Oh, some golden oldie who doesn't seem to have a problem getting younger men. Do you know she...' But before she could regale me with the salacious gossip, I heard the sound of a gong. 'Got to go, Ellie. You watch that Inigo. He's like Aidan – a charmer who could whip the skirt off you quicker than Buck's Fizz.'

I had no idea what she was talking about but got the gist.

'Before I go, any further info on young Kitti?'

I briefly explained about Reverend Rosie and me taking her back to Newcastle and that I was going to talk to Kitti later.

'You ring me soon as you hear anything, okay? And Ellie, me and Bert would take her in, if need be. You know that, don't you?'

'It won't come to that, Meg, but I know you would.' We said our goodbyes and hung up, then I made my way back outside towards my gorgeous rock god and the intriguing silver fox.

'Inigo was just telling me he arrived late last night and didn't want to disturb us, so just went straight into the apartment and put the heating on, which is what I heard clanking.'

'It's bloody freezing in there without the heating, and having just come in from Ibiza, the weather here is Baltic.' He shivered, zipping up what looked like some kind of sailing jacket.

'I didn't get up until late this morning, and when I went over to see Meg and Bert there was no one around.'

Zen explained about the blessing and honeymoon, and us staying in the cottage, juggling our various jobs, hence not being in when he called.

'Not to worry. I told Aunt Grace I didn't want to put them to any extra trouble, so not to ring with advance notice of my arrival. I can imagine they would have been straight in, cleaning and preparing the place, and I reckon they must be getting on a bit now.'

'Never let them hear you say that,' I smiled. 'They're both really well and enjoying life, but you're right – Meg would have had poor old Henry Hoover worn out.'

I liked that Inigo had thought of the older couple. He certainly wasn't coming across as entitled. Not yet any-way.

'So, just fancied a break away?' asked Zen.

'First time in years I've been able to leave the business in capable hands without lots of forward planning. Uncle James was bored and offered to caretake for me if I wanted to take a break.'

'Inigo charters luxury yachts,' explained Zen.

'I split up from Lucia not that long ago, and it's been less than harmonious, so just needed to get away.'

'Sorry to hear that,' said Zen. 'I liked Lucia, but I was terrified of her and her fiery temperament.'

'You and me both, mate.'

'What about Viviana and Santiago. They must be head-ing towards becoming teenagers?'

'My kids,' he smiled at me.

'Yes, Santo is twelve and Vivi ten.' He got out his phone and showed us a photo of two beautiful kids. 'They're with Lucia at the moment until we can sort out access arrangements, which won't be easy with my darling wife, so when James offered to cover things, I just decided to come away and sort my head out.'

'Why here?' I asked, thinking he probably could have gone anywhere in the world.

'Listen to that, Ellie,' he smiled.

'To what?' I asked.

'Precisely. Nothing. I came for some peace and tran-quillity, and to do some thinking without distraction.'

'You do know the holiday season gets underway in earnest next week?' I asked.

'Yes, I do. James mentioned it, but we get this place almost to ourselves when the tide is in, or so I'm told. I'm also intending to do some soul searching by hiking across the wilds of Northumberland, and there's not many peo-ple up on the Cheviots.'

It sounded like Inigo had a lot on his mind. Hopefully, he had come to the right place for contemplation.

<h1 style="text-align:center">Chapter 14</h1>

'It's getting cold out here now,' said Inigo shivering. 'I'll adjust to island temperature soon enough, but how about we go over to the Crab and grab a bite to eat – my treat?'

I was just about to explain about us having guests staying, when the door inside the wooden gates opened and the dogs shot off to greet Tara and Kitti, who were propping up a very wobbly Sophie between them.

'Oh, no. I fear the worst,' I glanced at Zen.

They made it across to the table, and as I stood up, Sophie plonked down into the vacant chair and Kitti shot off down the cinder path to see the animals.

'Tara?' I raised an eyebrow questioningly.

'Sorr…' she began, then stopped mid-sentence as her eyes alighted on Inigo.

'Erm, hello,' she grinned, sticking out one hand towards him, the other smoothing her hair down. 'It's grand to meet you. I'm Tara one of the besties.'

'Inigo,' he replied. 'Great accent. I take it you're not from around these parts?'

'I'm from near Tipperary in Ireland, she replied, taking what seemed like ages to actually remember where she was from, such was her admiration of the new arrival.

'Tara's married to Toby, the Lindisfarne Estate Custodian.'

'Ah,' said Inigo. 'I was going to call into the office first thing tomorrow to introduce myself to him.'

Tara looked puzzled.

'Inigo is Sir James nephew,' I explained. 'He's going to be staying in their apartment in the castle for a while.'

'Cool,' said Tara, unable to hide her delight at such news.

Suddenly, Sophie appeared to return to the land of the living... just. Noticing our guest, she stumbled out of the chair, drew herself up to her full 5' 2" height and peered at Inigo.

'Was it you in the castle last night? You're the ghost? If you don't mind me saying so, you look very real to me. A proper filver sox.' And she leaned forward, grabbed his upper arms and gave them a squeeze, while I found myself hardly able to breathe with embarrassment.

'Yesh, affirm...aff... you are real and are very, very handsome. Just like a young Wayne Rooney.'

Zen, who had been watching proceedings with a straight face, burst out laughing.

'I think you might mean George Clooney, Sophie.'

'That's what I said,' she muttered.

Inigo took the exchange in his stride. I imagined that he was quite used to people being rather awe struck by his physical presence.

'I don't know who you are, but I am Sophie, the real bestie,' she glowered at Tara. 'I'm on holiday, and perhaps you are too, so would you like to take me to the Crab for a drink?' My eyebrows shot up and landed somewhere on the stable roof. 'Coffee, Ellie Nellie, before you get a hernia. I know when I am broken.'

'I only left her for two minutes when I went to see to Farne,' whispered Tara, 'and she was off to Ethel's and on the happy juice.'

'I can hear you, you know. So, Mr Fox, are we going?'

'Actually,' laughed Inigo, 'I'd just asked Zen and Ellie to come with me for something to eat, so why don't we all go?'

'Ah, thanks, Inigo, but count me out. I really need to speak to Kitti tonight, but Zen will go.'

'I will?' he questioned.

'Yes, to keep an eye on Soph,' I whispered in his ear.

'Gotcha,' he smiled.

'Sorry, I must get back for Farne,' apologised Tara. 'Tobes has had him most of the day, so tell you what, why don't I send him across? He'd enjoy some company that doesn't involve Peppa Pig. Ellie, can I come and grab Sophie's bag?'

Tara and I walked to the cottage to collect Sophie's belongings.

'That was a bit embarrassing,' I laughed.

'He seemed to take it all in good grace. He's like, well fit, isn't he? If I was single, I'd be on it like a car bonnet!'

'As long as Sophie isn't. She's not single... yet, anyway, and I for one don't want it to come to that, as her and Jake are meant to be together.'

We went back into the yard, and Tara called to the others.

'Come on, I'll drop you all off in the village. Sophie tucked her arm into Inigo's and made her precarious journey across the cobbles.

'Keep an eye on her, please,' I said to Zen, giving him a hug.

'I'll text you if she doesn't come home tonight, the lucky bag,' Tara grinned.

'Tara! She'd better, and once she does, lock her in and don't let her out until the morning.'

Once they had all gone, I went down to the paddocks, where Kitti was gazing at the Alpacas and talking gently to them.

'Getting some love?' I smiled.

'I'm sure they understand everything you say to them,' said Kitti. 'They look so wise.'

'I'm sure they do,' I replied. 'I know – I often chat to them. Not just the alpacas but most of the animals. Maybe not the hens,' I laughed. 'Anyway, Kitti, fancy helping me do the lock down for the night, then you and I can get comfy in the cottage, and we can have a talk? The others have all gone to the pub, so it'll be nice and quiet, just you and me.'

'Yep,' she replied. Just tell me what you want me to do now. Is it okay if I see to the goats? I want to say goodnight to Holly before I have to go back tomorrow. I really wish I didn't have to.'

I wished she could stay as well. The animals were proving to be just the kind of therapy Kitti needed right now.

Chapter 15

Once back in the cottage, Kitti sprawled out on the sofa, and I took advantage of Bert's comfy chair. I saw how relaxed she looked, nothing like the broken young woman we had met just yesterday.

'Have you enjoyed today, Kitti?'

'I really have, Ellie. Ethel's so funny – she just says whatever she likes and doesn't care.'

'Yep, she's a one off, that's for sure,' I laughed. 'How was Sophie? Those two can be a nightmare when they get going.'

'She's canny too. They got some old bottle from underneath the sink, and after a couple of glasses they were both singing their heads off to Ethel's records. She's still got a one of those old things with vinyl – it's cool – but the music wasn't,' she smiled.

'They didn't give you any alcohol, did they?'

'No, and I wouldn't have had it anyway, but Ethel told Sophie I wasn't to touch it.'

'Good. It's homemade hooch. Been brewed on this island for years by the local fisherman to an ancient old recipe. No one knows quite what goes into it – I hate to think. Maurice, who was driving the cart yesterday, is chief brewer these days. He runs the oyster farm, which has been in his family for years. Wouldn't be surprised if he slips a few of those in the mix.'

'Eurgh,' said Kitti, twisting her face.

'Anyway, Kitti, I wanted to talk to you about a few things – is that okay?'

'Yes.'

'You know you said something about your mam mentioning Lindisfarne? Do you have some kind of connection to the island?'

Kitti looked at me, her big blue eyes unblinking, and I worried I had touched a raw nerve.

'You don't have to tell me, you know,' I said gently.

'No, it's not that, Ellie. Just trying to think of the words. My mam came to Lindisfarne when she was sixteen. She was on a school environmental trip. Mam loved wildlife, especially birds, and she had been so keen to study them on the island. Thing was, her mam and dad hated Lindisfarne.'

'How could anyone hate Lindisfarne?' I wondered out loud.

'My mam didn't know why, but they said she couldn't go. They said it would be all parties with sex and drugs. Suppose they got the sex bit right,' she said wryly. 'Anyway, Mam used some money she had saved and paid for herself to go and didn't tell them. She met a boy…'

'On the study?'

'No, he was on holiday on the island. I think he was called Adam and from somewhere down south. Mam really liked him – said he was like no other boy she had ever met.'

I saw where she was going with this tale.

'Did they keep in touch after the week?'

'He had given Mam his phone number on a slip of paper, but when she got home, she couldn't find it. She didn't even know his surname or where he was from, so she just accepted it as a holiday romance.'

'And then she found out she was pregnant with you?'

'Yes. And when her mam and dad discovered that, they kicked her out. How could they do that? Then not long after, when Mam had been put into a mother and baby hostel, like I already told you, they moved away without even telling her, so she never saw them again, and I never ever met them.'

I went and flopped on to the sofa next to Kitti and gave her a hug.

'Their loss, chick.'

'And this boy? Did your mam ever try to track him down? It sounds as if she really liked him.'

'No, Mam said she didn't want to. I was too young to care really, and happy just with Mam. She told me about it years ago when I was quite little. She used to bring me to the island during the summer holidays before I started school to see if he might be back, but he never was, and I can't even remember being here. Then when I grew up a bit, we just stopped talking about him. There wasn't much point, but Mam always talked about the island'.

'You could always look for him yourself, when you're ready?'

'Maybe one day, but not yet.'

'So, I'm guessing that's how you got your beautiful name – because of your mam's love of birds?'

'Mam loved watching the kittiwakes on the island. She said they were fiercely protective of their young, and if the babies made it to be grown-ups, they became strong, independent adults who soared on the wind, which is what she wanted for me.'

'Your mam sounds like a wonderful woman; I know she and I would have got along if we had ever met. What was she called?'

'Loveday. It's Cornish and she hated it, so just told people she was called Daisy.'

'So, you really do have island ties, Kitti. Far more so than me. Listen, Reverend Rosie and me are going to take you back to Newcastle tomorrow–'

'You don't have to. If you lend me the money, I can get the bus, and I promise I'll pay you back,' she said hurriedly.

There was that fierce Kittiwake spirit of independence coming through.

'It's fine. Kitti, I want to explain something to you, but before I do, I need to say please don't get your hopes up, because you've been through enough. If we could do this without asking you, we would, but it's so important to hear what you think.'

Kitti's unblinking eyes rivetted on to my face.

'Rosie used to be a social worker before she became our Vicar. She knows a lot about the care system, and I asked her to come with me to see if we could talk to someone about your situation.'

'Rigggght,' she murmured, without moving her lips.

'Kitti, if it was possible for you to come and live and work on the island, even if it's only for a short while, would you be interested? You don't have to tell me straight away; you can sleep on it tonight.'

'I don't need to. Yes. I would. I really would.'

'You would need to sort out your education, Rosie was very explicit about that.'

'I'm not going back to school. I'm on bereavement absence now, and I had already decided to leave school. I need to work to support myself.'

'What about you wanting to become a vet?'

'I can always go back and study later.'

'Yes, you can,' I said. 'You're still very young, and a little delay wouldn't hurt, I suppose, but you'd probably have to talk to someone about that during the holidays.'

'Mam said I had to follow my dreams. She couldn't follow hers because of me, so I will do it for her when I can.'

'What did your mam do?'

'She had wanted to be an environmental lawyer but was working in the office of a solicitors. She was a volunteer with the RSPB, though, and loved that.'

'Where will I work if I can come?' asked Kitti looking excited, which filled me with trepidation. If this didn't fall into place, it could make things worse, but I didn't want to start discussing things with her social worker if she wasn't interested in the proposal. It really was a Catch-22.

'The island gets very busy over summer, and I know that you would be a great help in different places.'

'Could I help with the animals, though?'

'Yes, of course you would be able to do that. Bert would be delighted.'

'And where would I live?'

'One step at a time, eh? I still want you to think about this tonight. And please, Kitti, it's not cast in stone. We all want it to happen, and will do everything we can, but you know yourself, sometimes these things don't go the way we want them to.'

'I'll be coming, Ellie. I know that. Mam used to say that if it's in the stars then it's in the stars, and I know it is. It's funny, when I crossed the causeway on the way here, I had this feeling like I was coming home. Does that sound stupid?'

I felt a tingle sweep across my body because I could hear myself saying the very same thing.

'No, not at all. I often wonder if it has some kind of magical powers.'

'I will think about what you've said properly, Ellie, but I know I'm still going to want to come. Anyway, is it okay if I try and get some sleep? I want to be up early with you and Zen in the morning to help with the animals before I go.' She got up and headed to the bathroom.

And that was it. End of conversation. Kitti's mind was made up, and I prayed things would work out for us all.

Chapter 16

♥

It was gone eleven, and I was settling down in the top bunk when I got a text from Tara:

She's back. She obvs didn't take her own advice to have coffee. She wouldn't have been able to do a thing, even if she had got lucky and gone back with George Rooney. Imagine not remembering that! See you in the morning x

I heard the dogs making a fuss as Zen came into the cottage. He crept into the broom cupboard and climbed into the bottom bunk after giving me a kiss.

'Have a good night?' I whispered.

'It was great craic. Sophie was a bit worse for wear, but Toby and I got her home and she's safe.'

'Was she embarrassing?'

'More funny, actually. I'm not sure if Inigo quite knew what to make of her, but she didn't disgrace herself... too much! Anyway, Ellie,' he whispered, 'I've been thinking about Kitti and...'

'I've had a long talk with her tonight,' I said interrupting him, 'and I'm more determined than ever to help her.' I told him of the conversation we'd had.

'No way. I can hardly believe that. Kitti was con-ceived on this island?'

'It seems so. Can you remember any school trips coming for environmental studies? I know it's a long time ago, but you never know, you might have even met her mam. She was called Loveday, or more likely Daisy. You'd have been just a little older than her.'

'Ellie,' he laughed, 'there were school trips virtually every week in the outward-bound centre. And yes, I hold my hands up – sometimes I would meet girls. I met a Rose, an Iris, a Poppy, a Lily, and a Daisy... just joking! I don't think I ever met a Daisy,' he laughed, 'and if I'd met a Loveday, I would never have forgotten that.'

'I'm not suggesting that you actually, erm, met her, met her,' I laughed. 'Kitti thinks the boy was called Adam and was here on holiday. I just thought it would be bizarre if you had met Daisy and could remember her.'

'Sorry, no, I can't. Anyway, the answer is yes. I'm up for letting Kitti stay with us temporarily – maybe until the end of the school holiday period, then they'll have to sort her out with something longer term.'

'You are an absolute diamond, and it was worth nearly drowning to have met you. I love you so much.'

'You're still not ganging up on me to watch *Love Is-land*,' he laughed. 'Right, Miss Montague, even though I would dearly like to attempt to make mad passionate love to you right now in this creaky old bunk bed, I'll just dream about you instead – safer for my back. Night night, gorgeous. Sleep well.'

'You too. Sweet dreams, but not of young female bird watchers called after flowers. You're not a hormonal teenager anymore!'

'I am hormonal right this minute, Ellie, but only for you – although I seem to recall Rose was rather accommodating and might make for a good dream.'

'Hoy, I'll give you accommodating,' I grinned, swinging my legs out of the bunk and dropping down to the floor. 'Shift over, and if you put your back out don't blame me!'

***

The next morning, I was getting ready to go across to the Crafty Lindisfarners meeting when my phone rang. It was Sophie.

'Hey, nice to know you're still in the land of the living. What happened to sticking to coffee?'

'Oh, Ellie – don't. I feel awful. My mouth feels like the bottom of a budgie's cage, as Granny Ethel is always saying.'

'Serves you right – totally self-inflicted.'

'It's all coming back to me in waves. Am I imagining it or was there some very good-looking guy there, a bit like a younger version of George Clooney?'

'That's not what you called him last night,' I laughed.

'Oh, my God. Was I awful? What did I say? Who is he?'

'More funny than awful. You said rather a lot, or so I'm told, and he's Inigo Lindisfarne, Sir James's nephew. He's staying in their apartment for a while.'

'That makes it even worse, knowing he's not some random holiday maker who will be gone from the island today. On a scale of one to ten, how bad was I?'

'Oh, at least an eight point five, I reckon!'

'I'm mortified.'

'Mortalfied more like!' I quipped. 'Listen, Soph, we can talk more later, but I'm off to the Crafty Lindisfarners meeting at 10.00 am. Do you want to come?'

'No. If you don't mind, I think I'll go for a stroll to blow the alcohol out of my system and have a good talk to myself.'

'Sounds like a good idea. Will you take Kitti with you? She hasn't really seen around the island, and you know your way about now, so perhaps give her the full tour. I'll meet you both in the café for lunch?'

'Yes, of course. She seems like a nice kid.'

'She is,' I confirmed. 'I'm taking her back to Newcastle this afternoon.'

'It's a shame she has to go. Right, Ellie, I'll see you later, and no more alcohol for me.'

'I've heard that before. Just make it none today – it's a start. And Sophie, we really do need to have that proper chat on our own. You can't just keep burying things under red wine.'

'Yes, you're right, and we do,' she said, suddenly sounding serious. 'Love you, bestie.'

'Love you too, you drunk. See you later.'

Chapter 17

The back room of Love Lindisfarne was alive with chatter as I went in. Ethel had managed to walk down and was on top form, sitting at the head of the table next to a plate of Dora's homemade sausage rolls.

'Here, Ellie, Linda was just telling us about Sophie being a bit lively last night.'

'She's like a younger version of you,' tutted Muriel.

'How lively, Linda?' I asked, thinking I had maybe only been given an abridged version from Zen.

'Ellie, your face! She was okay. Not offensive – just full of beans and wanting to dance with Inigo,' laughed Linda.

'You don't have dancing and music on a Sunday,' muttered Muriel.

'I'd dance with him any day of the week,' Dora smirked. 'If only I was ten years younger…'

'Try twenty-five years, pet – that's closer to the mark,' said Ethel, her cheeks bulging with treats.

'I could be ten years younger… sort of,' said Linda, counting on her fingers.

'You're no Carol Vorderman, Linda, but you have got her backside, if that's any consolation.'

'Ethel!' Aurora burst out laughing. 'Anyway, never mind Sophie. What's Inigo Lindisfarne doing on the island?'

'He's come to find himself,' I grinned.

'We'll all help him do that,' said Linda lustfully. 'Is he any good at crafting, do you think?'

'I'll show him how to do an in, over, through and out with me,' said Dora, licking her lips.

'You're all sex mad,' muttered Muriel, the most chaste of the group.

'Can't fault our memories, though, Muriel,' Ethel laughed. 'I've never had an organism since about 1984, after a night out in Seahouses with a fisherman from Iceland – the place, not the shop. Mind, came close when I watched that *Rivals* on the telly, but probably not good for me blood pressure these days.'

Glancing at Muriel, it looked like her blood pressure wasn't doing so well either – she was the colour of a boiled lobster.

'Some of us in this room remember organisms quite well – don't we... Ellie? Aurora and I are with the others, us being so knackered looking after a baby and a toddler,' Tara grinned, a mischievous twinkle in her eye.

'Apparently, Inigo's split from his wife,' I jumped in, before my love life got dissected, tipping poor old Muriel right over the edge.

'She was at a do in the castle once,' said Linda, 'and they all came across to the pub. Spanish she is, and very fiery. Lovely looking woman, mind.'

'Where's Meg when you need her? She knows all the goss,' said Dora.

'Erm, attention,' coughed Imogen from the other end of the table.

'Oh, sorry, Imogen. How rude of us! You have our full attention now,' apologised Muriel.

'Let's do the business first, then we can get back to the gossip when it's time for some more tea,' smiled Imogen. 'I'm rather intrigued by our new resident myself!'

Imogen explained about her plans to go and live permanently on the farm with Harriet.

'We totally understand,' said Linda. 'It's your shop to do with as you wish, but we'll be sorry to lose it. Since you took over Love Lindisfarne, it's become an integral part of island community life.'

'The shop doesn't belong to the Lindisfarne Estate, does it?' asked Muriel.

'No, it's freehold like the Crab.'

'So does that mean whoever buys it can change it to whatever they like?' asked Dora.

'I suppose, within reason,' said Imogen. 'It was easy for me because it was already trading as a gift shop, so I just expanded on that.'

'What happens if someone wants to turn it into a naughty knicker shop?' Ethel chuckled.

'I think the Lindisfarne Estate and Parish Council might object to something like that,' I smiled.

'Will we lose our space?' asked Muriel, looking around what was originally a stock room but had been taken over by the craft group.

'You might,' admitted Imogen. 'Suppose it depends on who takes over the shop and what for. I'm thinking of letting rather than selling. I don't need the capital with moving in with Harriet, so the rent will give us a good income. What I was thinking was to advertise it, then perhaps a few of us can interview any interested parties. Suss them out – see if there are any that would fit. How does that sound?'

'Imogen, sweetheart,' said Linda, 'there's no sentiment in business, and none of us would hold it against you if you had to let it go to someone who wanted to change it.'

'That's because you're in business yourself,' retorted Ethel. 'If it turned out to be one of those mini pubs which Zen was telling me are all the rage these days, I bet you'd not be so keen.'

'It could be another butchers,' mused Muriel, looking at Dora.

'We've been on this island since Stan's family opened the shop in 1948, and we struggle to keep afloat, despite us having loyal customers and Stan delivering on the mainland,' said Dora. 'We want to retire next year, and I doubt whether we'll be able to pass the shop on as a going concern, so be prepared for yet more change. Probably end up as another holiday let.'

'It's your famous pies and sausage rolls that keep you going, Dora – the tourists can't get enough of them.'

'That's as maybe, Ethel, but I'm sick of the blinking sight of them.'

'I'm not,' said Ethel, batting flaky crumbs off her jumper to prove the point.

'Our island is changing, ladies, and there's not a lot we can do about it,' said Linda matter of factly.

'Well, as long as the Crab stays the same,' said Aurora.

'Not much chance of us moving on quite yet,' said Linda, 'and we certainly can't afford to glam it up. We've got about ten years until we get our pensions, so it's business as usual for us. Unless we win the lottery, of course.'

'Anyway, Imogen pet, back to your suggestion. If you have the time, then I think that's a great idea and I would like to be on the panel. I'm the oldest, therefore have been on this island the longest and should take priority as a judge,' said Ethel.

The looks on the faces across the room were priceless, ranging from mild amusement to all out horror.

'Ellie, would you and Meg join us? asked Imogen, mouthing "please" at me while she nodded at Ethel, knowing full well that only Meg had any chance of keeping her under control.

'I'd be happy to, and I'm sure Meg will agree, but does no one else want to do it?'

Tumbleweed blew across the room. They were probably all realising what it would be like with Ethel on the panel.

'That's agreed then,' said Ethel. 'Can I be Alan Sugar? I've always wanted to say, "You're fired!"'

Chapter 18

After the meeting, I went across to the café with Tara and Aurora. It was a bright blustery day, and the tourists were out in force, even though the tide was in until 2.00 p.m.

Sophie and Kitti, looking rosy-cheeked and windswept, were sitting at an outside table at the back of the garden, sheltered by the roastery, from which a gorgeous aroma of coffee was permeating the air, meaning Zen was busy cooking the beans or whatever it was he did with them.

'Enjoy the walk?' I asked, as I sat down.

'Cobwebs well and truly blown away,' smiled Sophie. 'It was bracing, but Kitti kept me on my toes. She was determined to see as much as she could in the time we had, and quite frankly I'm exhausted. I feel like I've done a marathon.'

'I've had a great time. Sophie showed me everywhere, including the hotel where that poison woman used to live. She sounds awful.'

'I might have known you'd be sharing the local gossip, Sophie,' said Aurora, bursting into laughter.

'I did show her the priory and St Cuthbert's Island too, so it wasn't all scandal,' Sophie tutted.

'Pleased to hear it,' I smiled.

'You're right though, Kitti,' said Tara. 'She was awful. We used to call her the Poison Pylon. Wonder what happened to her?'

'We don't get to hear anything now since Dora finished cleaning at the hotel. The last thing she found out was that Isla was living in America. I was going to google her but just never find the time, and, quite frankly, I'm not that interested.'

'America's not far enough away,' grinned Aurora. 'Right, let's decide what we want to eat as it's busy, and Ellie and Kitti need to be away soon. If you lot look after Hettie, I'll go in and lend a hand and sort out our order. Poor Pip is working so hard. I really need some extra staff,' said Aurora, casting a very unsubtle glance at Kitti.

Between babies, toddlers and gossip, there was no time to have a quiet word with Soph. It would just have to wait until I'd got back to the island after taking Kitti to Newcastle.

'What you going to do this afternoon, Sophie?' I asked.

'I think I might go and have a nap with Farne,' she smiled. 'Kitti has worn me out, and I could do with a rest.'

'Are you going to phone Jake?' asked Tara, in her usual forthright manner.

'Jake hasn't phoned me,' Sophie retorted stubbornly.

'I could crack your heads together, you pair of eejits,' said Tara. 'Someone has to make the first move.'

'I didn't shout at Jake,' muttered Sophie.

'And Jake didn't get sa...' began Tara, then for once managed to keep quiet.

'Soph, just promise me you'll think about things when you have your rest,' I said gently. 'I'm hoping to be back about 7.00 p.m. so fancy coming over for supper and we can talk properly?'

'Okay, will do. See you then.'

When it was time to leave to catch the tide, a tearful Kitti and I said our goodbyes and went to meet Reverend Rosie, leaving Tara and Aurora giving Sophie chapter and verse on why she needed to contact Jake. I knew from past experience that the more they pushed, the more she was likely to ignore them, but I lived in hope that by the time I got back, maybe she would have had a change of heart, and our inner circle would be back up to full strength. I really wished that the other two members of our group, Stanislaw and Aleksy were in London and not Poland, where they'd gone to visit family, because I know they might have managed to help Jake. If Sophie didn't contact him soon, I was seriously wondering if Zen could find the time to go to London and make sure he was okay, rather than just speaking to him on the phone.

***

I got back to the cottage just after 7.00 p.m to find Zen and Sophie sitting at the farmhouse table, a delicious smell coming from the Aga.

'Zen said it was okay for me to come and cook for us,' smiled Sophie. 'I've made your favourite curry, although I had to improvise a bit with what I could find. There's no mini mart to pop to for the bits I didn't have!'

'Great,' I said, giving her a hug. 'You feeling better?'

'I am,' she grinned.

'And you look nice,' I said, noticing she had put on a gorgeous pink top and her heels.

'Oh, well, you know – if you look good on the outside, you feel good on the inside, and all of that positivity malarky.'

'Anyway,' said Zen, handing me a glass of sparkling water and whispering 'we're doing alcohol free tonight,' before continuing in a normal voice. 'How did you get on? I half expected you to have kidnapped Kitti and brought her back.'

'Well, it was—' I began, then heard someone come into the porch and tap on the inner door.

The door opened, and there was Inigo, casually dressed but still looking like a menswear model in an M&S advert filmed on a sailing sloop in the Med.

'Come in,' said Zen. 'Just shove the dogs out of the way. Second thoughts, I'll put them in their kennel until we've eaten.'

'I'll give you a hand,' said Inigo, putting a bottle of something expensive down on the table, probably liberated from his Uncle James's cellar.

As soon as they'd gone through the door, I stared at Sophie.

'What on earth is he doing here? Did Zen invite him?'

'Erm, no, it was me.'

'You?' I asked incredulously. 'How?'

'I did think about things when I got back to the Holiday House this afternoon like you said, Ellie, but my head just kept going back to what I might have done or said last night in the pub. I decided that the best course of action was to go and apologise in person, and then maybe I might feel better.'

'You what?'

'He was very gracious. Made me a coffee and we had a lovely chat. He's a nice man – very interesting.'

'Nice?' I felt my insides constrict. 'And the fact that he's drop dead gorgeous hasn't got anything to do with it, I suppose?'

'No, it has not. I couldn't even remember what he looked like, so you can't put that one on me. But he is rather fit, isn't he?' she laughed.

'Sophie Olatunji, do not even go there. You love Jake. I know you do. *You* know you do. So, you're having a rough time, but this is not the way to deal with things. You and me really do need some time on our own to talk. I'd hoped that would have happened tonight, but it would appear not, now that we are entertaining Lindisfarne's answer to Ryan Reynolds – even though he is a nice man,' I added hastily, realising how churlish I sounded.

'I'm having dinner with friends. I'm not exactly ripping his clothes off, am I?'

But I'm getting the feeling you'd like to, I thought.

'Keep your own shirt on, Ellie Nellie. Let's just relax, enjoy the night, and you can tell us all about what happened in Newcastle. We will get the chance to talk about Jake. Just not now, eh?'

Chapter 19

'So, it's a case of waiting to see,' I said, explaining about what happened on our trip to Newcastle. 'It was too short notice to talk to anyone directly associated with Kitti's case, but Sue, her foster carer, was lovely, and we had a long chat with her. She thought that in her experience it would be possible to put a short-term plan in place to see how things go. Kitti is sixteen, after all, so in effect can make some decisions for herself. Rosie talked to someone she knew from her days in Newcastle Social Services, and they know Kitti's case worker, so we're hoping that things can slot into place within a couple of weeks.'

'That's great, Ellie,' smiled Sophie. 'Who would have thought it? You with a teenager, eh! I hope it works out for all of you.'

'Kitti is very mature for her age. She's had to grow up fast and, even though it is early days, I just know that bringing her here onto Lindisfarne is the right thing to do. Don't ask me why.'

'Sometimes gut instinct is the only way to go,' mused Inigo. 'You can do what you think is the right thing, but deep down know it isn't, and it usually turns out that your instinct was right in the first place.'

'More water, anyone?' asked Zen. 'I think that bottle you brought would have gone well with this curry, don't you, Inigo?'

'I do, but a break from the old vino will do me no harm. We drink it like tap water in Ibiza, and since my marital issues, well, it's become a bit of a prop. I'm here to sort myself out, so while I'm in Northumberland I'm going to cut right back.'

'Leave a bit of space for the Spring Fling at the fishing club, though,' laughed Zen.

'What on earth is that?' asked Inigo.

'Just an excuse for the island to gather to welcome the forthcoming summer and get ratted on the famous island hooch, brewed by Maurice. You know, the oyster farmer.'

'Your cousin Aidan participated in the winter gathering last year,' I laughed, 'and ended up wearing trawler gear covered in fish guts.'

'That sounds about right for Aidan. Although, now he's a celebrity he might think twice. Imagine if any photos of that got on his social media... might be good for bribery purposes,' smiled Inigo.

'Have you seen him recently?' I asked.

'Only on the television. Honestly, if my dear cousin Aidan fell in a cow pat, he'd come up smelling of roses. Who manages to get paid shedloads for lounging about on the world's best beaches, eh?'

'He nearly wasn't quite as lucky,' I mused. 'He might have been married to Isla by now.'

'I never met her, although I saw the media coverage when they got engaged. From what I hear Aidan had a lucky escape. Still, he's with Beth now. It's the first time I've known Aidan to be settled. They seem very much in love and might well be the next Bamburgh wedding – if he beats cousin Violet to it.'

'And what about you, Inigo? asked Sophie. 'Are you hoping to get back with your wife, or might you be the next divorce in the family?'

I kicked Sophie under the table and glowered at her.

Inigo burst out laughing. 'Just say it how it is, Sophie! Seriously, I don't know. Just let's say, Lucia and I were as bad as each other. Fifty-fifty split of the blame, right down the middle. We've almost been here before but always rescued it for the kids. This time, well, they're a little older and can deal with situations better. Half of their schoolfriends are in blended families. Living in a place like Ibiza, there's a lot of swappery as I call it. Lucia is currently seeing some American tech guru. These super rich burned-out CEOs come to Ibiza to escape through yoga, or some form of alternative therapy, and to try and find themselves again but then end up finding someone else's wife. It's just how it is. So, I came to another island to find myself. One that is far more grounded, without the fakery. I know which one will be best for the soul.'

Sophie was looking intently at Inigo, drinking in his every word. It worried me.

'You've come to the right place for grounded,' smiled Zen. 'Tell you what, mate, talking of grounds, do you fancy coming and putting in the odd shift at the roastery? A few hours of good honest graft will help both you and me.

I'm struggling at the moment as young Ethan from the farm, who works for me when he can, has actually left the island.'

'No way!' I exclaimed. It was a standing joke that young Ethan had never been across the causeway.

'He's gone to some agricultural machinery fair in Harrogate with his dad. You'd think he was going on a long haul to Australia the way he was flapping.'

'I'd love to come and lend a hand, Zen. I drink enough of the stuff, so it'll be interesting to find out more about the process, but it'll have to fit in around some of my planned hikes if that's okay?'

'Absolutely. Any time you can give will be a help. Where are you thinking of going walking?'

'I'm going to start off tomorrow with a nice easy thirteen miler from Warkworth to Craster, part of the Coastal Path. Have you done it?'

'I have, but in sections – never found the time to do the whole thing in one go, but that's a very scenic part of the route you've chosen,' said Zen.

'I like walking,' said Sophie.

How a lightning bolt didn't come down from the sky, strike her full on and turn her hair into candyfloss for telling such an outrageously blatant lie was beyond me.

'Since when?' I gasped.

'Always have, as you well know, Ellie,' she glared at me as her foot got to work and encountered my shin. The two of us were going to have more bruises than a couple of ripe pears at this rate – it was just like the old days!

'I'd like to see more of Northumberland,' she continued. 'Maybe I can come? I need to find myself too...'

'You know, Sophie, it would be nice to have some company on this particular walk. I can leave the soul searching for when I'm doing the real extreme stuff across the Cheviots, unless you'd like to do a bit of that too, perhaps?'

'Erm, I'll see after this one,' she gasped.

'I like walking too,' I blurted out, hoping that the bolt hadn't just been delayed and was now going to strike me down.

'You do?' Zen raised an eyebrow. 'When I suggest we go off for the day, your main focus of interest is which cafés we pass en route.'

'Well, priorities of course. Need to keep the calories up when you're walking. I've read about the coastal path, and that section sounds so interesting.' This was true. I had read up on the walk, and Zen and I had planned to do sections of it together. 'Is it okay if I tag along too?' I smiled, hoping that saving Sophie from herself was worth thirteen long miles. Even the thought of it wore me out and made my feet tingle.

Sophie's pretty face was contorted into a scowl, and I didn't need to be Mystic Meg to read her mind, which was probably also thinking about a bolt from above – one that would strike me down to prevent me from attending the hike.

'Why not?' smiled Inigo. 'The more the merrier. Zen, you up for it too?'

'Count me out, bud. Far too busy, especially since my partner here,' he gestured towards me, 'seems to have awarded herself the day off, which means I'm going to be far too busy.'

I leant over and kissed his cheek, whispering in his ear at the same time, 'Crisis intervention.'

'Got it,' he whispered back, returning the kiss.

'Okay, ladies, just us then. 7.00 a.m. sharp in the morning.'

Sophie's face rapidly changed expression when she learned of the early start.

'I've already arranged a lift with one of the staff from Bamburgh, so we're sorted. A nice, gentle thirteen mile stroll,' smiled Inigo.

Gentle? I could think of other ways of describing what amounted to a half marathon.

'Hopefully we can do about three miles an hour,' Inigo mused.

Maybe for the first three miles, I thought wryly. After then it might all go belly up. Of all the things Sophie had got me into, this had to be one of the most challenging. If I had any energy left afterwards, I might just kill her on the spot!

'The weather is meant to be dry but breezy. I take it as you both enjoy the outdoors that neither of you are fair weather walkers? There's no such thing as bad weather according to Wainwright, only unsuitable clothing,' he laughed.

Enjoy the outdoors? That might be true of me, as I'd adapted due to living and working on the island, but city slicker Sophie, whose idea of an outdoor adventure was a flat white and a pastry on the dock at Chelsea? My bestie nodded like she knew what Inigo was talking about, then whispered, 'who's Wainwright?' in my ear. But I was distracted; I couldn't quite get past the word breezy.

I'd seen 'breezy' before on the Northumberland coast and it was a misnomer if there ever was one. I had a feeling that Ms Olatunji and I were going to live to regret our sudden interest in hiking!

Chapter 20

The alarm went off at 6.00 a.m. the next morning, which was quite usual for us these days, so I got out of the bunk and headed to the Aga to pop the kettle on. Tea in hand, I gave Sophie her early morning wake up call. It took a few rings for her to answer, and when she did, I could tell that she had just woken up from a deep sleep.

'Ellie, it's still dark,' she croaked. 'It can't be time to get up yet, surely?'

'It's not dark. The sun has risen, and it's gorgeous, so get your backside out of bed, open the curtains and get your gear on. Did you borrow some stuff from Tara, like we discussed last night?'

After Inigo had left the previous evening, Zen and I tried to prepare Sophie for what she had signed up to.

'Ellie, Toby told me all about that Wainwright chap, and he seemed to know what he was talking about, but I refuse to look like a charity shop reject in Tara's stuff, which is far too big for me.'

'And what about your feet?' I asked.

'What about them? My feet are in perfect condition. Bear in mind, until a few days ago, I was one of London's leading podiatrists. There's nothing much I don't know about feet. I've got my trainers – they'll do.'

She wasn't really selling herself to me as a podiatrist, leading or otherwise. Maybe it really was time for a career change. Although, thinking about it, at least she'd be able to treat herself, and me, after the walk if need be.

'Have it your own way, but don't whinge to me when they begin to get sore.' After the first couple of miles, I thought to myself. I was in for a long day. 'At least let me lend you a hat – keep the wind out of your ears. And you can borrow the yellow coat too, if you want – it's windproof.'

'Ellie, have you lost your marbles? Me in a hat and that disgusting yellow coat? Absolutely not, no way, Jose. I'll be fine. I really don't know what all the fuss is about. We're just going on a nice walk at the seaside.'

'Erm, well, if you're sure. Right, we'll be picking you up in half an hour, so be ready.'

'I will be. That gives me plenty of time to do my hair and put my makeup on.' And click, she hung up.

We picked Sophie up from the Holiday House in the Bamburgh Castle Land Rover and bumped our way across the quiet causeway to the mainland. I loved the island at this time in the early morning, after the sun had popped up to the east and welcomed in the day to come. The birds were circling ready for what lay ahead, their chatter getting increasingly louder by the minute. Grey seals could be spotted in the distance, bobbing up and down on the waves like they were taking their early morning baths, and there was an unmistakable sense of serenity and calm in the cobbled village streets before the throng of day trippers descended. In a couple of hours, the island would be filled with tourists who, for a short while, would rejoice in the natural beauty that we were lucky enough to see every day.

Sophie was dressed slightly more appropriately than I had expected. She'd given in at the last moment and had borrowed a puffa type jacket from Tara and had rolled up the sleeves. It was the full face of makeup and her faux eyelashes that she insisted on wearing when she was going out that made me chuckle. Well, good luck there, I smiled to myself. If they made it through Warkworth without blowing down to Amble along with the rest of her cosmetics sliding off her face, she'd be lucky. Inigo had been right, it was breezy. And by breezy, I mean Northumbrian breezy – in other words blowing a hoolie.

Warkworth lay some thirty-four miles south of Lindisfarne. As we drove into the village, it was clear to see that it was yet another ancient Northumberland gem, steeped in history.

'It's a hugely popular place,' said Inigo, as Sophie and I looked out of the window at the picturesque village which lay in a curve of the river Coquet and was a treasure trove of historic buildings and artisan shops.

'I thought Warkworth was on the coast,' I said, looking around for any sign of a way to a beach.

'It's about a mile inland, but fear not, we're going to be walking along the coastline, and it's spectacular.'

As we ascended the steep main street, it was easy to spot the piece de resistance, yet another huge castle, perched on top of a hill surveying the surrounding lands.

'I thought you might want to start by seeing Warkworth Castle,' said Inigo, as we piled out of the land rover. It's managed by English Heritage these days and shut to visitors until later this morning. It's rather majestic, is it not? Obviously, it's no longer habitable, but it's still fairly well preserved for a medieval building dating way back to the 1100s. It was once home to the infamous Harry Hotspur.'

'Is there a castle in every village in Northumberland?' shouted Sophie above the noise of the wind.

'Not quite,' grinned Inigo.

'I must come back when it's open,' I said, drinking in the sight of the almost golden building, which had stood on guard for so many years.

'If you do, Ellie, you must try and take a trip to the Hermitage. It's a hidden gem, reached only by boat.'

'What's that?' I asked.

'It's a chapel and priest house, built into the cliff on the river Coquet, and is one of those places that has a special atmosphere all of its own.'

'Where did you grow up, Inigo? You seem to know the history of around here.' I asked.

'As a Lindisfarne, we have our history drilled into us from an early age. My father is James' younger brother, and the pair of them grew up in the castle, but as is the way in our ancient families, as James is the eldest he inherited Lindisfarne. When Pa got married, he and mother moved into her family's... erm, property, near Corbridge, which is where I grew up.'

'Property?' queried Sophie. 'Go on, spit it out. It's another castle, isn't it?'

'Oh, okay, hands up – but a very modest one, as castles go,' he laughed. 'It's just the way it is with us landowner families who've been around for aeons. The estates got passed down the generations, and very rarely do they end up outside of the family in question, but that's happening more these days. Some do come on the open market as they're so expensive to maintain and tend to swallow up the lives of the custodians, who may want to pursue other interests or just have an actual life. Giving your entire being to preserving a historic building can be thoroughly exhausting and sometimes thankless.'

'So will you inherit your *small* castle in Corbridge?' smiled Sophie.

'Yes, one day, but I won't have any issues in letting it go if I don't feel I'm the right person to carry it forward into the future. It's not something I feel duty bound to pass on to Santo either, unless he really wants that kind of life. I suspect he'd rather be a professional sportsman of some sort; he loves tennis and is incredibly good at it. I don't live in a castle in Ibiza, by the way. Far from it – it's an ultra-modern, whitewashed villa and only has five bedrooms. Anyway, are you both ready?' Inigo checked his watch. 'It's just gone 8.00 a.m. so let's get going.'

We walked down the main street, but before we had even reached the footbridge over the river, towards the coast, Sophie began to complain. The wind was full on into our faces, and her hair was already doubled in size.

'I told you to bring a hat,' I said. Inigo, who was striding ahead, was sporting a beanie, and I was wearing my alpaca Viking hat with the little horns, which was keeping me toastie warm.

'How far to a shop that's open?' yelled Sophie, holding down her hair.

'We should get there in a couple of hours, if you two speed up a bit. Would you like my beanie, Sophie?'

'My hair will never fit under that,' she exclaimed.

'You can have my hat, if you like,' I offered.

Sophie took one look at the colourful number with the dangling plaits and the little ecru horns and shook her head.

'Hell would freeze over,' she muttered.

'Suit yourself.'

'I'll put my hood up; that should help,' she replied, bundling her hair together and pulling tightly on the drawstring under her chin. Quite frankly, she would have looked more attractive in the horns.

'Better?' I asked, but she couldn't hear a thing and started to march on ahead to catch up with Inigo, who had just reached an official sign pointing us to the Coastal Path.

After meandering along a road then through sand dunes, we eventually joined a path which ran along the top of the beach. The view was panoramic on this bright day, looking over miles of beach and shoreline, a vast expanse of cornflower blue skies with snow white cotton wool clouds moving along at a lick, and a small island, complete with lighthouse, in the bay beyond.

'Coquet Island,' explained Inigo, as we stopped to look at the amazing vista. It's a little bit like Greater Reef, in that it's a wildlife haven and not open to visitors.'

'Lovely,' said Sophie dismissively. 'Are we nearly at the next place yet? I could murder a coffee and a sit down.'

I checked my watch.

'Soph, we've only been going half an hour and probably done less than two miles. I'm thinking we've got at least another hour to go unless we speed up.'

'Speed up? I'm five foot two. It stands to reason I'm probably doing double the steps you two are,' she grumbled, 'so I must have walked at least four miles already.'

'I don't think it works like that, Soph,' I laughed. 'Come on, we'd better catch Inigo or we'll end up lost, knowing our luck. Best foot forward and all that, and just think of coffee and breakfast, like an oasis in the desert.'

And tempted though I was of reminding her that this had been her idea, I didn't. Even if she wasn't enjoying it, I was absolutely loving seeing more of the special place I was lucky enough to call home.

Chapter 21

We trekked on, with Sophie probably expending more energy on moaning about her feet, her hair, her tiredness, her anything and everything, than on the actual walking. We had hardly even spoken to Inigo, who had always been many steps ahead, so if this had been her idea of getting to know him better it had already backfired. When we eventually got to the outskirts of our first stop, Alnmouth, we could see the village in the distance, and it looked very inviting – picture perfect, with pastel-coloured houses and small boats bobbing on an inlet.

'Wow, that looks lovely,' I smiled, and then it dawned on me. It was the scene I had seen from the train window when it had broken down on my journey up to Lindisfarne for the first time. It really was that memorable. 'Not much further to go now. Just think, soon you'll be intravenously caffeinated,' I laughed, 'then you'll be raring to do the next section.'

Sophie peered at me from inside the hood, shaking her head. As suspected, the eyelashes had escaped to goodness knows where, and what was left of her makeup consisted of a couple of tramlines down her cheeks.

'Lead me to the coffee drip. Why is Inigo walking down there?' She pointed to him strolling along the path in the distance. 'Look, we can cross over that way, like the crow flies,' she gestured to her right. 'It'll be so much quicker.' She set off, a newfound bounce in her step.

'Er, Soph, there must be a reason we need to stick to the correct path. Wait, let me get Inigo's attention.' But she was having none of it, and marched on, desperate for what treats lay ahead in the village.

I ran to catch up with Inigo.

'Where's Sophie?' he asked.

'She's taken a short cut.' I pointed back to her figure striding out towards the village.

'She's not going to get far,' laughed Inigo. 'There's an estuary between her and the village, and she's not going to be able to cross it. She'll have to come back and walk this way – no other choice. Will I run and get her?'

'You know what, Inigo, just leave her. She'll find her way... eventually. We'll text her the name of the café.'

I only felt a little mean. I'd listened to Sophie moaning almost non-stop for the last two miles, the oasis was in sight, and I was ready for that coffee too!

***

'Thanks very much, I've had to walk an extra mile,' Sophie grumbled as she came into the deli. Flopping into a chair, she then immediately got back up to go to the loo. On her return, her face could have curdled the milk of my creamy cappuccino, which was akin to nectar, and I was savouring every mouthful. I'd had a proud girlfriend moment when I noticed Zen supplied this gorgeous little deli with his Island of Beans products.

'Have you seen the state of me?' she wailed. She'd taken off the coat and her hair looked like it might never go back to normal, it was so frizzy, and her eyes had been streaming due to the constant force of the wind in our faces.

'Sophie, none of us look exactly glam.'

'Inigo seems to have managed it,' she said, and she was right. When he took the beanie off, his hair had sprung naturally back into place, and the amber eyes had returned to their customary sparkle, thanks to protection from his very expensive Raybans, so he didn't have quite the watery style that Soph and I were sporting – Inigo still managed to look like a model on a shoot for a great outdoors commercial.

'The good news,' he said, 'is that the wind is meant to drop soon, leaving us with a bright afternoon ahead and perfect walking conditions.'

'Better go and find some sun protection,' I smiled, thinking that would be the next thing on Sophie's list to complain about!

'How much further to go?' asked Sophie, beginning to remove her trainers to inspect her feet.

'Sophie! You can't take them off. Not in here. And anyway, if you do, you might not be able to get them back on. Are they really hurting that much?'

'My pride hurts more,' she muttered, and re-tied the laces.

'Don't focus on the distance, Sophie. One step at a time, remember,' said Inigo, checking his app.

'I'll one step at a time him,' she grumbled in my ear, 'you tell me, how far?'

'Seriously, I'm not too sure. Maybe about nine miles?'

From the expression on her face, I thought Sophie was going to keel over at the very idea of how far we had left to walk, but we were saved by our brunch appearing. For the first time that day she went quiet and tucked into her eggs Benedict.

Sophie and I left Inigo having a third espresso – maybe that was his secret – and hit the few shops on the main street of the village. There wasn't a pharmacy, but there was a convenience store with all kinds of things that I hoped would make the next section of the walk more bearable for Sophie. We came out with a cap, a pair of sunglasses, insoles for her trainers, a lip salve, sun cream, a big bag of fruit gums and a newly upbeat Sophie.

'I'm sorry, Ellie Nellie, and I'm going to apologise to Inigo too. I know I've whinged, but I'm going to try my best on this next section, honest. I was half tempted back there in the café to call it a day, but no, I'll soldier on and try to enjoy it because it's so very beautiful. It's just the circumstances and my head not being in the right place, I suppose.'

I gave her a hug.

'That's the spirit. Try and use the quiet time to think about things, Sophie. Walking is meant to be therapeutic, after all.'

We went back to the deli to collect Inigo. A virtually disguised Sophie, in cap and sunglasses, said sorry and gave him a brief hug.

'I know it's not easy when you have the weight of the world on your shoulders pushing you down, Sophie. It makes every step harder. My advice is, think of this in small sections, and concentrate on getting to our next destination, which is Boulmer, where there's a great pub. It's less that you've already done so far today, so you know you've got this!'

Chapter 22

Refuelled, refreshed and revived, we walked through Alnmouth, yet another charming place to add to my list to visit again, and made our way to the path that would take us further north. Inigo slowed down to make sure we all stayed together, and the path was mainly flat and easy to walk along, with more stunning views of the coastline below us. It was incredible that even on the expansive golden sandy beaches, there were hardly any people about – a few dog walkers and some hikers on the actual shoreline, but otherwise deserted and in stark contrast to Brighton, where Sophie and I would head to for our seaside fix when we lived in London.

'How long had you and your wife been together?' Sophie asked Inigo, as we ambled along.

'About fifteen years,' he replied. 'Married for coming up fourteen, so it's a long time to give up on things without careful thought. I need to keep a clear head to think and learn to enjoy my own company. My propensity to be easily led is legendary, and it hasn't helped that my wife shares the same trait too.'

I glanced at Sophie. She didn't look overly disappoint-ed by his reply, and it seemed Inigo was taking his breakup seriously, working out the best way forward, so maybe Meg's warning about him whipping skirts off was out of date. We strolled along, basking in the miles of open space around us. We had passed two other walkers heading the other way and a couple walking a huge dog, and that was it, but by the halfway point, the colour of the sky began to change, and we could see storm clouds gathering on the horizon.

'I thought you said it was going to be nice this after-noon, Inigo? Those clouds look ominous to me. Zen and I once got stuck on Greater Reef when a squall blew in out of nowhere. Could it be something like that?'

'It could. The app doesn't always get it right, and as a sailor I'm all too aware that sometimes the weather can be unpredictable over the ocean.'

'Just what I need,' said Sophie, whose sunny mood had reverted like the weather to battleship grey.

'Tell us about Boulmer,' I said, trying a bit of distraction therapy.

'Boulmer was notorious for its smuggling activities. It's alleged that one of the most well known smugglers was a chap called William Faa, the King of the Gypsies. He didn't live in Boulmer; he came down from Kirk Yetholm in the Scottish borders, because in the 18th century this was the place to be for illicit cargo. Much of the activity took place in the village pub, where we're going to be stopping next.'

'Great. Wonder if he could smuggle me an umbrella,' said Sophie holding her hand out as the first few drops of rain began to fall. Then without much warning the heavens opened, like someone had purposely put the rain cloud right above our heads, and within a matter of seconds we were drenched to the skin.

'No such thing as bad weather just...' began Inigo, who was protected by his hi-tech gear.

'I'm going to punch his lights out,' hissed Sophie, looking down at her soaked trainers. So, the interest in Inigo was on the wane and might have just come to its natural conclusion.

We marched on in silence, the rain continuing to play cat and dog with us. We eventually got to the pub in Boulmer and went inside, Sophie and I dripping a trail.

'It gets busy in here, so I booked us a table,' said Inigo, and we were shown to a window seat with a panoramic view of the bay.

We took off as much wet gear as possible, and this time Soph did remove the soaked trainers. Who could blame her? She was probably in danger of getting trench foot, her feet were that wet. Inigo ordered three glasses of robust red wine – so much for the pledge to remain teetotal – but there are times when the odd glass can really help take the chill off, and this was most definitely one of them.

We were perusing the menu when a group approached the table next to us. There were two men and three women, who clearly hadn't been caught out in the downpour. One of the women, a tall brunette, maybe just a few years older than Soph and me, was wearing one of those wild swimming robes that only stick thin willowy people can get away with – the rest of us lesser mortals more likely resembling Sumo wrestlers heading for the ring in our branded dressing gowns.

'I bet she's been to Waitrose,' whispered Sophie. 'I see loads of them in the Kings Road branch, swimming up and down the aisles!'

The woman took off the robe, and underneath she was wearing very tight and expensive looking gym gear, which clung to her slender, very toned and honed gym body. She hadn't been for a dip in the North Sea, that much was clear.

'Inigo! I don't believe it! It can't be, surely?' gasped Ms Swimming Robe, as she hung the garment on the back of her chair and noticed us on the next table. 'But then, there aren't two people who look like Inigo Lindisfarne.'

'Cressida Armstrong, as I live and breathe,' said Inigo, jumping up and giving the woman a hug and air kissing both of her cheeks. It's been years.'

'It's Cressida Armstrong-Carmichael now,' she said, 'although, actually, I'm back to being just Armstrong.'

'No way – don't tell me you married Atticus? I heard that you were seeing him.'

'I was, I did, and now I'm not. Let's just say it was one of those impulsive decisions you live to regret; however, I don't regret my two beautiful boys, even though they tie me to Atticus, and I'd like to cut the strings. And his balls come to that,' she glowered. 'And you? I heard on the grapevine that you and that fiery Spanish wife of yours have parted ways, and she's hooked up with some eye wateringly rich American guy. Pity, I could have helped him spend it, but then if that means you're available...'

'Cressida, give the bloke a chance,' boomed one of the men on her table. 'He's probably battle scarred and goes for a different type of woman these days.' He stared at Sophie and me. 'Ones that don't spend hours in front of a mirror.'

Sophie and I looked at each other in sisterly dislike of the buffoon across the table.

'Inigo prefers us both to go for the natural look, don't you darling?' said Sophie. 'We come as a pair, you know, like two for the price of one.' She cackled. 'My nights are Mondays, Wednesdays and Fridays, and we get to share him on Sundays.'

The man's eyes widened suddenly, taking much more interest in us, and the woman next to him, who I assumed was his wife, gave him a swift poke in the ribs and told him to shut up.

'Sorry, where are my manners,' said Cressida. Her hormones, all but exploding on seeing Inigo again, seemed to have settled down to a mild throb. 'Pull up your chairs, join us and let's do some introductions.' She looked at Sophie and me with puzzlement in her eyes.

We shuffled chairs, and Inigo stopped laughing long enough to introduce us as his friends (without bene-fits) from Lindisfarne. Then we learned that we were in the esteemed company of Cressida 'gagging for it' Armstrong (no longer Carmichael), Andrew 'something to do with politics' Buffoon Barrington and his wife Bunny, and Sir and Lady Alderley, who just happened to own a holiday house near Craster, where they were all staying after coming up from London.

'And what do you both do? asked Bunny, sipping her gin and tonic like it was drain cleaner – but then being married to Andrew the Buffoon, who could blame the woman for having a permanent scowl?

'I'm unemployed, and Ellie shovels shit for a living. That just about sums it up,' said Sophie, looking far more chipper than she had done all day.

Bunny's eyebrows raised into two perfect arcs.

'Oh, how very fascinating,' she replied, pulling her chair away from us.

'And how do you come to be living on Lindisfarne?' asked Alice, Lady Alderley, who in fairness seemed a genuinely nice woman and, it transpired, went to boarding school with Grace. 'Neither of you have local accents.'

'Long story,' said Soph, warming up to the role and talking in a fake cockney accent that would put Bianca from *Eastenders* to shame – I half expected her to say, 'Cor blimey guv,' and start to do the moves to 'The Lamberth Walk'. 'The gist is that Ellie and I lived in Peckham, in a flat above a Turkish barbers. Mehmet's lovely and does a great mullet if you're interested, although maybe not...' she stopped and stared at Andrew's balding pate. 'Anyway, Ellie's ex-fiancé, Matt the Prat, who worked in Randy Parrot and erm, actually, was a randy parrot with Karen the Cougar and—'

'-the rest is history,' I jumped in, shutting her up. 'Shall we order some food? I'm starving.'

'Good idea,' howled Inigo, wiping his eyes. 'I might go for a jellied eels and mash stottie, if they've got one!'

'With liquor,' Sophie winked.

It was so good to see my bestie more like her usual hilarious self.

Chapter 23

Lunch turned out to be quite a jolly affair. One glass of red wine led to two, then a third, by which point the rest of the walk was postponed.

'We're not cancelling this altogether, you two,' smiled Inigo. 'We'll come back another day and start afresh from here to do the rest, okay?'

'Yes, fine by me,' I replied.

'No, I think we should finish it now, today, in fact right this very minute,' retorted Sophie with a straight face, before holding out her glass for a top up.

It was fascinating listening to the group chatting about their circle of friends and the exploits they got up to. Not much different to ours, really, except the situations usually happened in far more exotic locations. Apart from Andrew the Buffoon, who was loud, bumptious and whose hand kept 'accidentally' landing on my knee, the rest of the group were quite sociable and inclusive – even Bunny who, by four double gins, had lost the scowl, except when she looked at her obnoxious husband.

Cressida turned out to be fun. I had wondered on first seeing her if she was going to be another Isla, but

I hadn't taken into the equation that Cressida was proper posh, not jumped up pretend posh like Isla, and had very few of the airs and graces that Isla carried around with her in abundance. The one similarity they shared was that they both appeared to have very rampant libidos. As it happened, Cressida had a long-time infatuation with Inigo, and they had shared some flirtations when they were young but had never 'fully done the deed' according to Cressida, in her own words. She had no problem relaying this information to the whole table, and not one of them batted an eyelid, unlike Sophie and me who were goggle-eyed, hanging onto every word.

Inigo seemed delighted with the way the day was progressing, and his statement from earlier about 'sorting himself out' seemed to have flown out of the coop quicker than a champion racing pigeon. I looked at the way he was staring at Cressida. I knew that 'look'. It was just like Aidan when he had seen Isla for the first time, and his testosterone had taken over his brain. Meg was right – Inigo was another charmer. Highly likeable, but a player, who, I suspected, might never find the time to find himself!

The afternoon continued to go swimmingly, until Bunny caught sight of Sophie's lovely engagement ring. I had noticed that she hadn't removed it, and it had given me great hope that she wasn't ready to call time on her relationship with Jake.

'Oh, my dear, what a beautiful ring! I take it your fiancé mustn't be on benefits like you, as that is rather lovely.'

Sophie looked down at the ring Jake had commissioned especially for her, and which he had concealed inside a shell for her to find on the beach in the Maldives. She looked up at me, her bottom lip trembling and her eyes filling with tears, which began streaming down her face. Then she jumped out of her seat and ran barefoot to the toilets, as if she was being chased down the smugglers tunnel which probably lay under this ancient building.

I had known this moment would come. Sophie had been bottling her real feelings up for days, and it was obvious to me that she had tried to distract herself with alcohol – and Inigo – to some degree. Being her stubborn self, Soph had prevaricated and dug her heels in over contacting Jake, but I knew that she would eventually come out the other side and see sense. Her timing could have been better, however.

'Let me go and sort this out,' I said to the table, who were all silent, probably wondering what on earth had just happened. Even the buffoon seemed lost for words.

'I hope it wasn't something I said,' hiccupped Bunny. 'It really is a beautiful ring.'

'Don't worry, Bunny, it wasn't you. Just continue without us for a while, and we'll be back soon.' And off I went to find my bestie.

'Sophie,' I tapped on the toilet door. 'Come out here this minute and have a hug.'

The door swung open and Sophie, with her mad, damp frizz, big tear-filled eyes and a bottom lip that was wobbling like a jelly, fell out of the cubicle into my arms.

'I miss my Jake,' she sobbed. 'I love him. I've been such a daft cow, haven't I?'

'Oh, Soph, it'll all be okay,' I said, stroking her frizz at the same time as trying to flatten it.

'Do you think he does want to marry me, though?' she muttered, self-doubt beginning to creep back in.

'Of course he does. Listen, Sophie, Zen's been checking in on Jake, and, well, this situation is all to do with his job and money and nothing to do with you. It seems that he's been struggling with work lately; that's why he's not been coming home until late. He hasn't got another woman, you dafty. He's been trying to play catch up, and it has literally worn him out.'

'Why haven't you told me this before?' she asked, fear now having crept into her watery eyes. 'And more to the point, why hasn't he told me?'

'Sophie, you know Jake. He's a proud man and one who would go to the end of the earth to give you what you wanted. He didn't want to spoil your wedding dreams. And as for me telling you, you probably wouldn't have listened, and we hoped that you would have talked to him yourself long before now. Jake made Zen promise not to tell you any of this, but I'm overriding that now – it's gone too far. We're really worried about him, Sophie. We don't think he's coping. You losing your job was just the final stick to be pulled out of the Kerplunk. All the balls came tumbling down, and he saw red.'

Her eyes looked in danger of pinging out of her face as she stared at me.

'Are you saying he's unwell?'

'I think so, chick,' I nodded.

'I need to talk to him... now.'

'Good. I'll go and fetch your phone, and you can ring him.'

'No, not on the phone – I need to see him. I want to go back to London. Now.'

'What, like, right now?'

'Yes, right now. How can I get there?'

I looked at the forlorn figure standing in front of me, who looked like a little street urchin with no shoes, urgently in need of a shower and some dry clothes, and was about to reply when the door opened.

'Hey, everything okay in here?' Cressida smiled, then at once went to Sophie, put her arms around her and gave her a hug. Conclusive proof that this was no Isla.

'I'm suspecting this is a matter of the heart, and as such I have a lot of experience of sticking those back together – both metaphorically and physically, as it goes. I happen to be a cardiothoracic surgeon, so, as with all my patients, I've come to help put a plan in place.'

I stared at Cressida. A surgeon? I'd have to come back to that revelation later.

'So, Sophie, what is it that you need right now that will help you?' asked Cressida.

'I need to go to London.'

'I was just about to say to Sophie that we actually need to get back to Lindisfarne so that she can change, and we can take her to the station in Berwick later.'

'That will take hours, and knowing my luck the bloody tide will be in, out, or a giant whale will be washed up blocking the causeway,' Sophie wailed. 'I want to go NOW.'

'Sophie, chick, your coat and shoes are still soaking. I didn't mention her hair or streaky face.'

'Okayyy,' said Cressida, taking charge. 'Alice is the driver today. We have a car at our disposal that will take you to Alnmouth Station, which is just down the road, and from where you can go direct to Kings Cross without changing at Newcastle. You leave the clothing to me.' And off she went back into the restaurant.

'She's a surgeon!' I gasped, looking at Soph.

'I don't care if she's a blinking alien, as long as she gets me to London,' retorted Sophie, splashing some water on her face and patting down her hair.

We went back to the table to find the men had retired tactfully to the bar, and both Alice and Bunny had been brought up to speed with the situation, or as much as Cressida knew of it.

'I'll take you to the Station, my dear,' smiled Alice, 'and I'm going to pop out to the car as I have something you might be able to wear.'

'Here, take this,' said Cressida, shoving the swimming robe into Sophie's hands. What size shoe are you?'

'Four,' sniffed Sophie.

'Bunny?'

'Erm, yes, I'm a four.'

'Well, hand them over.'

Bunny stared down longingly at what looked like an extremely expensive pair of shoes like she was about to say goodbye to a best friend.

'Andrew will buy you another pair. The least he can do after his latest indiscretion with that dreary Daphne, Shadow Minister for Tartery. I really don't know why you put up with it, Bunny,' said Cressida.

'Chanel... Dior... and the fact I no longer have to sleep with the bald old coot,' smirked Bunny.

'Look, I'll get Inigo to carry you barefoot back to the house, which will give you more of a thrill than Andrew or those shoes ever could,' laughed Cressida.

'Well in that case...' said Bunny lasciviously, immediately taking off the shoes.

Cressida ended up swapping her dry leggings for Sophies damp jeans, which looked like a pair of shorts on her long legs. Sophie rolled-up the leggings which were teamed with a brand-new camel-coloured cashmere twinset that Lady Alice had just bought from a very chi-chi shop in Alnwick, a pair of eye wateringly expensive designer shoes which had probably cost more than I earned in a month, and a designer swimming robe which was almost trailing the ground.

'You look, err, lovely,' I grinned, trying hard not to laugh.

'No need to overplay it, Ellie Nellie,' Sophie managed a smile. 'I don't care what I look like. I just need to go and see my Jake.'

Chapter 24

It was after five by the time I got dropped off at the cottage. Inigo had gone back with the others to the Alderleys', much to the delight of Cressida and Bunny.

'Hey, gorgeous.' Zen greeted me from Bert's armchair, where he was sprawled out, beer in hand. 'I've not long been in myself. Had a really busy day and I'm whacked. I popped the dogs in the kennel, if you were wondering where they are.'

I went across and dropped a kiss on top of his unruly hair.

'You must be whacked too, Ellie,' he said, getting up and wrapping his arms around me. His familiar aroma of pine nuts and extra strong coffee washed over me like a soothing balm.

'You've been roasting again?'

'I have,' he grinned. 'You chill out on the sofa, and I'll go and make you a tea. Thirteen miles is gruelling when you aren't used to it. How are the feet? I'm longing to hear how it went. Did Sophie cope? Has she gone straight back to Tara and Toby's? She's not with Inigo, is she?'

'Oh, that reminds me, I need to call Tara,' I replied. 'Soph's not coming back to the island. She's gone to London.'

'She's what?'

Zen made tea, and we sat side by side on the sofa as I told him all about the day's events.

'Sorry for laughing, but it all sounds quite funny. The main thing is she's going to see Jake, and I hope that by later we'll get a call to tell us that they've made up.'

'Me too. She said she would ring me when she was home, but she won't get there until later tonight.'

'They've still got a lot to sort out, though,' said Zen. 'But you know what this means, don't you?'

'I do?' I asked, puzzled.

'Both runaways have gone, and for the next couple of days there's just you and me and a menagerie of animals to think about. Even Inigo might not reappear for a while.'

If Inigo was getting up to what I thought he might be, then I wondered if he would be back at all, but plenty of time to tell Zen about that bit later.

'Let's go over to the Crab tonight and treat ourselves to a nice meal out together. Just you and me. A date night, which we don't often get. I can drive us over if your feet aren't up to it.'

'Actually, a lift across would be good. It's not my feet, more the three large glasses of red wine I had this afternoon. Wear your wedding suit,' I whispered. 'Let's recreate that moment like we said we would!'

He raised an eyebrow.

'If you put that gorgeous bridesmaid dress on, I will. And don't forget the wispy lingerie,' he countered.

And so, Zen, suited and booted with Northumbrian tartan cravat in place and me in the minty sea foam dress and slinky underwear, made our way to the Crab, looking like we should be going to the Ritz and not the island pub.

'Hey, seeing as we are in our finery, we could splash out and go to the hotel, if you want?'

'Zen, I've only ever been in there once, and once was enough. Isla's mam and dad are not my favourite people on this island. Elspeth is like an older clone of her odious daughter, and her dad, well he was so far up Aidan's backside I thought he would disappear and never be seen again. More's the pity that didn't happen. Besides, I love the food at the Crab. It's Aye's Pies tonight – Dora will have been baking them all day. Hope her veggie balti one is on the menu.'

We walked into the pub hand in hand. It was busy with both tourists and locals, and there was a noticeable hush as we entered the room.

'Bloody hell,' shouted Dean, one of the island fisher-men. 'It's Bond and Moneypenny.'

'Double oh eight, licenced to grind,' guffawed Maurice.

'Martinis, shaken not stirred, I presume, my darlings,' smiled Linda. 'Seriously, what's all this in aid of...?' Then she stopped mid-sentence. 'Oh, I see!'

She did? Well perhaps she could enlighten us.

'Champagne, is it? Nice little table in the corner? Hang on, stay there and I'll go and shift those two tourists – they've got the best table in the house. I'll tell them it was reserved for Lindisfarne royalty.'

'No, please don't do that,' shouted Zen as she scurried across the pub, but to no avail. The two tourists, looking dumbfounded, followed Linda as they were unceremoniously seated at a table next to the draughty door.

'It's okay, my darlings,' she said when she came back, 'a few free drinks and some of chef's Spotted Dick, and they'll be happy. They said congratulations.'

'Congratulations?'

But Linda was off with her mobile hurriedly texting someone, so Zen and I went and took our seats in the 'VIP' corner next to the fireplace.

My phone buzzed. It's a text from Meg,' I said, reading it out to Zen.

You little tinkers. You know me and Bert wish you all the absolute best, my pets, but we really would have liked to have been on the island for such a special occasion. We're thrilled for you both, but now we want to come home and celebrate with you xx

'What on earth is that all about?' asked Zen.

'I've got a sneaky suspicion,' I grinned, not really wanting to tell him my theory, but at that Linda came and put an ice bucket containing a bottle of Champagne on the table.

'On the house, my darlings, with mine and Paul's congratulations. I can't believe I'm going to see the ring before Meg. Come on then, let's have a look!'

'Erm, I think there's been a bit of a misunderstanding,' began Zen, before our phones began to beep with messages.

'Linda, who did you text?'

'Well, I might just have put it on the village group chat. News like this deserves to be shared across the island.'

At that, the pub door burst open, and Aurora ran in, wearing her dressing gown and slippers.

'Is it true?' she demanded. 'I'd just got Hettie down when I saw Linda's post. How could you keep this from me, your little sister who shares everything with you? And you Ellie, you turncoat.'

'Here, sis, sit down. I'd offer you a glass of this, but I know you can't at the moment. I take it Jack's watching Hettie?'

'Yes, he is. He said to say congratulations.'

'We're sorry to disappoint you, but no one has got engaged. We just thought we would get dressed up for our date night,' I smiled.

Linda raised her eyebrow looking at us suspiciously.

'There's dressing up, and then there's dressing up, my darlings.'

I could feel my face begin to burn.

'Erm, well, we were er, just role, I mean recreating...'

Aurora burst out laughing. 'I think I can guess, you pair of sexy beasts!'

'Linda, just put the Champagne on my tab, and come and have a glass with us. Give Maurice and Dean a pint of Lindisfarne Lil on me too – after you send out another group message saying there's been a mistake, otherwise we'll have half the island in here on false pretences.'

Zen looked at me, a twinkle in his gorgeous coffee bean eyes.

'Ellie, I hope our day isn't too far away,' he whispered in my ear.

'Me too,' I smiled, as the butterflies in my stomach began to flutter enough wing beats to launch a jumbo jet.

Chapter 25

We had just got back to the cottage when my phone rang. It was Sophie.

'Hey, how are you? Was the journey okay?'

'Yes, fine. I got a few strange looks, but I think looking like Hagrid from *Harry Potter* stopped anyone from wanting to sit next to me and talk.'

'And how are things…?'

'Oh, Ellie,' she said in a noticeably quiet voice, 'Jake's broken.' She began to sob. 'I've never seen my Jake like this before, and it was a shock. Even though it's not been many days, he looks like he hasn't slept in months, and he's lost weight. We're going to be okay, though. We've a way to go, but we'll do it together and try to sort out our lives going forward, especially Jake's. I'm not going to go into all the details now. It's late, and it's been a long day, but just wanted to say thanks to both you and Zen for being there for us – and Tara and Tobes too, of course. First thing in the morning we're going to try and get Jake a doctor's appointment and go from there, so I'll ring you and let you know what's happening.'

'Okay, bestie. I'm so pleased that you and Jake can work through this together.'

'Nighty night, Ellie Nellie. Love you.'

'Love you too, Soph. Sleep tight, and you know I'm here anytime for you.'

'Suppose if the worst comes to the worst,' she added with a tiny hint of humour in her voice, 'at least I can sell those shoes! Night, Ellie.'

***

After an early start on the animals, Zen went off to catch the tide, as he had some deliveries on the mainland, and I made my way up the back steps into the castle, to meet with Toby and the rest of the staff and volunteers for the forthcoming season. As I walked through the hallway connecting the outside door to the inner stairwell of the castle, I knocked on the door of the Lindisfarne's apartment to see if Inigo had returned overnight. There was no reply, so I went straight to Toby's office as arranged, half an hour before our main get together.

'Morning, Ellie. I hope you appreciate I literally had to hold my wife back from coming down to the pub last night to tell you off for not informing her of your big non-news,' laughed Toby.

'That's okay. Aurora got there first – in her dressing gown and slippers. I can promise, you will all be the first to know if and when we do decide to become "official",' I smiled, my heart still warm from Zen's declaration last night.

'Down to business,' said Toby, looking far more serious. 'Ellie, I know you'll appreciate that what I'm about to say stays with just us for the moment, Zen excluded, naturally. I've spoken about this to Tara already; I need to run things past an independent ear.'

'Okay,' I replied, already worrying about what was going on.

'It really pains me to say this, but to some degree Aidan was right.'

I raised my eyebrow.

'The estate, whilst far from being in financial crisis, is just about holding up, and Aidan's protestations that we need to offer more wasn't far from the truth. Now I'm at the helm, it's my role to keep Sir James and the board happy, and I'm not going to be able to do that if we just keep ambling along.'

'You're not planning on us all being involved in a new reality show, are you?' I quipped. 'Sorry, Tobes, couldn't resist. Please go on.'

'We're treading water at the moment, Ellie. Maybe wrong choice of phrase, as our most recent building survey informed me that an area of the roof needs to be overhauled very soon, otherwise we'll be facing actual water and a much bigger bill, not to mention the unthinkable prospect of losing valuable historic artifacts. Gate money is healthy – we'll always have visitors – but we need to either plan some additional events that will be ticketed separately or come up with other ventures to bring in revenue, like the café idea Aidan mooted originally, I suppose.'

'Oh, not that again,' I muttered. 'I thought TEA at the Castle was the perfect compromise.'

'It was at the time, but it's not a long-term solution. Ellie, you three pay peanuts for the space because we understand that with such a small selection of drinks and packet snacks to offer, you aren't really making any profit. None of you are actually getting paid any-thing, are you? I know Tara keeps pleading poverty.'

'Erm, no, but we have made a little money, which we keep in an account to use to buy our stock, pay the rent etcetera. Toby, as you well know, we did it to support the estate.'

'I appreciate that, Ellie, and I know it's partly Tara's baby, and she loves it too. I'm right behind the sen-timent… but being realistic, we need to think of how we can make more from it. Or from something else. Perhaps I can get together with the three of you soon and thrash the whole issue of a food offer out. By the way, have you sorted your rota for the van for this season? Your two co-owners have little ones to think about; I can't imagine a baby or a toddler cooped up in a camper van for hours at a time when it's Tara and Aurora's turn, but it can't all fall to you.'

Toby was right about TEA at the Castle, and it had bothered me for ages. I suppose I had put off tackling the topic as I seriously couldn't see a way around how we were going to manage this season, other than for it to remain closed for the foreseeable. I was really beginning to feel the strain of juggling.

'Let me meet with Aurora and Tara, and we'll see what we can come up with. There's got to be something.' I sounded far more confident than I was actually feeling.

'Morning everyone,' said Toby, as we settled down in the Henrietta Room. 'Thanks for coming along this morning. I'll start by congratulating Ellie and Zen on their happy non-engagement.' The room descended into laughter.

'The power of the Lindisfarne grapevine,' I smiled.

'Okay, down to business. I just want to start by saying that we do really appreciate everyone's input into the Lindisfarne Estate. Without you all helping in whatever role you've chosen, we wouldn't be able to even open the castle to the public. We do well, but we can do better. By that, I don't mean in terms of customer care as you are such a warm and welcoming team, but we need to start to think strategically about getting the best out of the castle itself. I'm starting to look at what we might do to broaden events, and I want you all to think about what additional activities may look like, because if you leave it to me, it will be all very academic and not that appealing to a wide audience.'

'We're open to all ideas,' I chipped in. 'Please help by giving us some inspiration – doesn't matter how daft you think your ideas might be.'

'As long as you're not expecting us to get dressed up like Vikings,' muttered Muriel. 'I said the last time that was suggested that I do not suit those long tunic things. I'm far too short, and I'd look more like Friar Tuck without the sunroof in my head.'

'That's it,' shouted Maurice. 'No Vikings, but we can all get dressed up as monks as a homage to St Cuthbert and island history.'

'We won't be dressing up as anyone, Maurice,' Toby laughed, 'unless it's for something specific, but in essence Aidan was right, we do need to maximise our potential. What I can guarantee is that whatever we come up with, it will all be done openly and transparently – no hidden surprises. Anyway, Ellie is going to go through the rota. Let's look forward to a fantastic new season coming up. My door is always open if you have anything at all you need to talk to me about. Now, if you'll excuse me, I need to see a man about a roof.'

Toby had managed everything beautifully – no one needed to know that things were a little more serious than he had alluded to, and if I knew the team, they would be doing everything they could to support the castle.

<h1 style="text-align:center">Chapter 26</h1>

As soon as the meeting was finished, I checked my watch. I had an hour before I was due to help in Aurora's café for the afternoon shift, so I went to the dogs' kennel, grabbed their leads and headed down to the bench on the shoreline next to the derelict fishing shack. It had originally been Zen's special place where he would go and think, and now it was mine too. It was lovely to go and just switch off and be at one with the nature surrounding us. As usual, there wasn't a soul in sight in this corner of the island, which the tourists hadn't really discovered in any great numbers. As I sat down, I re-read the brass dedication plaque on the bench to Ethel's father, which always made me smile.

In loving memory of Septimus Fish. A thinker, a drinker and forever the island tinker.

One day we might just add Ethel's name, as they sounded like two peas in a pod.

The day was bright and clear. The bench had a stunning view out across the bay, beyond Greater Reef with its red and white striped lighthouse, to the smaller, uninhabited islands, also looked after by Zen's parents,

Mike and Simone. The sea was relatively calm, reflecting cerulean blue from the sky above, which today had very few clouds. As usual, the noise from the seabirds was intense, but rather than irritate me, I loved to hear them as they swooped and darted about, chasing each other. The phrase, 'free as a bird' ironically sprung to mind. Here I was, on a tiny island in the North Sea, running about from job to job more than I had ever done in London. This was part and parcel of island life, where most of us had more than one role, and I wouldn't swap back to my London life for all the pebbles on this very beach, even if every one of them were solid gold, despite how tiring it got at times. I closed my eyes, breathed in the sharp clear air and lost myself in the distinctive wheel of kittiwake calls, which of course led my thoughts straight round to Kitti, and I began to think about what would happen when she arrived. So much for my switching off. I called the dogs and headed back to the castle, where I needed to get ready to go to the café.

***

Before I started my shift, I called in to Aurora's flat.

'Hi, how's my favourite niece?' I said in a whisper, peering into the crib where baby Hettie was sleeping, looking all pink and cherubic, as if she was straight out of a renaissance painting.

'She's just gone down,' said Aurora. 'It's hard work this baby malarkey, I'll tell you that now. Stick with dogs,' she laughed.

'Can you manage half an hour to chat after I finish work? I've asked Jim to go and sort the animals as Zen is on the mainland today. We really need to start talking about the van.'

'Yes, that should be fine. I was just thinking about that.'

'Oh, and can you get Tara along too? Come downstairs when we're closed, and we can pretend we're doing afternoon tea in a café like normal people – I'll hold back some cake for us. If that's okay with you,' I added quickly. 'I don't want to eat your profits.'

'Make sure it's the lemon meringue; Pip is amazing at making those,' smiled Aurora, 'and I know we all love it.'

'Okay, boss, will do. See you later. I'll try to be nice to your customers!'

***

Aurora, Tara and I sat blankly looking at each other in the now empty café.

'I don't even know what to suggest,' said Aurora, 'other than pass me another piece of that lemon meringue. How on earth can we make the van work this season?'

'I hear what you're saying, sister. Farne is at the stage where it takes all my time just watching over him to keep him out of harm's way. I couldn't take him with me to the campervan. It was okay when he wasn't crawling, but he'll be on his feet soon. He nearly is now, and then I'm packing my bags and leaving him to Toby! Seriously, Aurora, you couldn't take a newborn with you and try to work. It would be far too cold, for one thing.'

'I wish my mam was on this island,' said Aurora. 'I really could do with a pair of helping hands, but she's not. She did say she would try and get across once or twice a week, but with the weather situation, it wouldn't be a particularly reliable arrangement.'

'What about Nana Louise?' I asked about Jack's mam.

'Nana Louise is still working in the family business, and she'll kill you if she hears you call her 'nana'. I have been given my instructions that Hettie is to refer to her as Lou-Lou the minute she starts to speak. She said I could drop Hettie off when she's working from home in the afternoon, but by the time I get to Seahouses and back to Lindisfarne, I'd need to go straight off again to collect her. And that's before I take into account our favourite nemesis, the flipping tides. Jack could bring her home, but it's not practical if he's out at sea. Even when he's on the island cruises, he can be working until late at night.'

'I'm sure Meg might help out,' said Tara, pouring us more tea.

Aurora and I gave her such a look it's a wonder she didn't wither on the spot.

'No!' we said in unison.

'I want Meg to have Hettie, but not for hours at a time, and certainly not regularly. Her and Bert do far too much as it is, and I don't want to add to the load. Although in fairness, she would jump at the chance and probably enjoy it.'

'Aurora's right. Meg has been doing so much more for Ethel lately; she's almost taken on the role of carer. I do worry about her – and Ethel, come to that,' I added.

'I hear you both. Just a suggestion. Anyway, this could all be irrelevant,' said Tara. 'Ellie, I know you've spoken to Toby this morning, and I asked him if we could discuss things with Aurora and he agreed.'

'Intriguing,' mumbled Aurora, devouring a piece of Victoria sponge now that the lemon meringue was all gone.

I explained Toby's concerns about how little our van enterprise raised, both for the Lindisfarne estate and for us as business owners.

'He's right. We must be mad,' laughed Tara. 'Imagine us working for Randy Parrot for free, Ellie. It just wouldn't have happened.'

'But it brings us full circle as to how the castle can offer refreshments without it affecting Aurora's business,' I said, sweeping my arms around the café.

'The answer is simple, really,' mused Aurora, 'although the timing stinks. I could branch out, take on some suitable space within the castle and open a second café. That way the estate will be getting a proper income from a lease, and I wouldn't be in competition with myself. But frankly, I'm not sure I could afford the startup costs, and it would be too much to take on with Hettie being so young.'

'I know you've got more energy than the Duracell Bunny, Aurora, but even you couldn't take that on at the moment.'

'You're right, of course. And then...' she faltered.

'What?' I asked, hearing the hesitation in her voice.

'Remember I said I wanted to talk to you. Well, Jack and I have been considering whether it might be better if we moved over to Seahouses. Then I would have Lou-Lou and all the aunties, and Jack wouldn't have all the to-ing and fro-ing he has to do at the moment, which doesn't bother him that much, but it all adds to our long days. It makes a lot of sense.'

'Oh, no, Aurora, you can't. You're part of the fabric of the island, and what about the café, and Bert and Meg, and Ethel... and us. I'm an auntie, always at your disposal, right here on Lindisfarne.'

Aurora wiped a stray tear that had fallen. 'Don't mind me, blooming baby hormones. I don't do tears... well, I didn't, but I do now. I hear what you're saying. It would probably break my heart, but I must also go with what my head is telling me. The other thing is living in the flat. Getting the baby gear up and down those stairs isn't easy, and I want a garden for Hettie eventually, like you have for Farne,' she smiled at Tara.

'Could you not buy something on the island?' I asked.

'Ellie, you've been here long enough to know that the prices on the island are so much more than somewhere like Seahouses. We could get a much bigger house on the mainland for less. Plus, the fact is, houses don't come up that often. Well, not the kind we want.'

'Toby and I were incredibly lucky. We sold our house in London for a ridiculous price for what basically was a two up two down but in a sought-after area. We were able to buy the Holiday House outright. I can't help you with the stair situation, Aurora, but you can borrow our garden anytime. In any case they'll be playing together and...' Tara stopped abruptly. 'That's it!'

'That's what?' I asked.

'Why didn't I think of that before? We become each other's babysitters. When it's your turn, I look after both little ones, and when it's mine, you do the honours. Honestly, Aurora, going to the van for a few hours will be grand. It'll be like having a rest.'

'Are you okay about doing that, Aurora? You're meant to be on maternity leave,' I asked.

'It'll only be a few hours, and my mam will be able to cover some of the time, and she'd do that for you too, Tara. Give you a few hours off every now and again. I'm interviewing someone tomorrow for a full-time job in the café,' said Aurora. 'She comes recommended, as she ran a tea-room at a farm shop up from Berwick. Her husband has just accepted a job on the oyster farm with Maurice, and they're going to live on site in the lodge, so no tide worries. It would also take the pressure off Pip, who's been amazing, but she's only just turned nineteen. I'll still be needing temporary help, though, if your Kitti comes back. Any news on that front?'

'She texts me every day. Seems very buoyant and hopeful that things are moving in the right direction. It might be another week or so before she can officially join us, but only until the end of the school holidays. They are determined she needs to continue her education, although she seems reluctant as she wants to provide financially for herself. She's a very independent young woman.'

'Kittiwake by name, kittiwake by nature,' smiled Aurora.

'Aw, I'm so pleased about that, Ellie,' smiled Tara, 'but back to the van. Keeping it open this season doesn't really solve the long-term problem of raising income at the castle, but it's better than us remaining closed, as then there are no winners. Perhaps we can think more about helping you come up with an expansion plan… if you stay on the island.'

'I'm telling you now, Aurora, if Meg and Ethel get wind of you even thinking of leaving Lindisfarne, they'll probably bulldoze the causeway so no one will be able to go anywhere!'

'Ha, you're right there. Okay, another pot of tea? We need to get down to the important business of the day – I want to know exactly what's going on with Sophie and Inigo!'

Chapter 27

The next few days flew by in the usual haze of busyness. The farrier was coming today to check over Hannibal and Stout, and it was not a job for the faint hearted. Stout was a darling, and she just stood patiently while Will did his thing, nuzzling his ear while he was at work. On the other hand, Han would rip Will's ear off given half a chance. Because Han and me got on best, I was always nominated to be the one to oversee the visit.

It had taken me ages to catch Han earlier; he had a sixth sense when it was time for his feet to be checked. Will came every three months to trim the heels to stop them cracking, and I was always sure that my nerves were going to crack long before Han's tiny feet. Will was so gentle with all the horses he worked with, but he made no bones about saying that his worst client was our cute little Hannibal the Cannibal!

I had just taken a deep breath while holding on to Han's halter for Will to begin, when a familiar voice came drifting down from the cinder path.

'Hang on, Ellie, lass, or he'll have your fingers off quicker than a starving crocodile.'

'Bert!'

Bert came into the paddock, gave me a hug and shook Will's hand.

'You're back early. I wasn't expecting you till the second tide.'

'Truth be told, Ellie, whilst we've had a lovely time, both of us have been itching to get back to the island to see our friends, including the furry and feathery ones,' he smiled. 'Go on – you go and see Meg and leave our Hannibal to Will and me today. We'll be up later for a cup of tea and a bandage or two.'

I didn't take telling twice as I handed Bert the rein and almost ran back up the path towards the cottage.

'Meg! How lovely to have you back,' I said, as I went into the kitchen and gave her a hug.

'Eeh, it's so lovely to be back, Ellie pet. I don't mind telling you that me and Bert both had to stop ourselves from coming home early. Not that we weren't having a good time as it was lovely, but there just seemed so much going on here that I was missing, and you know me – finger in every pie!'

'Go on, you carry on putting your bags away and I'll pop the kettle on. Would madam like a specific type of biscuit today? I'm thinking of some scrummy Empires I got from Aurora's to welcome you back.'

'Suits me, as long as it's not shortbread for a while.'

Big brown teapot and biscuits on the table, we sat down to catch up on the island events, and considering Meg and Bert had only been away a week, there was so much to discuss.

'And you're sure Jake is going to be okay? Poor Sophie – it sounds like she was all over the place too. Is she okay? And Inigo, what of him? Has he reappeared yet? Is that woman with him? A surgeon eh, who would have thought that? But he really should be concentrating on sorting out his marriage, shouldn't he? And Kitti? I need to hear everything about her. She's one of the reasons I really wanted to come home. She's stolen my heart has that one...'

Meg fired questions at me, not giving me any time to answer.

'Whoa,' I laughed. 'Slow down – one thing at a time. I need to ask you something first. I explained to Meg about the forthcoming interview panel at Love Lindisfarne.

'So, will you join us and keep Ethel on the straight and narrow?'

'Of course I will, but I can't promise to stop Ethel from being Ethel. How has she been? I've rung her a few times and she sounded fine. I know you wouldn't have told us if anything had happened while we were away, though.'

'No, nothing, I promise. In fact, she's been on top form, walking around the village with Duchess and generally being, erm, well, as you say, Ethel!'

'I'll try to get over to see her later this afternoon, once I've checked out my girls and seen the goats. I don't suppose those two turkeys have shuffled off their perch since we've been away?'

'Meg! No, Sage and Onion are still with us and look like they're not going anywhere anytime soon.'

'Pity,' Meg winked.

The door opened, and Bert and Will came into the kitchen and sat with us at the table, both still sporting all ten digits, thankfully.

'Cup of tea, Will?' asked Meg. 'How's your mam?'

'She's fine, thanks, Meg. Her and dad are busy building a greenhouse, or should I say, trying. I fear that there won't be much glass left by the time they're finished.'

Meg handed Bert and Will a mug each and shoved the biscuits towards them.

'Now that we can concentrate, lad, and aren't in danger of a kicking from Han, continue telling me about old man Sparks.'

'He's had the animal welfare sniffing around,' replied Will. 'You know he was going to start up that mini animal farm? Well, he never got round to it, and word is that he's not been taking care of the animals very well. In fact, I've not been paid for doing the ponies for months, but I can't bear not going because it would be them that suffered, not him. Anyway, he's decided to sell up before they come on an official visit. They'd probably remove all the animals and likely prosecute him, so he's putting all the minis up for sale next week, I heard.'

'I never liked Sparks. He's a rogue,' said Meg vehemently. 'Those poor wee animals.'

'What's he got lad?' Bert asked.

'Well, there's a couple of tiny Shetlands, even smaller than Han and, bless 'em, as good natured as they come.'

'Aw, they sound cute,' I smiled.

'Then there's three mini Highland cattle, who are in serious need of some attention.'

'How adorable,' said Meg, wistfully.

'I wonder where he got those from, as they're not really recognised as a breed here. There's a risk of defects if they're cross bred, but it's not their fault, the poor beasts,' Bert exclaimed. 'Sparks wouldn't be dealing with reputable people for sure.'

'And that leaves two tiny donkeys and a pair of the smallest goats I've ever seen,' Will smiled.

'How delightful,' I grinned.

'Word on the street is that he bought all of the animals as a job lot from a 'breeder' in Ireland, but you know Sparks – he'll have gone over on the ferry, done a deal in a lay-by somewhere and handed over a bag of cash, no questions asked,' said Will angrily.

I studied Bert's face; he looked like he was going to burst with rage.

'Sad thing is,' said Will, 'he's talking of splitting them up as they'll be easier to shift, but none of them have ever been apart from the others of their breed.'

'Oh, no, that's too much. Imagine trying to take Han away from Stout, or Wonky from Wilma. It doesn't bear thinking about,' I cried. 'What can we do, Bert?'

'I'll get Maurice to come with me tomorrow, and we'll go down to see Sparks. Is he still on that smallholding outside of Ashington?'

Will nodded.

'Now, Bert,' said Meg, looking concerned and clearly beginning to think with her head and not her heart, which was probably full to bursting with love at the idea of tiny, cute animals. 'I know what you're thinking, and whilst I don't want to see those poor animals separated and go goodness knows where, don't be too hasty. Where are we going to get the money from to buy them, as they won't be cheap? And then we'd have to find space for them. We'd need money for fencing and new shelters. And how much are we going to have to find every month to look after them, and where's that coming from? Our lot cost a fortune already, and whilst Grace pays for most of the upkeep, we couldn't ask her for any more money.'

'If Grace were here, she'd be sending me with a wagon this very minute to pick them all up.'

'You're probably right, Bert, but we still need to speak with her. And Toby, to get permission and work out where to put them. It's not cut and dried, and we need to consider it carefully before you wade in. I know you, Bert Shafto.'

'I hope so, after fifty-five years, and I'm not going to change now, but I hear you and I promise we won't do anything rash. You leave it with me, Meggie lass. Let's see what Sparks wants and go from there.'

Bert had that look of a man who was on a mission, and I doubted that nothing much was going to stop him.

'You've only been back about an hour,' I laughed, 'and see what's happened already. One thing, though, Bert – please take Zen with you when you go. And Maurice. I don't like the sound of that Sparks chap.'

'Okay, Ellie, we will, but don't worry. If Sparks thinks he's going to get money out of us, then he'll be charming. He's a wily old fox, that one, but then it takes one to know one,' he tapped the side of his nose, straightened his cap, and went back out into the yard whistling.

Chapter 28

'It's good to be back home,' said Zen, as we got in from the cottage after tea. 'Just think, we've got that big bed to stretch out in.'

'Is that a euphemism, Zen Chambers?'

'Well, now you come to mention it! Actually, Ellie, we'd better make hay while the sun shines because frankly, I'm not sure about us doing anything other than stretching out when Kitti comes to stay. She'll be right there in the next room, and this being the attic, there's not much sound proofing going on.'

'Oh, I never thought of that,' I frowned. 'On second thoughts, it might be exciting.'

'Exciting how?' he raised an eyebrow. 'Pray tell.'

'We can have secret assignations when we know Kitti's at work,' I smiled.

'Then we'll just make her work sixty hours hard labour a week,' said Zen laughing. 'That'll give us lots of time to ourselves.'

'I'm speaking to her social worker tomorrow, to agree how many hours work is appropriate and whether the

café is suitable, but she also wants to help with the animals.'

'Seriously, I could do with an extra pair of hands every
now and again in the roastery, even though Ethan is back
tomorrow.'

'Kitti isn't coming to be our fill-in wherever there's a gap
in the workforce,' I laughed. 'We've got the social worker's
visit at the end of this week too, so try and make sure
you don't leave your smelly socks behind the cushions
like you usually do, and keep the place tidy.'

'Erm, pot calling kettle, Ellie. You're just as bad as me.
In fact, worse, considering that most days you've been
wearing stinky wellies! I was just joking about Kitti, but I
was hoping Inigo would rise to the challenge and come
to the roastery. He said he would.'

'I think he's rising to another type of challenge altogether,' I giggled.

'I thought he'd come here to find himself, not find
another woman so quickly.'

'I don't really know whether he has found another
woman, I'm just guessing. They were all old friends, and
Cressida, who clearly had a major thing for him, was
really nice. When I first saw her, I thought she might be
another Isla because, apart from being attractive, she
was extremely confident – very assertive and maybe a
little cold, but when she found out Sophie and I weren't
competition, she warmed up immediately. Thankfully,
she was nothing like the Poison Pylon. Like proverbial
chalk and cheese, as it happens.'

'Well, let's hope he turns up tomorrow and fancies
grinding of an entirely different kind.'

'Talking of tomorrow...' I told Zen all about the mini animals and nominating him to go with Bert and Maurice as the minder.

'Ellie, I'm stowed off. That will take...' He counted on his fingers, 'I guess at least four plus hours if it's straightforward, but with Bert and Maurice, well I imagine a full day. Seriously, I don't know if I can spare the time.'

'Oh, Zen, please. Can I go and do something in the roastery, like packing, or cleaning or whatever? I've got a couple of hours spare between the castle and Love Lindisfarne. You said Ethan was back tomorrow, so can he not just hold the fort? I really don't like the sound of that man, and well, Bert and Maurice are notorious for getting into bother – they lead each other astray.'

'Maurice can take care of Bert; he's years younger. I've seen him in action and wouldn't like to cross him.'

'That makes me feel worse, not better. They need the voice of reason, which is you,' I simpered, stroking his arm. 'Pleeeeease. I'll make it worth your while.'

'Oh, okay, okay, and don't think I don't know you're buttering me up. If I go bankrupt because I'm never at work it's all down to you, and you'll have to keep me in the style to which I've become accustomed. Now then, one good turn deserves another, seeing as you're offering, how do you fancy making some hay? The sun may not be shining anymore, but I am going to make it my mission to make the most of the time we have left alone, starting right now. I love you, Ellie Montague, but please do not go inviting anyone else to stay for a while. I just want you all to myself.'

'Come on then,' I said, dragging him off the sofa. 'We're wasting valuable time. I love you too Zen Chambers, and one of the reasons why is that you don't mind me inviting total strangers to stay, and you go out of your way to help people. You've got a good, kind soul, Zen, and I think things with Kitti and us two are going to work out just fine. And Bert and Maurice will get back in one piece tomorrow, probably having bought a load of tiny, very cute animals. I for one can't wait!'

***

The next morning, I was on duty at the castle. I was walking around the parapet, checking for any stray litter that had been dropped or had blown in from the strong North Sea wind. It was a grey, blustery day, but as I stared out over the bay, even on a day full of mizzle, as Bert called it, the view was still spectacular, although I could hardly make out the buildings on Greater Reef for the sea fret. The miles and miles of sea in front of me was school blazer grey today, but that only served to make the tips of the waves appear whiter than white, and they bubbled and crashed forward to the shoreline as if racing with each other. I scanned the sea for any sign of grey seals, but if there were any they would probably have just blended into the dirge.

My phone rang. 'Morning, Meg.'

'Morning, Ellie. The boys got off okay this morning, but I'm worried about our Zen taking so much time off.'

'Don't be. It's all fine.' I kept my fingers crossed.

'Listen, why don't you come over for your tea later when they get back, and we can hear all about what happened. I'm excited – are you?'

'I am, but what happened to you being so cautious?'

'Oh, I still am, Ellie, but I keep visualising those poor little lambs in need of a good loving home…'

'Not sure there are any lambs, Meg,' I laughed.

'Figure of speech, pet, but you know what I mean.'

'I do, and yes to tea, so we'll see you later. I'm on the parapet and can hardly hear you, the wind is so strong today. Anyway, I'll pop over at lunchtime and give the dogs a run down to the paddocks before I head over to Love Lindisfarne. I'm covering a shift in there, and it'll give me a chance to speak to Imogen about the potential interviews. She's had a few responses from her campaign on social media, so fingers crossed we find somebody who just wants to keep the shop exactly as it is.'

'If I ask Ethel for tea, can you pick her up and bring her across? You've got Zen's van as they've gone in Maurices.'

'Yes, that's fine. Tell her I'll be there just before six. See you later.'

I picked up my rubbish bag and was heading back inside when the main front door of the castle squeaked open.

'Inigo, you're back.'

'I am, but come in, it's freezing out here.'

We went inside to the entrance lobby of the castle and shut the door against the wind.

'I've just got back. I've tried to phone Zen but can't get through. I was going to offer my services today.'

I explained that Zen was on the mainland for the day.

'I'll still go over to the roastery, Ellie. His young helper is called Ethan, isn't he? He might need a hand.'

'That's really kind of you. Fancy a coffee before you go?' I asked, heading towards the kitchen. 'I've got half an hour before we open up.'

We sat at a table nursing steaming cups of one of Zen's experimental roasts, which he donated to the castle helpers in return for feedback (usually 'send more'). The kitchen was just about as cold as outside. I had long since decided that whilst castles were wonderfully historic buildings, being in one for any length of time required a certain amount of tolerance towards the cold, which I didn't possess. In some respects, I was still very southern!

'How's Sophie?' asked Inigo, undoing his coat. He was probably adjusted to the arctic temperatures found in these old buildings, seeing as he grew up in one.

I told him as much as I felt he needed to know, and he nodded.

'That all sounds positive. Sophie is highly entertaining. I wasn't too sure when we first met on account of the fact she was pickled and, erm, a little OTT, but as I got to know her better, I saw more of what I hope is the real her: a funny, feisty woman who was going through a hard time. I'm so pleased that she and her fiancé have begun to work together to put things right.'

'And what about you putting things right, if you don't mind me asking? Or have things got more complicated with Cressida turning up out of the blue?'

I swear his handsome tanned face took on a wash of shell pink blush.

'Erm, let's just say we concluded our unfinished business. Cressida's an amazing woman, but the timing is so wrong. Both of us are adjusting to life outside a marriage, so it's not right for either of us to jump straight into a relationship, serious or otherwise. Plus, she's in London, and I'll be heading back to Ibiza at some point until I get things sorted. My kids are my priority, and I wouldn't be here now if it wasn't for the fact that Lucia has taken them over to the States for a month – without my permission, I hasten to add.'

'That's tough,' I replied. 'I hope it all works out for you. Maybe you and Cressida can be friends – with benefits, perhaps.'

'Oh yes,' he said emphatically. 'Bring on those benefits!'

'Are you going to see her again while they're in Craster?'

'It was left open. Cressida has to get back to work by next week, so who knows. But Ellie, I'm still going to do all that soul searching I said I'd come for. Cards on the table, I'm a born flirt. I'm told I'm as bad as Aidan, although it should be that he's as bad as me seeing as I'm a few years older than him. The chance of a night with a beautiful woman like Cressida was just too much temptation to put in my way, but hey, I've seen Aidan reform, so there's hope for me yet.'

He stood up, put his jacket on and ran a hand through his hair, which immediately sprang back into shape. He smiled at me, his autumn gold eyes crinkling at the corners, and it was easy to see why he was probably always facing a lot of temptation.

'I'm off to the roastery, hopefully to do some manual labour. Will you speak to Ethan and let him know I'm on my way, otherwise he won't have a clue who I am.'

'I will,' I nodded as we went back into the hallway, where the volunteers had already begun to take their places by the doors, ready to open them.

'Thanks, Inigo. Would you like to come to the cottage for tea tonight? Call it payment for your help today. Meg always cooks enough for an army. About six?'

'Thanks that'll be great. I will. Six it is.'

Chapter 29

We all gathered around the farmhouse table later that evening. Maurice had dropped Bert and Zen off but had gone straight back to catch what little light was left at the oyster farm. There was a tap at the door, and Inigo poked his head around the frame.

'Come in, Inigo. We don't stand on ceremony here; it's only a bit of tea,' said Meg, stirring a huge pot of bolognaise sauce. 'Bert, get the boys a beer.'

'Never mind just the boys – I'll have one too,' Ethel cackled. 'Here, son, come and sit beside me,' she patted the chair next to her, gesturing to Inigo.

'Thank you. It's Mrs Fish, isn't it?'

'Miss Fish,' she replied, with a heavy emphasis on the word Miss, 'but you can call me Ethel. I'm single, you know, and I hear you are now too,' she grinned. 'Maybe you like the more mature lady? According to *This Morning*—'

'Ethel!' Meg shouted, banging her wooden spoon on the pot for effect. 'Don't scare our guest like that.'

Inigo burst out laughing. 'I'm not scared, Meg. Flattered, actually.'

Ethel needed no encouragement.

'Your cousin Aidan and I used to step out, you know. He would take me to the Crab and buy me drinks.'

'Well, in that case, I think it's only fair that I carry on the family tradition. We shall go on a date.' He smiled a smile that could have lit up the lighthouse, even though it was decommissioned.

'You're very handsome. And charming,' said Ethel, peering at his face. 'I shall look forward to it.'

'Here, don't get too excited, Ethel. It's not good for your blood pressure,' laughed Bert, handing her a glass of beer.

It was a jolly affair, but as soon as we had finished eating, Meg banged on the table.

'Right, Bert, I've waited long enough. I need to know exactly what happened today.'

'Me too,' I grinned.

Ethel and Inigo looked at us blankly.

'It'll all become apparent,' I smiled, giving them a brief rundown of the situation.

'And so, the upshot is, that if we want to rescue all of the animals – that's two Shetland Ponies, two alpacas, two donkeys and the three Highland cows – it's going to cost thousands,' said Bert.

'They're all tiny,' said Zen. 'Smallest I've ever seen of their breeds. I've seen bigger dogs! I tell you what, you two,' he gestured to Meg and me, 'you had better get in an industrial sized box of tissues because I can guarantee when you see them, it'll be tears. Of the happy kind, that is, because they are all incredibly cute. There's no doubt about that.'

'Sparks said that he would get more if he sold them individually, and he's probably right,' continued Bert, 'but that's not what's best for those beasts. They aren't in the best of condition, and the priority would be getting them some urgent veterinary input. They need nursing back to full strength, so there's potentially more thousands.'

'He wouldn't care who he sold them to, would he?' I said angrily.

'No, he wouldn't,' Zen agreed. 'He made my skin crawl. First time I'd met him. He has no regards for the animals – just sees them as things to trade.'

'He was charming, though, like I said he would be,' continued Bert. 'He knows that selling the whole lot to us in one fell swoop would be the most straightforward way of getting in the cash, so he'll keep us sweet for now.'

'I'd like to castrate him with me da's rusty pliers,' said Ethel, shaking her head.

'I'll hold him down for you, pet,' nodded Meg. 'Anyway Bert, how long have we got?'

'That's the thing. Until the end of the week. He has someone coming back over from Ireland soon to look at the cows, and from what I gather, it's people he's dealt with in the past on the same level as him – in other words, highly unscrupulous – so I'd like to get in there first and secure them.'

'So how many thousands to buy them, put aside for Vets bills to get us going and sort out the logistics?' I asked, not really wanting to hear the answer.

'About eight to ten I reckon,' said Zen.

'Ten thousand pounds,' gasped Meg. 'We haven't won the lottery, Bert. Where on earth would we get that kind of money at such short notice?'

'We've got a bit put aside, Meggie lass. We can contribute some towards it, and we got some cash as presents for our blessing. What better use for that?'

'I'm so sorry,' Zen said. 'Everything I have is tied up in the business, but I can ask Mam and Dad to lend me some.'

'Don't even think about that, Zen. They're coming up to retirement and will need what they have for any plans they might have.'

'I've got a little bit left over from when I sold that engagement ring Matt gave me. I'd happily put that in,' I offered.

'No, you won't,' said Meg firmly. 'That's for your future.'

'I'll buy them,' said Ethel, who had remained quiet to that point. 'I have the money, and at my time of life what else do I spend it on?'

'No, Ethel,' said Meg. 'You might need your savings to do alterations to the cottage.'

'Meg, I've got a bit put aside – enough for both. I want to do this,' Ethel replied, with determination.

'I'll match you, Ethel,' grinned Inigo. 'Also, I know if I were to mention this to my family, they would all want to donate, so maybe we won't need anything from you at all, Ethel, or from Bert and Meg either. Ethel, you especially must keep your savings to make sure your cottage is suitable for your needs in the future.'

'The future is already here, Ethel, but we can talk about that another day,' smiled Meg, with a determined glint in her eye.

'At the very least, I want to buy those tiny cows,' said Ethel, 'and that's the end of the matter. I've always loved hairy coos. Who wants a stuffed one when you can have the real thing? I get to name them, though. That's the deal.'

I couldn't help but laugh. Goodness knows what they would end up being called, but that was the least of their worries.

'Hear you loud and clear, Ethel,' said Bert, 'and we all very much appreciate it. And that's amazingly kind of you too, Inigo. Talking of your relatives, we need to run this past your Aunt Grace and Uncle James, and Toby the custodian before we go any further.'

'You talk to James and Grace, and leave Toby to me... and Tara,' I smiled, knowing he would be putty in our hands.

'Site visit down at paddocks first thing in the morning,' smiled Bert. 'Let's see what space we might need and get something drawn up.'

'Sorry to be the doom bunny, but was that guesstimate including the fencing and shelters as well?'

'Ellie, just leave that to me,' smiled Inigo. 'Uncle Lance has a workforce at his disposal over at the castle, and I'm sure he can find us some wood. Am I right in thinking he owns a sawmill up near Wooler?'

'You are, lad. Why didn't I remember that?' said Bert. 'And as for the building of them, there'll be plenty of volunteers from the island to help.'

Meg put a bottle of Prosecco down on the table. 'Let's toast to our proposed new arrivals. I'm hoping we're not being a little premature, but I've a feeling it's in the stars; it's all been decided already by a greater power than us.'

'I'll drink to that,' said Ethel. 'Here's to my hairy coos!'

Chapter 30

By nine thirty the following morning, everything was sorted regarding the arrival of our new mini friends. I thought Toby was going to have a heart attack when he learned of the proposal, but Bert had spoken to Grace and James first. As predicted, Grace had told Bert to go and get the animals immediately and that she and James would contribute towards the upkeep.

'How much of the land do you require?' Toby asked, fiddling with his glasses, which meant he was stressed. 'I had a plan in mind for a new history garden celebrating edible plants over the ages on Lindisfarne. I thought it might prove popular with our visitors.'

Ethel's eyebrows shot up.

'Toby, pet, if it's between a cute hairy coo or a rhubarb patch, I know which most people would like to see.'

'But the animal paddocks are private,' said Toby. 'It's not a visitor attraction, and nor can it be; we can't afford the insurance, and the legal fees it would take to set something like that up... I really must put my foot down.'

'Keep your hair on, lad,' smiled Bert. 'No intentions of that, but people can see the animals from up there.' Bert pointed upwards to the castle walls. 'And from the road as they walk along. The animals we already have are loved by the folks who come to the island, so a few more little 'uns will just add to the experience. As a man of the soil myself, gardens are hard work, son, and you'd end up having to pay a gardener to constantly keep on top of it.'

'I know when I'm beaten,' said Toby, 'besides which, Tara said she wouldn't cook for me again if I put a spoke in the wheel, and she makes a wonderful colcannon, does Tara. But, and there is a but, I really cannot allow all the flat land to be taken over. I'm going to mark out a section I want to hold in reserve, and you're going to have to work around that.'

'What for?' I asked, curiosity getting the better of me.

'I don't know yet, Ellie, but my grandfather always told me to never give away 100% of anything, and it's stood me in good stead up to now. By the way, are you not on duty this morning?'

'Yes, boss. I'll be up in a sec. Thanks, Tobes – we all love you, you know.'

Toby's face flushed as he said his goodbyes and headed up the cinder path.

'One final thing,' said Bert before we all went our separate ways. 'We already have an official bank account for the animals' welfare, so any donations can go in there and be looked after by the Trustees – that's Grace, Don from the Post Office, Meg and me. The thing is, we're going to need cold, hard cash for old Sparks, and I can't draw that amount out.'

'Not a problem,' said Ethel. 'I've got the readies.'

'What do you mean by that, Ethel Fish?' asked Meg, looking at the older woman suspiciously. 'Don't tell me you've got money stuffed under the mattress?'

'As if. Me da, and his da before him, never trusted banks. Said they were all charlatans, so they kept all their money in a hole in the ground underneath the pig swill trough. Those pigs wouldn't let anyone other than me da in their pen, so it was as safe as houses.'

'Don't tell me you're still using that,' gasped Meg.

'And why not? I might not have any pigs anymore, but that sty stinks more than Duchess, so no one would ever want to go rooting around in there. And before you get all uppity, Meg Shafto, I do have a bank account, but I still like to have some tucked away for emergencies. You'll thank me one day when t'interweb blows up, and mark my words, it will. It's only a matter of time. That nice fellow on the morning news that used to be a judge said so, and he knows what he's talking about. When it happens, none of you will be able to pay for as much as a pint of Lindisfarne Lil, but I'll be okay... just like a pig in muck.' She chuckled at her own joke.

I glanced at Inigo, who was struggling not to laugh.

'Ethel, there's no need for you to use your rainy-day fund. I'll sort the finances out with Bert, but would you come on that date with me this evening? I'd like to take you out before the system explodes and I can still pay for it. I think your company is just what I need!'

'You can pick me up at six o' clock sharp because I need to get back early. Fisherman's Cottage on Gospel Lane, and just to let you know, there'll be no benefits as you youngsters say. Not on a first date, anyway.'

'I shall be the perfect gentleman,' replied Inigo, struggling to keep his face straight. 'Why the rush home, though?'

'I need to be back at seven for *Emmerdale*. That Cain Dingle is about to get his comeuppance, and not before time,' she tutted, her eyebrows knitting together.

'Come on, I'll drop you off at home,' said Zen, laughing while taking Ethel's arm. 'You can go and check on your readies. Please tell me it's not in old pound notes?'

'Red ones,' replied Ethel, winking, 'but they might still have the queen's head on them!'

Chapter 31

When the rest of the islanders heard about the potential new arrivals, it was all systems go, with offers of help and ideas for fundraising. Linda and Paul from the Crab came up with the idea of something we named the Mini Fest, and it was now in the planning stages.

True to his word, Inigo had approached his uncle, Lord Bamburgh, and the foreman from the wood yard rang Bert straight away to find out what was needed and to put everything into action.

I was frantically tidying up the attic in advance of the visit from the social worker. I was dreading it, as Kitti had been so depreciative of Mrs Monster, as she called her, and I was expecting us to be grilled. I ran downstairs to Aurora's, to make sure she hadn't forgotten that we would be calling in to discuss Kitti's job in the café.

'Nope, I'm all sorted, Ellie. I've worked on the original suggestion of 25 hours a week, which is way within the guidelines, and of course we'll be as flexible as we can. As you know, Julia who came for the interview accepted the full-time job, so it's all looking good. Julia seems down to earth, and I'm thinking she has management potential in the future, erm, should I, I mean we, decide to move off the island.'

'Not that old chestnut again,' I grinned. 'You're not going anywhere, but it's good to hear that Julia sounds exactly the right choice. I hope we find the same sort of person for Love Lindisfarne. The meet-and-greets are tomorrow, so we can suss them out. What are you up to now?'

'I thought I'd have a stroll over to the paddocks with Hetti – find out what's happening and pop in to see Meg. It all sounds very exciting. Jack and I have talked to Tara and Toby, and between us we'd like to 'adopt' the two Shetland ponies for Farne and Hettie and con-tribute towards their upkeep. We'd get to name them!'

'You sound just like Ethel with her hairy coos, but that's great. Bert and Meg will be so pleased, but Hettie isn't going to see much of her pony friend if she's in Seahouses, is she?'

'Fair point,' said Aurora, her forehead furrowed in concentration.

'I'll walk over with you. I need to catch up with Toby, then we can come back across in time for the social work visit. Perhaps we can all meet for tea in the café when she gets here? Butter her up with some nice cake and some of Zen's best coffee. Kitti tells me she's an ogre.'

'Sounds like a plan. I'll tell Pip to reserve us a table in the corner.'

'I hope your brother gets back in time to brush his hair and change into something more, erm, responsi-ble adult.'

'Are you sure you're doing the right thing?' asked Aurora, a hint of concern in her voice. 'Kitti seems lovely, but she's been through so much, and you know teenagers – their moods can swing like the mast of Jack's boat in a storm. And that's without everything that Kitti's endured.'

'I hear you, but it's only for a couple of months. Quite frankly, I think she's going to be kept quite busy, and hopefully that will give her less time to think too deeply, although I know she's still so very vulnerable.'

'I know what you mean. I just hope it doesn't impact on you and my bro; you seem in such a good place now. I was so disappointed when it was a false alarm the other night. I really am looking forward to you being my official sister-in-law.'

'Hey, who knows. Maybe one day, but we are good at the moment, which is why I'm confident that Kitti isn't going to impact on us at all. Well, maybe a little,' I smiled, thinking about the sound-proofing situation.

'Well, you know I'm right here, underneath you, if things get stressful and you ever need to talk, don't you?'

'Yes, I do, which is why I'm never going to let you move off this island. I got to thinking, what about asking Zen if you can store the pram and buggy over in the posh shed, then that's the stairs taken care of?'

'Are you kidding me? My brother would never see his precious roastery turned into a baby store – not even to keep me here. I can hear him now, jabbering on about health and safety, and Hettie and I would probably have to wear hairnets just to enter! Anyway, just think – if we move you can have this flat, and I thought Mam and dad might fancy the attic as their bolt hole when they retire.'

'There has to be another answer to this,' I said. 'We just haven't thought of it yet. Would Jack be happy to stay if you had a house of your own?'

'Jack loves the island, but he does feel that we should have somewhere to call our own and not live above the shop forever. I'm sure he could deal with the commute as he's got the choice of car or boat. Nothing's going to happen immediately, Ellie, and if we don't see anything we like and can afford we might be here until Hettie goes to school.'

'That's another reason you need to stay; Hettie is needed to keep school numbers up or it will end up being closed, and that would be on your head,' I laughed.

'Actually, you have a point. I'd always thought that Hettie would go to the island school, so if we move to Seahouses I'd probably end up commuting in reverse. This does require more thought, doesn't it? Anyway, let me get madam sorted. You carry the pram down, and we can go to see Grand Nanny Meg as she's chosen to be called – none of your Meg-Meg. On the way you can fill me in about Inigo. I hear Ethel's going on a hot date with him tonight.'

'How do you know that?'

'Oh, you know – the island grapevine never fails!'

***

'Well, that went far better than I expected,' I said to Zen, as we cuddled up on the sofa in front of the television that night. 'Mrs Monser, or Mrs Monster as Kitti calls her, wasn't anywhere near as officious as I thought.'

'You know why that is, though,' he replied as he flicked through the channels.

'Why?'

'Because we presented her with a ready-made placement that required her to do very little, except cross the i's and dot the t's.'

'Zen Chambers, you cynic. You could be right, though. She was colder than Maurice's oyster house – anything for an easy life, I suppose. Still, I don't care. Kitti is coming in a couple of days, and I'm so pleased she's going to be here to see the arrival of the minis. She's going to be so excited.'

'So, we have a couple of days left to ourselves,' said Zen, switching off the telly and giving me *the* smile, the one that even if I lived to be a hundred would never fail to constrict my insides into a scrunchie.

'Ellie,' he said, 'promise me that we're going to have some us time when Kitti is here. I don't just mean our haymaking,' he laughed. 'Just normal couples time for me and you. We're always so busy, and I want more time with my best friend, not less.'

'We will. I promise. Let's maybe try and do some walks together. Get away, just you and me.'

'Good idea. We'll go somewhere no one knows us and switch off the phones. Maybe we could do more of the coastal path, seeing as you didn't get very far last time. Leave it with me, and I'll have a think. We'll diary it into the calendar and stick to it, even if St Cuthbert comes back from the dead that day. Right, grab your phone now, and let's set a date for our date.'

I wrapped my arms around him, breathing in his oh-so-familiar scent. Holding him tightly, I could feel his strong heart beating rhythmically beneath his shirt.

'Maybe we'd better go and make some more hay?' I smiled, and suddenly his heart went from a slow and steady bass beat to rapid orchestral manoeuvres as he began to kiss me.

Chapter 32

We gathered in the back of Love Lindisfarne the next morning, a debate going on as to how we should set up the chairs for the meet-and-greets.

'I think we should keep it all very informal,' said Imogen, 'so they relax and feel at home.'

Ethel shook her head.

'Have you not watched *The Apprentice,* Imogen? We sit in a line behind the table, and I should be in the middle. Show them who's boss.'

'But you won't be the boss, Ethel, and neither will I. They're going to lease the shop, so it won't have anything to do with us.'

'Yes, it will. We still want to meet in this room, so I think we should spell it out from the beginning that we're in charge.'

Imogen and I both turned to Meg, our eyes pleading for intervention.

'If anyone's sitting in the middle, it's Imogen,' said Meg tutting. 'I vote we go in a circle, with no middle – all equals. We're only here today to support Imogen and help her decide what's best for *her* and *her* shop. Our needs as Crafty Lindisfarners are secondary. You got that, Ethel?'

'Okay, okay. Keep your gansey on, Meggie.'

'How many have we got coming?' I asked, changing the subject as Imogen arranged the chairs in a circle.

'Five. Just a brief chat with each – twenty minutes max – with a ten-minute break in between to catch our breath and see what we think.'

On the dot of ten the first of the interested parties rang the shop bell. A woman with long red hair, dressed from head to toe in Viking clothing, came into the room and took her seat. My heart was hammering, wondering what the heck Ethel was going to say, and it didn't take her long.

'Are you off to a fancy dress party after here?'

The woman glowered at her.

'No, this is me. It's how I choose to dress and live my life, in the way I want to, without comment, thank you very much.'

That's you told, Ethel, I thought.

'Right, erm, Brunhilda,' smiled Imogen, looking at her list.

I thought Ethel was going to choke. 'Brun what—' she began.

Meg jumped in.

'Lovely to meet you, Brunhilda. Tell us, what interests you in running a shop on a tiny island like ours?'

'It's actually not your island. It's ours,' retorted Brunhilda. 'We arrived on the eighth of June, in the year 793. The island should still belong to us, so we're going to reclaim it.'

'Listen Brunhilly, your lot came to plunder *our* island and the monastery, and sadly they succeeded, but they didn't come to take charge,' said Ethel.

'You don't know that unless you were around in 793, which you very well may have been,' Brunhilda retorted spitefully.

'Ladies, ladies,' said Meg, looking like she wanted to shove a Viking seax into Brunhilda's back.

'Erm, back to today,' interjected Imogen, her eyes getting wider and wider as they darted from one woman to the other. 'What role would the shop have in your erm, takeover plans?'

'We'll open a Viking experience—'

'And who is we?' asked Meg, suspicion dripping from her every word.

'My clan. We want to regain our presence on the island. How many do you think can sleep in the flat above the shop?'

'She's fired,' I heard Ethel mutter under her breath, and for once I agreed with her.

'I'm not sure we're ready for that much change, Brunhilda, but thanks for coming. Have a safe journey back to... to... well, wherever you Vikings live these days,' said Imogen, bringing things to a close.

'Wallsend,' retorted Brunhilda as she stomped out.

We all sat in silence, even Ethel for a nanosecond, before bursting into laughter.

'Well, let's hope the second ones are better. It's a husband and wife next,' said Imogen.

The doorbell rang, and a middle-aged couple came into the room.

'Welcome, Mr and Mrs Timperley. Thanks for coming. I see you live in Bedlington, so not too far away.'

'That causeway is a pain in the arse,' said Mr Timperley, a thin, sour-faced man. 'Is there any chance of them raising it so the road stays open all the time – turn it into a flyover or something?'

This was not getting off to the best of starts. After the preliminary chit-chat, Imogen asked Mrs Timperley what they intended to sell.

'Well, gifts, of course.'

That sounded more promising.

'But not like what you've got in here.' Her powdery over made-up face twisted far too easily into a scowl. 'Who wants handmade things like this?' she said, reaching out and picking up a beautifully made beanie. 'Too expensive, and far too old fashioned. I'll get some nicknacks from China off the internet, like some of those nodding plastic cats. And if it's hats you want, there's some lovely washable acrylics with huge pom poms.'

'That hat was crafted on this island by Muriel, an islander, using wool from island alpacas, and it will not be replaced by mass produced imports. Thank you for coming, but I don't think this is the right business for you both,' Imogen said curtly.

'Too right it's not. If you go now, you can catch the tide, I'd hate for you to get stuck, but believe you me, you'll have a long wait for a flyover being built.' Ethel glowered at the pair, who rushed for the door.

The next two applicants proved just as fruitless. One chap wanted to change the shop into an amusement arcade and the other a natural health centre, called Get Naked with Nature. We didn't ask.

'This is pointless,' wailed Imogen, after the fourth applicant had gone. 'Maybe my wording on the ad wasn't specific enough. I understand that a new owner will want to make changes, but the ideas we've heard today are all so inappropriate. I'm not letting my baby go to someone as undeserving as they've all been so far.'

'Oh, I don't know. That Get Naked with Nature one did sound interesting,' said Ethel. 'You should have let me ask more questions.'

'Ethel, pet, my body has gone as far south as Watford Gap and yours – well it's probably heading over the English Channel by now – so getting naked with anything is no longer an option for us,' chuckled Meg.

'Look, we're running early seeing none of them have lasted more than ten minutes, so let's have a cuppa. You never know, number five might just be the one,' I said, ever the optimist.

Chapter 33

The appointment time of applicant number five came and went. And another ten minutes. And then another.

'They're not coming, are they?' Imogen sighed. 'Back to the drawing board.' But just at that the shop door burst open.

'Cooeee! Anyone there?'

Imogen went into the front shop to introduce herself and bring the man to the stock room.

'Everyone, this is Mr Bell.' She introduced us to a young man, whose grin spread from ear to ear like a huge slice of watermelon.

'Just call me Barry, or Big Lad. Everyone else does,' he squealed. 'Eeeeeh, I am *so* sorry I'm late. I'd just crossed the bridge thing, and there was a seal at the side of the road on the shingle.'

Barry Big Lad began clapping like he was a performing seal himself.

'Oh, My Gawwwwd! How cute was it? You don't see many of them in Fenham, where I live. Anyway, it must have been injured, but there was this absolute rock god there – all Heathcliff with his long dark curls, the kindest eyes I think I've ever seen, and his muscles… oh my days! I came over all a quiver.' Barry's hands began theatrically slapping together again. 'I just had to stop and make sure it was okay,' he guffawed, 'and erm, maybe to meet the rescuer. He's called Zen. I mean, how cool is that, and there's me newly single and…'

Barry didn't stop for breath!

'Hands off. Zen's mine,' I butted in smiling, liking Barry from the very minute he had walked through the door.

'Barry lad, slow down. You're going to knock yourself out. Meg, go and make the boy a cup of tea – he's all a dither,' said Ethel.

Imogen began the questions.

'So, Barry, what brings you to the island?'

'Did I mention I got dumped recently? He was called Tristan. Pur-lees tie me up if I ever go near a posh boy again! Well, he's gone back to Persephone and—'

'So, you wanted a new start?' I jumped in before we got chapter and verse on Tristan and Persephone, which one day I would love to hear more about – just not right now.

'I did. And when I saw this advert and showed it to Old Joe he said, "Bazza lad, this has got your name written all over it."'

'Old Joe?' queried Ethel, her eyes twinkling, no doubt at the idea of a potential new 'friend'.

'From Lockley Knit and Natter Group,' explained Barry. 'Eeh, they're a lovely lot. Old Joe was in the navy, you know, and he can knit better than any of them. He made this especially for me to wear today.' Barry pulled down the extra-large jumper, which had a seagull devouring an ice cream on the front.

'Very nice,' said Meg. He's got that expression perfect with its beady eyes. I detest seagulls.'

'You belong to a craft group?' asked an astonished Imogen, a huge smile on her face.

'I do. I don't live in Lockley, but they took me under their wing when my shop, erm, shut, after Christmas.'

'So, you have experience in running a shop?' asked Imogen.

'Yes, I ran a haberdashery store.'

Everyone's eyes shot up on hearing this revelation. It was like manna from heaven.

'And where was that?' I asked.

'Only inside the biggest department store in New-castle,' said Barry proudly.

'No way. I've never seen a haberdasher's store in there before,' said Imogen.

'Erm, it was a pop-up shop for Christmas,' said Barry, 'so it's finished now.'

'And what's your favourite craft?' asked Ethel.

'Anything involving glitter,' said Barry firmly. 'I loves a bit of sparkle. Does us all good to shine don't you think?'

We all nodded in wonderment at this gift from above who sat in front of us, beaming.

'And what would you do with the shop, should you be lucky enough to be offered the lease?' asked Imogen.

'Old Joe looked over the figures you sent me. He said, "Bazza lad, if it ain't broke, don't fix it," so I would continue just the way it is, with a little bit of Barry bants and magic thrown in for added effect,' he grinned.

He picked up the beanie discarded by Mrs Timper-ley.

'Take this, for example. Look at how gorgeous it is – the work that must have gone into it. But I might just add a bit of Barry magic and attach a vintage brooch. It would look good with a big diamante star on it, and that would give it even more va-va-voom. How good would that look on Insta?'

We all remained silent, in awe, until Meg managed to pull herself back into gear.

'And would you have any plans for this room we're in now?'

Barry stared around the small room.

'I'd love to just have a space where people can drop into for a chat or a cup of tea and a bit of banter with me. What does it get used for now?' asked Barry.

We explained about the Crafty Lindisfarners using the space for meetings, get-togethers and crafting sessions.

'That's perfect. Eventually, I could organise for visiting craft groups to come to the island and do different types of sessions. Obviously, if I got the shop, I'd have the Lockley Knit and Natter up pronto. You'd love them.'

'And outside of crafting, do you have any hobbies, Barry?' asked Meg. 'Small island life can be boring for some young people.'

'And there's no takeaways, pet,' said Ethel, looking pointedly at Big Lad's girth.

'Great – I need to get some of this timber off me, so I can be Barry Slim Lad,' he chuckled. 'As for hobbies, I love to sing.' He jumped out of his chair and burst into a unique version of 'Any Dream will Do', his jazz hands all aflutter.

Meg stood up and cheered. 'Barry, you are just what The Lads are crying out for.'

'Ooh, I do hope so,' said Barry winking, 'but what lads?'

'The Lindisfarne Amateur Dramatics Society. We were thinking of doing *Joseph* for Christmas.'

'Sign me up,' said Barry, 'I'd look amazing in that coat, pardon the pun.'

'Can I say it? Can I say it?' shouted Ethel.

Imogen nodded.

'Barry, lad, you're hired!'

'All subject to references, of course,' said Imogen, 'but welcome aboard, Barry. I think you're going to fit in on Lindisfarne perfectly.'

The squeals that came out of Barry were ear-piercing as he ran around the room, high-fiving us all.

'Thank you, thank you, thank you. You won't regret it,' he yelled.

'Barry, would you like to accompany me to our local to meet—'

'Plenty of time for Barry to get acquainted with the Crab,' interrupted Meg.

'Why don't we all go over to the café and have some celebratory cake instead, and we can tell Barry more about the island?' I suggested.

'Sounds good to me. Slim Lad Barry can wait a while longer. Lead me to the biggest, fattest cream cake they've got!'

<h1 style="text-align:center">Chapter 34</h1>

'I can't believe that Kitti is going to be with us in a matter of hours,' I said to Zen, as we sat at our tiny kitchen table eating breakfast. 'Do you think I got enough things in to eat that she might like? She probably won't enjoy this muesli stuff you concoct yourself, though; it's like eating the shingle off Brighton beach!'

'Hey, no one forces you to eat it, and in answer to your question, you can't fit any more in the cupboards, so I'm sure she's not going to starve until we find out her dietary likes and dislikes. Besides which, there's a café two floors down, and I'll make sure Aurora sets up a tab for her.' He stood up and put his bowl in the sink. 'I'm heading to the roastery early to work for a couple of hours, before going to Ashington with Bert and Maurice to collect the new arrivals. Please tell Kitti I'm sorry I can't be here when she arrives.'

'I will. Without telling her why,' I grinned. 'It's a day off for me, so I can be around for her coming, but I'll go straight over to the castle now and see if Bert needs any more help with the animals or last-minute preparations for the minis coming. I can't believe we managed to get the new paddocks and shelters all up and fenced in such a short space of time. Everyone has really put a lot of effort into this.'

I walked across to the castle with Nacho scampering ahead, past the fishing club and the upturned boats on the scrubland. I had hoped for bright sunshine today, but as usual, the weather didn't play according to my rules, and it was a dull, grey day with a sea fret hovering over the coastline.

'Morning, Bert,' I shouted. He was leaning on one of the fence rails, surveying the new paddocks. 'Everything okay?'

'Morning, Ellie. I was just having a moment, thinking about all the good things I've got in my life. When you get to my age, lass, you'll not be able to help your mind casting back across what you've done with your time on this earth. I hope I've made some contribution and that it won't stop until I'm six feet under. It's a lucky person who gets to my age with nowt more serious than a dodgy hip, but none of us knows what's around the corner.'

'That's true of all of us, Bert,' I said, feeling a sense of melancholy coming from him. 'What's brought this on today?'

'Well, lass, I was watching the swallows diving around the stables this morning.'

'The swallows?'

'Yes. Just think, Ellie, they've already flown all the way from Africa – about six thousand miles, can you believe? They've beaten the odds to fly to us here on Lindisfarne, eating whatever they can from the air as they go. Then they get here and have to find the strength to build their temporary homes and produce their young. It got me thinking that they pack in a lot into their short lifespan on this earth, and I was hoping I had too. Swallows probably don't live more than two years, if they survive that long, because like the rest of us, they don't know what tomorrow might bring either. It's the circle of life in speeded up form.'

'Oh, I see, I think,' I said. 'Like on David Attenborough, when they fast forward a life cycle kind of thing?'

Bert nodded. 'Swallows are magnanimous, or whatever you call that thing. You know – being with one mate for life.'

'You mean monogamous?'

'Aye, that. Anyway, if one goes, the other is left alone, and it got me thinking about me and my Meg. And then, bringing in the new animals. Shetlands, for example, can live up to thirty years or longer, and our two new ones are just youngsters. Am I doing the right thing bringing them here with an old duffer like me?'

'But it's not just you, Bert. There's lots of us here to share the load. With age comes experience, and we need you for that. And you're not an old duffer, by the way.'

'Ellie, lass, when we started the sanctuary, it was always expected that Grace would be here long after me, I've got about fifteen years on her, then look what happened – she had that stroke out of the blue. I'm just being realistic.'

'That's why it's good to try and live in the moment, Bert. Take today, for example. This is the day we get to see Kitti arrive, to spread her wings and hopefully find some peace after the trauma she's been through. And we also get to do the right thing by nine tiny animals who otherwise might have had a very different life, ending up goodness knows where, so I would say today is a very good day.'

'You're right, of course, Ellie, but I want you to promise me that should anything happen to me, you and Zen – and Aurora, of course – will look after my Meg. I don't ever want her to be on her own. The thought cripples me, lass.' His eyes, which were clouded with pain at the thought of him and Meg being parted, sought out mine and silently beseeched me to agree.

I laid my hand gently on his arm. 'Bert, I promise you, and I know if Zen and Aurora were here too, they would say the same. Meg will never want for company, and we will all care for her just like she looks after us. And as for the menagerie, don't you worry about them. Between us, your legacy will live on.'

'I don't want you to ever feel that you must give your entire life to this island like me and Meg have, Ellie. It's a different world now. Eventually, you and Zen might want to see more of it together, and I would hate that you felt you had to stay on Lindisfarne because you're tied in some way.'

'We won't be tied. There's a few of us "younger ones" as you put it living on the island now. We're all friends who will look out for each other in exactly the same way that you and Meg have done with Ethel, Maurice and all your island family, because that's what you all are to each other. One day I'll not be so young, and I hope I still have that close bond with lifelong friends like you and Meg have. That kind of thing is priceless, Bert.'

'Aye, lass, it is. You'll always be a young 'un to me, Ellie,' he smiled. 'Right, now I've got that off my chest, let's go and get a nice cup of tea with my Meg and put the world to rights.'

'Maybe the world on Lindisfarne. We haven't got enough time for the rest of it,' I laughed, feeling so much better seeing Bert smiling, his tweed cap askew on his head.

'Meg's ready to bust her bloomers, she's so excited,' he smiled. 'She had the hens and turkeys out of their coops by dawn this morning. I don't think they knew what had hit them, having to get up so early!'

I took Bert's arm, and we made our way back up the cinder path like Darby and Joan.

'Did Meg tell you about Big Lad Barry, who's coming to take over Love Lindisfarne?' I chattered as we walked, and as I burst into an impression of Barry singing 'Any Dream will Do', Bert was back to being Bert, laughing like a drain at my warbling then joining in with me and singing just as badly as me.

As we were crossing the yard to the cottage, Inigo came down the back stairs of the castle.

'Morning. Where you off too looking so, erm, outdoorsy?' I laughed.

'This is the day, Ellie. The day I am going to stride across the Northumberland National Park and reflect on where I have gone wrong in my life,' he grinned. 'The day I will finally get my ducks in a row and find myself.'

'Good luck with that. We've got a busy day here as the mini animals are coming later.'

'I know, Ellie, and I'm sorry I'm going to miss out, but I really need to do this hike. My time has been totally taken up since I got here, not that I'm complaining – it's great – but I came with the intention of doing some walking.'

'I understand. Thanks for all the help you've given us. Not only financial, but Zen also tells me you're a dab hand with a hammer.'

'You know, I really enjoyed building the new fences and shelters – the banter with the boys and just keeping it real – it was fun. Anyway, I shall see you all later tonight. Perhaps we can go and toast the new arrivals in the Crab?'

'Not sure. Kitti's arriving today; you caught a glimpse of her the day you arrived. Anyway, she's staying with Zen and me for a few weeks, so we'll not be leaving her on her own on her first day. She's sixteen and been through an unbelievably tough time, which puts all our woes into perspective.'

'Aw, poor kid. Not much older than my Santo. I'll see you soon. I'm going extreme today, so better get on.'

'Where're you off to?'

'I'm doing Hethpool to the Curr, over the Cheviot Hills. Eleven and a half miles.'

'That's less than we were meant to be doing on the coastal path, you slacker.'

'Slacker? This isn't a stroll along a flat path. It's probably the most extreme walk on offer, estimated to take seven hours. It takes me past a memorial to airmen who lost their lives in the hills, around the time of the second world war. It's going to be tough; Sophie wouldn't have made it out of the car park! Incidentally, have you heard from her recently?'

'Yes, every day. Her fiancé is taking some time out of work, so I'm half expecting to hear that they're going to come back up here soon.'

'I hope I'll still be around if they do. Be nice to meet him.'

'Well, shake a leg or whatever the saying is. If you don't come back, we'll send out the mountain rescue.'

'Ah, thanks for the vote of confidence. Catch you later. Good luck with all the new arrivals today. It's a good thing you're doing, Ellie.'

'Not just me,' I smiled. 'Joint effort. See you later.'

Chapter 35

Kitti's foster carer, Billy, dropped her off but headed straight back to Newcastle.

'It's a shame that him and Sue weren't able to come and spend the day here as arranged,' I said as we carried Kitti's bags up the stairs to the attic.

'That was all down to Paige. The police were around again last night about her, and Sue had to take her to the police station this morning.'

'That doesn't sound very good,' I replied.

'It's a regular thing; she's always up to all kinds and will probably have to go into something Sue called a 'secure training centre' the way she's going.'

'Will you miss Sue and Billy?'

'I like them. They've been kind, but I hated being in the house with Paige being there, so I'm just pleased to get out.'

'I'm so sorry it didn't work out that well for you. Right,' I said, opening the door to her tiny room, 'I hope this will be okay. We've done what we can with it...' But Kitti didn't even hear me. Her eyes were fixed on a big canvas on the wall. It was hard to miss in the small space.

'Oh, Ellie, did you get this done for me?' she gasped, looking at the picture of a kittiwake standing proud on a carpet of extra-large daisies.

'Zen and I got his dad to paint it for you.'

'It's beautiful. Is that Greater Reef?' She pointed to the image of the cute lighthouse behind the bird, the buttery yellow sun high in the sky and the sparkling blue sea beyond tipped with the whitest of waves.

'Shh, I'll let you into a secret. I had to twist Mike's arm to agree to do an artist's impression, so to speak. He normally does extremely realistic, serious bird paintings. It is Greater Reef, but there's no grassy meadow like that over there. I've never seen the island look so colourful, but it's just how I imagined the picture. Zen and I love it, and we hope you do to. We want you to have happy memories of your mam, Daisy, every time you look at it.'

'I will,' she said quietly. 'Mam always used to say this island was special, and it is.'

'You haven't got a huge amount of luggage,' I said, changing the subject. 'I was wondering where we were going to put all your stuff.'

'I just brought my clothes and a few special things I could carry, which I had to hide at Sue's because Paige would have just come into my room and helped herself if I hadn't. The social worker organised a storage place for everything from our old house. She said that it might be useful for when I get a place of my own. At least they didn't just put it in a skip; I couldn't have stood that. Mam had worked hard for what we had, and she enjoyed going to sales and charity shops for vintage things. I loved our house. It was full of bright colours, just like the picture,' she smiled, looking at the canvas again.

'Your things will be safe here, Kitti. This is your space, and Zen and me won't ever come in unless invited. Okay, let's go downstairs and have some lunch with Aurora and baby Hettie, and you can meet Pip. You'll get on well with her. There's a new manager called Julia starting on the same day as you, so it will be good not to be the only new starter. You can make mistakes together.'

'Where's Zen? I thought he might be here.'

'He would have been, and he said to say hello. There are nine very good reasons why he can't be here right now, and all will be revealed later. When you find out, I'm sure you'll forgive him for missing your arrival.'

'Ooh, sounds interesting.'

'Just you wait!'

***

Zen phoned to say they were about to drive along the causeway. Kitti and I had been chilling out, eating ice cream and watching an episode of *Gilmore Girls*.

'Time to go.' I jumped up.

'What? Now? The programme isn't finished yet.'

'Never mind that. Get your coat on, and let's go.'

'You're very excited, Ellie, and a little bit crazy. But good crazy,' she laughed, tying the laces on her trainers.

My phone beeped again – Meg telling me to get our backsides across. Aurora was waiting for us at the bottom of the stairs.

'Where's Hettie?' I asked.

'Imogen's got her over at the shop. She says it's just like looking after one of the baby lambs, which is quite reassuring.'

'Just as well she hasn't got an Aga,' I laughed, 'or Hettie would be in it!'

We began to hurry across to the castle.

'Are either of you going to tell me what the rush is?' asked Kitti, looking perplexed.

'Nope!' we replied in unison.

We got to the road in front of the paddocks where Meg, Tara, Toby and Farne were waiting by the entrance gate.

'I thought half the island would be here,' said Tara.

'Bert told everyone to hold back until we know that everything is okay.' I gestured towards Kitti and mouthed, 'don't you dare blab!'

'Oh, right – gotcha,' laughed Tara.

'Where are all the animals? asked Kitti, noticing the empty spaces. And what are those for? They weren't there before.' She pointed to the newly created paddocks.

'Erm, the animals are all up in their stables for now because...' but I was saved from explaining by the wagon pulling up at the gate.

<h1 style="text-align:center">Chapter 36</h1>

'Eeeh, they're here,' said Aurora, letting out a high-pitched squeal that could have shattered glass.

'Shush, Aurora,' said Meg. 'You'll terrify them.'

'Terrify who?' asked Kitti, looking puzzled, as the men climbed down from the front of the wagon.

'Did everything go okay, Bert?' shouted Meg.

'Fine. He got his money then buggered off and left us to it, which suited us down to the ground.'

Maurice and Zen undid the back ramp of the wagon.

'We loaded them in order of who goes into the furthest paddock,' said Bert, who had been planning their arrival like a military operation, telling us that each breed would be kept apart from the others and away from direct contact with our own animals until the vet gave them the all-clear. If there wasn't anything causing concern, the segregation might only last a couple of weeks.

'I'll see what the vet says, but I hope we can fetch ours back down here so that they can all see each other over the fences at a distance. Then I can work out who can live with who and think about ground rotation and all of that.'

When it came to animal husbandry, Bert knew his onions.

'You said Zen had nine reasons for not being here when I arrived,' said Kitti, her cheeks glowing and a smile so wide I thought her face might split in two. 'So, what's in there?' She pointed to the wagon.

'Nine tiny bundles of joy,' I smiled.

The first newbies were brought down the ramp together – two tiny Pygmy goats, about the same size as Holly Goatlightly. Both goats were heavy-coated and predominantly black, with white markings across their heads and legs.

'Oh, my God,' gasped Kitti. 'They look like baby pandas. They're not quite as pretty as Holly, but nearly. And soooo cute.'

'They are that,' agreed Meg. 'Poor old Nanny isn't much of a looker, but I still love her, especially now she doesn't need milking anymore.'

Next came the two donkeys, who were both long coated in shades of fawn, and on first sight they were identical to each other.

'Are they twins?' asked Tara. 'I can't tell one from the other. Look, they've even got the same white star mark on their muzzles, and their ears are all rimmed in dark brown. Oh, my god – I think I'm in love.'

The donkeys broke the silence by braying in unison.

'Listen to that. They even talk at the same time,' laughed Kitti.

Bert then led two tiny, cartoon-like Shetland ponies down the ramp towards Aurora and Tara.

'I believe these two are yours and that you are going to look after them – muck them out day and night and do everything to care for them.'

Tara's face was a picture.

'I think we said we'd sponsor them, and we'd like to name them, but I'm up for helping more with all the animals. It'll be good for Farne to learn. I helped in our stables when I was a child.'

'And I'll help too,' said Aurora, 'whenever I can fit it in.'

'You'll not be able to help if you move,' I hissed in her ear.

'Take no notice, girls. He's winding you up. You've got the bairns to look after – they're your priority,' Meg said firmly.

'That's as may be,' said Aurora, 'but with all these extra residents we are all going to have to lend a hand more, and I promise I will be over as often as time allows. I'll be able to bring Hettie, and you can look after her while I muck out.'

'Fine by me,' Meg smiled.

Tara and Aurora studied the two ponies like they were at a top racehorse sale. They were both undeniably cute with their rotund tummies, short legs and long, dark manes. Unlike my own little favourite Hannibal, they seemed quite happy to be fussed over, and neither of them demanded Chianti once! I had no clue as to how Aurora and Tara were going to decide which one they would each sponsor.

'Aurora, you choose. You're family and should pick first,' said Tara.

'How can I? They are equally utterly scrumptious.'

Both ponies were piebald and looked almost like Dalmatian dogs. Zen handed Aurora the pony with more splodges, and Tara the other lesser marked one.

'There – decision made. Happy to help,' he smiled.

'Farne, look at your new friend,' said Tara to her son, who was watching proceedings from the safety of Toby's arms.

'What will we call them?' asked Aurora.

'They support the Toon,' said Maurice, 'both being black and white, so how about Shearer and Keegan?'

'Who?' asked Kitti.

'Joelinton and Big Dan,' laughed Zen.

'Who?' I asked.

'Jackie and Bobby,' joined in Bert.

'Bert, pet, you're going back some years. None of those names are right,' said Meg, scratching her chin in contemplation. 'Got it. How about Jimmy and Perez? I loved *Shetland* when he was in it. He was a bit of a dish, and he knew how to solve a crime, just like Vera.'

Tara and Aurora smiled at each other and nodded.

'Meg, that's inspired. Welcome to Lindisfarne wee Jimmy,' said Aurora to her adopted pony.

'And to you too, Perez,' smiled Tara. 'Do you approve of the name, Tobes?"

'I do. Very fitting for a pair of Shetlands. I'd love to go there. Did you know, you can explore over 5,000 years of human history on some amazing historic sites. Take Clickimin Broch for example—'

'Okay, Tobes, one day we'll go there, but let's get these animals sorted first, eh?' smiled Tara.

Bert came back down the ramp with two of the tiniest Highland cows I'd ever seen trotting down behind him. Kitti's eyes took on the appearance of two flying saucers hovering in space as she gazed at the minute animals. One cow was mid-brown with greyish flecks, huge brown liquid eyes like the darkest of hot chocolate and a big black nose. The other was the reddish-brown typical of highland cattle, and it at once snuggled next to the other. It also had huge brown eyes and a slightly paler, more milk chocolate nose. Both were undeniably adorable.

'And last but not least,' said Bert shouting up the ramp. 'Bring her down, Zen.'

Zen came down the ramp carrying the tiniest of the three. It was an off-white shade, or at least it might have been underneath all the dirt. It shared the dark eyes of her friends, but unlike the first two, this little one had a rosy pink nose.

'Bert, I don't like the look of this little girl,' said Zen. 'Her legs just about buckled, and she seems quite lethargic. Maybe it's the journey, but I'm thinking she's dehydrated and possibly suffering from malnutrition. All three of them are very underweight.'

'Oh, no,' cried Kitti, running towards Zen and stroking the small cow, which lay limp in Zen's arms.

'Right, lad, straight up to the isolation stable in the yard with you, and Meg, you call the vet. Zen, make up some electrolyte solution and see if she'll drink. I'm thinking she might need to be rehydrated intravenously, but we'll let the vet decide the best course of action. No doubt he'll want to check the others too. I'll be up in a minute.'

The poor little cow looked so sorry for itself and made no protest as Zen gently carried it up the cinder path.

'It's not going to die, is it?' asked Kitti in a shaky voice, her face clouded with concern. Immediately I understood that for her, this was all too raw.

'I don't think so, lass. Try not to worry,' said Maurice. 'She just needs a good drink and a feed, and she'll be right as rain.'

I hoped so, because this was not the happy introduction to Lindisfarne that I had envisaged for Kitti.

'Oh, dear lord,' said Aurora, wiping away a stray tear, 'blooming baby hormones again, but she looks so dejected and poorly. I just want to give her a cuddle.'

'Me too,' I echoed.

'Me three,' said Tara, sniffing into a tissue.

'I'm going with Zen. I want to help,' said Kitti, and she ran up the path towards the yard like an Olympic sprinter.

The other two cows stood in their new paddock, their long eyelashes fluttering as they sniffed the air and adjusted to being back on solid ground after their ride in the wagon. They huddled together, their mouths chewing on hay that they had been eating in the truck. The pair looked unkempt and far too thin.

'They're hungry,' said Aurora, 'and they look sad.'

'They won't be for long, lass,' said Bert, and he was right. It didn't take much time for them to find their voices and begin to moo. It was joyous to hear them and watch as they explored, beginning to look a little more confident as they began to sample the grass.

'What are their names?' asked Tara, her eyes rivetted on the tiny creatures.

'Nothing yet. Don't think they've ever had names, but they might prefer that in the long term, as Ethel gets to name them. I fear the worst, knowing Ethel,' laughed Bert.

'How old are they, Bert?' I asked.

'Sparks had no idea, but I'm thinking about two, it's quite hard to judge as they are so underweight that I don't think they've reached the appropriate size, but their horns are not quite fully grown yet, so maybe under three. Right, I'm away up to see the invalid.'

'I'll come with you and make sure Kitti is okay,' I said.

'We'll all stay down here and keep an eye on this lot,' said Meg. 'Vet said she'd be here as soon as she could. It's Jilly on duty today, and for once the bally tides are in our favour.'

Chapter 37

'She's not interested in drinking, Bert,' said Zen, as we went into the stable. The cow looked like a tiny bag of bones and lay on the sawdust, showing no interest in what was going on around it.

'I'm worried,' said Kitti. 'Can we not just squirt some down her mouth?'

'The vet's on her way, young Kitti – try not to panic.' said Bert. 'When you start helping with the animals, you'll begin to learn that sometimes, like humans, they get poorly, and we follow procedures and processes. Why don't you go and get a dish of warm water and some clean cloths? Meg keeps them in the cupboard in the goat's stable. Give her face a gentle wipe; her eyes and nose are looking a little dry. No cross-contamination, though – clean, separate cloths for eyes and mouth.'

'Got it,' she said, running to get the gear.

'That's it, Kitti,' I said when she came back and carefully wiped the lethargic animal using clean cloths, taking care to change the water between wipes.

'You're doing a grand job, lass. Now then,' said Bert, 'as a welcome to the island you get to choose the names for the goats. You don't have to decide now. Have a think about it and see what they look like in a few days' time. I know you're going to be helping me look after all of these while you're here, and I can see you're a natural.'

Kitti turned pink and gulped.

'That's really cool. I need to have a think. I'll come over as much as I can when I'm not working in the café. I don't start until Monday, so I'll be here first thing in the morning, if that's okay, Ellie?'

'That's perfect. Then you can maybe pop into Ethel's afterwards – she's longing to see you. Zen and I are working but will be around on the island if you need us.'

'So, that just leaves the donkeys without names for now, but I thought we could get Linda to run a competition at Mini Fest to raise some dosh. Winner gets to name them,' grinned Bert.

'How's she doing?' said Meg, popping her head in the door. 'Oh, the poor wee thing. She looks so sorry for himself, but I'm sure Jilly will put her right,' she added quickly, seeing Kitti's worried face. 'I'm just going to pop the kettle on if anyone fancies a cup.'

'Grand,' said Bert, 'just what I need – a nice cup of tea.'

The vet arrived not long after, and it was just as Zen and Bert had suspected; the tiny cow was severely dehydrated and malnourished, so was given an intravenous injection and was to stay in isolation until she was back on her feet. We left her peacefully resting in the stable and went down to the paddocks with Jilly the vet. After checking the other two cows, who were also underweight, Bert and Jilly came up with a feeding regime. Kitti hung onto every word.

'See, I told you that young girlie up there in the stable was going to be fine,' smiled Bert. 'You're in charge of keeping an eye on her. I can almost guarantee she'll be on her legs later tonight, and we'll probably get her back down here with her sisters tomorrow.'

Kitti smiled, the anxiety disappearing from her face. I had no doubt that she would follow Bert's instructions to the letter and make sure the cows were nursed back to full health.

'Fancy a pint, anyone? I'm parched,' said Maurice.

'Not tonight, son. I'm going to ask young Kitti to bring me down a flask, and I'm going to sit and make sure our new arrivals are all happily settling in.'

'I'll help Kitti with that,' said Zen. 'I wasn't able to welcome her today. Bert, get the chairs sorted from the storage shed and we can sit with you and have a bit of a welcome party down here, now the crisis is over.'

Maurice went off to the pub. Tara, Toby and Aurora made their way back across the island with baby duties in mind, and Zen and Kitti went up to the cottage, leaving Bert and me alone.

'How are you feeling now, Bert?' I asked, as once again he leant on the fence, only this time he was looking at the eight mini animals who had taken up residence in the new paddocks at the base of the castle.

'I'm feeling grand now, Ellie. It wasn't so good seeing that wee beast so poorly – I could swing for that Sparks – but you were right. Today has been a good day. I enjoyed the craic with Zen and Maurice on our little road trip. We're not out of the woods, though. Somehow, we have to raise enough money to keep these lads for the next umpteen years, but I'll worry about that tomorrow. It's another day.'

'Exactly,' I replied.

'Look at that, Ellie,' Bert gestured towards the cinder path where Zen and Kitti were walking down carrying bags from Meg. 'It makes my heart sing to see the young lass happy.'

I watched the pair as they chatted away to each other, Kitti laughing at something Zen had said, and I felt a lump form in my throat. Despite his concerns, Zen was getting fully behind welcoming Kitti into our lives.

The four of us sat inside the storage shed, with the doors wide open, as the day turned to dusk and the stars started peeping out of the navy blue night sky. There was a cluster of them twinkling like Tinkerbell's wand, and I'd like to think they were welcoming the newcomers to the island. As the light began to fade and the sky fell silent as the birds turned in for the night, the minis seemed quite at home. The cows and ponies were grazing happily, the donkeys were snuggled together in the corner looking out across the island, and the goats had already found the way into their shelter for bed.

'It's getting dark, so I'm going to go up and see Meg before we go home,' I said, dropping a kiss on Zen's head. 'I'll leave you lot to pack up, then I'll come back and collect you both, and we can walk across together.'

I gave Bert a hug and made my way up to the cottage. As I was going across the yard, the door in the big wooden gates opened and Inigo came through. He wasn't alone.

'Ellie, how did it go with Kitti, and the animals? Oh, excuse my manners. Ellie, this is Bree.'

Bree was stunning, in the most natural kind of way – not a scrap of makeup, and her huge smile revealed white, even teeth, twinkling more than my cluster of stars. She looked about twenty.

'G'day,' she said in a broad Australian accent. 'Nice to meet you, Ellie.'

I muttered hello back, not quite knowing what to say next but wondering if she was Margot Robbie's younger sister, as she looked just like her. Inigo sensed my astonishment and filled in the gap.

'I met Bree on the walk; she thought she might have twisted her ankle so...'

'So, Inigo said he would kiss it better,' she interrupted, laughing.

'Er, right... well, er, have a good night both of you.'

'Oh, we will,' smirked Bree, with Aussie forthrightness. And off they went up the stairs to the castle – without a limp in sight. I guess Inigo finding himself might have to wait for another day!

Chapter 38

Kitti was up with the larks the next morning and eating cereal at the breakfast table.

'Sleep well for your first night?' I asked as I went to put the kettle on.

'It was a little strange, but not bad strange. I like the tiny room, and I just kept looking at my picture and then fell asleep. Hope you don't mind me helping myself to cereal,' she said. 'I want to get over to help Bert. Jilly the vet's coming back later this morning, and I want to watch and listen to what we need to do afterwards.'

'You just help yourself to whatever you want. What's that you've got there?'

'From the big container. It's really nice.'

Zen walked into the kitchen, fully dressed in his T shirt and jeans rather than his usual birthday suit. Oh well, we sometimes had to make sacrifices, I suppose! He ruffled Kitti's hair.

'Good choice. Just call me Mr Alpen. I make that myself, and Ellie reckoned you would hate it. No one could not like my muesli.'

'Mam was into all kinds of natural produce,' said Kitti, a faint shadow of sadness crossing her face, 'but at Sue and Billy's the nearest we got was an apple or banana. Not that Paige would eat healthy things, and the only fruit she got came out of a vape.'

'Have you decided on a name for the goats?' I asked, trying to raise her mood.

'I have,' she replied, her face returning to a smile. 'I'm going to name them after black and white birds.'

'Your mam would have liked that,' smiled Zen.

'I thought maybe Penguin and Puffin.'

'Great choices, Kitti, though you do know there aren't any penguins here?'

'I do, Zen,' she said indignantly, 'but they're both black and white birds.'

'Ellie didn't know that there weren't any penguins here, did you?'

'No,' I laughed. 'At my leaving party fancy dress, they gave me a puffin costume to represent Northumberland, and I thought I was a penguin! But I think Penguin and Puffin are ridiculously cute names and suit the goats.'

'I'm going now,' said Kitti, jumping up and rinsing her cup and bowl then grabbing her coat from the back of the chair. 'See you both later.'

'What have you got on your feet?' I asked, no longer feeling like the new girl.

'Trainers.'

'No good. Go to the cottage first. You'll find wellies in the porch, and put that yellow coat on. It'll protect your clothes from stinky stuff!'

And she was gone, looking happy and relaxed. Zen and I looked at each other, smiling.

'Day one, and I think we're doing a good job, don't you?' I said.

'So far, so good. We'll make canny parents one day soon, I hope. In fact, how about starting that process right now?' He winked.

I glanced at the clock, grabbed his hand and we took advantage of our new offspring leaving us alone!

***

That afternoon it was my turn to run TEA at the Castle. The arrangements between me, Tara and Aurora were working out so far, and we had managed to keep to our reduced opening hours. We still weren't making any real profit, but the van was definitely an asset to the castle.

'Hi, Ellie.'

I looked up from my phone to see Kitti.

'Hello, you.'

'I've just been to see Ethel. She sends her love, but I'm going back to the cottage now to see what else Bert needs me to do.'

'What did the vet say?'

'She thinks there's not much wrong with them apart from being underweight and the white cow suffering from dehydration, but she took blood tests and skin swabs, and they'll need to be kept away from the others until she gets the results. They all need to be treated for potential parasites too. The farrier called Will is coming later to make sure their feet are okay, and I want to be there to watch. Penguin and Puffin like their names, I can tell! They were munching away and seemed really at home.'

'I hope you aren't going to forget about Holly while she's up in the stable.'

'Never,' smiled Kitti. 'I've been around all of them this morning to say hello. Your Hannibal was not happy at being kept in. He was stamping his little foot, but Stout looked really pleased. Bert says she loves her stable.'

'Have you had lunch?' I asked, sounding like a mother hen.

'Yes. Meg made me and Bert sandwiches. Maurice is coming across later, too. This van is so cool. Would you like me to help in it, if I can? We can change the name to TEAK at the Castle,' she laughed.

'That would be great, but let's get you started in the café first. You can learn how to use the coffee machine and find your feet there before you work in here. There's only space for one person at a time, so you'll need to be already able to operate the equipment.'

'Okay, that sounds good.' And off she dashed again, back to her new best friends – Bert and the animals.

I was kept busy with customers until late in the afternoon when the tide had gone out, which meant that most of the tourists had departed. I was about to pull the shutter down and close a little earlier.

'Noooo!' shouted a voice, rushing towards the van – it was Inigo. 'I need coffee. Flat white, preferably.'

'How many would that be? Three, perhaps? One for you and one each for Cressida and Bree?' I asked, trying to keep my face straight.

'Cutting, Ellie!' he laughed. 'I've just dropped Bree off in Berwick, so she can catch the train back.'

'Where to? School?'

'She's twenty-five, as it happens. She's backpacking around Britain and stopping in Newcastle for a few nights. I won't be seeing her again, even though she's a great girl and lots of fun.'

'I could see that,' I smiled, 'and I'm only pulling your leg.'

'Before you say it,' he said, draining the cup and asking for a refill, 'I hold my hands up. I'm a lost cause. I've decided that maybe I have found myself. I'm single, I know Lucia and I are done, so maybe this is me just being me. I'm not giving out any signals of anything other than a brief connection.'

Looking as good as him, I don't suppose he needed any signals at all!

'One day I hope I might find someone to share my life with and commit to fully, I do believe in that, but even when I was married, the commitment bit very soon went out of the window, on both sides. I've not experienced the together thing like you and Zen have going on. The pair of you are blessed to have found each other, and I can see you're a perfect fit. I know Zen was much younger when he came to Ibiza with Beth, but I never for a minute thought they would stand the test of time, and I was right. There was one night I'd gone down to the cellar for a bottle of wine, and she followed me and made it crystal clear that she wanted me, right there and then amongst the Rioja!'

'No way. And did you?' I asked, not convinced he could have resisted anyone as sensual as Bethania.

'No, of course not. They were guests in our house, and I've a lot of time for Zen. He's the kind of guy I wish I could be – a deep thinker with a core of kindness – and I wouldn't ever have disrespected him like that. Mind you, don't mind saying I was sorely tempted. She's a very vibrant woman is Beth. Please, Ellie, don't say anything to Zen. It's years ago now, and he doesn't need to know.'

'I won't. I do hope Aidan and her manage to be magnanimous, as Bert calls it! They seem very much in love, but they've both got a track record of infidelity, and moving in the circles they do, lots and lots of partying from what I gather. There must be so much temptation put in front of them.'

'Let's hope they make a go of it. Talking of Aidan, he's coming across to Bamburgh soon as it's Lord B's birthday, so I'm going to hang around until then, at least.'

'It'll be good to see him – and Beth, if she comes too.'

'Right,' he said, finishing his second cup, 'I think I'll wander over to the village and see if I can be of any help in the roastery for a couple of hours. Then I'll take your boyfriend for a pint. Fancy joining us?'

'Not tonight. I promised Kitti we would make pizza. You can come for tea, if you want?'

'I'll not gatecrash when she's just got here. I'll grab something in the pub, but thanks, anyway.'

Inigo ran his hand through the steel blue hair, put the Raybans on, and like a Hollywood A lister strolled down the hill towards the road.

Chapter 39

'Hi, Meg,' I said, giving her a hug. 'I've just shut the van, so thought I'd pop in and say hello and see if I can prise Kitti away to come home with me.'

'Cup of tea? You look tired, Ellie. Hope you're not burning the candle at both ends. It's a massive thing taking on a teenager and trying to juggle everything else around it.'

'I've hardly seen her,' I laughed. 'She's been here nearly all day, other than a quick visit to Ethel. Thanks for looking after her.'

'She's not a pick of bother. Her mam did a grand job bringing her up. She's polite and very thoughtful. I'm way down in the pecking order, mind. She seems to have formed a strong bond with Bert because of the animals. She's not stopped asking him questions, and he loves it! They're down the paddocks now with Maurice, like the Three Stooges.'

'Who?'

'Oh, just some ancient comedy trio. Even I don't know, really. It's just a saying. Anyway, young Kitti is getting them organised. I think I know who's boss, even though Bert and Maurice both think they are.'

Meg put the teapot on the table alongside a plate of digestive biscuits.

'Hoy, what's going on? Where's the chocolate? These are not up to our usual standard. I've had a busy day and need a treat, not these cardboard cut-outs.'

'Ah, well, Ellie lass, I don't want you getting chocolatey fingers because I'm going to show you something.'

Meg went off into their bedroom and came back with a large parcel wrapped in brown paper.

'Remember on our blessing day I told you I had spent all our savings on a whim?'

'I do,' I smiled. 'Ooh, is that it, whatever it is?'

Meg laid the parcel on the table and carefully undid the string. Then she unwrapped the brown paper and held up the most beautiful wedding dress I think I'd ever seen.

'Meg! That's stunning.' I looked at the amazing gown, taking in the exquisite detail. 'Where did you get it? And is that what you wore to get married?'

'I'd been shopping in Newcastle with Muriel and Dora, and at that time there was an arcade area with various second-hand shops.'

'You mean vintage,' I laughed.

'It was so exciting, especially to us from a tiny island. It was where the hippies would hang out, and the place was alive with music, chatter and the smell of patchouli oil. It nearly choked you.'

'Are you sure it was patchouli?' I winked.

'Don't know, pet, but it stank! Anyway, there in the window of a shop called Fynd was this 1920's art deco style wedding dress, and I fell in love with it on the spot.

It was £25, which sounds nothing now, but was a lot of money to me and Bert back then. Probably about a month's wages. I didn't have enough money, so Muriel, Dora and I pooled what we had, but still I didn't have enough to buy it, and I began to cry in the shop…'

'Oh, not that old stunt,' I laughed, squeezing her arm.

'Anyway, the lovely man said I could have it for £20. We couldn't even afford to go to our favourite Italian coffee bar afterwards, but I didn't care, and Muriel and Dora are such good friends that they didn't either.'

I looked at the dress. It reminded me of something that might have been worn in an episode of *Downton Abbey*. It was a silk shift dress in ivory, with an overlay of the most exquisite silver and white beadwork. The pattern on the lower part of the dress almost resembled a silvery mermaid's tail, which fell away to the floor in folds. V-necked and cap sleeved with beaded fringing, the dress was sheer simplicity, but that didn't take away from the impact. It was perfection.

'I bet you looked stunning, Meg. Please show me a photo of you on the day.'

She went to the sideboard and retrieved a photo, which she handed to me. It was of a very young Meg and Bert on the steps of Alnwick Registry Office, and Meg was wearing what looked like a floral Laura Ashley type dress.

'Of course,' I exclaimed, suddenly remembering 'You didn't get your church wedding, so you couldn't wear this beautiful dress. That's just too sad.'

'Ellie, lass, I would have worn it to the registry office, but when I brought the dress home me mam took one look at it and said, "Meggie, you'll not get one arm in that, never mind the Potts parcel shelf."'

'Potts what?' I asked laughing.

'The posterior all of us female Potts were blessed with. You can line your shopping on it. It turned out that mam was right. Look, you can see here – the seam began to give in the backside department, and I hadn't even pulled it over more than one buttock.'

Tears of laughter begin to drip down my face.

'Sorry, Meg. I know it wouldn't be funny to you at the time, but it's just the way you're describing your erm, anatomy. People pay to have backsides like that these days!'

'So I hear. The world has gone mad,' Meg tutted.

'Did you not try the dress on in the shop?'

'No. Rose coloured specs, pet. I just convinced my-self it was going to fit. Besides which, there was no way I was getting undressed in that hippie commune. Who knows what might have happened to me. I might have ended up in a cult.'

'So, even if you'd had a church wedding, you couldn't have worn it?'

'Not without lots of alterations, and that would have spoiled it. It's meant for someone taller and slenderer than me. I had hoped Aurora might have worn it for her wedding. She tried to try it on, but it was too tight for her too. It's like Cinderella's slipper, waiting for the right person.'

'That's such a shame; Aurora would have looked lovely in it.'

Meg looked me directly in the eye. 'I think it might fit you, Ellie, and nothing would give me greater pleasure than to give it to you. Even if you don't wear it as a wedding dress, maybe to a posh ball or something. It needs to be worn once in my lifetime. I want to see it being enjoyed and know that our £20 was not spent in vain. That would have got us two weeks to Lloret de Mar on a coach trip, that would.'

'I'd be honoured to wear it, if it fits, Meg,' I said, kissing her on the cheek. 'I'll try it on soon, when we're not in danger of prying eyes.'

I didn't say to Meg, but like her all those years ago as a young woman staring at the dress in the hippie shop window, the moment I clapped eyes on it my heart had raced too. If Zen and I ever did get married, there was nothing I would like more than to be able to wear Meg's beautiful dress. It would be a very fitting tribute to this wonderful woman who, despite the forty-odd years between us, had become one of my best friends.

As Meg carefully wrapped the dress back up, I went to the cupboard to search for the Jaffa Cakes and put the digestives back in the tin.

'Kitti opened up a little to Bert and me at lunchtime. What a lovely young lassie she is, God love her. She was telling us that her and her mam came back to the island every summer until Kitti went to school, to see if the boy was here too.'

'Yes, she told me that,' I said. 'It's sad, isn't it? I wonder what would have happened if Daisy and the boy had kept in touch?'

'Who knows, but it wasn't meant to be. Plus, they were both so young. It may have meant that Kitti would have had more family around her now, though, as it sounds like her mother's lot were right rotten eggs. Who could just go off and leave their sixteen-year-old pregnant daughter behind without so much as a goodbye?'

'Horrific,' I shuddered. 'Still, we've got the opportunity for the next few weeks to make Kitti as happy as we can. She's got an online bereavement counselling session later tonight, and I'm hoping her counsellor will be able to come up to the island to see her in person. He did say he would be happy to do that.'

'Good, pet. She had a bit of a twinkle in her eye when her and Bert came up for lunch with Will.'

'Will, the farrier? How old is he?' I demanded.

'Twenty-one,' replied Meg, chuckling. 'Ellie, your face. You're already looking like an overprotective mam.'

'Twenty-one is far too old for her,' I laughed. 'And, yes, I'm feeling very protective of our Kitti.'

'Listen, pet, she may have had a twinkle – he's a very handsome young man – but our Kittiwake has got her head well and truly screwed on, thanks to her mam. You've no need to worry in that direction.'

'I hope not,' I replied, thinking back to me at sixteen and reassuring myself that I had been sensible. But then I thought of Sophie!

The door burst open, and the dogs charged in, including Tri, which meant Maurice wasn't far behind. The Three Stooges came in and sat at the kitchen table in a huddle.

'Meg, have we got a notepad and pen, please?' asked Bert. 'We need to make some plans.'

'What are you three up to?' I asked.

'Nothing,' Kitti laughed.

'In my experience nothing always means something,' said Meg, handing Bert the stationery.

'Just animal business,' said Maurice. 'Two sugars, please, Meg.'

'I'll two sugars you, Maurice. Go and freshen the pot, and keep your grubby hands off the Jaffa Cakes.'

'Come on, Meg, let's go and sit on the sofa and leave these three to their board meeting. Kitti, twenty minutes and then we need to go and crack on with the pizzas.'

'Okay, Ellie,' she replied, and turned back to her partners in crime, as they all giggled over whatever it was they were planning.

Chapter 40

♥

Kitti began her job in the café and took to it like a duck to water. She and Pip hit it off straight away and both bonded with Julia, the new full timer, from day one. Julia was a real find and a mother herself to two teenage boys.

'You enjoying your job?' I asked, as the three of us sat around the breakfast table on a bright Lindisfarne morning.

'It's great, Ellie. Pip is hilarious – I keep telling her she needs to get off the island more, but actually I understand. I'm quite happy staying on it now, too.'

'Are you missing the city at all?' asked Zen. 'I'll be delivering coffee around Newcastle soon, and you could always come with me. I could drop you off so you can catch up with your schoolfriends, or just go shopping or whatever, and then I can collect you.'

'No, thanks. I'm too busy,' she said, straightening her T shirt with the Northern Lights and Bites logo on the front. She was getting ready to head downstairs for her shift, but not before checking her phone and grinning.

'Are we missing out on something?' I smiled.

'Erm, just a project I'm doing with some, erm, friends. Don't worry – it's nothing dodgy.'

'That's okay, then,' laughed Zen. 'Nothing dodgy is fine by us!'

Later that morning it was the Crafty Lindisfarners meeting, and we gathered in the back shop, the usual array of treats on the table.

'How's the packing going, Imogen? asked Dora.

'Just about there, thanks. Harriet came down with the horse box, and we got most of my stuff out from the flat. Barry is happy to have whatever I don't want to take,' she smiled. 'Talking of, he rang me – wants to come and see us all, so I said he could come to today's meeting. He'll be here soon. He sounded worried about something, to be honest.'

'I hope he's not going to back out now,' said Muriel. 'We liked the sound of him, and more importantly, we get to keep our room.'

'Not to fear, Muriel.' cackled Ethel. 'We've always got the nudie thing to fall back on.'

'I don't think it was naked in that respect, Ethel, although you never know,' I winked.

The shop bell tinkled, and Barry breezed in. He was wearing another huge jumper, but this one had a lighthouse on the front.

'Cooeee, I'm on time today.'

'No injured seals or my boyfriend at the side of the road then?' I laughed.

'No seals, but there was a silver fox strolling across the beach beside the bridge thing.'

'It's called the causeway,' tutted Muriel.

'Okay, hun – *causeway* – got it. Anyway, back to the hottie. He looked like a lead in a romcom. He was well fit, whoever he was.'

'Inigo,' we all said in unison.

'Ini-who? He sounds posh and Barry does not want posh, but perhaps in his case I might relax the rules. Does he live here?'

'Just visiting,' said Imogen, stopping him in mid-flow.

'Is that another of Old Joe's creations?' I asked, pointing to his jumper and quickly moving the subject away from Inigo. 'I feel like I know Joe, even though we haven't met.'

Barry nodded. 'Since I saw the advert, he's got a seaside theme going on has Old Joe. Says it reminds him of the Navy.'

'Was he a captain?' enquired Ethel. 'I bet he looked handsome in his uniform. All the nice girls love a sailor, you know. Me especially.' She patted her hair.

'Erm, actually, Joe was a cook in the galley,' replied Barry, 'but his whites would have been pristine. He's very particular, is Old Joe.'

'Barry, we haven't introduced you to Dora and Muriel,' said Imogen, trying to steer things back on track. 'The rest of us you've already met. You'll meet the others as time goes on... that's if everything is still okay? We're all worried you've changed your mind.'

Barry took a big gulp of air, then looked around the table at us all. He began to pace around the room, his hands flapping nervously.

'Erm, well, I've come to make a confession,' he said dramatically.

'What have you done? You're not a serial killer, are you? If you are, son, I'd ditch the jumpers – you'd stand out a mile in an identity parade. Better get yourself a nice black tracksuit and a balaclava. You can knit him one, can't you, Dora?'

'Ethel!' I squeaked.

'Erm, Barry's squeamish. I don't like the sight of blood, so no murders, Ethel.' He glanced around the table. 'I have a feeling that I might have misled you at my meet-and-greet. When I got home and told Miss Primm about how everything had gone, and how nice you all are, and how lovely the island is, which she already knows because she's been loads – she's into all that stuff about the monks and the man in the coffin who got carried to... wherever he got carried to...'

'Durham... eventually,' answered Muriel.

'Aw, thanks, hun.' Barry beamed at Muriel. 'Anyway, she was so pleased for me, but then when I mentioned that maybe I hadn't told you the full story about my haberdashery shop, she said it was dishonest of me not to have told you... but you know... then even Old Joe said I had to come back and tell you the truth, and he's as slippery as an eel is Joe. Not that I lied... I just kind of...' Barry was garbling at the rate of knots and making no sense.

'Barry lad, spit it out, I've not got long left in this world, and I need to hear whatever it is before I shuffle off,' chuckled Ethel.

'Well, thing is, I haven't actually run a haberdasher's shop. Well, I have, but it wasn't a real shop. It was for kids... truth is, I was Haberdashery Elf in the department store's Christmas grotto. I even had a wig that looked like a giant ball of wool,' he blurted out, his face turning the colour of the red stripes on Greater Reef Lighthouse.

Imogen was struggling to keep her face straight.

'So,' I asked through clenched lips that were itching to burst into laughter at the thought of Barry Big Lad in an elf costume, complete with a ball of two-ply on his head, 'what is it you actually do?'

'I work in the warehouse for the department store. Have done since I left school, and I was so bored that, when the chance of working in the Christmas grotto came up, I jumped at it. I was born to entertain, you know,' he said, trying to prove the point by pirouetting around on one leg and almost crashing into the craft cupboard in the process.

'I'm not sure I have the experience you might have expected,' he said sadly, 'but I really didn't think I could live with myself if I continued the deception. I'm bigger than that... much bigger,' he guffawed, patting his middle.

'Tell us what you do in your warehouse job, Barry,' said Imogen.

'Well, I liaise with the store managers, order in stock, keep inventories, check deliveries, rotate stock as it comes in, chase orders, and then I deliver the various goods to the departments across the store.'

'That sounds a bit like running a shop to me and on a much grander scale than this small operation.'

'Hmmm,' said Barry, 'suppose it does. I never thought about it that way. Did you get my references?'

'Yes, I did. I got one from the son of the owner of the store, no less. You have friends in high places, Barry, and the other was from your Miss Primm, who sang your praises loud and clear.'

'So, is it still okay? I've got my finances sorted and really will work hard to keep Love Lindisfarne just the way you like it, but more sparkly!' He stopped to take a breath.

'Barry, pet, just have a sausage roll and calm down. You're still hired, and you'd better get your backside up here in time for Mini Fest. Remember Meg, who was here last time? Well, she's already got you down for a medley of show tunes, so you'd better get gargling, son.' Ethel patted him on the arm.

Barry let out an ear-piercing screech that could have cleared the skies above the island of birds.

'What's Mini Fest?' he shouted. 'Oh, my God, never mind what it is – I'm up for it. How many tunes? Do you have any requests? What will I wear?'

Barry was in seventh heaven, and the future of Love Lindisfarne was in a pair of very enthusiastic jazz hands. I had a feeling Barry was going to add a whole new colourful dimension to island life and stir us all up a bit in the best possible way!

Chapter 41

When the meeting finished, Ethel asked me if I would take her across to see the cows so that she could give them their names.

'Have you decided yet?' I asked.

'I saw some photos, but me eyes aren't great on this tiny screen.' She waved her mobile about. 'They could be elephants for all I know.'

Ethel had an ancient phone, so small it was like one of those burner things favoured by criminals, which they could hide down their socks.

'No elephants,' I laughed. 'Zen and Kitti were trying to guess what you might call them. Zen said it might be Rump, Sirloin and T Bone, but you can't. They're far too cute!'

Ethel scratched her chin. 'Hmm, maybe, Ellie, but I need to see them with my own eyes, and then it'll come to me.'

The paddocks were a hive of activity when we got there.

'What's going on?' I asked Bert.

'The vet gave the go-ahead for the others who go in the paddocks to be brought down from the yard. We still need to keep them apart, but this way they all get to see each other and make friends from a distance over the fences. I can't wait to see what your Hannibal makes of them all.'

'Not a lot, probably,' I laughed.

'Have I missed the big announcement?' shouted Kitti, her face red from running across from the café. 'I've got twenty minutes of my break left – I couldn't wait to hear what Ethel was going to call the cows.'

'Can't wait either,' said Bert. 'I'm sick of calling them one, two and three!'

Ethel surveyed the three mini cows, the smallest white one now happily back with its sisters. They looked at her with big Malteser eyes, their long lashes fluttering in the breeze. They'd all had a hose down, and Kitti had groomed them, so they were looking so much better than they had on the day of their arrival.

'Eeh, my, oh my! Aren't they just lovely,' smiled Ethel. 'How tiny. Wouldn't get much of a steak pie out of the three of them put together, would you?'

'Ethel, you can't say that,' Kitti grinned.

'Hmm,' she said, 'they need to keep their heritage, so it'll be something Scottish. By jings, I think I've got it. Look at the colours – that one's all brown with flecks, her in the middle is almost orange and then the weeny little white one. Yes, perfect.'

Ethel turned round and surveyed her audience, which was me, Bert, Maurice, Kitti and about twenty people leaning across the castle walls, looking down on the mini animals way below them.

'Is it always like that up there? I asked, pointing to the audience. I know we always had people looking down, but the numbers seem to have increased a lot.'

'Nearly always,' said Bert. 'People seem really interested in what's going on down here. I've had to make sure the gate at the road is always locked too, because when they come out of the castle they sometimes try to come across to get a closer look. Don't blame them, though. I'd want to see them close up as well.'

'Erm, about to make an important announcement, you two,' said Ethel, looking at Bert and I. 'A bit of hush, please. Ladies and gentlemen,' she began, 'let me introduce you to my three new mini hairy coos, Haggis, Neeps and Tatties.'

'Ethel, lass, you've surpassed yourself,' laughed Maurice. 'Priceless!'

'What's a neeps?' asked Kitti, who had been filming the whole thing on her phone.

'Turnips. Haggis, neeps and tatties is a Scottish meal people serve for celebrations such as Burns Night. Haggis is made from, erm, well, things to do with sheep, and oats, I think,' I replied, 'I'm not actually quite sure. Then neeps is turnip and tatties potatoes, but you know those already. I see where Ethel is coming from, because the cows are all the same colours as the three items of food.'

'Ethel, we'll get them a nice little sign for their shelter door with "as named by Ethel Fish" inscribed on it.'

'Do I get a sign for naming Penguin and Puffin?' asked Kitti.

'Of course,' smiled Bert.

'So, we've now got Penguin and Puffin the goats, Jimmy and Perez the Shetlands, Haggis, Neeps and Tatties the cows, and the donkeys still to be named at Mini Fest,' said Bert, counting on his fingers. 'That means, all told, we have a total of thirty-three animals in the Lindisfarne Sanctuary, and seriously, I mean it this time, no more room at the inn.'

'Thirty-three!' I gasped.

'Aye, Ellie, lass. That includes the chickens and turkeys, four horses, four goats, five donkeys, three cats, two alpacas, three cows, five dogs and a partridge in a pear tree.'

'I can understand why you're worried about the food bill, fella,' said Maurice.

'Come on then, Ethel. Say goodbye to Haggis, Neeps and Tatties, and I'll take you up to see Meg.'

'Hope she's got some shortbread. We need to toast the hairy coos, and knowing Meg, she won't be giving us a wee dram. I know Bert's got some good whisky because me and him have a nip in our tea when she's not looking. If I tell you where it is, perhaps—'

'No!'

'Oh, okay. Can't blame a girl for asking. Shy bairns get nowt, Ellie.'

'So you all keep telling me,' I laughed.

Meg was knitting when we went in the cottage, *The Archers* playing on the radio in the background.

'What a lovely surprise! You can tell me all about the meeting – I couldn't get over because my sister and Ernie were popping in to see us. They've just gone, and

I thought I'd have half an hour on this – I'm making Kitti a scarf for her to take with her when she goes as a kind of reminder of her time on the island.' Meg's face clouded over. 'That's going to be a sad day. Anyway, before I get all maudlin, put the kettle on, Ellie. Sit yourself down in front of the fire, Ethel, and tell me what the heck you've called those hairy coos!'

Chapter 42

♥

I'd been speaking to Sophie most days since her return to London, even if it was only for a few minutes. Jake had been put on sick leave by the GP and was taking medication for stress, as well as seeing a counsellor. Sophie hadn't even begun looking for another job, throwing herself into taking care of Jake, and, despite the circumstances, they seemed to be even closer than they had been before.

'I'm thinking it might do Jake good to come up to the island. Get away from London and relax,' she said during one particularly long phone call. 'I've already asked Tara if it's okay for us to come, and she said yes.'

'She mentioned it, Soph, and I think it's a great idea. Just the thing you both need right now. Give you a chance to unwind and make some decisions about your future.'

'You're right. We've already talked about the flat and are both agreed that we'll sell it and move somewhere more affordable. Jake is saying he doesn't want to go back to the city. He seems adamant, but it's early days, and he's maybe not yet in the right mindset to make big decisions.'

'And what about the wedding?' I asked gently.

'I spoke to my mum and sisters. They're obviously very upset at what's happened to Jake and didn't even get on my case when they found out about my job. I've told them that whatever happens about the wedding, it will be Jake and me deciding together, and Uncle Tom Cobley and all will not be invited.'

'Good for you, chick. Sounds like you're taking control. Listen, there's so much going on up here, I can't wait for you to come and catch up on all the goss.'

'Is Inigo still around?'

'Yes, him and a procession of women that he seems to meet when he's out walking. He's started three routes now and never finished one! There was Cressida, of course, then we had Bree, an Aussie doppelganger for Margot Robbie, and just yesterday he went to finish the coastal path walk we started and ended up with a Claudia, who, along with her husband, owns a posh wedding venue near Berwick! We might get a discount if either of us ever get that far, if they stay "friends",' I giggled.

'He's such a tart,' laughed Sophie. 'But a very handsome one.'

'Anyway, Soph, sorry, but got to go. Kitti's counsellor is coming soon, and I need to tidy the attic. There's sooo much more to tell you, but it can wait until you arrive. Please make sure you're here for Mini Fest. It'll be a great day – a proper island get-together. I wish Stan and Aleksy could come up too, but they're catching up on the workload since they got back from Poland.'

'They're doing great. Jake and I went over to the café for lunch with them. It was really busy, and I hear that they're talking to Zen about opening another branch in Primrose Hill.'

'Yep, from Peckham to Primrose Hill – talk about aspirational.'

'I just hope they don't take on too much, or your Zen. Look at what happened to Jake, and he seemed as tough as old boots.'

'I hear you, Soph. We're all working too hard.'

'Hmm, not me at the moment, but you're right – all work and no play makes our inner circle a very knackered group!'

'I really must go this time,' I laughed. 'Love you, bestie. And Jake.'

'Love you and Zen too, Ellie Nellie. Can't wait to see you soon.'

Later that day Kitti and I were catching up on another episode of *Gilmore Girls,* which I was now quite hooked on, thanks to her.

'How did it go with your counsellor today, if it's okay to ask? He seems nice.'

'He is. He was really pleased with me and said that what you and Zen and the other islanders have done for me is amazing, and that he couldn't have achieved the same results in such a short time. I can't believe I've been here nearly three weeks now, Ellie. The time is rushing, and every day I think it's another day nearer to me having to go somewhere else. Errol said I wasn't to focus on that and just concentrate on one day at a time, but it's hard when I feel happy here, and I'm going to have to leave all my new friends and all the animals behind, especially Holly, Puffin and Penguin.'

'I do know, Kitti, but Errol's right. Let's just take things a day at a time, and, as Meg is always saying, let tomorrow take care of itself.'

A tear suddenly rolled on autopilot down Kitti's cheek and plopped onto her lap.

'Oh, Kitti, don't get upset. You're doing so well, and everyone loves having you here. It's still weeks before we need to think about the next steps.'

'Ellie, I have been so much happier since I came to the island, but then should I be? Mam hasn't been gone very long, and I feel guilty; it's like I'm disrespecting her.' She dissolved into sobs as the floodgates opened and tears fell in torrents, soaking her T shirt.

'Sweetheart,' I said, folding her into my arms, 'your mam would want you to be happy. I think you know that deep down, and it's not being disrespectful at all. It's actually respecting her memory, being the strong young Kittiwake she wanted you to be. I never met her, but I reckon she would much rather see you smile than cry, am I right?'

'Yes,' she sniffed. 'Mam said feeling happy was a free gift that we should always show gratitude for.'

'I like that; it is a gift, and we should be so thankful for it. Right, I think this calls for ice cream, don't you?'

Kitti gave a little smile, wiped her eyes and grabbed the remote to rewind the programme. I went to fetch the ice cream. I wasn't going to admit to Kitti that I too had begun to worry about what was going to happen at the end of the summer holidays when decisions would be made about her future. I got as far as questioning myself whether I had done the right thing in even bringing her to the island, but Zen had reassured me that whatever happened, Kitti would be leaving us stronger and that she would always be able to come back and stay with us. And he was right; she would be stronger. The days she had counselling might unsettle her, but long term it would help her recover, as would her time with us, and I hoped Kitti would carry on being happy for as long as she was with us on Lindisfarne.

We had nearly finished a tub of raspberry ripple when Zen came in with Nacho. 'What's this? Where's mine? Have you two scoffed the lot? There's me walking Duchess and Nacho after a gruelling day down the coffee mine, and the thought of that ice cream had kept me going.'

'Sorry. Kitti and I needed it to get through this very emotional episode,' I winked.

'I'll feed Nacho,' said Kitti, scraping out the remnants of the ice cream then licking the spoon.

'And I'll feed us soon,' I smiled. 'Fish pie. Maurice gave some fresh cod to Kitti for us.'

'Great – I'll go and grab a shower. The footie's on tonight, and now I'm in ice-cream withdrawal it would be very cruel to deprive me of that as well.'

'Shall we let him watch it?' I grinned at Kitti.

'I suppose so, if we must.'

As I was popping the pie in the oven, I glanced at the calendar and noticed the date. I went to our room. Zen was sitting on the side of the bed with only a tiny towel around his waist, and I sat down next to him, breathing in the scent of the eucalyptus and pine nut shower gel that he favoured.

'Have you come to give me a massage? It's only fair after you scoffed the raspberry ripple,' he smiled, putting his arms around me. As I ran my fingers over his damp skin and pushed back the tendrils of hair falling over his face, all thoughts of Kitti and fish pie began to fade fast.

'Erm, I'd love to but...'

'I know, Ellie, I'm messing. Well, only partly, but I get it. Send Kitti out to check the tide or something!'

'I wish. I came in to...' I hesitated. What had I come in for, other than a massive surge of libido. 'Oh, yes, do you know what day it is tomorrow?'

'Erm, Saturday?'

'It's our date day – the one we said nothing was going to stop us from going on.'

I could see by the horrified look on Zen's face that he had forgotten all about it.

'Oh, Ellie, I'm so sorry. I can't. I've just got a new customer lined up in Morpeth who could be big, so I can't turn that down. I'd send someone else but...'

'Hey, it's okay. Confession time – I'd forgotten too, and I'm working in the castle tomorrow, as ironically, Toby and Tara are having a family day out.'

'I feel quite sad now. We've become *that* couple who just don't have enough time to themselves, and it's not just Kitti causing this,' he whispered,' it's everything. Right, we're going to fix a new date, and I'm going to set every device I have so that we don't forget – okay?'

'Right,' I said, looking into his soulful coffee bean eyes then kissing his gorgeous minty mouth, my hand trailing down his smooth, now dry back until it reached the top of the towel, and with all the resolve I possessed, I stood up and went back to the kitchen to check on the fish pie.

After tea, the three of us lounged in the small living room. Zen in his old Brazil T shirt and board shorts, beer in hand, glued to the footie, me trying to sort out our busy timetable and find that elusive date date, and Kitti, head down, scrolling on her iPad and laughing out loud every now and again.

'Care to share?' I asked, 'I could do with a laugh.'

'All will be revealed soon, I promise,' she grinned. 'Nothing dodgy.'

'So you keep saying, but you seem to spend a lot of time on that,' I said, sounding like an old fossil.

'Ellie, chill. I'm not on the dark web or anything, I promise, and all is going to be revealed very soon.'

'Has it got anything to do with Bert and Maurice, by any chance? Meg tells me that you three are as thick as thieves.'

'No comment,' she replied, grinning. 'You'll just have to wait and see!'

Chapter 43

The next week flew by. We were in high tourist season, and everywhere was busy from the minute the tide went out.

'Don't forget we're going to the Crab tonight to finish the arrangements for Mini Fest. I can't believe it's only two days away,' I said, clearing the table.

Kitti fleetingly lifted her head from her phone and nodded, as Zen shouted, 'see you there,' racing downstairs for work. I went to the fridge to put the milk away, and there was yet another Post-it note reminding me of our date day. Since our failed attempt at having some time to ourselves, Zen had taken to sticking Post-its everywhere, so it was impossible to forget – I found them in my shoes, in my bra, wrapped around the tea caddy, stuck on the remote control, on the top of the kettle and on every packet of crisps and biscuits in the attic (my boyfriend clearly knew me well). Our date was tomorrow, and whilst I couldn't wait for us to be together without any distractions, the timing wasn't great as we had so much to do before Saturday and the festival. Sophie and Jake were arriving later tonight on the second tide, and Big Lad

Barry was taking over the shop as from tomorrow. The Crafty Lindisfarners had promised to help him sort things out and help him settle in.

'I could do with two pairs of hands,' I sighed.

Kitti looked up, this time concentrating on what I was saying.

'Is there anything I can do to help? It's my day off tomorrow, and I was going to go and see Ethel then go over to help Bert.'

'No, you do that. You've worked extremely hard this week; the café has been so busy. Tell you what though, how would you like to go with the Crafty Lindisfarners to welcome Big Lad Barry to the island when he arrives tomorrow? He's from Newcastle too. You'll love him, I'm sure – he's very funny. I don't think I can go, as Zen and me are on our date day.'

'Even I haven't forgotten about that,' laughed Kitti. 'Can't help it thanks to those notes stuck everywhere. Ethel was telling me all about Barry; he sounds cool, and I can't wait to take him to meet the animals,' she grinned, 'especially Hannibal.'

'Hannibal? I'm not sure that would be a good idea. Maybe start with Jimmy and Perez. They're so cute and love the attention.'

'Hmm, maybe,' she replied.

I was getting used to this parenting malarkey, and I'm sure she was up to something, but as long as it wasn't anything dangerous or dodgy, and she kept telling us it wasn't, then it really wasn't any of my business.

'Anyway, I'm going – working at the castle until lunchtime. Are you ready to leave?'

'Erm, not quite, Ellie. Got some things to post.' Her head was back in its usual position of eyes down, grinning away at whatever she was looking at.

I called into the roastery before I walked over to work.

'Did I forget something?' asked Zen.

'Erm, I just got to thinking, I know we said tomorrow for our date, but maybe we should postpone it, just for a little while. There's so much going on here.'

The look on Zen's face was answer enough to let me know what he was thinking without him saying a word. He looked absolutely dejected, and I immediately began to feel guilty for even suggesting changing dates, especially for something so non-urgent.

'No, Ellie, absolutely not. We agreed. We both chose tomorrow. I've cleared my work diary, and I know you have too, so why the need to change our plans? I've gone—'

'Oh, you know – just the usual,' I interrupted him.

'Exactly – the usual. If we swap this time, it'll just happen again, so please, let's stick to our plans and have some time to ourselves. I just want us to make a memory together,' he said solemnly.

'Are you okay? You're not ill, are you? I asked, starting to feel uneasy. 'There's something you're not telling me. I can see by your face you're keeping something from me.'

'No, of course I'm not ill,' he laughed. 'Why shouldn't we make some memories of just us? What's wrong with that? I want us to be sitting next to the fire, holding hands when we're ancient, saying things like, "can you remember when...?" At this rate all we'll have to say is, "can you remember when we were at work?" I love our friends dearly, and we're so lucky having lots of good people around us, but sometimes I just want it to be me and you.'

'As long as you really are okay,' I replied, still thinking he wasn't being quite open with me. My duplicity detector was perhaps on full alert because of Kitti and her teenage ways descending on us!

'Maybe we won't take the whole day out – how would that work?' said Zen.

'It might, but no. I know you're right, and I do really want for us to have some time alone. It goes without saying I'd rather have a full day with you than half a day.'

'Me too, Ellie.'

'Anyway, you haven't told me what we're doing or where we're going?'

'I thought we had agreed on a walk,' said Zen. 'The weather is meant to be good tomorrow, and for the next few days, which bodes well for the festival.'

'So, just casual?' I asked.

'You can turn up in that yellow coat for me, as long as you turn up, although we could wear the suit and dress combo again for a laugh.' He smiled *the* smile which lit up his entire face and made my knees knock together like a pair of castanets. I must have been mad even contemplating changing our date. What was more important than spending time with my boyfriend? Absolutely nothing.

'Okay, it's a date,' I said, putting my arms around him and giving him a hug. 'Love you.'

'Love you too, Ellie, and I think we're going to realise that even more tomorrow, when it's just you and me and no distractions.

***

The Crab was busy that evening as the Mini Fest committee sat huddled in the corner, Linda taking charge.

'Okay, my darlings, I think we've got everything in place. The marquee is going up tomorrow, but we may not need it because the weather forecast is looking good.'

'The barbeque food is almost ready,' said Dora, 'and I twisted Stan's arm to make veggie alternatives. I wasn't sure at first, but I tell you, they're delicious. Me and Stan have sampled every one of them.'

'Music, Zen?'

'Yes, all sorted. I'm opening with a few acoustic songs, then from what I gather, Lindisfarne's newest resident, Barry Big Lad is going to outshine Michael Ball with some show tunes. The boys and I will be doing our usual electric set later.'

'Fundraising, Aurora and Ellie?'

'Yes, raffle, tombola and various other fundraising ideas all good to go.'

'Who's on the door collecting the entrance money?'

'Ethel. There's no chance of anyone getting in the garden without them coughing up at least double with that old reprobate on the case,' smiled Bert.

'Beer, Linda?' laughed Maurice.

'Plenty of that, don't you fear, my darling,' said Linda.

'And me, Maurice and young Kitti here have our special presentation, which she's organising,' chipped in Bert.

'What's that about?' I asked.

'I keep telling you, you'll have to wait and see,' said Kitti.

'It sounds like it's going to be a reet grand day,' said Bert, 'and hopefully we'll raise enough to keep us in animal feed for the next few months without me having to go cap in hand to Grace.'

'Just as well, as no one could get that cap off your head, bonny lad,' chuckled Maurice.

'Room for two more?' said a familiar voice.

I looked up to see Sophie and Jake. Jake was looking very pale but had a big smile on his face.

'Jake! Soph!' I jumped up to give them both a hug. 'It's so good to see you.'

'I'm pleased to be here, Ellie Nellie; it's been tough but I'm getting there, and this place will sort me out,' Jake whispered in my ear, and I squeezed his arm.

'Budge up you lot,' shouted Bert. 'Seats for the guests. Now then, we'd better find them both jobs... no idle hands on this island!'

Chapter 44

Date day dawned bright and clear. Zen was up early and straight out with Nacho, who was going to be going over to the castle with Kitti for the day.

'I was just going to make some tea,' I said, as he came back through the door.

He threw his arms around me, swept me off my feet, twirled me around then kissed my cheek before putting me back on the ground.

'What's all that for?'

'I'm excited,' he smiled. 'You, me and the sun beating down on us. What's not to love?'

'I haven't organised anything for today,' I said. 'Sorry, just been so busy.'

'Just as well I have it all under control, then,' he smiled. 'Organised is my middle name.'

'Zen Chambers, your pants are going to set on fire. You couldn't organise a chimps' tea party!'

'O ye of little faith. Right, come on. Get dressed and let's get out of here – our chauffeur will be here soon.'

'Chauffeur?'

'Ellie! Just go and get ready.'

Ten minutes later a voice shouted up the stairs.

'Your carriage awaits.' It was Aurora.

'Kitti, we're off,' I shouted through her closed bedroom door. 'Time you were up. Don't forget to go to Love Lindisfarne to help Barry.'

'I won't,' she replied, still sounding half asleep. 'Hope you both have a lovely date.'

'I thought we were going walking,' I said as we got into Aurora's car.

'We are,' replied Zen, 'but first I thought we could go to Alnwick. See the gardens again. Remember last time? We had Isla trailing around complaining about everything, and it kind of took the shine off things.'

'How could I ever forget that; she was dreadful. It's a lovely idea, but I'm hardly dressed for the occasion. I'd have put something nicer on if I'd known. I could have put my walking stuff in a bag to change into later.'

'You look beautiful to me.'

'Yuck, bro. Too early in the morning for that mushy talk,' laughed Aurora.

'Never too early,' I smiled.

'Have a great day, both of you,' said Aurora as she dropped us off in Alnwick. 'Jack and I need to take a leaf out of your book. Mind, his idea of a day out would be on a boat! If you change your mind about the walk back, just shout, and I'll get Tara to look after Hettie.'

'No, we won't, but thanks. See you later, sis,' said Zen, as Aurora spun the car round and headed back towards the A1 to make sure she caught the tide in time.

We had a leisurely breakfast outside in the sunshine overlooking the fountains and then wandered around the garden hand in hand. Late spring was such a good time to visit, when everything was bursting into life, creating so much colour. An abundance of floral scents hung heavy in the air as we walked.

'This was where we came on our first date, I suppose,' I said, 'even though it wasn't a date, but it was really. It was December, though. Cold and mostly only evergreens to look at, but I won't ever forget how magical I thought it was.'

We sat down on a bench in the rose garden and breathed in the gorgeous aroma coming from the multitude of magnificent blooms around us. It reminded me of the rose perfume favoured by my gran.

'I love roses,' I said. 'I used to collect the petals when I was a kid and try to make perfume from them. Unsuccessfully, I hasten to add, but my mum pretended it was the best thing since Chanel No 5.'

'I used to collect stuff that landed on the beach and make models from it, and likewise, Mam and Dad would display them and tell me I was a genius.'

'We're lucky having supportive parents. I hope one day I might be a good mum. Or mam, as you lot say.'

'Ellie, I've watched you with Kitti. You're a natural.'

'As are you. How have you found it in general?' I asked.

'I adore Kitti. She's such a strong young woman, and I've watched her slip into Lindisfarne life like she was born to be here, which she kind of was,' he smiled. 'You?'

'It's been easier than I thought,' I said, 'apart from the odd moments of grief, which is totally understandable. I'm sure when she's on her own she has meltdowns, but she's managed to begin to live again. I wish...' I began but then stopped. 'Today is about us. Let's talk more about Kitti later.'

'Okay.' He squeezed my hand. 'Let's continue, and we'll finish off at the poison garden because last time we hardly had any time in there, thanks to Isla.'

'She's got more poison in her little finger than what's growing in the whole of that garden. I'm looking forward to going around it again, though. It was so interesting.'

'Anyone you want to poison at the moment?'

'No, I'm all about love today, especially for you.' I brushed his hair out of his face and stared into his eyes as I kissed him. 'Remind me, why don't we do this more often?'

'We will, Ellie.'

We set off again, and I could have floated around the gardens. As long as Zen and I were together, everything in my world was going to be okay.

'Fancy a cocktail?' Zen asked as we passed a mobile drinks cart.

'Why not? We can do what we like today,' I replied, surveying the list of what was on offer.

'Oh, look, there's one called The Duchess. We have to have one of those.'

'I think it might be named after the Duchess of Northumberland, not Ethel's smelly old Patterdale terrier,' he laughed, 'but it's got Northumbrian gin in it, so sounds good to me.'

'Perfect.'

We lounged in deck chairs, the sun warming our faces, doing nothing more than sipping our cocktails and watching the world go by.

'What's next?' I asked, seeing Zen consult his watch for the hundredth time.

'Sorry, Ellie, just need to keep an eye on the time. That's living on an island for you. We have to fit in with the tides today.'

'So where exactly are we going to walk? I'm quite happy sitting in this deckchair getting merry on cocktails, as it happens.'

'All I'm telling you is that it's going to be about a two hour walk, so no more cocktails, but I promise I'll get you some at Mini Fest tomorrow. As many as you like.'

'Oh, okay. Deal. Is this a difficult walk? It's not like one of Inigo's extreme thingies, is it? Not that he ever seems to finish one,' I laughed.

'Hmm, it can be a little trickier than a usual path walk,' he said mysteriously. 'Just wait and see.'

After lunch we had a browse in the gift shop. I bought Zen a book about growing organic vegetables, although why I don't know as the attic didn't have so much as a window box, but it was what he wanted. Maybe one day we'd have a garden, and he could fulfil his ambition to win the Lindisfarne Biggest Pumpkin Competition!

'Right, Ellie, we've got to go. We need to grab a taxi to take us to the start of the walk.'

'Have we got to?' I smiled. 'I'm so enjoying just wandering around here.'

'Yes, I'm sure, Ms Montague, but you're not wheedling out of it, so best foot forward. Trust me, you're going to love it... I hope!'

Chapter 45

The taxi dropped us off at Beal, by the causeway to the island.

'Why are we getting out here?' I asked, starting to feel uneasy. 'You aren't going to make me walk across the causeway, are you? I've not quite recovered from the last time, and I said I'd never do it again. Are you trying to make me face my fears or something?'

'Ellie.' He smiled reassuringly, took me by the shoulders and looked directly into my eyes. 'I'd never do that to you, unless you asked for my help. We aren't walking across the road causeway; we're going over there.'

Zen pointed towards the first of the tall poles embedded into the sand to our right.

'We're going to follow the Pilgrim's Walk. It's been a walk of pilgrimage since way back in the 600s when King Oswald gave the island to St Aidan to start up the monastery. It was the only way to walk to the island up until 1954, which, in the grand scheme of things, isn't that long ago. The poles, as you know, are markers to keep people on track and safe.'

'How fabulous,' I said. 'I know about the walk, of course. It's not easy, I understand. Can't the sand and mud just about suck you down in places?'

'You might lose a boot, but it's not like quicksand, so you're not going to sink. I hope! The conditions underfoot depend on the weather, and it's been good lately. We'll be wading through water and walking on the seabed, though, so it might all feel a little strange. Then there'll be mudflats to plough through, then some drier areas where we'll be on firm sand. Are you going to be okay with all of that?'

'As long as you're there,' I said, but all the while thinking I'd rather be downing another Duchess cocktail, lounging in a deck chair, people-watching.

'We've got our walking boots on, but for authenticity we could do it barefoot, if you want, because they're going to get soaked anyway?'

'Let's maybe do the last bit barefoot; otherwise, we're just going to have to lug these heavy boots, and that backpack of yours looks full already. What've you got in there?'

'Mr Organised, remember. All kinds. First aid kit, water, survival blanket, flare, umbrella, camping stove, kettle, hammer, Nacho...'

'You're pulling my leg!' I grabbed his hand. 'Let's go. About two hours, you say? Are we okay for the tide?'

'Ellie, I followed Bert's example and planned this like a military operation, so yes, all good. We're setting off at the safest time of two hours before low tide, so we can take our time and enjoy the peace, the birds, hopefully a seal or two. And maybe the odd pilgrim, but I can't see anyone else about, so I reckon it might just be us and the wilderness.'

Walking was exactly as Zen had said. At times we were almost knee deep in water, at others, thick mud just about sucked our boots off, then there were periods where we were walking on sand. It was nothing if not different. As we approached the safety box, which was about midway along the marker poles, Zen said we should climb up the ladder so we could get a panoramic view of the bay we were walking across.

'I'm not going up there; it looks like it's been made by the scouts.' The 'shelter' was a square, roofless wooden structure on poles which were fixed into the seabed and sat in a pool of water. A rickety, straight ladder with dubious looking rungs led up to the box.

'It's perfectly safe,' laughed Zen.

'What happens if it's raining and you're stuck?' I asked. 'At least the causeway shelter has a roof. This is very, erm, basic.'

'I don't imagine that anyone needing to use it for safety reasons is too bothered about it being basic, plus, they'd probably be already quite wet by the time they got in here. Come on, follow me. You'll not regret the view from up there.'

Zen climbed up the ladder first then held out his hand from the top, which I reached out for, and he pulled me into the box. He was right; the view was spectacular, and I gazed around the landscape in awe, looking across the bay to the undulating hills on the mainland then towards the island, with the ancient castle dominating on the hilltop.

Zen opened his backpack and pulled out a blanket.

'Thought we might need a little rest up here, and I do just mean a rest,' he grinned, laying the blanket on the damp wooden floor. We both sat down, out of sight from everyone, cocooned in our own little bubble on stilts in the North Sea, with no other pilgrims in sight.

'Your face,' I laughed. 'It's splattered in mud.'

'So's yours,' he grinned. 'It reminds me of the night we met, just over there. You were like the swamp monster then too.'

'Charming! But you're right. I looked like I was auditioning for a part in *The Creature from the Black Lagoon*.'

'I didn't care, Ellie. The minute I saw you, mud and all, I was hooked. Still am, and always will be.'

'Same here,' I said, taking his face into my hands and kissing him. 'The minute I saw your eyes peeping out at me from beneath your beanie and scarf, that was me gone, and I still am. It really was kismet, don't you think? Like it was all mapped out in the stars for us. I do believe that.'

Zen began to get up.

'Have you got cramp?' I asked, as he stopped awkwardly on one knee.

'Nope,' he said, delving into the backpack again and this time bringing out a small box.

'Ellie, I was determined to bring you somewhere where we would have no interruptions, where there was just you and me, and where better than near to the place where it all began...'

I could hardly hear what he was saying, I was so focused on the box. He flipped it open and took out a ring. I almost forgot to breathe.

'Marry me, Ellie Montague? As soon as we can – no long engagement. Please be my wife, and I promise I'll try to be the best version of a husband that I can be.'

I opened my mouth to reply but no sound came out, I was so stunned.

'Ellie?'

'Yes... yes! Of course I'll marry you,' I squeaked, my voice sounding like I'd inhaled the contents of a helium balloon. 'In fact, shall we get married right now, here in this box? Let's just make up our own ceremony so we don't have to wait. Of course, I want to marry you. I love you so much, Zen Chambers. My love for you is bigger than the quantity of lugworms underneath those mudflats we've just walked on.'

Zen burst out laughing.

'And that's why I love you; you say the most romantic things.'

He took my muddy hand in his.

'Hang on a minute,' I said, searching in my own little rucksack for a wet wipe. 'You are not putting anything on my finger until it's a little bit cleaner.'

Once scrubbed, I held out my hand, and he placed the most beautiful ring I'd ever seen on my finger.

'Hope it fits. I had to use one of your dress rings as a guide.'

'The pearl one? I wondered where it had gone.'

I gazed at the ring, which fitted perfectly. It was gold and platinum, set with a big yellow stone in the middle that was surrounded by a circle of small diamonds. It looked like a daisy. It was totally understated and exactly the type I would have chosen if I'd picked it myself. I could feel the tears welling up in my eyes as I continued to stare at it.

'Do you like it?' Zen asked, sounding nervous.

'I absolutely love it,' I said, tearing my eyes away from the ring and gazing into his dark roast coffee bean eyes with the shards of golden demerara sugar reflecting the sun and shining almost as brightly, thanks to a few un-shed tears. I stared unblinking at his finely chiselled face with cheekbones like shark's fins, his pearlescent skin as pale as a mistletoe berry and his dark wayward curls blowing in the wind. Zen, my handsome boyfriend, who was the kindest man I'd ever met, who wasn't afraid to show his feelings, and who I loved beyond words.

'I'm so relieved,' he exhaled. 'I would've hated to have got it wrong. It's antique, from about 1905, and the stone in the middle is a yellow diamond; they're rarer, appar-ently, than clear diamonds. The woman in the shop told me they're associated with warmth, radiance and new beginnings, which sounded perfect to me.'

The tears began to fall, and Zen took the scrunched up wet wipe from my hand and gently dabbed them away.

'Ellie, the mud is running down your face with the tears,' he laughed.

'Yours too,' I wiped his face gently with my thumb, 'but I don't care because WE'RE ENGAGED!'

He went in the backpack again and this time brought out a couple of crystal flutes, carefully protected in bub-ble wrap, and two mini bottles of Champagne.

'You weren't kidding about having the kitchen sink in there, were you? You haven't got a mirror and a makeup bag? I want to look my best for you.'

'Ellie Montague, soon to be Chambers, or whatever you want to be called because all I want to do is marry you, you will always look your best to me, no matter what. Even in the yellow coat and that Viking hat, I still fancy you.'

'And I fancy you, even in that raggy Brazil T shirt and your ancient joggers.'

He popped the corks on the bottles and filled up our glasses.

'To us, Ellie. You have made me the happiest man on the planet.'

'To us. Zen, my soulmate and my best friend, except don't tell Sophie that! I cannot wait to marry you.'

We sat side by side in the damp little box, my head resting on his shoulder. The sky was turning into strands of citrus shades, from the palest lemon through to rich orangey tangerine, as the sun began its descent for the day. The birds flew over us, creating a cacophony of sounds as they headed towards the Holy Island of Lindisfarne, where our story first began, and now it had set the next chapter. We toasted our future in blissful solitude with eyes only for each other, and I gave a little smile upwards to the sky where the stars would soon be twinkling, silently thanking the universe for making me the happiest woman in the world.

Chapter 46

We may well have been levitating across the rest of the walk to the island, as neither of us really noticed if we were walking through water, mud or on sand.

'Did you keep this a secret?' I asked, taking yet another admiring glance at my ring, which was taking on the colours of the fading evening sun.

'Not a word to anyone. It's just about killed me keeping quiet, though. I was so keen to tell Meg and Bert, and of course Aurora and my mam and dad, but I didn't. Then when you mentioned changing the date we'd set, my heart sank. I couldn't have kept it up for much longer.'

'So, what happens now?'

'Well, as the date has more-or-less coincided with Mini Fest, why don't we just announce it tomorrow when most of the island will be there anyway? It will be like an engagement party we don't have to pay for!'

'I like your thinking. Even your mam and dad are coming across...' I stopped suddenly.

'I know, Ellie, you're thinking about your own family not being there. Why don't we speak to them online tomorrow, and we'll organise them either coming up here or us going down to Cambridge as soon as we can fit it in?'

'Perfect.'

'What do we tell Kitti tonight?' I asked, as we approached the café building.

'Hide the ring. Let her find out with everyone else tomorrow.'

'I can't bear to take it off ever again!'

'Well, keep your hand in your pocket,' he laughed.

But there was no need to worry, as when we let ourselves into the attic it was in darkness, with no Nacho at the door to greet us when he heard our footsteps on the stairs. There was a note on the kitchen table.

Went with Barry for tea to Meg and Berts, so me and Nacho staying there tonight. Kitti xx

'I bet that was Meg's idea, to let us have the attic to ourselves on date night,' I smiled.

'I didn't think my day could get any better. Are you coming in the shower to scrub my back, future wife?'

'Try and stop me, future husband!'

***

Zen and I overslept the next morning. After the walk, the excitement and hardly having time to sleep a wink, we were both exhausted. The bedroom door burst open and Nacho took a flying leap at the bed, followed by a snuffling Duchess, who stuck her head up for a stroke then promptly farted. Zen, Nacho and I all retreated underneath the duvet.

'Kitti!'

'Sorry, I'll just grab Duchess. Barry carried her up the stairs; we're just going to have some breakfast. Will I make you some coffee? You both need to get up.' She sounded like the grown up.

'Great, thanks, Kitti,' I said, as she took the dogs and shut the bedroom door.

'So much for the morning wake up I had planned,' smiled Zen.

'Yep, back to earth with a bump,' I smiled, taking one last look at my ring before I took it off and put it on a chain hanging it around my neck, out of view.

Barry was at full volume when we went into the kitchen.

'Eeeeeeh, hello! I've had such a good time since I got here yesterday. I can't tell you how lovely everyone has been,' he squealed, the hands flapping. 'I did a trial run of my set for Meg and Bert last night. It was great, wasn't it, Kitti? I'm sooo excited for today – to sing and meet everyone.'

'It was, erm, memorable,' said Kitti, tactfully.

'And I'm still not sure what to wear. Old Joe said if I wear the Lycra I'll be sweating like a fat lad in a chippie.'

The very thought of Barry in Lycra was not a good one.

'We're going over to Barry's to look through his outfits,' said Kitti, 'then I'm off to help Bert. We're getting everything done this morning so we can all have the afternoon off.'

'I'll come with you both,' I said, hurriedly finishing my coffee and thinking it might be wise to help Barry choose something to wear for his introduction to the islanders that the hooch swilling fishermen wouldn't ridicule... too much!

'Love you so much, fiancé,' I whispered in Zen's ear, giving him a hug.

'Enough of the PDA, pur-leese,' Barry grinned. 'I'm a saddo singleton, remember.'

'Love you too, fiancée,' Zen whispered back, and I patted where my ring was hiding underneath my shirt, leaving my new fiancé to tidy up the kitchen.

***

'That'll be five pounds, Ellie. Young Kitti can come in for free,' said Ethel the Bouncer, as we arrived at the entrance to the garden of the Crab.

'I'm a helper on the committee,' I smiled.

'No discounts for friends or family on my watch. Here, Dean, get your twenty quid ready,' Ethel shouted down the queue.

'Twenty quid, Ethel? I'm playing in the band.'

'I'd pay thirty quid not to have to listen to you,' quipped Don, who was in the queue behind him.

'I hear you brought in a good catch this morning, Dean, so it's twenty of your readies. All in a good cause,' cackled Ethel. 'Those lobsters I hear you caught would be worth more than that.'

Dean laughed and handed over the money to the old reprobate, who put it in her capacious handbag where she was collecting all the gate money.

'Thirty quid, Don, and I'll unplug the speakers,' Ethel laughed raucously. She was on top form today, no doubt helped by a nip of the happy juice.

Kitti and I made our way over to the trestle table Meg had reserved for us all. Tara, Toby, Sophie and Jake were already there, with Farne sitting on Jake's knee, looking so cute in his T shirt and shorts with baby animals on them. I said hello to everyone and wandered across to the marquee, which was the domain of the Crafty Lindisfarners, who were in charge of the refreshments. Stan the butcher was set up outside, a set of tongs in each hand. He was alternating between two barbeques like he was Ringo Starr playing a double drum kit at Wembley.

'One for meat, one for veggie,' muttered Dora. 'He thinks he's Gordon Ramsay.'

'As long as he doesn't swear like him,' tutted Muriel, arranging a plate of cupcakes, complete with hairy cow chocolate horns.

'If there's one thing this island can do,' smiled Meg from behind a steaming tea urn, 'it's put on a bally good party, and that's not swearing, Muriel! Kitti, pet, have a cupcake,' said Meg. 'Where's Barry?'

'Propping up the bar. He seems to have made friends with the fishermen.'

'He's what?' gasped Meg, throwing down her tea towel and almost sprinting out of the marquee. 'Watch the urn for me, Kitti. If that lot start him on the hooch, it'll be a disaster.'

'Let the boy have some fun,' Linda laughed.

'Linda, lass, we heard him sing last night, and let's just say what he lacks in tone he makes up for in enthusiasm, but if he has so much of a sniff of that stuff his island dreams will be over before they begin. We need him for The Lads – tone issues or not!'

Chapter 47

Zen arrived, carrying his battered acoustic guitar. Fresh out of the shower, he was wearing a black ruffled shirt and tight jeans, with the silver coffee bean dangling around his neck. His hair was still damp, the tendrils falling around his pale face. I couldn't take my eyes off him, he was so captivating. He began with a medley of songs from all eras. It was the perfect start to the afternoon, and people were singing along with the songs they knew.

'This one's for my very own Lady Eleanor,' he said, looking directly at me while striking up the chords to my namesake's song. I felt for my ring, hidden away under my shirt, crying out to go back on my finger, and lost myself in the soulful words of the song that he sung so beautifully. I was so proud of him and couldn't wait for us to share our news with everyone. He finished his set to rapturous applause and came and sat next to me at the big table, with all our nearest and dearest round us.

'You were on top form today, son,' said his dad, Mike.

'Aren't I always?' Zen laughed.

'Always,' replied Simone, his mam, her face beaming with pride.

'Hoy, what about me?' quipped Aurora. 'I might not be able to sing and play the guitar, but I've produced your first grandchild – and I can bake a mean cheese scone.'

'I'll say you can, Aurora,' said Maurice. 'I've had three already.'

'Barry's up next. Did you save him from the hooch, Meg?'

'I tried, but he'd had a tipple before I got there. It's usually not a great experience when you drink it for the first time.'

'Precisely,' said Maurice. 'That's why you need more than one glass!'

Barry Big Lad literally bounced onto the makeshift stage. He was wearing my suggestion of his navy blue velvet jacket, a sparkly bow tie and... oh, my God, he'd ditched the trousers we'd chosen for a pair of sequinned shorts.

'Hello, Lindisfarne,' he boomed down the microphone like he was on an arena tour. 'I'm Barry Big Lad, the island's newest resident, and I am thrilled to be here. Thrilled, I tell you! I can't wait for you all to call in to Love Lindisfarne. We've got a 'Welcome to Bazza' sale happening next week, so why not pop in for some Barry bants and a little bit of Monday magic?' He twirled and once again nearly fell over but somehow steadied himself.

'Hey up, Bazza lad, has the hooch got you going?' shouted Dean, laughing,

'It's the only thing that has since posh boy dumped me,' Barry chuckled, 'but without further ado... doo doo...'

Barry launched into his version of 'Agadoo' and began shaking his pineapples all over the place.

'What musical is this from?' Muriel tutted. 'I thought he was doing show tunes.'

'So did I. He must have changed his mind,' said Meg, the tears already streaming down her face from laughing, as Barry gave the performance of his life. By the time we got to 'Hey Big Spender' and a few attempted high kicks, Barry's face was the colour of the village post box and the shorts looked in danger of bursting at the seams, but the whole of the garden were on their feet singing and dancing along. Barry went down like an island storm to demands for more and promising to do some songs with the band later that night.

'Not sure about that,' laughed Zen. 'I'll be redundant!'

Next up was Kitti, Bert and Maurice with their secret project. A giant screen was placed on the stage, and Bert did a little cough as he tapped the top of the mic.

'Testing, one, two – can you hear me in the concert room?' he laughed. 'First off, thanks to all of you for coming today. The weather has blessed us, and if you're enjoying yourselves half as much as me, you'll be having a wonderful time. As you know, today is about the Lindisfarne Animal Sanctuary. Our numbers have increased with the arrival of all the mini animals we took in recently, and we need to make sure that we have enough in the bank to pay for food and vets bills for all our furry and feathery friends. We thank the Lindisfarne and Bamburgh families who continue to support us financially – it is very much appreciated. Is Inigo here today?'

'Cooeee,' shouted Barry, pointing to the corner. 'Mr Silver Fox is over there... with a very foxy lady, sadly.'

We all swung round to see Inigo looking like he had just stepped off a movie set, along with yet another glamorous woman – identity unknown!

'We've done well with the fundraising so far today, and before I show you our little film, we're going to pick the winner of the Name the Donkeys Draw. This alone raised over £200. Kitti, lass, put your hand in there and pick out a winner – but don't let it be Ethel. I couldn't take any more Haggis, Neeps and Tatties.'

Kitti pulled out a name from the bucket and shouted gleefully. 'It's Barry!'

'Me?' squealed Barry Big Lad, jumping back on the stage and grabbing the mic out of Berts hands. 'Oh, my days. I'm honoured. I met the cuties yesterday, so had a little think, and I know already what they're going to be called. Drum roll please... I name those donkeys Persephone and Pandora. They were two women I used to work with, who both had long faces and brayed like the pair of asses they were.'

A big cheer went up from the crowd.

'Erm, right, lad. Thanks,' said Bert, taking back the mic. 'We welcome Pandora and Percypony, or however you say it. You'll be getting a naming plaque above their door as part of the prize. Right, back to the exciting bit. Young Kitti here knows all about your internet malarkey – the social media I'm told it's called, like... erm...'

'TikTok, YouTube and other platforms,' laughed Kitti.

'So, Kitti began filming me and Maurice when the animals arrived. She gave us a name – we're called *Castle*

Capers – and from the minute the minis arrived, Kitti has been making little post-it things, and videos and ...'

'Reels and stories,' smiled Kitti.

'Aye, them things. They're not like fishing reels, mind, lads,' said Maurice, nodding towards Dean and his buddies.

'She began putting them online, and knock me down with a cormorant's feather, but we went and got a virus.'

'Went viral,' corrected Kitti.

'We broke the internet,' said Maurice. 'Well, nearly.'

'We're now content creators,' said Bert. 'Did I say that right, pet?' Kitti nodded. 'And already have begun to get asked to do advertising in exchange for animal food and supplies. Kitti says if we get enough followers, we might get actual real money.'

The crowd clapped in appreciation.

'We might even get asked to do a reality show,' smiled Kitti.

'Not on my watch,' yelled Meg. 'We've had enough of those to last a lifetime.'

'Spoilsport, Meggie,' said Ethel. 'I'd be up for it.'

'Anyway, let's run the tape, except it's not tape these days, is it?' Bert chuckled. 'So without further ado, here's a little film Kitti has put together of some of our clips and reels. We hope you enjoy it and follow *Castle Capers* on those things I mentioned.' The entire garden got out their mobile phones and started tapping away.

'Did you know about this, Meg?' I asked, astounded after watching the film of clips the three had collaborated on. They ranged from hilarious, with Bert and Maurice like a hapless Geordie version of *Laurel and Hardy*, to extremely cute, with the tiny cartoon-like animals with their big beseeching eyes, to heartstring-tuggingly sad, when the vet pronounced all the animals underweight and neglected. The content was set against the stunning backdrop of the island and castle. The entire project was a stroke of genius, and I had no doubt that *Castle Capers* would end up with thousands of followers.

'I didn't,' said Meg. 'I knew they were up to something, but not this. Eeh, my Bert is an internet sensation.'

'Meg, pet, you'd better watch him. He'll be getting all kinds of offers now he's famous,' cackled Ethel. 'I want to be in on this, Kitti. Just you remember your Granny Ethel – you'd better cut me in.'

'I'm so proud of you, Kitti,' I said, giving her a hug. 'I can't believe you did all of that yourself, because I know Bert and Maurice don't have a clue about the technical side of things.'

'I told you it was nothing dodgy,' smiled Kitti, 'and Barry says he's going to help me from now on, so I think it will get even better. Is it okay if I go over to see the animals now? I want to check on them.'

'That's fine,' I said, knowing how much she would prefer being over at the castle. We could tell her about the engagement later.

Kitti went off, and the rest of us sat around the table, marvelling at Bert and Maurice's new career while enjoying a few drinks and some fabulous food. It was the perfect time for our news. Zen and I had decided to tell our table, as all our friends and his family were present, and we knew that from there it would take only seconds to spread around the rest of the party. I clutched Zen's hand and whispered in his ear.

'Now? I can't wait, can you?'

'No, I can't,' he whispered back. 'I'll get their attention. But just as he got ready to speak, Meg jumped up and began glaring at a woman who had just come through the gate.

'What's up, Meg? Shall I go and make her pay to come in? She's missed half the afternoon,' hiccupped Ethel, 'might as well let her in for nowt.'

'I don't bally believe it,' Meg gasped, shielding her eyes. 'That's Gloria Penaluna. I'd recognise that bust anywhere. What on earth is she doing back on the island?'

Chapter 48

The older contingent at the table all swung round to look at the woman.

'So it is,' said Dora. 'She must have some scaffolding going on to keep those upright these days, mind.'

'The last time I saw a bust like that was on the front of the *Cutty Sark*,' tutted Muriel.

'Penaluna,' shouted Ethel. 'That's it!'

'That's what?' asked Meg.

'The name Penaluna. It's Kitti's name, and I knew I had heard it before but couldn't remember where from.'

A silence descended on the table like Lindisfarne fog, so thick you'd need scissors to cut your way out.

'Please tell me this is some kind of joke?' said Meg, a look of horror on her face.

'No, Meggie, lass. We must have found that out when you were in Scotland. It really is Kitti's name, and it's too much of a coincidence not to be connected. It explains the whole Cornish thing,' Ethel mused, her eyebrows knitted together in one long line.

'Oh, my God,' I gasped, finding the power of speech. 'You mean that woman could be Kitti's grandmother?'

Gloria Penaluna had a face harder than the granite cliffs on Greater Reef. Even the overload of baby blue eyeshadow and bright pink lipstick did nothing to soften her pinched features.

'Yes, Ellie. And just in case you haven't put two and two together, she's the one that wrecked mine and Bert's church wedding by running off with that randy beanpole who called himself a vicar,' Meg huffed, smoke almost coming out of her ears.

I turned to Zen, all thoughts of announcing our engagement now forgotten. 'Thank God Kitti went over to the castle. What are we going to do?'

Bert stood up. 'I'm going to go over there and find out what that blousy bissom wants. It must be fifty-five years since she stepped foot on this island.'

I think I already knew what she wanted, and it filled me with a creeping fear that gripped me from my head right down to my toes. But before Bert moved, Gloria made her way across to our table and stood at the helm like the ship's figurehead Muriel had mentioned.

'Well, well, well,' she exclaimed in a throaty Cornish drawl. 'Look who we have here. I thought half of you lot would be long gone by now.'

'Pity you weren't,' muttered Ethel.

'Meg Potts, as I live and breathe.'

'It's Shafto now,' growled Meg, 'no thanks to you and that robbing string bean who called himself a man of the cloth.'

'Whatever,' drawled Gloria. 'Time hasn't been too kind to you, has it? And Ethel Fish. I presume it's still Fish, as who in their right mind would have ever married you?'

I could see Bert getting angrier by the minute. This woman was toxic; she reminded me of a much older version of poison Isla. Had she been her grandmother then I wouldn't have batted an eyelid, as they were like peas in a pod.

'Who do you think you are?' said Muriel, 'we thought we'd seen the last of you when you made off with our silver, you thief. Your fingers should have dropped off.'

'Oh, Little Muriel actually has a voice now. Wonders never cease. And Dora, I can see you've eaten your way through most of Stan's profits.'

'That's enough,' said Maurice, getting up out of his chair and looking like he was about to flatten her. He was joined by Barry, and the pair of them eyeballed Gloria like it was a standoff in a comedy western. The fact that Maurice was wearing a T shirt with 'Nowt Moister than an Oyster' on the front and Barry's girth was straining in the sequinned shorts suddenly gave me hysterical giggles, as the whole thing was so surreal.

'And what's so funny?' Gloria turned to me. 'Which one of these do you belong to?'

'Hoy, don't you speak to Ellie like that,' squealed Barry Big Lad, wading in to my defence. 'I don't know who you are, but believe you me, you're a nasty piece of work, and I think you should just take a hike, lady. I've met lots like you, and just because you're old it doesn't give you the right to speak to anyone the way you have.'

I saw Gloria visibly flinch at the word old.

'Maybe we should just all calm down a bit,' said Bert, ever the peacemaker, even though he was fuming. 'What is it you want, Gloria? You made it plain that you hated this island and us islanders, and it would seem you haven't exactly mellowed over the years.'

'I'm here on a personal matter,' she spat. 'I hear my granddaughter is on the island, and I've come to take her home with me to Cornwall. If you're Ellie,' she turned to me, 'you and I need a little chat. And where is the other one she's staying with, him with the funny name?'

'You mean Zen, my grandson,' said Meg. 'You'd just better watch what you are saying, Gloria, because as God is my witness, I'm going to come over there and wipe that smile off your wrinkly old face.'

Ouch.

'Your grandson? Just my luck,' sneered Gloria. 'Anyway, where is my granddaughter?'

'Your granddaughter, if she really is that, because believe me, Gloria Penaluna, we'll be checking you out long before you get to even lay eyes on her, isn't here, thank God.'

'I'd heard she's called Kittiwake. What kind of damn fool name is that? It might not be too late to change it; she should be called something Cornish like her mother.'

'How dare you,' I exploded, feeling my blood pressure hit the roof. 'How you have the nerve to come here and say things like that after what you did to Kitti's mother is just unbelievable. You abandoned Daisy in her hour of need. What kind of woman are you?'

'The worst kind,' said Ethel, glaring at Gloria.

'I'll thank you to call my daughter by her proper name, Loveday.'

'She liked to be called Daisy, which you would have known if you had hung around, you...'

'Ssh, Ellie, don't stoop to her level.' Zen put his arms around me and I held on to him feeling like I was going to topple over.

'I think it's time you left,' said Zen in a calm, measured voice.

'I'll leave when I'm good and ready and not before,' shouted Gloria. Everyone was now aware of the exchange, turning their heads and watching the drama as it unfolded.

'Right, lady, you'll leave now,' said Linda. 'I've heard enough. This is my pub, and I get to say who stays and who goes, and you're not welcome. Not now, not ever – you're barred.'

Gloria momentarily went silent.

'It was much better management in here in my day,' she growled. 'I'm staying at the St Cuthbert's Way Hotel...'

'Best place for you. It's like a witch's coven over there; you'll fit right in,' muttered Dora.

'You've got until lunchtime tomorrow to contact me, then I'll be seeking legal advice, because you cannot keep me from seeing my granddaughter.'

'Pet, you can contact Judge Judy for all we care,' said Bert. 'We will do what is best for young Kittiwake, make no bones about that.'

'I'll be in touch tomorrow,' said Zen, taking control, 'and I think it's best you leave now, seeing as Linda has asked you nicely.'

'Oh, I'm going. Tomorrow, then. You can tell my granddaughter that I'll be taking her back with me, make no bones about that,' she said, quoting Bert as she looked him directly in the eye. She swaggered off out of the garden, leaving the rest of us feeling like we'd been in the eye of a tornado.

'Oh, my God,' gasped Sophie, 'what an absolutely revolting woman. Come here, Ellie Nellie. You need a hug; you're shaking like a leaf.'

'Kitti's been through enough. She didn't ever want to meet her grandmother after the way she treated her mam, and I can't say I blame her,' I gasped.

'Jeez, that woman is toxic,' said Tara, immediately going into organisational mode. 'We can't let her take Kitti, so here's the plan. Ellie, you get straight back to the attic and see who you can talk to on the phone, it's Saturday night now, so you may not have any luck but worth a go. Sophie and Jake, you two go and fetch Kitti and take her straight back to the attic before anyone else has the chance to tell her what's going on. You know how fast things spread on this island. Toby, darling, you're so good at research, so take Farne home and see if you can find out what Kitti's rights are, and the rest of you have all had a shock, so Aurora and I are going to the bar to get you a brandy, and you're all just going to sit there and calm down.'

'What about the band?' asked Barry. 'There's another set to do – we can't let everyone down. I'm not being unkind because, even though I've only met Kitti, I really like her, but the show has to go on. Everyone has been so generous with their donations today.'

'Barry's right,' said Bert. 'The rest of us carry on for now as if nothing has happened. Zen, go and get the lads ready, and Barry, mind those shorts, son. No more high kicks, or we'll be seeing something even more unpalatable than Gloria bloody Penaluna!'

'Are you okay with me staying, Ellie? I can come back with you now; the band will manage without me,' said Zen, holding my hand.

'No, you stay. I'll be on the phone anyway, but you will come home the minute you're finished, won't you?' I said, hugging him.

He nodded, kissing me. 'Of course. I'll let Barry do the encores.'

'You and Zen will have to talk to Kitti later,' said Meg sadly. 'I don't envy the pair of you, but you need to do it. It's best coming from you two.'

So instead of happily announcing our engagement, Zen and I were going to have to break Kitti's heart instead. Life sometimes really did have the habit of turning everything on its head in the blink of an eye.

Chapter 49

'What's going on?' asked Kitti, as Sophie and Jake dropped her back off at the attic. 'Sophie was being weird – more weird than normal. She kept saying you needed me to come back. I was in the middle of sorting Penguin and Puffin out. Are you okay? Is Zen okay?'

'Zen's fine. I've got a headache,' I said, which was perfectly true. My temples were throbbing like a Harley Davison in full throttle.

'Can I get you anything?' Kitti asked.

'No thanks, chick.'

'I can hear Barry singing from here, so if you're okay I think I'll go back down and watch. He's so funny, I don't want to miss it.'

'Kitti, would you mind staying in with me? I don't feel like being on my own. We could find something to watch, and I brought loads of things home to eat?'

Kitti eyed me suspiciously.

'Suppose, if you really need me to,' she muttered. 'I hope Barry doesn't think I'm ignoring him after he's offered to help me with *Castle Capers*.'

'I'm sure he won't,' I said, looking at the clock and willing Zen to come back soon, as this was one job I was not going to do on my own. Sometimes time moved more slowly than the outgoing tide when you're waiting to cross the causeway.

'Hey,' said Zen, when he eventually bounded in. 'I've left it with Barry; he doesn't know the lyrics to half our songs, but he's very good at improvising and has the audience eating out of his hand.'

'Why have you left him?' demanded Kitti. 'That's a bit unfair when it's his first time performing on the island.'

Zen and I looked at each other, neither of us quite knowing what to say. I clicked off the television and Zen sat down in the chair. Kitti and I were side by side on the sofa.

'Look, tell me. I know there's something not right. I can feel it,' Kitti said, her voice full of trepidation.

'Kitti, you need to hear this from us, before anyone else on the island tells you—'

'Tells me what?' she said, her eyes growing wider by the minute. 'You're sending me back, aren't you?'

'No! Of course we're not. Kitti we both love having you here, as does every single person you've got to know on Lindisfarne. The thing is, a woman appeared this afternoon...' I faltered.

'A woman? So, what's that got to do with me?'

'It was your grandmother, Kitti,' said Zen, taking charge and looking at her directly.

'My grandmother? What grandmother?'

'Your mam's mam, Kitti. She's called Gloria Penaluna,' he said quietly.

I watched as Kitti's face crumpled, like it had on the day we met her. She began to sob, and I wrapped her in my arms.

'Let it out, Kitti. It's a nasty shock to take in.'

'What does she want? she replied in a small voice, 'although don't bother answering that. She's here for me, isn't she?'

'Well, I think she'd like to meet you,' I said gently.

'And how does she know I'm here? It'll be that Mrs Monster; she can't wait to get rid of me. I don't want to see her, whoever she is, and no one can make me.'

'Kitti, no one is going to make you do anything you don't want to do. I tried to speak to Sue earlier, but her and Billy are away, and we'll have to wait until Monday to speak to the social worker. Anyway, you need to take time to process this. It's a huge thing, and it'll take time to sink in.'

'It won't because I'm not seeing her. She can go back to wherever she came from. She's not my grandmother any more than she was my mam's mam – end of.' And she jumped up, ran into her room and slammed the door.

I got up to follow her, but Zen shook his head.

'Let her have some space, Ellie. It's been a hell of a shock for the poor kid. We'll give her a little while and then see if she's okay.'

'Since when did you become so wise?' I managed a smile. 'Oh, Zen, what a shambles. Gloria is worse than I could have ever imagined. I wonder what she's up to, because I can tell from just meeting her once that she's not doing this due to a change of heart and wanting to put things right.'

'I agree. She's here for something, that's for sure, but we're only the people giving Kitti a place to live temporarily, Ellie. We're no more than landlords, really, and we have no input into decisions over her care.'

'I know that, but someone has to be on her side. I hope Toby has come up with something. Shall I ring him?'

'It's late. Just leave it for tonight. You can find out tomorrow. We'll sort this,' he said, grabbing my hand and kissing the empty finger where the ring should have now taken pride of place. 'What an engagement announcement, eh? We're never going to forget this in a hurry, for all the wrong reasons.'

'We'll just keep it to ourselves for now, eh? It doesn't feel right to be all smiley and happy when we've got all this going on,' I replied, and I took the ring from under my T shirt, kissed it then popped it back.

'As long as we know that's all that matters, Ellie.'

'It's Meg,' I said, as my phone started to ring.

'Me and Bert are back home having a cup of tea and worrying ourselves sick about that poor lamb. Have you told her?'

'We have. Oh Meg, it was awful. She got very upset, then angry. She went to her room, and we're giving her a bit of space, but I'm going to check on her in a minute.'

'Time has done nothing to soften that old crow,' said Meg. 'I can't believe she had the audacity to come back on this island. Me and Bert both think that she's after something. Has Kitti ever mentioned any money left to her?'

'I don't think they had much, Meg, but her mam was killed in a road accident which wasn't her fault, and whilst

I haven't probed too much, I suspect there maybe compensation involved.'

'That'll be what she's after, then, as sure as eggs are eggs. I wonder where the randy rev is? Mind, she might have dumped him years ago. I notice Kitti and her mam both went by Gloria's name, not Richardson, which is what he was called.'

'Who knows, Meg. It'll all become clear eventually, I suppose. Right, got to go and check on Kitti.'

'You do that, my pet. Sunday lunch here tomorrow, all three of you. I asked Barry Big Lad, seeing he's on his own, and he's bringing Ethel across. I won't take no for an answer from you three. We must show Kitti love and stability, so don't let her fester in that bedroom. Get her out into the fresh air in the morning and send her across to Bert and the animals. There's no finer medicine than that, and Gloria can't get at her here. We need to keep young Kittiwake occupied until this thing sorts itself out.'

'You're right, as usual,' I smiled.

'Love you all. Oh, and just before I go, Barry's shorts eventually gave up the ghost. I got a right eyeful of his scanties when he was doing "YMCA".'

'Meg, you're incorrigible. Night night, love you both lots.'

Chapter 50

'Kitti?' I knocked lightly on her door. 'Are you going to come out and have some hot chocolate with Zen and me? We don't need to talk about you-know-what if you don't want to.'

'No, don't want any,' she replied in a sullen voice.

'Are you okay?'

'Stop asking me that, Ellie,' she replied sharply.

'Well, we're here for you, I just want you to know that. Meg and Bert send their love. They've asked us for Sunday lunch tomorrow with Barry and Ethel. That'll be fun, won't it?'

No reply.

'I'll let you sleep, then. But please, Kitti, just shout if you need us.'

Silence.

'I'm not sure what to do,' I whispered as I went into our bedroom. 'She's gone in on herself. If she's no better tomorrow, I'll try and find a contact number for Errol, her counsellor.'

'Good idea. My immediate concern is that she might decide to do a runner in the middle of the night.'

'Oh, my God, you don't think she would, do you?'

'I've no idea. I hope not.'

'Let's leave our bedroom door open. If she gets up, we'll hear her. I doubt I'll sleep anyway. It's a pity Nacho is over at the castle; he would make a noise if she woke him up in the night.'

***

After a virtually sleepless night, I got up early to make a drink and a very pale faced Kitti came in and sat down at the kitchen table. It was killing me, but I didn't ask how she was.

'Hot chocolate?' I smiled.

'I'm sorry,' she murmured in a tiny voice.

'You have nothing to be sorry about. Did you manage to get any sleep?'

'A little bit, but I had horrible nightmares where this old witch came and picked me up on her broomstick. She took me to Cornwall and made me do all the housework.'

I wondered if Kitti was psychic, because I'd lay money on that not being far from the truth.

'I kind of don't want to know, but I do. What was she like?'

How on earth did I answer that truthfully? I might as well have said, just like the witch in your dream.

'Erm, she was, erm, very strong willed and erm, vocal.'

Kitti looked at me through red eyes, which were boring into me like laser beams.

'Did she ask about me or my mam?'

'Erm, she mentioned you both.'

'Did she seem kind?'

At this point Zen appeared, and I silently thanked the stars above as I was seriously way out of my depth.

'She didn't seem very kind, Kitti, but then maybe she will be to you. Your grandmother—'

'She's not my grandmother.'

'Okay, Gloria has a history on the island, and I think it's only fair we tell you. We only just found out ourselves recently, but what it meant was that all the older people around our table have bad memories of her, and I think that made her angry.'

Zen told Kitti the whole sordid tale of her grandmother and Reverend Richardson, the missing silver and Meg and Bert's cancelled wedding.

'I don't believe it,' said Kitti. 'So that's why she hated Lindisfarne and tried to stop mam from coming on the environmental trip.'

'It would seem so,' I nodded.

'So, is the old vicar my mam's dad then?'

'Only Gloria will be able to answer that, Kitti. Meg asked that you go and help Bert this morning. He had a long day yesterday, and he's not as young as he used to be, so really needs you. I think Maurice is going too, so perhaps you can do some more content or whatever it's called. I kept my fingers crossed under the table; a little white lie was okay every now and again, after all.

'I don't feel like doing any social media today, but I will go and help with the animals. Will she be able to get to me though?'

'No, Bert keeps the gate locked at the paddocks, as you know, but anyway, why not do the yard chores today? She can't even see you there.' I was really tempted to say, 'those walls are as thick as her,' but stopped myself.

'Ellie and I will walk you over to the castle, and then we're going to see Toby. Is it okay if we go and see Gloria and tell her that until we've spoken to whoever we need to, she'll just have to be patient?'

'Suppose so. But nothing's going to happen, anyway, 'cos I'm not seeing her, so just tell her to go back to wherever she came from.'

***

'Come in,' shouted Tara from the kitchen. 'Just getting Farne sorted for the second time today. How is it that little fingers can make such a big mess? Tobes is in the study, if you want to go and talk to him.'

Toby explained to Zen and me what he had found out online.

'Kitti, at sixteen, can leave home without parental consent, but her parents, or guardian in her case, would still have to ensure that she had a suitable place to live,' said Toby, 'just like what happened when she came to stay with you.'

'Well, that sounds positive,' I said.

'Not if they appoint Gloria as her guardian,' said Toby, because she could still make things difficult, although she would have no right to see Kitti unless Kitti herself agreed. Gloria would have other responsibilities too, like signing off on a housing lease, for example, and she could make finding somewhere to rent difficult if she chose not to.'

'But she couldn't take her to Cornwall?'

'In effect, no, but if Kitti doesn't have a place to live then that might change. Gloria is Kitti's next of Kin. Then there's the matter of any monies coming to Kitti via an insurance payout and, of course, what effects Kitti has left of her mam.'

'So, there might be some conflict around finances because of Kitti's age,' said Zen. I suppose Gloria would be the nominated responsible adult, after all, she is the mother of Loveday.'

'I don't like any of this,' I said. 'Even though it sounds like Kitti at this stage doesn't have to see Gloria, I actually think she needs to.'

'So do I,' said Tara, coming in the door. 'It really might help if she meets her face to face and hears what the old bag has to say.'

'We're going over to the hotel now. Zen texted the old bag, as you so delightfully call her, and we're going to tell her she's just got to be patient until Kitti is ready. If she ever is, of course. By the way, where are Jake and Sophie this morning?'

'They've gone over to the paddocks to help with the animals,' smiled Tara.

'Are you kidding me? Is it some kind of therapy? I know they like the animals but voluntarily mucking out at this time in the day – there's a rabbit off here somewhere!'

'They're on a scoping mission,' said Toby mysteriously-ly.

'A scoping mission? What's that supposed to mean?'

'All in good time, Ellie,' said Toby, his face turning Barbie pink.

'You're up to something, Toby Butler. Tell me.'

'Client confidentiality,' he laughed. 'I promise I'll tell you soon. If the idea I had comes to anything, you and others will be the first to know.'

'Others? You're lucky I've got Kitti to focus on right now, otherwise I'd stay here until you told me. Do you know, Tara? Bestie loyalty and all of that?'

'No, not a clue, Ellie, but I know some very good ways of getting Toby to talk. Just leave it with me.'

'Ellie, we need to go to the hotel and get this over with,' said Zen. 'Wish us luck guys.'

'I really hope it goes well,' said Tara, giving me a hug. 'Kitti's lucky that she's got you two in her corner, Ellie.' She whispered in my ear, 'if Sophie and Jake go to the Crab for Sunday lunch, and Farne is having his nap, I might be in a position to tell you everything you need to know by later this afternoon!'

Chapter 51

'Ellie, Zen,' said the ever-haughty Elspeth looking down her long nose at us. 'Gloria is waiting for you in the conservatory; can I get you some coffee?'

'Tea,' jumped in Zen.

'Tea?' I whispered. 'What's got into you?'

'The coffee they use here is like cat's pee; it's cheap and nasty. I offered them a good deal, but they refused.'

'How's Isla?' I asked, out of absolutely nothing more than curiosity.

Elspeth swung round and looked at me shrewdly but then couldn't resist an opportunity to brag about her daughter.

'She lives mainly in Texas now. She got married to her fiancé, Howard, recently. A billionaire, you know. They live a quiet life, flying to their various homes across the world in Howard's private jet. I do believe they're on their Caribbean island at the moment. It's so difficult to keep up,' she boasted. If her head got any bigger it would knock the very ostentatious chandelier down.

'Did you go to the wedding?' I asked.

'No, far too busy here,' muttered Elspeth, her face turning the colour of a clown's nose, before quickly turning away to go and collect the tea.

'I reckon they weren't invited,' I said to Zen. 'Oh, well, good luck to Howard, whoever he is. I hope he got a pre-nup.'

'I'm surprised you haven't looked him up online,' laughed Zen.

'Oh, I will, when I find the time.'

Gloria was sitting staring out at the garden when we went into the conservatory. With the full glare of the sun on her face, it was difficult not to see her as anything other than an old woman. Until she opened her mouth.

'You're late,' she spat.

'Sorry, just talking to Elspeth.'

'Right, let's get down to it. When is the child coming to see me?'

'Firstly, Gloria, if it's okay that I call you that?' said Zen. She nodded belligerently. 'The child, as you so indelicately put it, has a name. She's called Kitti, and she's a young woman, not a child.'

'Kitti's had a big shock, you turning up like this. It's a lot for her to take in. She's still newly bereaved and has just begun to find a little joy in life again,' I added.

'Well, no one told me about Loveday until social services eventually tracked me down, so I'm in shock too.'

'And how many years is it since you even saw your daughter? I asked, 'just in case you can't quite remember, I'll remind you. It's sixteen.'

'Loveday never once tried to contact me or her father,' she replied bitterly.

'So where is her father?' I asked bluntly. 'Is that Mr Richardson? Why isn't he here?'

'That's the Reverend Richardson to you.'

'Oh, I thought he was struck off, or de-robed, or whatever happens to vicars when they do things like steal the church silver.' I glared at her.

'He passed away,' she continued, choosing to ignore my outburst. 'And in answer to your very impertinent question, yes, he was Loveday's father, so now I'm on my own, and it might be beneficial to have some company.'

'Beneficial to whom?' I fumed.

'Both of us. I thought the chi... Kitti, might be able to help around the house and be there for me. I'd give her a roof over her head in return.'

I couldn't quite believe what was coming out of Gloria's mouth. It really sounded like what she was after was a live in carer.

'Kitti isn't the hired help,' I said. 'She's a bright young woman who wants to become a vet one day. She needs to restart her education when she's up to it and achieve her dreams, not become a live in housekeeper to a complete stranger.'

Gloria glared at me.

'Don't you dare talk to me like that. She's my granddaughter and I am not a complete stranger; blood is thicker than water, missy. Did you pick her,' Gloria jabbed her ring clad finger at me while looking at Zen, 'because she's like your granny, Meg?'

'Okay, okay – time to calm down,' said Zen, reading the look on my face. 'Let's try and remain civil, shall we? What we came to say to you is that we will try and encourage

Kitti to meet with you but cannot guarantee that she'll agree, so you'll need to be patient and give her some time.'

'I have things to do. I can't stay on this Godforsaken island indefinitely. Besides which, how much do you think it's costing me to stay here? I'll be making sure it's paid back to me once the comp...' she stopped abruptly.

I could feel my face beginning to outdo Toby's in the Barbie stakes. Zen gripped my hand and shook his head, gesturing for me to remain calm.

'Mrs Penaluna,' I said, in as steady a voice as I could, 'you haven't asked one thing about Kitti, about what she likes, what her aspirations are, about her beautiful relationship with Daisy—'

'She was called Loveday, not Daisy,' interrupted Gloria. 'So disrespectful, trying to change her name into something she wasn't. Daisy! Pah – her God-given name was Loveday Penaluna.'

'That's as may be, but you haven't asked one solitary thing about either of them,' I continued. 'Shame on you. Kitti is an amazing young woman, which is all down to *Daisy*,' I said pointedly. 'Sadly, we never met her yet feel like she was an old friend. We will talk to Kitti, and we'll be backing whatever she decides she wants to do. If she doesn't want to meet you, then so be it, because it's her choice, not yours.'

'Well, we'll see what social services have to say, shall we? Mrs Monser seems like a very competent woman who can see the benefit of my granddaughter coming to live with me. And don't forget I can take legal steps, you know. I am Loveday's mother, and there's nothing you or anyone else can do about that,' she said threateningly.

'We'll leave it there, shall we?' I said, having heard enough and getting up to go, just as Elspeth carried in a tea tray.

'Sorry, no time for tea now,' said Zen to Elspeth. 'I'm sure Mrs Penaluna might want some while she considers our discussion.' Zen placed a £20 note on the table. 'Have this on us, Gloria. No need to add it to your claim. We'll be in touch, but until then, please do not try to contact Kitti.'

'I shall do as I please. Just leave the tea, Elspeth, and perhaps some scones, if they're fresh? Those ones you gave me yesterday could have passed for ancient rocks from Tintagel,' barked Gloria, sitting back in her chair like nothing had just happened.

***

'She what?' said Meg, beating the Yorkshire pudding mix with such ferocity that it was a wonder it didn't evaporate. 'The brass neck of the woman. So, what I'm hearing is that she just wants Kitti for whatever compo might be coming her way and as a free skivvy? Well, over my dead body.'

'Meg, unfortunately it really has little to do with us. I know it sounds crazy because that woman is truly toxic, but I do think Kitti should meet with her because when she does, I'm certain that she won't ever want to see her again. That might help if Gloria applies to be her guardian because if Kitti hasn't met her, the courts might suggest that they meet and get to know each other, and it would drag things out even longer.'

'You're right, pet, but don't let her go alone, will you? I know it's not your responsibility, but it would be like throwing her into the lion's den.'

'We won't, Meg, don't worry. Anyway, maybe you've beaten that yorkie batter enough. They'll rise like the tide!' smiled Zen.

'What time are the others getting here?' I asked, but no sooner than the words had come out of my mouth than the door opened and in shuffled Barry and Ethel, looking like two extras from *The Blues Brothers* in their big, dark sunglasses.

'Cooeeee, we're here,' said Barry Big Lad, in a much more subdued voice than usual. 'Eeh, my days. She gave me that hooch stuff. I'll never ever drink it again.' He slumped into a chair at the farmhouse table and held his head in his hands. 'It would strip paint. I might change the colour of the shop door, and I know what to use.'

'You young ones have no stamina,' said Ethel, re-moving her glasses and looking remarkably chipper as she unclipped Duchess from her lead.

'Let me sort out some coffees,' I said. 'Dinner might be a while.'

'Thanks, Ellie,' said Barry. 'You're a life saver, hun.'

'Nothing stronger than coffee?' muttered Ethel.

'Not a chance, Ethel Fish. No hair of the dog in this house.'

'I think you'll find there's lots of hairs of lots of dogs in here,' laughed Ethel.

'Yesterday I had the best day that I've had since I met Tristan in the Christmas Cottage,' said Barry, from behind the dark glasses. 'Thanks for giving me the opportunity, Meg. I hope I didn't let you down. Mini Fest was a blast.'

'Not at all, pet. You were fab. I was expecting show tunes, but perhaps next time, eh?'

'Blame Ethel – last minute change of set. She said that show tunes might be too tame for the audience, and I think she was right.'

We were soon joined by Bert, Kitti and the motley crew of castle canines. The small cottage filled with chatter and laughter, and even Kitti seemed to relax a little, as Meg bustled about doing what she absolutely loved, the delicious aroma of Sunday lunch drifting out of the Aga.

'Young Sophie and Jake were across helping this morning,' said Bert, stretching out in his armchair, cap still on his head at the jaunty angle. 'She was acting odd.'

'What, more odd than usual?' I laughed.

'Yes, and Jake was looking a bit shifty n'all, although it's great seeing the lad looking so much more like his old self. He says being on this island away from the Canary Whatsit is just what he needs.'

'What were they up to?' I asked, remembering Toby's words about a 'scoping exercise'.

'They seemed to be taking a great interest in the parcel of flat land that Toby has reserved for something. Asking me all kinds of things about drainage and power.'

'Odd,' said Meg.

'Very,' I agreed. Just wait until I got my hands on Toby. If Tara didn't manage to get whatever it was out of him with some afternoon delight, then there will be some less delightful morning interrogation, for sure.

'Did you speak to *her* then?' Kitti asked, breaking into my reverie.

'We did, but not now. Let's just enjoy lunch, and we can talk later when we get back to the attic. Nothing to worry about, though. Nothing was arranged, Kitti,' I said, keeping my fingers and toes well and truly crossed.

'Okay,' she nodded. 'Barry, we need to work on the rest of the videos from Mini Fest and get them posted. The ones I did yesterday, even though I didn't feel like it, have had loads of views. Let's get started while we wait for lunch – can't expect our views to go up with you just sitting there like a seal with a hangover.'

'Gawd, Kitti, ever thought about a career in the diplomatic service?' said Barry, removing the glasses to reveal pink eyes not too dissimilar to Tikka, one of Meg's chickens. 'Come on then – Barry Big Lad won't let the side down. Hangover or no hangover, *Castle Capers* will take priority.'

Chapter 52

'You really think I should meet her?' asked Kitti in a tiny voice when we got back to the attic.

'We do. Listen, Kitti, we won't lie to you. We found her to be a difficult woman, but then, that was to us; we hope she might be better with you. Let's wait until you speak to Mrs Monser tomorrow and find out what she has to say.'

'*If* I agree, will you come with me?'

'Of course. If we're allowed, then we'll definitely be there.'

'I'm asking you to come, and I should get to choose. I don't want that Mrs Monser to be there with just me and that woman on my own.'

'Let's try not to jump ahead, Kitti, but we won't let you go alone.'

I felt so scared that I was making promises I couldn't keep, but Kitti looked terrified, and I was frightened for her. The idea of Gloria taking legal advice was stuck in my head like a bad song on repeat, and I couldn't shake it off.

I was just about to suggest a diversionary game of Scrabble when my phone pinged.

'Hey, Zen, it's a message from Tobes. He says can we meet at theirs in half an hour?'

'What for?' Zen replied, still full of Meg's giant Sunday dinner and just about asleep in the chair.'

'Don't know. I imagine it's about whatever Jake and Sophie are up to. Do you want to come too, Kitti?'

'Might as well, I suppose.'

I'd noticed that since the arrival of Gloria, Kitti didn't want to be on her own.

The three of us made our way along Main Street to the Holiday House, Nacho on his lead trotting along next to Kitti. We passed Love Lindisfarne, where Barry was busy re-dressing the window for his very first day in charge the next day. There was a lot of sparkle going on, and a large home-made banner strewn across the front proclaimed 'Under New Management. Grand Opening Monday. Call in for some bants and bargains with Barry!'

We all waved and gave him the thumbs up.

'I think I'll go and help Barry, if that's okay?'

'Of course – we'll collect you on the way back.'

'Come in,' shouted Tara, when we got to the Holiday House. 'We're in the sitting room. Toby has the place organised like a care home,' she laughed, and I noticed the furniture had been arranged in a circle.

'So, what's going on?' I asked Tara, as I followed her through to the kitchen.

'Sorry, Ellie, I failed in my mission. Farne didn't have his nap, which is why he's fast asleep now, and Sophie and Jake didn't go for lunch, so I never got the chance to use my feminine charms. More's the pity, as there's not a lot of action going on in that direction, let me tell you.'

'Hellooo! It's me,' shouted Aurora coming into the kitchen. 'Jack is looking after Hettie; it seemed such a shame to disturb her. Did he need to be here?'

'I have no idea,' said Tara. 'What would you like to drink?'

'I'll just have a glass of council pop, please,' grinned Aurora.

'Council what?' I asked.

'Tap water,' giggled Aurora. 'Mam and Dad used to con us with that all of the time! 'How many more weeks until I can have a proper drink?' she laughed, taking a glass from Tara.

'You're in good company tonight as Jake and Sophie are on a health kick, and Toby and I have decided to join them, so apple juice all round, unless you fancy a glass of council pop too, Ellie?'

Drinks in hand, we sat in a circle, all focused on Toby, waiting for the big reveal.

'This had better be good,' I said, 'we were just about to thrash Zen at Scrabble.'

'You wish,' he grinned.

'Thanks for coming to this evening's meeting,' began Toby formally.

'Toby, they're our friends not flipping board members,' Tara laughed. 'Just get on with it, whatever *it* is.'

'Sorry. I just go into work mode when I'm in a circle,' he said seriously. 'Okay, remember me talking about the need to raise additional income for the upkeep of the castle, and we discussed the tea van and the refreshment idea first mooted by Aidan?'

'I do,' I said, 'and then me, Tara and Aurora talked about it and sorted it out for this season. Didn't we?'

'You did, Ellie, but like I said at the time, the small rent the estate gets from you three, not to mention the fact that you are all working for nothing, isn't really the kind of business that is going to work long term for either side. Sorry to be so blunt.'

'He's right,' said Aurora. 'Something needs to be done, especially if we move...' she stopped mid-flow, looking at her brother, who stared back at her open mouthed.

'You what? Move? Move where? And why don't I know about this?'

'Keep your hair on, bro,' replied Aurora. 'There's nothing set in stone. Just an idea we had that if we want to buy somewhere, our money will stretch further on the mainland.'

'Do Mam and Dad know about this? And Bert and Meg?'

Toby coughed.

'Erm, I'm shocked at that too, but maybe we can concentrate on the matter in hand and come back to it?'

'Of course, Toby. Sorry, I didn't mean to blurt that out. Soz, bro, we can talk later.'

'Well,' Toby continued, 'when the mini animals arrived, I had no idea how popular they would be with people visiting the castle. I've been keeping an eye on the ramparts, and every day there are people hanging over and watching what's going on below.'

'It's always been like that,' said Aurora.

'Yes, but not the numbers that you see now,' I said.

'The volunteers have reported back to me that they're always getting asked if they can get closer to the animals and whether they are part of the castle.'

'Bert keeps the gate locked,' I said, 'and Toby, you were quite firm about the fact that we couldn't open up as some kind of animal farm to the public.'

'And I'm still clear on that, Ellie; however, Jake and I were chewing the cud the other night...'

'Did you really mean to say that, darling?' laughed Tara.

'And,' Toby continued, 'it suddenly came to us that we have the spare parcel of land, we need a café, and that land looks directly over the paddocks...'

'So,' continued Jake, 'we thought it might be possible to build a wooden building with a viewing platform – no access to anywhere near the animals – but from where the visitors would be able to see them more clearly. They'd spend money in the café and generate the much-needed income.'

We all turned and looked at Aurora, who seemed deep in thought.

'Hmm,' she mused, 'I can see it, and it sounds great, but that would really affect my business. I couldn't afford to take on a huge project like that. I thought of running a small offer from inside the castle some-where, but this is a new proposition entirely.'

'We thought about that,' smiled Toby. 'What I would like to propose would be a partnership arrangement. A private enterprise between the directors,' he laughed out loud, 'of TEA at the Castle joining forces with a new venture capitalist who will very soon be moving onto the island, and who would invest the lion's share, project manage and get the whole thing up and running.'

'What's going on?' I asked, my mind whirring round like a wind turbine. 'Do you mean Jake? And Sophie? Moving here?'

'Yes, us!' Sophie yelled. 'Jake and I have had enough of London, which I never thought would happen, especially for Jake,' she turned to her fiancé and gave his arm a squeeze, 'but times change, life moves on and since we came back on the island, we've both felt so much calmer. Neither of us has any desire to go back to Chelsea. This island is as magic as you always tell me it is, Ellie. It's cast its spell on us.'

'I don't want to go back to Canary Whatsit, as Bert calls it, either,' laughed Jake. 'I'm much better than I was; I'm thinking clearly now and realise that I can't go back into the cutthroat world of financial dealing yet, if ever. So, when this potential new opportunity came to light, I felt so positive, and I hope we can all do this together.'

'And where are you going to live?' I asked, shocked by the whole revelation.

'Well, double bonus,' said Toby. 'Sir James and Lady Grace have agreed that Jake and Sophie can rent the guest apartment long term, which means extra income coming in immediately.'

'We're selling the flat in Chelsea,' explained Jake.

'I'm going to be living in a castle,' squealed Sophie, 'I might turn into the Poison Pylon, mind, and expect you all at my beck and call.'

'You're too short for that,' I shouted, jumping up to give her a hug, and we both started squealing, making the others put their fingers in their ears.

As I reached out for Sophie, my shirt button popped open and the chain with my beautiful engagement ring fell out for everyone to see. Sophie, never one to miss a trick, clocked it immediately.

'Oh, my God,' she yelled, the decibel level going up several more notches. 'What's this? Is that an engagement ring? You sly dogs...'

The room erupted as our closest friends all jumped up and began congratulating us, firing questions at the speed of light at the same time.

'Why have you kept it a secret?'

'Does anyone else know?'

'When did it happen?'

'Can we call Stanislaw and Aleksy and tell them?'

'Slow down, you lot,' Zen grinned.

Zen and I filled them in on our engagement and how we had been going to tell everyone at Mini Fest.

'It just seemed so inappropriate to announce it when that awful woman turned up out of the blue and Kitti was so upset, and since then there just hasn't been a moment spare. Honestly, guys, it wasn't because we didn't want to share our news, because we did, but we wanted to sort things out for Kitti first.'

'We understand, Ellie Nellie,' said Sophie. 'But now we know, what happens next? Are we all sworn to secrecy? Ooh, it's just so romantic.'

'Bro, Mam and Dad will kill me, not to mention Meg and Bert,' smiled Aurora, 'but if it's what you want, then I'll do my best to remain schtum.'

'Can you just give us a few more days?' Zen asked. 'We should know more about the Kitti situation, and then we can think about a way to celebrate with everyone.'

'I'll try,' said Aurora. 'I'm telling Jack, though!'

'You lot are going to have to watch me like a hawk,' laughed Tara, 'you know how I just manage to put my foot in it all the time. Does this call for Champagne?'

'Let's keep that for when we celebrate properly,' said Zen.

Toby coughed again.

'Erm, I don't want to be a party pooper but…'

'I know, darling, you want us to finish off the idea about the café,' said Tara.

'I do,' he said seriously. 'At least establish in principal that you are all on board to take it to the next step, then Jake and I can start talking to people?'

There were nods all round, and we all clinked glasses of council pop to both our engagement and new joint venture, and it couldn't have tasted any better than if it had been *Moet et Chandon!*

Chapter 53

Mrs Monser eventually found the time to call me back. Nice to know Kitti was a priority.

'Yes, you go with Kitti. It's a long way for me to come, and it's only an introductory get to know each other session, after all. When it gets to the legal bits, then of course I'll be on hand to ensure that Kitti's voice is heard.'

Why didn't I believe that? Mrs Monser was not at all the type of social worker I'd want in my corner, and as for the get to know each other and legal bits, none of the conversation filled me with any confidence for Kitti's future, because it felt to me like all Mrs Monser wanted to do was write 'case closed' across the file.

***

It was a dull, rainy day as Kitti and I walked along Main Street towards the St Cuthbert's Way Hotel. The greyness matched our moods. Kitti had been monosyllabic all morning, and I felt like I was marching her to the gallows.

Even Barry rushing out into the street to wish us well didn't raise so much as a flicker of a smile on her face.

'Do you want me to come with you too, hun?' Barry asked. He was sporting his newest Old Joe creation; this time the huge jumper had an octopus on the front. 'I'll sort the old bag out for you.'

'Erm, thanks, Barry, but we need to do this on our own. Oh, and by the way, that octopus has far too many tentacles,' I grinned.

'Has it?' he said laughing, beginning to count, 'it's probably genetically modified. Either that or Old Joe is number-lexic.'

'It's still lush,' whispered Kitti, the longest sentence she'd strung together today.

We arrived at the hotel, and once again we were shown into the conservatory by a sour faced Elspeth. No mention of refreshments today, I noticed.

'I hope you get this sorted out quickly,' she muttered. 'That woman could make St Cuthbert swear. She's forever complaining. There's nothing wrong with chef's scones, nothing. They're far superior to those powdery things you get in the café; chef follows Mary Berry, you know.'

I didn't know, and I didn't care, but as much as I wanted to put her straight on Aurora's gorgeous bakes, today wasn't the day.

We walked into the conservatory, Kitti hiding behind me like I was a shield. Gloria looked up.

'Come on then, maid, let me have a look at you,' she said, without a trace of warmth in her voice.

She looked Kitti up and down like she was a prize specimen at Crufts.

'You're blonde. Dyed I expect? Us Penalunas are dark haired. If it wasn't for the hair and those blue eyes, you'd look just like your great grandma Demelza. She was tall like you. That's who you should have been named after, not some bird.'

'My name's Kitti, and my hair is natural,' said a tiny voice.

'From the father's side, no doubt,' said Gloria with a scowl on her face that would turn the tide. 'Except we don't know who he was. We should have tracked him down and made him face up to his maintenance responsibilities.'

I had vowed not to speak, to let Kitti and Gloria find their feet without me butting in, but it was so difficult and virtually killing me to keep quiet. I was nearly biting my tongue in two. The woman was odious, and far from wishing they had found Kitti's dad for support, her only concern was that he should have been made to pay financially, which at sixteen would have been fruitless.

'You should have faced up to *your* responsibilities,' said Kitti, her voice getting stronger. 'You put my mam out without any money and then disappeared.'

'Your mother disobeyed us by coming to this island and look what happened. We brought her up to be God-fearing, but the minute she goes off on her own she's having sex with boys and...'

'I heard that you went off with the vicar, and he was married. How was that God-fearing?' Kitti interrupted, now at nearly full volume.

'Do not speak to your elders and betters like that. I can see that Loveday wasn't very firm with you. Still, there's time to learn yet.'

'Mam preferred to be called Daisy.'

'Pah,' hissed Gloria. 'She was a Penaluna. Loveday was her God-given name.'

I couldn't hold back any longer, feeling I needed to try and steer things on a more even keel.

'So, Gloria, perhaps you'd like to ask Kitti about her interests? She's doing some amazing things online.'

'Online? That's the Devil's breeding ground, and you already told me she wants to be a vet. I don't hold with women doing jobs like that. Once she comes to Cornwall, I'm sure she'll give up on that nonsense and eventually settle down with a good Cornish husband who will provide. Just like the reverend did for me.'

'When did you marry *the reverend*?' asked Kitti pointedly. 'You haven't got his name.'

Gloria glowered at her.

'That pitiful excuse of a wife he was forced to marry by his parents wouldn't give him a divorce. Said it was a sin, so we weren't able to get married, but we loved each other right up until the end.' Gloria dabbed her eyes with a tissue, but there wasn't a hint of tears, and I just didn't believe the narrative.

'I don't want to come to Cornwall,' said Kitti bluntly.

'You're sixteen. Until you're eighteen you need someone to guide you, and I'm your next of kin.'

'I don't have to live with you, though. I can make my own choice at sixteen.'

'You sound wilful, just like your mother. Where else are you going to live, and how will you be able to afford it? I'll no doubt be given control of your finances until you reach eighteen. Anyway, you'll love Cornwall. You're a Penaluna; it's in your blood.'

'I won't,' said Kitti. 'I like it here.'

'This is only temporary,' responded Gloria. 'The social worker told me that. I gather that her,' she pointed her finger at me, 'and him with the funny name, you know, Meg Shafto's grandson with the hair that could do with a good cut, are only giving you a place to live for a couple of months. They're not responsible for you. You can't stay here indefinitely.'

Tears began to trickle down Kitti's cheeks, splashing onto the new sweatshirt Meg had bought her.

'You'll be coming to Cornwall, maid; the courts will see to that. It's just a matter of time.'

'I won't,' shouted Kitti, suddenly popping with rage. 'How can a person like you be my lovely mam's mam? We were better off without you. She never once said anything bad about you because she was a kind person, so I'm going to say it for her now – you're a bitch, and I don't ever want to see you again. I'd rather live on the streets than live with you.'

And at that, Kitti bolted for the door and ran out of the hotel.

'Is that your doing?' glared Gloria. 'Have you been filling her head with nonsense?'

I ignored her question. 'I don't think there's anything left to say.' I got up and headed for the door.

'I'll be speaking to Mrs Monser as soon as I can and then instructing my solicitor to start whatever process is necessary to ensure Kitti comes back to Cornwall with me. She might be a flighty little thing at present, but we'll soon sort that out.'

I followed in Kitti's footsteps and hurried out of that door as fast as my legs would take me, otherwise I might be spending the next few years detained at his Majesty's pleasure, because that woman tested every ounce of restraint I possessed.

Chapter 54

I ran down Main Street like I was being pursued by a clan of raging Vikings then jumped up the stairs two at a time and burst into the attic.

'Kitti! Kitti, are you here?'

There was no reply, so I opened her bedroom door. The little room was empty. I ran down to Aurora's flat.

'Aurora, have you heard Kitti come back?'

'No. I can see from the look on your face that it didn't go so well?'

'It absolutely did not, but I need to find Kitti,' I said, exasperated.

'Ellie, you're worrying me. Where is she? Why do you need to find her? Is she okay?'

'Seriously, I don't know. She bolted out of the hotel upset. I just need to find her.'

I dashed across to the roastery.

'Hey,' began Zen until he saw the look on my face. 'What's happened?'

'No time – it was terrible. Gloria was worse than awful, and Kitti ran off, and she's not here. I need to find her.'

'I'll come with you,' he said, pulling off his overalls. 'I knew I should have been with you today, but Kitti was insistent that it would be better just you and her.'

'I wondered why she said that, but then I got to thinking, there was always just her and her mam so maybe she was more comfortable with that sort of arrangement. I know it's not because that she doesn't want you around, Zen; she's told me how much she likes you.'

'That's good, and I was cool with her choosing to meet without me being there. Anyway, what did the old witch say?'

'Not now, Zen. We've got to find her.'

'Right, you ring Meg and Bert, and I'll do the Holiday House. Between us we'll find her – don't worry.'

We set off, phones clamped to our ears, but no one had seen her.

'I'll go down and check the shelters,' said Bert. 'Meg's going to go around the yard.'

'Put it on the island chat, Zen, please.'

'Isn't that a little premature? Kitti would hate people knowing her business.'

'Yes, you're right, but if we haven't found her soon then she'll have to forgive us because I don't want her on her own.'

Barry came running out of Love Lindisfarne as we were passing.

'What's going on? I saw you belting down the street before, like the hounds of hell were after you. Where's Kitti?' I briefly explained, and Barry began to lock the door of the shop. 'I'm coming to look too.'

'Barry, you can't. You might lose business, and you're just getting going,' I said.

'Kitti is more important. Look, I'll stick a note on the door offering free sparkles or something if they come back.'

The three of us were about to set off when Aurora, pushing baby Hettie in her stroller, came out of the café, and Jake and Sophie came down the street from the Holiday House.

'You two do the village and the shops and pub,' said Zen to Aurora and Sophie. Barry, can you and Jake go along to the far side of the island and check the sandy beaches. She likes going there. She can't have got off the island because the tide is in, thankfully. Can you also go and check the oyster farm, I don't think she would have gone there, but you never know. She likes Maurice.'

'It would be quicker to put it on island chat, bro,' said Aurora.

'Just half an hour, and then we will. Let's just try and find her first – she can't have got far.'

'Ellie, let's you and me go down to the harbour and along the beach in front of the castle. She sometimes goes down there to look for seals.'

Zen and I virtually ran to the harbour. The weather hadn't improved all day. It was still grey and miserable and felt even more so, considering the sombre mood. There was no sign of Kitti.

'That's odd,' said Zen scanning the boats that were anchored to the harbour wall. 'The *Lady Eleanor* isn't there.'

I looked at Zen, my stomach doing somersaults an Olympic athlete would be proud of.

'You don't think Kitti...' I began.

'No, of course not. It's just odd that she's not in her usual place.'

'Kitti might have decided to go and be with the birds. She's been over there with you a few times; she might think she could sail herself across. Ring your dad now,' I screeched.

'Ellie, he would have rung me immediately if she had turned up on Greater Reef.'

'What if she's tried to get to one of the uninhabited islands?' I exclaimed, my imagination running on fast forward. 'What if she's capsized? Would she wear a life jacket?' I scanned the sea for any sign of the bright blue boat that Zen used to get back and forwards to Greater Reef, but there was nothing, other than a few birds bobbing on the waves.

I looked at Zen's face as he spoke to his dad and saw the relief that passed across his paler-than-usual features, but the coffee bean eyes were still clouded with worry. He was trying to be upbeat for me, but I could tell he was scared too.

'It's okay, Ellie. The volunteer warden went over in the *Lady Eleanor* this morning. You can breathe again now; she didn't take the boat.'

'Oh, thank God. One less thing to worry about,' I sighed.

'Where now?' I asked.

'Let's try the bench. You told her about us going there to think, didn't you?'

'Yes, I did.'

We set off to the secluded part of the island, but the bench was empty and there was no sign of Kitti.'

'Let's try the lime kilns next,' I said, starting to feel desperate. Then my phone rang. It was Meg.

'Ellie, we've found her.'

'Where is she? Is she okay?'

'She's terribly upset but managed to give me the gist of what happened. Bert found her huddled up with Puffin and Penguin. The first time he looked he hadn't checked behind the hay bales in the storage shed, then he noticed the goats were missing, so he went to check, and there they all were. She's safe and warm in the cottage, and her and I are just having a bit of a relax on the sofa until you get here.'

'We're on our way,' I said, disconnecting the call.

'Thank God,' said Zen. 'I was dreading having to tell that officious social worker we'd lost her.'

'I hope she doesn't find out. That's all we need. I've got a bad feeling about all this, Zen, and there's not a lot we can do about it.'

Chapter 55

Kitti was sandwiched between Meg and Ethel when we got to the cottage. The three of them sat in a line on the sofa like they were waiting for a bus. The two older women were watching over her like she was a fledgling chick trying to get out of the nest too soon. She held both their hands tightly, and the sight of the two kind older women, the antithesis of Gloria, filled my heart with love and my eyes with tears.

'We've had a little chat about why people are sometimes bitter,' said Meg. 'I reckon if we delved into your grand... I mean Gloria's past, then we would maybe find some explanation for her behaviour. Not that anything can justify what she's done.'

'But then sometimes people are just born wrong 'uns and will never change, and there's no reason, other than they know no different. Me da would say they just aren't wired right. Gloria was always as hard as bell metal, and even becoming a mam doesn't seem to have softened that crusty shell of hers,' said Ethel angrily.

'The older you get, Kitti, sweetheart, the more you'll learn about human nature, and it can be evil, that's for sure,' said Meg gently.

'I think I'll leave you four to it,' smiled Zen. 'That's if it's okay with you, Kitti? I'd better get back to work.'

Kitti nodded and gave a brief smile.

I sat down in Bert's chair and wondered what on earth I was going to say that would help the situation, but before I uttered a word, Kitti began to speak.

'She's right, though, isn't she? None of you on the island can really help me. It's social services and the court who are going to decide. I get that I can't be forced to go to Cornwall, but I might not have a choice if I don't have any money of my own, and she seems determined to get her hands on that.'

'We might not have any sway,' said Ethel, 'but we can get you a solicitor. I'll pay, and before I hear a word come out of your lips, Meg Shafto, I am telling you now, if I want to cover the costs of that I will.'

'You won't get any argument from me, Ethel – not this time.'

'Let's look into that before we make any decisions,' I said. 'Kitti, what we can all promise you is that we will do whatever we can. It may not be enough, but it's not going to stop us trying.'

'Do you fancy going down and seeing Puffin and Penguin?' Meg asked gently. 'You've disrupted their routine taking them into the storage shed – better make sure they're okay.'

'Yes, I'll do that,' said Kitti, letting go of their hands and getting up. 'It'll give me time to think, but thank you. I don't know what I would have done without you all. I'll never ever forget you, or the island, or the animals, no matter where I end up.'

She wiped her sleeve across her eyes and went out into the yard.

'Poor bairn,' said Meg once she had gone. 'My heart is breaking for her.'

'I'd like to go and break Gloria's jaw,' growled Ethel. 'I should have done when I was younger. Shutting that woman up permanently would give me great pleasure.'

'Now, Ethel, we don't resort to violence. We left that behind with the Vikings, but I get what you mean,' nodded Meg. 'It's tempting. I nearly flattened her myself at Mini Fest...'

'Ellie, when you get home, start having a look at finding Kitti a solicitor who deals with this kind of thing, and see how much it might cost. We'll find the money somehow, if need be,' said Meg.

'I've already told you; I'll cover it. I'm worth a few bob, you know. The Fishes were always good at money management, long before that Martin fella came on the telly to help us with our finances. Us Fishes might not always have been, erm, on the right side of the law, especially our Ezra, me da's brother who was the slipperiest Fish of all, but a plentiful supply of fresh fish and bootleg whisky to PC McHue, the island bobby, and all was good. Anyway, like I've already said, it's left me more than comfortable and able to pay for this, so I'm going to, end of subject. I don't want to hear another word.'

'Okay, I'll get on to it. Maybe she'll be appointed legal representation through social services if she's contesting Gloria's interest. I'll check.'

When I got back to the attic, I was wading my way through online advice for Kitti's situation when my phone rang.

'Miss Montague, it's Mrs Monser here, Kitti's social worker.'

'Oh, hello,' I replied, immediately feeling uneasy, as she usually called me Ellie.

'I'm sorry to ring you so late, but I've had a very trying day, and I felt I needed to speak to you as a matter of urgency. I had an unexpected in person visit from Kitti's grandmother this afternoon. She was lucky to catch me in the office; I'm rarely there these days.'

'Right,' I said, dreading what was coming next.

'Mrs Penaluna left Lindisfarne as soon as she could after your meeting this morning. It sounds like it wasn't a success. Would you like to tell me how you found it?'

I explained in carefully selected words that the meeting had indeed been fraught, and that Kitti was still adamant that she didn't want to go and live with her grandmother.

'Mrs Penaluna has grave concerns that Kitti is being given false hope that she may be able to stay on Lindisfarne.'

'Absolutely not. We're so careful never to promise anything that might not be possible.'

'Mrs Penaluna feels that you and others living on the island are all conspiring to paint her in a bad light to

Kitti, and it's clouding Kitti's ability to make informed decisions.'

'Again, absolutely not,' I said, hearing my voice raise a couple of octaves.

'I must take what Mrs Penaluna says seriously, Miss Montague. As you are aware, Kitti is in our care for now, and it is my duty to ensure her safety. When a close family member steps forward and offers a longer-term solution to providing a home environment, quite frankly we dance for joy because that is always our preferred choice.'

'Even when the person has never met that family member, and there's a history of the abandonment of Kitti's mother?'

'Even then. We have no proof of what the relationship between Kitti's mother and Mrs Penaluna was like. Mrs Penaluna tells a quite different story.'

I bet she did.

'Naturally, we'll have social services in Cornwall do the necessary checks on Mrs Penaluna, but if she's found to be suitable, then in the best interests of Kitti we would recommend her to the family courts to take over Kitti's guardianship from us.'

'And Kitti doesn't get a say in the matter?'

'Yes, of course she does, but we look at the situation as a whole and consider what's best for Kitti until she turns eighteen, and believe you me, the alternatives aren't too great.'

There was a silence as I digested this information. But Mrs Monser was far from done.

'In light of what I heard today, I tend to agree with Mrs Penaluna that perhaps Lindisfarne is not the right environment for Kitti at present, and I have decided that she should come back to Tyneside as soon as I can find a placement for her. Mrs Penaluna is going to stay in Newcastle while this is sorted out. Unfortunately, because it's earlier than envisaged, she can't return to Sue and Billy, as they have taken in an emergency placement. I may have to seek a residential care placement or even look outside of our area.'

'You what? I yelled, unable to stop myself. 'You're telling me that you'll remove Kitti from a place where she's thriving and happy, and take her God knows where until you can go through the courts to place her with a grandmother she despises?'

'Miss Montague, I can hear the frustration in your voice, and I would remind you I am not the bad guy here. I have a huge caseload, with clients in far worse situations than Kitti, without any family at all. I work upwards of sixty hours a week and hardly see my own kids at times. I strive to do what I can in the best interests of each individual child or young adult on my caseload, but there's only so much of me to go around. Your angry response is only confirming to me that you have become too close, too invested, and that isn't fair on either you, or Kitti. You and Mr Chambers were merely giving Kitti a roof over her head, no more, no less.'

I could feel my blood pressure just about hitting the attic roof.

'And when is this likely to happen?' I asked, trying to calm my voice down.

'As soon as I've found a placement, but it won't be overnight, that's for sure. I should imagine it'll be by the weekend. I'll let you know.'

'And who breaks the news about this to Kitti?' I asked.

'I thought that might be best coming from you,' said Mrs Monser, a steely tone to her voice.

And there it was. Mrs Monser, the person who allegedly did everything she could for her caseload, might be overloaded with a stressful job, but she was still very good at passing the buck when situations got difficult. I was about to say to her that perhaps I was too close to impart this information, but then let Kitti hear it from her? Never.

'We won't tell Kitti until you let me know when she has to go. We'll make sure her last few days on the island are happy ones, and they won't be if she knows she's leaving.'

The only upside to this dreadful situation, as I saw it, was that the wicked witch Gloria had gone.

I hung up and took a deep breath, my hands shaking with the adrenalin coursing through my veins like a raging river. Even if we found a solicitor to help with any court proceedings, there was absolutely nothing any of us could do to stop Kitti having to go back to Newcastle sooner than expected. She was in the legal care of the social services for now, and that was that. I jumped up and ran down to the roastery. I needed Zen, my fiancé. Not that he even felt like that considering the ring was still hidden down my top, but I just needed a hug and some reassurance that everything was going to be okay, even though I knew deep down that it really, really wasn't.

Chapter 56

Zen and I made the decision not to tell a soul about Kitti having to leave early. That way we could be assured that she wouldn't find out by slip of the tongue, and everyone would just act normally around her. We did tell her that Gloria had gone, and it was like all the darkness that had seeped into her soul over the last few days had lifted immediately, and the sun had come out again. Kitti started enjoying life on Lindisfarne once more, darting between her job and the animals, she and Barry laughing like drains while they worked together on the content for *Castle Capers*. She still asked about what was going to happen longer term in relation to Gloria, but I told her Mrs Monser was busy, and that she was going to get in touch soon – no lies there – and Kitti seemed happy with that.

Meanwhile, I was breaking inside and finding it difficult to hold it together. The weight of knowing we had to tell Kitti she was going back to Newcastle was dragging me down. Zen was amazing. We kept sneaking off for walks around the island and to our bench, just drinking in the beauty around us, hoping it would work its magic, but even the sight of a school of bottlenose dolphins having a rare old time in the bay did little to lift our moods.

'I almost wish it was time to tell her, Zen. I know that sounds crazy because it would mean she has to go, but I can't bear the thought of breaking her all over again, and this will. We don't even know where they're going to put her. Imagine if it's a residential place full of druggies and kids with criminal backgrounds.'

'Ellie, stop it. You're torturing yourself. She might end up in a lovely foster home, yet.'

'She might not, as well.' I stood up. 'Right, she's over at the cottage, so I think I'll have a walk over there and see what she's up to.'

My phone rang, and a quick glance told me it was Mrs Monser. I sat back down and handed it to Zen. 'You speak to her, please. I don't think I can.'

I tried to focus on the now retreating dolphins who were heading back out into the North Sea, not a care in the world, wishing I was with them.

'Well?' I asked, as he handed me back the phone.

'Sunday at ten thirty. The woman was at pains to tell me it's her day off, but she'll "make an exception" and come and collect her. They've found her a placement in Low Fell, which is in Gateshead. It's not a residential home, Ellie; it's registered foster carers.'

'Thank God for small mercies,' I said. 'It's Friday today, so that means we tell her tomorrow. We can't leave it right up to the last minute. She might want to say goodbye to everyone, although she might choose not to, depending on what kind of state she's in.'

'Let's not second guess. We'll tell her tomorrow afternoon.' He took my hand in his. 'We tell her together, and we go from there; she dictates who she wants to see before she goes and things like that. We're just there to support her.'

'Do you think we'll ever get to see her again?'

'Of course, and I really mean that. As soon as Kitti can, I know she'll come back to the island and see us. I hope so, anyway.' He took my face between his hands and looked into my eyes.

'I adore you, wife to be. I'm sorry our engagement didn't turn out as planned, but I've also enjoyed just you and me knowing until the others found out. We'll get something sorted for a celebration soon, I promise. I'm going to miss Kitti too. I know I initially voiced some concerns, but it's been great having her to stay. We must try and think of our future too, though. I don't want a long engagement, so we have a wedding to plan,' he smiled.

'We can invite Kitti up for that,' I said, cheering up at the thought. 'I can't quite believe the inner circle have all managed to keep our secret.'

'Me too,' he laughed, 'especially big gob Tara. Right, come on. I'll go and see Bert in the paddocks, and you have a cup of tea with Meg.'

'They're going to be devastated about Kitti too. I hope we're doing the right thing keeping it from them.'

'We are,' he said, kissing me. 'We're saving them from the days of anxiety that we've had to endure. That has to be the right thing.'

'I love you, husband to be. I want to marry you as soon as I can.'

'Me too, Ellie. I'd do it tomorrow, if I could.'

***

The next morning came far too quickly. I woke up early, light streaming through the Velux window.

'You awake?' I whispered to Zen.

'Hardly slept a wink,' he whispered back. 'What's the plan?'

'I haven't really got one, except let her have her last morning doing what she loves. I know she's going over to the paddocks with Barry to film some content. Apparently, they reckon they've got Haggis, Neeps and Tatties to sing together as Barry's backing band.'

'Wonder what song they can sing?' Zen laughed.

'Oh, I can tell you that. It's a parody of the Proclaimers song, which just sticks in your head the minute you hear it. 'I would moo five hundred moos, and I would moo five hundred more, just to be the coo that mooed a thousand moos, to be who you adore.'

'Nah, na, na, na...' continued Zen, between belly laughs. 'That has got viral written all over it.'

'And even better, Barry has borrowed a kilt from somewhere. It's daft things like that, and her love of the animals, which have given Kitti some space from missing her mam. That's what bloody hurts the most – that she'll be right back at square one.'

Zen got up. 'I'll go and put the kettle on. Let's make a flask up and go down to the bench – watch the sunrise and see if we can spot the orcas. I was amazed when Dad told me that he'd seen a pod of them off the far Reef islands.'

There was no sign of the whales today, but as we watched, the sun came up, rising out of the horizon like a giant, glowing tangerine, and we were entertained by grey seals hauling their blubbery, wobbly bodies along the shore towards the sea for their swim across to Greater Reef, honking at each other as they went. The morning birds were circling above us, creating a joyous melody, and I tried to relax and let the natural beauty of the island wash over me like a balm. Taking a breath, I thanked the universe for all it gave us, then asked whether it could see its way clear to providing us with a miracle.

'Okay,' I said to Zen, as we walked back. 'I'll go over to the paddocks at lunchtime and think of some pretext to bring her back to the attic. You can meet us there and...' I couldn't finish the sentence. Zen squeezed my hand. He knew exactly what I was trying to say without the need of any words.

Chapter 57

I walked across the castle yard at lunchtime, feeling like a condemned woman. I was heading to give Kitti a shout at the five-bar gate, where I'd give her some spurious reason as to why we had to get back to the attic, which I so far hadn't thought of. Hopefully, the perfect excuse would just pop into my head.

'Well, if it isn't my favourite elf,' said a familiar voice.

I swung around, and there was Aidan Bamburgh: six aristocratic foot of hot, blond, Viking heritage, nicely tanned from his job of partying on the world's best beaches. He threw his arms around me and gave me a hug.

'How goes it, Ellie Elf? You're still as gorgeous as ever,' he grinned.

'What are you doing here?' I tried to smile, but it didn't quite reach my eyes. I wasn't feeling in a particularly smiley mood.

'You don't look too pleased to see me. Have I done something to offend you?' he asked, studying my face.

'Oh, sorry, Aidan. I am pleased, truly – just lost in my own thoughts. Got a lot going on at the moment. Anyway, what brings you here?'

'It's Papa's big birthday tomorrow. We're having a big party tonight.'

'Of course. Inigo mentioned it.'

'I'm here to collect my dear cousin to take him over to Bamburgh for a couple of days. It'll be great catching up with Ini. He's had a tough time lately.'

He's not the only one, I thought.

'Is Beth with you?'

'Sadly not. We get so little time off these days that when this week became free, she decided to go back to see her parents in Brazil.'

'Must be difficult being in such demand,' I half laughed.

'That's better. Where's my sunny Ellie disappeared to? You and Chambers haven't had a bust up, have you?'

'No! Of course not, in fact...' I started, then stopped before I blurted out about our engagement.

'Has he had a haircut yet?' he smiled, then his jaw dropped.

I had my back to the gate and watched as Aidan stared, open mouthed, as footsteps approached from behind me.

'Oh, my God. I thought for a moment that was my sister, Violet, when she was about sixteen. She's the ab-solute double.'

I swung round to see Kitti, who came and stood with us.

'You look just like my sister used to at about your age. It's uncanny.' Aidan laughed.

'Aidan, this is Kitti.' I struggled to get the words out. 'She's staying with us for a little while.'

'You're him off that beach programme on the telly. You're, like, really famous,' she grinned, looking at Aidan in awe. 'That must be such a cool thing to do.'

'It is,' he chuckled. 'Anyway, Ellie Elf, got to get on. Let's all meet up in the Crab for a drink before I head off. I'm here for a while. Nice to meet you, Kitti.'

I was speechless. I looked from Aidan to Kitti. No way. It couldn't be. But there was no mistaking the same colour of blonde hair and those bright Bamburgh blue eyes peeping out at each other. Oh, my God.

'Ellie, are you sure you're okay?' Aidan asked again.

'Yes,' I garbled. 'At least I think so, although I don't know, but probably...' I tailed off.

As they both stared at me gabbling, their faces held exactly the same expression, their raised eyebrows a mirror image of each other. I felt quite lightheaded.

'I'll be in touch, Aidan,' I managed to say, in a voice that sounded like I was being strangled, as he turned towards the castle.

'Why have we got to go back to the attic?' demanded Kitti, breaking into my thoughts. 'I'm in the middle of the best bit of video we've ever done.'

'You go back and finish it, Kitti. Never mind, the other thing can wait.' And she skipped off back towards the gate, leaving me reeling.

I immediately got my phone out of my pocket and messaged Aidan.

Meet me down at the lime kilns in ten minutes. It's urgent.

He replied instantly.

You've eventually decided I was the one you wanted all the time, haven't you? Followed by several smiley face emojis.

No jokes, Aidan. Just be there, and don't even tell Inigo.

Sounds serious. Are you sure you're okay? Anyway, see you soon x

I then sent Zen a message.

Got held up. I'll message you when we're on our way. Love you x

There seemed no point at this stage in telling Zen of my theory. I'd find out soon enough if truth was stranger than fiction.

I was nervously pacing about the cold, damp arched lime kiln when Aidan appeared.

'This is like déjà vu, Ellie. Remember the last time we met in here?'

'I do,' I replied, and I seem to recall it was for a very serious matter then, as is what I need to talk to you about now, and I needed to make sure that no one overhears us.'

He took off his jacket and spread it on the ground like last time, and we sat side by side with only a hint of a space between us.

'Okay,' he said, 'I'm all ears. I know I can be all bluster and bravado, but I'm actually quite worried about what on earth made you bring me here. You're acting very strange.'

'Aidan, cast your mind back to being about sixteen...'

'Sixteen? That's half a lifetime ago. I can hardly recall what happened last week, I move around so much.'

'Well, just try, please. Can you remember being on the island during the summer and meeting a girl called Loveday?'

'Loveday? Interesting name. No, it's a long time ago, but I think I'd remember that.'

Then it dawned on me – she would never have introduced herself as Loveday.

'What about a Daisy?'

His face completely softened, his eyes taking on a faraway look, like when you suddenly remember a time in your life that had imprinted itself on your brain. This was something he obviously hadn't forgotten.

'Daisy? Yes, why? Don't tell me she's on the island and you've met her? A lot of time has passed, and things have moved on, but I'd love to see her again...'

'I'm really sorry, Aidan. She's no longer with us. She died in a road traffic accident fairly recently.'

His face fell. 'Oh, no. I can't believe it. I've thought about her over the years and wondered what happened to her. I had her down as an ornithologist with an incredibly lucky husband and a couple of kids. Why did you need to bring me here to tell me about this, Ellie? And actually, how do you know about it?'

'I'll tell you that in a minute, but first, you tell me about Daisy.'

'I was sixteen, staying with Uncle James and Aunt Grace for the summer holidays when I got back from Eton. Ma and Pa were off on some adventures. Us kids were farmed out, and I drew the lucky straw to come here. There was an environmental study at the outward bound centre with loads of kids from Newcastle. Those studies happened all the time, which was one of the main reasons I wanted to come and stay on the island, because you got to meet girls.'

'Typical Aidan,' I smiled.

'I seem to remember Chambers quite liking the summer camps too, although can't recall much of him on this occasion. Anyway, I met Daisy. I was smitten from the off. Unbelievably, I hadn't had much contact with girls on any meaningful level until then – being at an all-boys school didn't help – so when Daisy breezed into my life I was mesmerised.'

'I can imagine,' I smiled.

'She was so vibrant, clever and not to mention absolutely stunning. Even though we were only together briefly, time back then seemed elastic – it lasted a lot longer than it does these days. She was kind of my first love, Ellie.' I swear his tanned face took on a rosy glow.

'So, how come you didn't see her again?'

'How do you know that?'

'I'll tell all in a minute, I promise.'

'No matter,' he continued. 'At the end of the week she had to go home. I wanted to ask her to come back and stay at the castle. She was from Newcastle, so it wasn't that far, but I hadn't told her about my background. Daisy was not the type of person to be impressed by castles and money. She was more about the environment and saving the planet, and I didn't want her to think I was just some rich kid. All she knew about me was that I'd come here from down south and was on holiday with family, all of which was true.'

'You really liked her, didn't you?'

'I did, Ellie. I think I did fall in love with her, even though we were just kids. I gave her my phone number and thought we could meet up in Newcastle. I expected her to call me, but she never did. I was gutted.'

'Did you not try to find her?'

'I had no idea how to. I did think about trying to ring the school, but it was summer holidays. Plus, I'll level with you – I thought I had been dumped, and at sixteen and besotted with someone for the first time, that kind of rocks the confidence a tad. I forced myself to accept it wasn't meant to be anything other than a holiday romance, even though it hurt like hell, and I had really wanted to see her again.'

'That's so sad,' I said. 'I wonder what would have happened if you had met again?'

'Who knows, Ellie, and now I'll never find out. Now then, please tell me where this is all coming from? It was the last thing I expected that you wanted to talk to me about.'

I sat quietly, staring at the assured man in front of me. The last time we had met in the lime kiln he had broken down in tears, and I hoped that there wasn't going to be a repeat when I dropped the bombshell.

'Ellie, you've gone all quiet on me.'

'Sorry, just thinking. Aidan, you know Kitti that you met earlier...'

'Yes, she did look like my sister Violet at that age. Bizarre, eh?'

'Well maybe not as bizarre as you might think. She's Daisy's daughter, and she's sixteen years old.'

I sat back and looked at his face. I could almost see the cogs turning around in his brain, a look of sheer bewilderment crossing his handsome face, the blue eyes wide with information overload.

'I think Kitti might be your daughter, Aidan.'

Chapter 58

It felt like we sat in silence for ages, but in reality maybe only a few minutes.

'My daughter?' he murmured, clearly shell-shocked. 'I think it's your turn to tell me everything now.'

I explained as much as I knew, telling him that the story he had just told me matched the one told by Kitti.

'The only difference is that Kitti thought her father was called Adam.'

'Adam, Aidan... maybe just lost in translation over the years,' he mused.

When I told him how I had met Kitti, and what had been happening to her since her mam passed away, his eyes filled with tears, which quickly turned to anger when I told him about the way Gloria had treated Daisy when she was pregnant, and that now she was back for Kitti. He went silent again, digesting the mountain of information I had just given him.

'Ellie, after seeing Kitti, I have no doubt whatsoever that she is my daughter. Oh, my God, I cannot believe I am saying those words out loud. *My daughter*. What the hell do I do now?'

'You need to go away and take all of this in, and talk to your family – and Beth, of course. This is huge, Aidan. Life changing.'

'And Kitti, what are you going to tell her?'

'Nothing. It would be irresponsible to say anything at all until you have had time to think this through. Besides which, she's being taken from us in the morning and being sent to live with foster carers in Gateshead until her grandmother can apply to become her guardian.'

Aidan's eyes just about popped out of his head and landed in my lap.

'And what does Kitti think about that?'

'She doesn't know yet. Zen and I were about to tell her this afternoon. We think it's all about money, Aidan. That, and Gloria wanting a live-in carer, but Kitti doesn't want to go anywhere near that poisonous witch.'

'And where is this Gloria woman now?'

'In Newcastle.'

'Do you know where?'

I gave him the name of the hotel Mrs Monser had mentioned.

'And you are absolutely certain that Kitti doesn't want anything to do with her grandmother?'

'I couldn't be more certain of anything else in my life,' I said bluntly.

He jumped up, held out his hand and pulled me onto my feet.

'Right, I'm off to see a woman about *my daughter*. Maybe I can't do much at this stage, but I can make sure that Kitti never has to see that woman again if she doesn't want to. I cannot believe what she did to Daisy when she was pregnant. The woman sounds evil.'

'She is, but how are you proposing to stop her?'

'Simple, Ellie. I'll eat that Viking hat of yours if me offering sixteen years' worth of back maintenance payments, plus interest, doesn't make her scarper back to Cornwall quicker than a starving mouse devouring a Cornish pasty. And I'll make sure she renounces all interest over Kitti as part of the deal. If there's one thing I have at my disposal, it's money. Along with top lawyers who will answer my call, even on a Saturday.'

'Are you sure about this, Aidan. It's not just a knee jerk reaction?'

'I'm certain. If this turns out to be the only thing I ever do for Kitti, at least it will be something positive. I know I need time to absorb all this, as it has come as one hell of a shock, but Kitti hasn't got much time, and I don't want her to have to go back into the care system. That's utterly barmy when she's happy here. She is, right?'

'As happy as she can be, Aidan, but she still might have to go back to Tyneside. She's in the legal care of the social services, and I'm not sure you can pay them off so easily.'

'I hear you, Ellie, but one step at a time. Just you leave the granny to me. Can you let Inigo know he'll have to make his own way over to Bamburgh because I need to attend to something urgently? Without telling him what, of course.'

'Sure. I'll take him over myself. Don't worry. Other than Zen, absolutely no one will hear about any of this. You have my word. And Aidan, for what it's worth, I think that you'll do right by Kitti when you get over the shock.'

He nodded, smiled and virtually ran out of the lime kiln towards the castle and his car.

***

'I can hardly take any of this in,' said Zen, when I relayed my shocking revelation. 'Are you sure?'

'As much as I can be. Honestly, Zen, when I saw them side by side, they're like two peas in a pod. Kitti has the Bamburgh genes, I'm almost certain of that.'

'Where is she now?' he asked.

'She's staying over at the cottage tonight. Meg is making her and Barry tea, and I suggested she stayed. You know how much she loves it there.'

'So, we're not telling her anything about tomorrow?'

'Not a word until I hear back from Aidan.' I checked my phone for the hundredth time.

'It's been hours now, and we haven't heard a squeak. You don't think he's done something stupid do you?'

'What, like kidnap Gloria and take her back to Cornwall?' He half laughed. 'No, of course not. Something like this might take time.'

'He needs to be back at Bamburgh by tonight. It's his dad's big birthday bash.'

I paced around the attic, wearing out the carpet. Picking things up, putting them down, turning the television on and turning it off again.

'Ellie, you're making me nervous. Come and sit next to me.'

But before I could, my phone rang.

'Thank god,' I exclaimed, but a brief glance at the screen told me it was Mrs Monser, not Aidan.

'It's the social worker,' I mouthed at Zen as I put it on speaker so he could hear. 'Hello?'

'Ellie.'

Good start, she was back to calling me by my name instead of Miss Montague.

'Calling me on a Saturday at this time, is everything okay?' I asked, feigning surprise.

'I'm not quite sure if okay is the way to describe it, but I've just had the most bizarre conversation with Mrs Penaluna,' she exclaimed.

'Oh, right,' I muttered.

'Well, the thing is, she no longer wishes to apply for guardianship. In fact, she's decided that she wants no further contact with Kitti at all.'

'None?' I squeaked.

'None,' she confirmed. 'She's catching the first train back to Cornwall in the morning. I don't mind telling you that I am very confused and a little angry that she has abandoned Kitti in this way, but despite me putting pressure on her, she was adamant that she was going.'

'She must have her reasons, I suppose.'

'Well, whatever they are, I'm not party to them. Do you know of any changes that might have contributed to her change of heart?'

'Erm, no,' I replied, keeping my fingers crossed. 'She did strike me as someone not to be trusted; I told you that.'

'Well, whatever. I'm ringing to say that now there would appear to be no reason for Kitti to leave Lindisfarne. Would it be okay for her to remain with you for the full duration we initially agreed, that's up until the end of the summer holidays?'

'Yes, that would be fine,' I said, trying to keep my voice steady and not give the game away.

'That way we will save on the expenses of the new foster carers, and I might actually be able to have a day off tomorrow, instead of traipsing up to the island.'

Mrs Monser remained true to character to the end, but I didn't care that she was putting funding and her time over Kitti. Whatever Aidan had managed to do, it had worked, and something told me that Kitti would never be returning to the care of the social services.

'That's the best news, Ellie,' said Zen. 'Say what you will about Aidan, but when he knows what he wants, he tends to get it.'

Just at that a message pinged through from the man himself.

Sorry, mad dash back to Papa's birthday party. Mission accomplished. What a horrible woman. She's cold and calculating, and I think I'd have taken drastic action rather than see K go and live with that battleaxe, but as expected, she took her pot of gold and is going back to Cornwall in the morning. Will come and see you soon for a proper talk. I'm still reeling from all of this, but tonight isn't the time to break the news to anyone. It really would be a birthday Papa wouldn't forget in a hurry, so mum's (or should that be dad's) the word for now x

I read it out to Zen while wrapping my arms around him, feeling all the anxiety we'd gone through for the past few days ebb away.

'Let's celebrate the best way I know,' I smiled. 'Kitti is out, Nacho is with her, so we're on our own for once. Come on, fiancé – let's go and make some hay, because the sun is definitely shining.'

'No can do,' he replied.

'Sorry, what? You're rejecting my very sexy offer?'

'I am. Well, at least temporarily. You and I are going to sit here and plan our engagement celebration.'

He unbuttoned the top buttons of my shirt, but rather than that leading to the bedroom, he merely took out my engagement ring.

'This needs to be on your finger, not hidden away. Gloria has gone, so Kitti will be okay until the next bombshell about Aidan hits, but I have a feeling that's going to work out just fine.'

He unhooked the ring from the chain, put it on my finger and kissed me.

'Right, where are we going to hold the biggest celebration party this island has seen since... well, since Mini Fest? Now then, do you think the village hall or the Crab? The beach? The castle, if we can swing it? Music? Food...

Chapter 59

We slept late the next morning. It was a rare day off for us both, and we hadn't made any plans, thinking that it was the day that we were about to say goodbye to Kitti.

'What shall we do today, fiancé? I asked, as Zen turned over to go back to sleep.

'I'm so tired, Ellie. The last few weeks have really caught up with me, so let's just have another hour. Then go down to the café for brunch and later catch up on that Netflix series that we started ages ago.'

'Fab, a duvet day. Suits me,' I said, snuggling back down beside him.

My phone pinged.

'It's Kitti – says she's staying over at the cottage today and that she'll see us this afternoon.'

'Even better,' murmured Zen, faint snores beginning to emerge.

When we went down to the café later that morning we stuck our heads in Aurora's flat, but there was no one home. The reason became apparent as we passed the café kitchen.

'Aurora, what are you doing working today?'

'Erm, rush on.'

The kitchen was buzzing, the smell of home bakes making me so hungry.

'Muriel,' I exclaimed, as I spotted her in her flour covered pinny. 'Are you a new member of the team?'

'Just lending a hand, dear. All hands to the pump for an important occasion.'

'So, what is the important occasion, Aurora?' asked Zen.

'Er, Lord B's birthday tea,' replied Aurora.

'Has he given his own staff the day off?' I laughed.

'Something like that. Now if you two don't mind, you're clogging up my kitchen, so if you go through, Pip will sort you out.'

'She's up to something,' said Zen, smiling as we took our seats.

'Don't be daft – it makes sense. She wouldn't turn an order from Bamburgh Castle down. What do you fancy? I'm going to go for the pancakes with fruit.'

'Sounds good to me. Make that two, and a bucket of coffee.'

The day passed quietly. Too quietly. No calls from Meg, or Kitti, or Barry, who had become my most frequent caller of late. There was no sound coming from Aurora's flat below, no Hettie crying to be fed, no dragging of the buggy down the stairs.

'I enjoyed that,' said Zen, as we finished watching the last of the crime series we'd finally had the chance to catch up on.

'Okay with you if I watch *Virgin River* now?' I smiled.

'Nooooo, please noooo – I can't stand that,' Zen laughed.

'Liar. I know you secretly like it.' But before we could decide the outcome of a trip to the mountains in America, crashing footsteps came bounding up the stairs.

'Zen! Zen, you need to come now. There's a seal washed up on the shore next to the old fishing shack, and it doesn't look at all well,' shouted Kitti.

'What were you doing over there?' Zen replied.

'Walking the dogs, what else?' she muttered. 'Anyway, you're wasting time. You need to come now.'

He jumped up, grabbed his kit bag and searched for his boots. I snuggled back down under the duvet on the sofa.

'You need to come too, Ellie,' she said, dragging my comfort blanket away. 'He might need help, and I don't know what I'm doing, I haven't learned about seals yet.'

'You'll manage,' I said, pulling back the duvet.

'No, I won't,' she pulled at the duvet again, until we were virtually doing a tug of war.

'Barry's over there watching it, and he's terrified of seals,' she said dramatically.

'Is he? He seemed to like them the other week.'

'That's, er, before one tried to bite him,' she muttered.

Zen shook his head.

'Come on, Ellie. We've not had a walk today. It'll do us good to have the cobwebs blown away.'

So, reluctantly I grabbed my hoodie, pulled on my old trainers and we set off behind Kitti, who might have well of been competing in the Great North Run as she broke into a fast trot.

***

'I've always been meaning to ask, who actually owns that old fishing shack near our bench?' I asked Zen as we marched along behind Kitti.

'Ethel. It was where her family used to land the fish, but they moved into the village, and it was just left to go derelict.'

When we turned the corner at the headland, we looked down towards the shore where the fishing shack lay, with a perfect view across to Greater Reef and the castle dominating the skyline to its right. But far from seeing an injured seal and Barry keeping his beady eye on it from a distance, the cottage had been turned into a grotto, surrounded by bunting and fairy lights, with a red and white striped circus type tent taking centre stage. As we approached, a homemade banner had been erected on two makeshift poles, blowing in the breeze proclaiming, 'HAPPY ENGAGEMENT TO ZEN AND ELLIE!'

'Oh, my God,' I gasped, as I looked around and saw all our nearest and dearest gathered to celebrate with us. The music came on as we got to what would have been the garden, and a delicious smell of grilled fish was coming from a barbeque, with Maurice on the tongs.

'Surprise!' shouted Aurora, emerging from the tent. 'We thought you two were never going to get around to organising anything, so we decided we would do it for you.'

'We hope you don't mind, but we told Kitti about your engagement,' said Sophie, giving me a hug. 'Once that awful Gloria woman had left the island, it seemed a good time to celebrate, and Kitti was so excited. Besides which, Tara had already blabbed, hadn't you, big gob?'

'Sorreee, Ellie – I tried, I really did, but it slipped out at the Crafty Lindisfarners meeting, and, well, you know, there was no taking it back. We're all dying to know why the granny from hell disappeared like that, though?'

'Oh, it'll all come out in the wash.' I grinned at the three women who were my absolute best friends. 'Time for that later – we've got a celebration to enjoy. Who's in charge of the drinks?'

There was a pop of a Champagne cork and flutes were thrust into mine and Zen's hands. Bert rattled his penknife on a glass, and everyone hushed.

'When Zen first found young Ellie on the causeway and brought her to our cottage, we thought he'd found a mermaid washed up by the tide...'

'More like a drowned rat,' I grinned.

'Although Ellie hadn't a clue about the animals she came to look after, she quickly adapted to her new life on the island, even winning over Hannibal, which said everything to me, as I'd been trying to tame the little bugger for years! When our Zen and Ellie became an item, no one could have been happier than me and my Meg, and it's the icing on the cake to know they're now engaged to be married. They're both an integral part of Lindisfarne life, and I want you all to raise a glass to Ellie and Zen. May the tides wash in with glad tidings every single day of their lives.'

'To Ellie and Zen,' shouted Meg. 'I love the bally bones of you both.'

Chapter 60

The party got into full flow. Barry was singing with the band, dressed for the occasion in shorts, wellies and a huge cable-knit fishing gansey, topped off with a pink sparkly sou'wester. As he burst into the opening bars of 'Islands in the Stream' with Kitti as Dolly, I knew we were in for a fun time. Zen and I split up and made our way around the guests.

'How are the café plans coming along, partners?' I asked, interrupting Sophie and Jake smooching, a sight that filled me with joy.

'Tobes and I are on it like a car bonnet,' laughed Jake. 'Any idea what we're going to call it?'

'Well, it's mainly yours and Sophie's, so you get to decide, but keep it local, because you are locals – nearly.'

'We're back off to London in a few days,' said Sophie. 'Believe it or not, we've had several offers on the flat, so need to sort that out and begin to pack our stuff.'

'Just think, you'll be living up there in that beautiful castle,' I said, pointing at the ancient building resting in the sunshine on the top of the hill.

'I still can't quite believe it. Jake and me, choosing to live in the back of bloody beyond, even if it is in a castle. I think we've both lost our marbles!'

'I think you've actually found them, and all we need to do now is get Stan and Aleksy up here.'

'Not sure that's going to happen, but they'll be coming up for lots of holidays.'

We were joined by Toby and Tara.

'It's all worked out well, eh, Tobes? The income from the café won't be immediate, but you know it's coming, and I'm sure that will keep Sir James and the board happy. What with the other suggestions of special events thought up by the volunteers and the rental income from the guest apartment, things are looking much brighter.'

'They are, Ellie, and I can't wait to start planning my 'Unearthing the brutal truth about the Vikings' lecture.'

'That sounds riveting, darling,' smiled Tara, winking. 'I'm sure it will be a great money spinner.'

I spotted Zen talking to Aidan and Inigo, so I went across to join them.

'Ellie Elf,' smiled Aidan, 'I'm devastated. I always thought that you and me... joking, Chambers! I'm so incredibly happy for you both. You two are meant to be together – a matching pair like Meg and Bert. When you do make it up the aisle, Zen, you might consider a haircut!'

'If Zen and me are like Meg and Bert in fifty-five years' time, I'll be a very happy woman,' I smiled.

'Massive congrats from me too,' said Inigo. 'Don't let my disastrous marriage put you off.'

Aidan's eyes had never left Kitti, even when he was talking to us.

'He told me,' said Inigo.

'I had to tell someone, otherwise I was going to combust. Look at her – she's so amazing, and whilst I'm sure everyone else will see her resemblance to the Bamburghs when they find out, I can see Daisy, dancing around the sand, barefoot on the beach as she got so excited seeing the kittiwakes. She was a special person in my young life, and I'm going to do the absolute best I can for *our daughter*.' He wiped a stray tear that fell down his cheek. 'I only wish I had known sooner.'

'We watched her content on social media,' smiled Inigo. 'She's a chip off the old media block.' He nodded at Aidan. 'That video of the cows mooing along with Barry over there was priceless.'

'She's great at that but wants to be a vet,' I said.

'Ellie, I'll make sure she gets to be whatever she wants to be. I'd be delighted if that's a vet, and I know that will make Papa happy – he'll save a fortune on his bills! I just want to give her the opportunities that Daisy was deprived of by her ghastly parents.'

'So, what happens next?' asked Zen.

'I'm speaking to my lawyer tomorrow to get advice. I imagine they will instruct social services of my involvement, and their lawyers will take it up from there with mine. If they say not to talk to Kitti until the legal stuff is done, then I won't, even though I really want to start to get to know her.'

'She's a great kid,' smiled Zen. 'Ellie and I were talking and agree that she can stay with us as long as she needs to.'

'Absolutely. I'm hoping social services will decide that she can stay with us until her future is sorted out properly,' I said. 'I hope she doesn't have to go back in September.'

'I'll do everything in my power to make sure that doesn't happen. Guys, this will all be about what Kitti wants. I appreciate it's going to rock her world again, and it might take her some time to decide whether she wants to become part of the Bamburgh clan – we're a crazy bunch after all – but she gets to decide how much involvement she wants with me. It's crazy to think of myself as a full-time dad, but if that's what she chooses, then that's what she'll get, or if she just wants me in the background giving financial support, then I'll have to accept that.'

'Sounds like you've really started to think this through, Aidan,' I said.

'The other thing I've been thinking about,' Aidan replied, 'is that at some point in the future, regardless of the outcome with Kitti, I'd like to fund some kind of memorial to Daisy, here on the island. Something to do with birds. Would you help me out with that when the time's right?'

'Of course. We'd love to,' I replied.

'Sounds a fitting thing to do, Aidan,' said Inigo. 'I'm leaving for Ibiza in a few days – going to see my kids and finalise my divorce with Lucia. Then who knows what, but I'm going to bring them back over here the minute I can for a holiday and hopefully to meet their new cousin, if things all work to plan.'

Meg came across to join us, so the Kitti subject was closed for now.

'Ellie, Zen, you're both summoned. Come with me.'

We followed Meg into the tent, which had been vacated by the Crafty Lindisfarners who had arranged an extensive buffet with a stunning engagement cake, courtesy of Aurora, as the centrepiece. Aurora must have worked during the night to finish such an exquisite work of art in such a short time. The cake was in the shape of a giant coffee cup and saucer, and on the top were tiny replicas of me, Zen and Nacho, with all the other animals at the castle surrounding us. It was far too good to cut!

Ethel sat centre table, glass of hooch in front of her, Bert on one side, and Meg took her seat on the other. Aurora and Jack, both with perplexed expressions on their faces, stood in front of the older islanders.

'I feel like I'm in court,' I laughed.

'If Ethel's the judge, I fear the worst,' chuckled Aurora.

'Bert. Do the honours,' said Ethel nodding.

Bert got up, retrieved a couple of brand-new shovels with big yellow ribbons tied on them, and handed one to Aurora and Jack and the other to Zen and I.

'What's this?' I smiled.

'Your engagement present,' laughed Meg.

'And ours?' queried Aurora.

'The engagement present you never got at the time,' cackled Ethel.

'Well, erm, thanks,' said Zen. 'I'm sure it will come in very useful.'

'It's from Ethel, not us,' laughed Meg.

'Just what we always wanted,' said Aurora with a straight face.

'Right, listen up,' began Ethel. 'I've been putting my affairs in order. Zen and Aurora, you're like family to me. I've known you since you were bairns. And then you brought Jack and Ellie into our lives, and baby Hettie too.'

Meg gave the older woman's arm a squeeze and handed her a tissue, before dabbing her own eyes with another.

'Aurora, I got wind that you and Jack are thinking of moving to the mainland,' said Ethel.

'Nothing gets past Ethel Fish,' chuckled Bert.

'And quite frankly, that's not going to happen,' Ethel continued.

'Tara big gob, no doubt,' I laughed.

'This island needs young, hard-working people like you all for it to survive, so with Bert's help I've been to see my solicitor, and this is for you.' She handed Aurora an envelope.

'What is it?' asked Aurora, as she opened the envelope and scanned the document. 'Oh, my God, it's the deeds to Fisherman's Cottage in the village. But that's your house, Ethel.'

'Not for much longer. It's yours and Jack's, to do up and enjoy and give Hettie that garden you wish for her.'

Aurora and Jack looked like they were about to keel over.

'But Ethel,' Aurora squeaked when she found her voice, 'it's your home. It's been in your family for generations, and you live there.'

'Look, pet, I'm the last Fish swimming, and the cottage is far bigger than I need. It would require a lot of alterations for me to live on the ground floor, so I'm moving.'

'No,' I shouted out loud. 'You can't... sorry, Aurora and Jack, but she can't move.'

'No, Ellie, you're right. She can't move,' agreed Aurora.

'I'm not going far, pet. You tell them Bert.'

'We've been making enquiries, and Ethel is going to live in the pigsty in the back garden.'

There was a silence as we all were probably thinking of the stinky old stone building at the rear of the garden, with the Bank of Ethel under the floor.

'Some might say that a pigsty is the perfect place for me and Duchess,' Ethel grinned, 'and they'd be right.'

'We're going to have it all renovated into the perfect small annexe for Ethel,' explained Bert.

'A Granny Ethel flat,' she grinned. 'I'm going to live with Bert and Meg while the work happens, so you two can make a start on the cottage as soon as you like.'

'I don't know what to say, Ethel,' murmured Aurora.

'Nor me,' said Jack, sounding shocked, 'except thank you, from the bottom of our hearts.'

'Eeh, well, pets, you can thank me with cups of tea and cakes, seeing as we'll be neighbours, and Jack, lad, you can pop to the offy in Seahouses every now and again for me. Now then, you two,' Ethel turned her attentions to Zen and I. 'You've got more time to sort yourselves out, not having any bairns yet, so you take this.'

She handed another envelope to Zen, which he opened, a look of sheer amazement crossing over his handsome face, which went from its customary ivory pale to baby rose pink in seconds.

'No way, Ethel. We can't accept this. Ellie, these are the deeds to the fishing shack and land – where we are standing right this very minute.'

'Aye, lad, you're probably stood in your future kitchen at the moment,' laughed Bert. 'You shouldn't have any planning problems because the foundations and some of the walls are still in place. It'll be amazing when you finish it.'

'I see nice big windows over there, and an Aga there…' said Meg, waving her arms around like a wind-mill.

'Oh, my God,' I gasped. 'You mean we could be looking out at that amazing view as we have our breakfasts?'

'Yes, pet,' said Meg, 'and your dinners and teas! You both deserve it.'

Zen was just about to protest when we were interrupted by Barry Big Lad, who came running into the tent squealing, hands flapping together like crazy and his wellies making squelchy noises as he ran.

'Eeeeh, come quick and see. Free Willy and his mates are frolicking in the bay…'

We all piled out onto the beach and stared across the bay as a pod of orcas treated us to a rare, breathtaking presentation. Majestic black and white creatures, their towering dorsal fins cutting through the foamy waves like huge antennae, and a formation team of youngsters, leaping out of the ocean in a display that would put a synchronised swimming team to shame. I clutched Zen's hand.

'How absolutely stunning,' I whispered, aware that not a peep was coming out of the party goers, the music cut as everyone watched the show open mouthed.

'Not something you see that often, Ellie. Dad was right when he saw the pod way out at sea.'

'They've come to wish us a happy engagement,' I smiled.

'How about we call our firstborn Orca, if he's a boy?' Zen smiled *the* smile. 'Orca Chambers has a ring to it don't you think?'

'Orca?' I laughed. 'Maybe, maybe not. I need to think about that one. It's different, though, I'll give you that. He or she will be called Chambers though, as will I. I'm going all in, Zen. You and I are going to be Mr and Mrs Chambers, and I can't wait!'

We watched, hand in hand, as the orcas made their way back out to sea, leaving no trace behind them, then everyone got back to the job in hand of doing what Lindisfarners do best – throwing an amazing party. Barry burst back into song with his very own version of 'I am Sailing', the crowd all swaying along, singing with him.

'Bazza, lad, do you know anything by The Police 'cos you're murdering that song, son!' quipped Maurice.

'Just you wait until later when I get you under house arrest in handcuffs. You'd better get scoffing some of them oysters of yours, big boy,' retorted Barry, quick as a flash, before bursting into a very wobbly version of 'Message in a Bottle'.

I felt like the luckiest woman in the world, standing on this tiny island in the North Sea, with so much love coming from the islanders, my friends, who felt more like family. I turned and surveyed the crumbling shack that was virtually on the beach, with the most amazing view that I would never ever tire of. The shack that was eventually to become our forever home, because I knew we would never leave. I turned again and looked across at my gorgeous fiancé hugging his mam, as she gazed at him with such pride and love, and I thought I might just burst into a million stars with happiness. Northumberland really was the gift that kept on giving. It had given me Zen, my soulmate, and now it had given us the most perfect place ever to start our new lives together as husband and wife on Lindisfarne, where dreams really can come true.

I hope you enjoyed your trip to Northumberland via the pages of Love Forever Lindisfarne. The story and characters are of course fiction, but the settings are all real. Whilst there are no Lords of Lindisfarne or Bamburgh, the castles mentioned exist, are all stunning and can be visited:

www.nationaltrust.org.uk/visit/north-east/lindisf arne-castle

www.bamburghcastle.com

www.english-heritage.org.uk/visit/places/warkw orth-castle-and-hermitage

You can also do the walks mentioned...

www.northumberlandcoastpath.org

www.northumberlandnationalpark.org.uk

Whilst the Reef islands don't exist, the Farne islands do and can be visited by boat from Seahouses harbour.

And for general information on visiting Northumberland:

www.visitnorthumberland.com

There are also lots of groups on social media promoting this wonderful county and don't forget - always remember to check the tide times if you are visiting the island!

www.holyislandcrossingtimes.northumberland.gov.uk

A thank you to...

Continuing the story of the islanders who are now like my friends has been a joy and without you readers it wouldn't have been possible, so my first acknowledgement is to all of you who have read the books and taken them to heart. Your support means so much.

To my team of creative professionals who support me in getting the words on a laptop into the pages of a book with the best ever covers! Sarah, the artist who listens to my visions and turns them into the most delightful images – and Love Forever Lindisfarne is no exception, the colours are stunning. To Rachel who takes the covers to the finished products by adding the graphics and ensuring the books all look like a matching set. And to Jo, my writing friend who painstakingly edited Love Forever Lindisfarne and turned it from my ramblings into something readable!

To all the bookshops and independent businesses who stock the book – believe you me Northumberland has some amazing retailers who work very hard to keep their small businesses going in such tough times.

To my writing buddies from the various groups that I participate in. The help and support I get from you all is very much appreciated and in the often long, lonely hours of writing, it's so great to know there's always someone willing to offer help, advice, and some much-needed positivity!

And finally, to my long-suffering family who endure me living and breathing writing, and organising my life around the whole book thing and are always there to lend an ear or some muscle to support me – those boxes can get really heavy and without them, they'd never get onto any shelves other than my garage! I really do appreciate everything you do for me.

Kim x

About Kimberley Adams

Kim was born in Corbridge in Northumberland and still lives in this gorgeous corner of the world. Passionate about the area, Kim tends to set her work in the northeast, and why not, considering the wealth of stunning scenery and the warm-hearted locals, both of which constantly give her ideas for future writing endeavours.

Kim's debut Love Lindisfarne was released October 2023 and from its first cover release on social media it gained momentum, taking Kim totally by surprise. Kim had never envisaged writing more than one book, but here we now are at number four, three Lindisfarne books and a Christmas novella called the Christmas Angel of the North which is about a nana and her granddaughter and set in Newcastle.

Kim finds most of her inspiration mooching around cafes across the Northeast where she 'overhears' some of the funniest and warmest things that are stored away for future use (anonymously of course!) If you see her, buy her some cake, then she promises never to write about you!

Kim is very proud of her ratings on Amazon and if you want to read reviews for her previous books just pop on and you will be able to see just why Kim gets quite emotional over some of the lovely things that have been said about the books! If you do enjoy the books, please try and leave a rating or review, you don't even have to have bought the book from Amazon, but each rating helps towards getting the system to recognise Kim and her books.

KIM'S OTHER BOOKS...
LOVE LINDISFARNE
LOVE BEYOND LINDISFARNE
THE CHRISTMAS ANGEL OF THE NORTH

All can be found on Amazon or from a host of stockists across Northumberland – just ask Kim for a list of where you can find them.

To keep up with what Kim is writing next from her little writing room find her on social media, she loves a bit of a chat so say hi to her and the other Lovely Lindisfarners...

Facebook – Kimberley Adams-Writer (Kim's main communication point)
FB Page – Love_Lindisfarne
Instagram – love_lindisfarne
X Twitter - @kim_adamsWriter
Or follow Kim on Amazon